Infatuation

NE LTD

BECAUSE NAUGHTY CAN BE OH SO NICE®

By Nicole Edwards

The Alluring Indulgence Series
Kaleb
Zane
Travis
Holidays with the Walker Brothers
Ethan
Braydon
Sawyer
Brendon

The Austin Arrows Series
Rush
Kaufman

The Bad Boys of Sports Series
Bad Reputation
Bad Business

The Caine Cousins Series
Hard to Hold
Hard to Handle

The Club Destiny Series
Conviction
Temptation
Addicted
Seduction
Infatuation
Captivated
Devotion
Perception
Entrusted
Adored
Distraction

The Coyote Ridge Series
Curtis
Jared

The Dead Heat Ranch Series
Boots Optional
Betting on Grace
Overnight Love

By Nicole Edwards (cont.)

The Devil's Bend Series

Chasing Dreams
Vanishing Dreams

The Devil's Playground Series

Without Regret
Without Restraint

The Office Intrigue Series

Office Intrigue
Intrigued Out of the Office
Their Rebellious Submissive

The Pier 70 Series

Reckless
Fearless
Speechless
Harmless

The Sniper 1 Security Series

Wait for Morning
Never Say Never
Tomorrow's Too Late

The Southern Boy Mafia Series

Beautifully Brutal
Beautifully Loyal

Standalone Novels

A Million Tiny Pieces
Inked on Paper

Writing as Timberlyn Scott

Unhinged
Unraveling
Chaos

Naughty Holiday Editions

2015
2016

Infatuation

Club Destiny, Book 5

NICOLE EDWARDS

Nicole Edwards Limited
PO Box 806
Hutto, Texas 78634
www.NicoleEdwardsLimited.com

Cover Images by: © Patrizia Tilly | 123rf.com
Cover Design by: Nicole Edwards Limited
Editing by: Blue Otter Editing **www.blueotterediting.com**

ISBN (ebook): 978-1-939786-03-6
ISBN (print): 978-1-939786-00-5

Erotic Romance
Mature Audience

Dedication

To my amazing husband.
Without you, I couldn't do this. Your unwavering support is
humbling. I love you!

Prologue

UNUSUALLY QUIET.

That's the only way Tag could describe the sound, or rather lack thereof, that greeted him the instant he stepped foot into the immaculately decorated, overly spacious house.

One week — seven *long* days — had passed since the last time he was here, the last time he had been privy to the sensual smorgasbord that he was sure to stumble upon at any given moment. He knew why he was here, and he knew what was going to happen, he just didn't know when, where, or how. He was pretty sure she liked to keep him guessing in that regard.

Tonight, for some reason, Tag was a little hesitant.

Okay, maybe more than just a little.

Not that he wasn't fully on board with the agenda for the evening. He just couldn't seem to shake that niggling little voice in his head that had him wondering whether he should be doing this. Honestly, he had never heard this voice before, never questioned his decisions in regard to this aspect of his life. But tonight he was questioning himself for one reason and one reason only.

Her.

The woman who had stepped into his path that one unusually warm October afternoon. The one who'd successfully imbedded herself somewhere in the dark recesses of his brain.

Tag knew her name, but that's about all he knew at this point. Well, other than the image he was intimately familiar with, the one that continued to haunt his dreams on those long, lonely nights. There was an intensity about her, one he couldn't shake regardless of how many times he tried to convince himself that it was only in his head. He didn't know her, but for some reason, she plagued his mind with thoughts that he knew were better left alone.

Which was why he was here, his legs carrying him through the vast open space as he took in his surroundings, attempting to predict what was about to happen before it actually did. Generally, that never worked for him, mainly because he had learned they liked to keep him on his toes.

He didn't doubt himself now. He knew what he wanted, or rather what he *needed*, and it wasn't some mystery woman disturbing his thoughts and making him anticipate something he knew was well out of his reach.

He was here now, and that was what he needed to focus on. A couple of hours of mind-numbing ecstasy at the hands of a woman who didn't threaten his resolve or have him wishing for things he had never wanted before.

This was the best of both worlds. The opportunity to explore his sexual fantasies while keeping himself detached from those pesky emotions that others around him had succumbed to in recent months. He wasn't interested in those things. He only had room for physical connections at this point in his life. These midnight trysts were all he needed in order to fulfill the areas he sometimes suspected were lacking but knew that wasn't the case.

And what better way to escape from his thoughts than to find gratification in the touch of a woman without the worry of discussions about something more. Logan and Samantha offered him that; they offered him the chance to erase all of the stresses of life for just a few hours and still give him the ability to walk away afterward without an ounce of guilt.

As Tag approached the living room, he was welcomed with even more silence. He knew the drill, knew that he would spend a couple of minutes anticipating the how and where before he stumbled upon what would ultimately allow his mind to clear for that short period of time. Tonight it wouldn't be in the kitchen or on the veranda because both of those places were empty. That meant there was only one other place they could be.

As he turned toward the master bedroom, Tag loosened his tie while welcoming the anticipation he sensed building in his gut.

Infatuation

Bypassing the bedroom, he turned the corner into the ostentatious master bath, with its floor-to-ceiling mirrors and expensively tiled floors, until his eyes landed on the wickedly hot scene already playing out before him. They hadn't made it into the shower yet, but Tag could hear the water as it ran on the opposite side of the wall. What he saw instantly had his dick swelling and his balls in desperate need of attention.

Sitting naked on the bathroom counter, her legs spread wide, her back pressed against the mirrored glass with her head thrown back, Samantha McCoy was completely unaware of his presence, although he knew she was expecting him. As was her husband, Logan, who was currently kneeling between her legs, holding her open as he devoured her with his tongue.

Without hesitation, but not rushing, either, Tag divested himself of his suit jacket and tie before slowly unbuttoning his dress shirt. His eyes were glued to the erotic display before him, allowing him the chance to push all other thoughts out of his cluttered mind.

At least for tonight, Tag was the third in this rendezvous, and he was satisfied with that just as he had been for the last few months, ever since Logan McCoy had approached him. With Sam's enthusiastic attitude toward sex, her ability to open herself up to exploring the pleasure that could be had from a threesome, Tag had nothing to fear except for the onslaught of physical gratification.

Tag liked Samantha; he liked her ambition, her intelligence, her drive, and he especially liked that hint of vulnerability he sensed each and every time he took her in his arms. This was still new to her, but she had finally given in to her salacious urges and accepted the fact that she enjoyed being the recipient of two men's attention for at least a little while. More importantly, Tag respected the connection between Sam and Logan and knew, without a doubt, why he was invited.

For the pleasure and nothing more.

Standing here now, his gaze drawn to the sexy blond laid out like a buffet for the taking, he attempted to force every other thought from his mind, focusing solely on the way Logan was feasting on her pussy while Tag watched.

That was Logan's fetish: watching and being watched. Tag didn't have any issues with that. He had his own kinks, his own forbidden desires, and just like Logan, Tag didn't make excuses for what he wanted.

Completely naked now, Tag remained where he was, stroking his erection as he allowed his mind to engage fully in the moment. Logan would ensure that this played out the way he expected it to, and Tag embraced the opportunity not to have to think. He spent too many hours a day doing just that, and this offered him the mind-numbing bliss he had come to enjoy.

When Sam's eyes opened, meeting his briefly, he smiled, watching as she writhed and moaned while Logan continued to lap at her sweet pussy. Her answering grin was brief before she closed her eyes, bowed her back, and allowed her orgasm to consume her.

That was another thing he enjoyed about Samantha; she was incredibly responsive, ensuring that he knew exactly what triggered that spine-tingling reaction that had her moaning Logan's name over and over.

"Come here," Logan instructed his wife as he stood to his full height. He offered his hand and then helped her to stand before heading to the fully open shower on the other side of the wall.

Tag followed, still in no rush but allowing his anxiety to ratchet up a notch or two as he made his way beneath the warm water behind them.

He had no way of knowing what would happen next because Logan's mind worked in mysterious ways. He was always coming up with ways to ensure they never got bored. It was true, pleasure was pleasure, but it was also true that, without spontaneity, it would become monotonous, something Logan appeared to be allergic to.

With his hands on her shoulders, Logan eased Samantha to her knees before him, his eyes seemingly locked on the woman's beautiful mouth.

"I want to feel your lips on me, Sam," Logan growled.

Watching as Sam teased the head of Logan's dick with her tongue, Tag moved closer. When he was no less than a foot away from her, she slowly reached out, stroking his fully erect cock with her soft, wet hand while she continued to suck Logan deeper into her mouth.

Infatuation

Needless to say, Tag was beginning to forget everything else that normally weighed heavily on his mind, losing himself in the sensation.

For long minutes, they continued this way until Sam pulled away from Logan, turning her attention on Tag. The heat of her mouth sent a chill racing down his spine as she slid her lips over the engorged head. He locked his knees as she continued to moan around his cock now filling her mouth.

Closing his eyes, Tag found it more difficult than ever to clear those pressing thoughts from his mind. Unable to forget the woman who'd made her presence known, inadvertently leaving him to wonder whether there was more to this than what he'd originally thought. But he demanded those thoughts to leave and allow him this one last night.

One last night to immerse himself in this diversion that had become crucial to his sanity, allowing him to pretend that one woman hadn't intrigued him with just a seductive, daring gleam in her crystal-blue eyes.

She was a woman Tag feared might just manage to push him further than he ever wanted to be pushed.

Chapter *One*

WITH A SLEW of reporters standing around, looking to pick up the tiniest bit of news that they could exploit, Tag Murphy did his best to appear unaffected as he made his way through the crowd. Although he wasn't Sierra's lawyer, Tag was still representing Club Destiny and felt it necessary to be present in the event Luke needed anything. As it turned out, he had. This was just part of his job that he wasn't all that fond of.

He didn't have any problem being the necessary distraction that would keep the media at bay temporarily for Sierra's sake, but he'd rather be doing just about anything else. If Susan Toulmin's rant of lunacy was anything to go by, the tactic appeared to be working.

Tag spared a glance at the immaculately dressed woman coming out of the courtroom spouting all kinds of crazy shit. As much as he'd like to be surprised, sadly, he was not. He didn't expect anything less from her today, especially after the judge had finally ruled in favor of Sierra Sellers.

He might have to endure a microphone or two that came just a little too close for comfort, but it was the least he could do to keep the attention from Sierra, who was now being escorted out through the side entrance by Luke and Cole. Better him than Luke McCoy, that was for damn sure.

"Mr. Murphy" — a microphone was jammed toward his face — "is it true that not only do you represent Club Destiny but you're also a member?"

Tag couldn't count the number of times he had heard that exact question in the last couple of weeks. And just like every other time, he ignored it and continued making his way through the hordes of people mulling about.

Another microphone.

Another question.

"No comment," Tag said as he shouldered his way through, only this time, something — or rather some*one* — caught his eye.

Stopping abruptly, his feet unwilling to continue, Tag searched the faces around him until his gaze narrowed on one woman. The same woman who had caught his eye every day for a solid month and captivated his thoughts for even longer.

McKenna Thorne.

After their first run-in, Tag had spent the better part of the afternoon digging for more information on the titillating redhead now standing just two feet away wielding a microphone and a seductive smile. The microphone he didn't mind, but the smile was more than just an intriguing tilt of her full, red lips. It was a dare.

His persistent research gave Tag quite a bit of information on the tremendously successful journalist. She wasn't just any journalist, though. McKenna was a relentless, highly admired entrepreneur who owned Sensations, Inc., a well-known online magazine geared toward swingers and the sexually taboo. In recent weeks, thanks to the loose lips of Susan Toulmin, McKenna's magazine had received more than its fair share of recognition.

He knew better than to provoke the intriguing McKenna. Not because he worried his life would become fodder for her daily newsfeed but because, quite frankly, Tag wasn't sure how far his control could be stretched, and the vibrant redhead, with her teasing smile and come-hither stare, seemed to realize that.

"Is it true, Mr. Murphy," McKenna drawled in that sexy, raspy voice that was better suited for phone sex than an interview, in his opinion, "that you're representing Luke and Logan McCoy in their newest business venture? Investing in a mega resort catering to the uber-wealthy and their kinky obsessions?"

Tag made sure his expression didn't change as he continued to stare into the most exotically intense eyes he'd ever seen on a human being. From a distance, her eyes appeared to be as crystal blue as the waters of the Caribbean, but up close, less than a foot between them, he could see that McKenna's eyes weren't blue or green or brown but a combination of all three. The iris consisted of a thin band of brown, encapsulated by a thicker ring of green, surrounded by an unusually bright teal blue. He didn't even think they could be called a specific color.

Her eyes weren't her only feature that Tag found appealing. Ever since the first day, outside of the exact same courthouse where they stood now, he'd been consumed by thoughts of her. It wasn't just the smooth perfection of her porcelain skin, her cute little nose, her luscious mouth, or all of those sinful curves that made men turn and watch while she walked away. McKenna had a confident sophistication about her, and when she had said his name that day, he'd been a goner.

His body hadn't known the type of lust she inspired for quite some time — an inferno of passion and need that all but consumed him. Only Tag was a smart man, and he'd been taught at a remarkably young age not to play with fire. And he sensed this woman was as fiery as the long, silky tresses upswept at the back of her head.

"No. Comment." Tag offered McKenna his signature statement and a sardonic grin, then turned and moved through the crowd. Had it not been for his momentary pause, he might've been able to avoid what came next.

"Mr. Murphy!" A voice rang out, all too familiar and more than a little irritating. "Don't you think it's time you came clean with the nice people of this city?"

Why couldn't the woman just keep her damned mouth shut?

Tag had initially found Susan's insistence on representing herself highly amusing, but it hadn't taken long before she proved not only to him but the judge as well that she was unquestionably batshit crazy. Now, apparently, she was out to ensure the world knew it, too.

He turned slowly, dreading the confrontation that had been a long time coming.

"Ms. Toulmin," Tag greeted her politely, although he should've ignored her.

With Luke McCoy, on behalf of Club Destiny, in the process of suing Susan for violation of a binding contract, Tag knew better than to invite trouble if he could avoid it.

Susan's reaction to Sierra's relationship with Luke and Cole had come as a bit of a shock to the three of them. She'd made good on her promise to sue Sierra for misrepresentation of her design experience, although Susan's retaliation was obviously due to her intense feelings for Luke and Cole. Tag knew for a fact that Sierra wished she'd never laid eyes on the high-maintenance, demanding attorney, so today's outcome had to be a welcome relief.

"When are you going to let these people know what Club Destiny is truly all about? The lewd and repulsive acts that go on behind closed doors?"

Funny how the woman hadn't found the club lewd or repulsive when she had been the one being nailed to the wall by one or more club members during her frequent weekly visits.

Tag raised his eyebrows as if to question Susan, knowing full well she was continuing to dig herself a deeper hole every time she chose to open her mouth.

He sometimes, like now, had trouble understanding what made the woman snap. Tag liked Luke McCoy well enough, but seriously? Could Luke have been that good in bed that the instant Susan felt he wasn't hers any longer, she went off the deep end? Shit, he'd engaged in some seriously intense sex in his lifetime, but no one had ever pushed him to his limits.

Then again, Tag never allowed himself to consider anyone *his* the way Susan mistakenly had. There might have been a relationship or two that Tag considered exclusive, but with those partners, they'd agreed up front, and they'd known full well what he was and was not interested in.

When it was over, it was over.

Another reason he liked the recent nontraditional aspect to his relationships. He was content with being a third because it allowed him the freedom he craved while also giving him the monogamy — for lack of a better word — that he desired. However, his current relationship status stood at single because he didn't have time for anything else. Or at least that's what he told himself.

For a solid month, Tag had managed to avoid Logan and Samantha McCoy's requests for him to join them in their infrequent rendezvous because … well, because of *her.* The sinfully beautiful woman, dressed in black from head to toe, pinning him with those exquisite eyes; the same one standing behind Susan Toulmin, pulling her bottom lip between her teeth in another attempt to fuck with him.

Instead of responding to either woman, Tag turned around and, this time, successfully escaped the throng of reporters eager to sling mud all over the front pages of whatever magazine or newspaper they represented.

Including McKenna Thorne.

If she knew what was best for her, she'd back off before she bit off more than she could chew.

MCKENNA WATCHED AS the extremely fine specimen known as Tag Murphy slowly disappeared from sight, appearing to be swallowed whole by the throng of reporters jumping for the chance to catch that one golden ticket comment that would rocket their career to stardom.

She didn't move until she couldn't see his sexy-as-hell bald head any longer. What she wouldn't give just to follow him. Thankfully, she had been blessed with enough common sense to know better.

From the moment she'd laid eyes on him nearly two months earlier, McKenna had realized Tag was one she didn't want to mess with. Yet she was captivated by him. Totally enthralled with every facet of the man to the point she was all but stalking him on the Internet, digging up as much information about him as she could, and absorbing it as fast as possible. It was a good thing that was her job, or she might be a little worried about her own sanity.

Oh, hell, who was she kidding? She *was* a little worried.

She found some consolation in the fact that Tag Murphy considered her the enemy and therefore thwarted any chance of her getting close to the man. Little did he know, McKenna was the least he had to worry about. But it was easier to accept his aversion to her than risk the chance of facing him one-on-one again.

Their impromptu introduction a couple of months before had left her reeling. Similar to today, McKenna had been at the courthouse in hopes of speaking to Tag in regard to his personal take on the trial. Considering he wasn't representing Sierra, she had been hoping to get his opinion on a future outcome.

From the moment she'd asked the question, McKenna had been caught up in the mesmerizing intensity of his beautiful green eyes. He never had fully answered her, but something else had transpired between them that day. Something McKenna had thought about often in the days since.

In recent days, she'd acquired a few juicy tidbits of information about the sexy lawyer that she was tempted to share with her readers, but for some reason, she felt it necessary to keep those intricate secrets to herself. After all, she hadn't become successful by exploiting people. No, her readers had come to love her online magazine for her insight and her honesty. But just like any other journalist worth their salt, McKenna had learned how to get the information she needed.

That was her job, and she was good at it.

Although, it didn't explain why she couldn't get her mind off of him and hadn't been able to for longer than she cared to admit.

Tag Murphy was sex personified, and she could only imagine what he'd be like between the sheets. Not that she would ever find out, but she could have fun pretending for a little while.

Her attention was pulled to the woman standing next to her, feeding a line of unsubstantiated bullshit into one of the lingering microphones. McKenna already knew what the bitter Susan Toulmin had to say. Same thing she always did.

According to Susan, the club Luke owned was one that dealt in raunchy, indecent acts of debauchery that were often orgiastic in nature. She continued to taunt the media by threatening to mention names of supposedly prominent members of society who frequented the club. However, whenever asked about her own membership, Susan often backtracked, hinting that she hadn't realized what she was signing up for at the time she'd applied, was accepted, and then paid the outrageously expensive membership fee.

McKenna knew she should be interested because, at some point, Susan was going to slip up. She just had an issue with taking her at her word because no one had the lowdown on the legendary Club Destiny, which meant there wasn't enough proof for her even to hint at a story and feel good about it. She was curious, though.

Figuring the day was already shot, McKenna switched off her microphone and turned to go. She didn't need to hear any more, and if she was honest, she hadn't come to hear Ms. Toulmin speak in the first place.

Her real reason for coming had just walked away.

Grabbing her cell phone from her pocket, McKenna dialed her assistant's number, wondering whether she'd been any more successful in getting information from Sierra or Luke.

"Whisper?" McKenna greeted when her assistant answered the phone.

Yes, her assistant's name was Whisper, and no one knew whether that was her birth name or if she'd changed it along the way. No matter what, the name didn't suit her at all. McKenna was pretty sure the term "quiet" wasn't even in the woman's vocabulary.

"Hey, Mac. You have any luck?" McKenna barely heard her assistant over the sound of a hundred voices speaking at one time, so she waited until she emerged on the other side of the group huddled closer and closer to the mouth at the microphone.

"No luck on my end," McKenna said, thinking back on that smoldering-hot look Tag had gifted her with seconds before he'd turned his back on her. "How about you?"

Any good reporter knew that Sierra Sellers was going to escape through the back doors of the courthouse while a diversion had been set up out front. McKenna had known, but she had also opted to take her chances on that diversion being Tag.

"No, Sierra wouldn't talk, and the glares I received from those muscles on her arm had me backing off. I'm not an idiot, you know."

McKenna laughed. Whisper might've been the loudest, most obnoxious woman she'd ever met — and she meant that in the most endearing way possible — but at least she knew when to back off.

Most of the time.

"I'll meet you back at the office. I've got something I want to write up for tomorrow's blog," McKenna told Whisper as she headed to her car. "Don't worry, it's nothing juicy, but I figure it's not a bad idea to dangle the carrot every now and again."

"McKenna." Whisper managed to drawl her name into way more than three syllables, which she recognized as a warning.

"Oh, hush. I've got this one covered," McKenna told Whisper.

"You're going to push that man too far, honey. I can feel it."

McKenna's sole objective these days seemed to be finding more and more ways to push him. The man was too self-controlled for his own good. She wanted to rough him up a little bit, and this little stunt just might get her what she wanted.

Chapter *Two*

WAS SHE OUT of her fucking mind?

Tag paced back and forth in front of his desk, certain he was going to wear a hole in the damn carpet if he kept this up. Hell, he hadn't even had his morning coffee, and he was subjected to this ... crap.

Staring at the tablet computer sitting on his desk, he still couldn't believe his eyes.

Secrets or Lies?

Tag Murphy, the attorney currently representing the infamous Club Destiny and its owners, hot, sexy twins Logan and Luke McCoy, might just have a few skeletons — or shall we say whips and chains — in his closet.

Is this mysterious man, who has captured the hearts of so many women as we swoon in front of the television waiting for him to lavish us with his seductively dark, rich voice, truly who he says he is? Or does he have a secret?

Considering Mr. Murphy is currently representing the very private, very exclusive Club Destiny in a lawsuit against former member, Susan Toulmin, inquiring minds would like to know.

Stay tuned as we expose some delicious details about the uber-sexy Tag Murphy and the rumor that he's got a few toys still hanging in his dungeon ... er ... closet.

Infatuation

He hadn't thought it possible, but McKenna Thorne was beginning to be an even bigger pain in his ass than she already had been. Didn't the woman know when to leave well enough alone? There was no doubt in his mind that she was playing a game, and that damn blog of hers was going to get her in some serious trouble if she wasn't careful.

Grabbing his cell phone, he went to the kitchen and poured a cup of coffee. There was no way he could face McKenna first thing without at least a little caffeine.

Toys?

Dungeon?

Seriously?

Tag didn't need any damn toys. He would gladly use his hand when he pulled McKenna's sweet little ass over his knee and showed her just what it meant to tempt him.

When his cell phone rang, Tag snatched it up from the counter and hit the talk button without even looking at the screen. He already knew who it was.

"So, Sam wants to know why you haven't introduced her to this dungeon of yours." Logan's deep baritone reverberated through the phone.

"Fuck off." Tag wasn't in any mood to play games right now, not even with Logan or Sam.

"Touchy, are you?" Logan laughed. "I think you might've just captured the attention of McKenna Thorne, my friend."

It appeared that way.

"That woman's beginning to piss me off." *And make my fucking dick hard.* Tag thought the last part, not willing to share that much with Logan.

"Well, according to what I read, you might just be well equipped to teach her a lesson."

Tag grunted, not dignifying Logan's sarcastic comment with a response.

"Seriously, man." All humor was gone from Logan's tone. "You need to figure out exactly what she knows. We can't have information leaking out about the club. Susan's already sharing more than we bargained for."

"There's no such thing as bad publicity," Tag stated, thinking back on the last conversation he'd had with Luke, Logan's twin brother and the face of Club Destiny.

Their membership applications had doubled in the last few weeks, and although they weren't currently looking to add new members, it was quite amusing the types of people interested in joining. Not that any of them had the kind of money required to be considered.

However, since the press release had gone out on a new resort that Travis Walker and his brothers were in the process of building, they'd been inundated with interest. Tag attributed it to a planted leak that Logan and Luke were interested in investing.

"That's what you think." Logan's tone was still firm. "Find out what she knows."

Tag nodded, knowing Logan couldn't see him. He fully intended to pay Ms. Thorne a visit soon.

Very soon.

Half an hour later, Tag was walking into the posh offices of Sensations, Inc. He hadn't bothered to call and make an appointment because he knew damn well McKenna wouldn't have made time to see him anyway. So, he'd decided to surprise her.

"Mr. Murphy." Whisper, McKenna's extremely attentive assistant, didn't sound all that excited as she greeted him, but she also didn't seem surprised.

"Whisper." He still had a hard time calling her that, even if it was her name. *Who the hell named their child Whisper?*

Then again, he wasn't one to talk. Tag wasn't a particularly common name, either, and since it wasn't short for anything else, people were often interested in how it'd come about.

The story his mother and father had told him wasn't one he cared to share with anyone. He'd been appalled enough when they'd informed him that, at the time of his conception, they were particularly fond of chasing one another. Around the bedroom.

"She available?"

"Actually…"

"Thanks. I know where her office is." Tag smiled, half expecting Whisper to try and stop him, but she didn't. However, he did hear her as she gave McKenna the heads up via telephone that he was coming down the hall.

"Mr.—" McKenna was standing at the door waiting for him.

Tag cut her off before she could greet him fully, grabbing her arm as she shrieked, then slamming her door and pressing her against it before she could catch her next breath. Lowering his mouth to her ear, Tag crushed his body against hers, careful to make sure he didn't hurt her but ensuring she felt his presence in every cell in her body.

He damn sure felt *her* presence. For weeks now, she had invaded his thoughts at the most inopportune times, making his dick hard as all of the things he wanted to do to her replayed over and over in his head.

"No need for pleasantries, McKenna." Tag breathed in her sweet, addictive scent and was immediately reminded of the last time he'd been there in her office.

It had been an innocent visit. At Logan's request, Tag had met with McKenna to get a feel for what her intentions were in regard to any stories related to Club Destiny. For about a week, she had been hinting at future details, but to this day, she still hadn't written anything about the club. Based on this morning's article, it appeared she'd taken a more personal interest. On one hand, that was a good thing for his client, but for him personally, it was proving to be a bit of a problem.

A physical one.

"Why—" The catch in her breath was evident, and he knew he'd taken her by surprise, but this was something else.

"Don't play dumb with me, darlin'. You want to find out what toys I keep in my dungeon? I'll be more than happy to show you, under one condition," he growled low in her ear, allowing his lips to brush lightly against the soft flesh of her lobe, using his teeth to nip until he felt her shiver.

Son of a bitch.

This woman was bound and determined to push him, and he knew it. So why was he letting her?

"What's the condition?" she asked, still breathless.

"I get to tie you up and use them on you." He slid his knee between her thighs, and he wished like hell she'd worn one of those short skirts she favored. Instead, she'd opted for jeans, but even through the denim, he could feel the heat of her pussy against his thigh.

When she put her palms on his chest and pushed, Tag conceded, backing away from her but not turning away.

"Who the fuck do you think you are?" McKenna bit out, glaring at him with those exotic eyes.

"*Me?* Honey, I'm not the one posting lies about you all over the fucking Internet."

"Lies?" The incredulity in her voice rang loud and clear. "I happen to have a very reliable source, *honey*," she retorted.

He didn't doubt there was someone out there who was willing to talk, but whether they were reliable was debatable.

"What's your fucking problem, McKenna?" Tag asked, feeling the anger roil in his gut. It didn't matter that his dick was like an iron fucking rod thanks to her or that he was turned on more than he had been in years by one single woman; he was still pissed.

"Problem?" That sweet, innocent tone of hers wasn't fooling him in the least. He watched as she walked over to her chair and then took a seat behind her desk.

He didn't blame her for wanting to put some distance between them. Whatever spark had ignited when Tag had touched her was roaring into an uncontrollable, scorching sea of flames that neither of them could get away from, let alone deny.

"Yes. Problem. Can't you just leave well enough alone?" he asked, perching on the edge of the long, leather sofa at the far end of her office.

"I happen to know my readers are curious about what it is you keep in your closet." She laughed, but Tag felt her tension.

Sexual tension.

"Darlin', you don't have to pretend it's your readers who want to know. If you're so interested, I'll be more than happy to give you a tour of my closet."

Infatuation

Tag knew her source hadn't revealed any such thing, but he wasn't going to deny that he did have a few toys on hand. Granted, they weren't in his closet or even at his house. They were at his private room at the club, which in no way resembled a dungeon.

If she was willing, and he'd bet money she was, Tag would be more than happy to show her where he kept them.

"Give me an exclusive," McKenna said, standing suddenly from her chair and damn near making his head spin from the abrupt change of topic.

"An exclusive what?"

"I want to do an exclusive story on Club Destiny. You can give me a tour. It'll satisfy my readers, and it will get the crazy lady off your back at the same time."

"Who? You?" Tag pretended not to know McKenna was referring to Susan. At the moment, he wasn't sure which of them was crazier — Susan for confusing lust for love or McKenna for daring to make this personal.

Either way, he had to admit, it wasn't a terrible idea.

Those inquisitive eyes of hers raked him up and down, and Tag fought the urge to press her against the wall one more time. Only this time, he was going to take what she was offering.

Tag was hypnotized as he watched McKenna pace back and forth, speaking out loud but obviously not to him. He was mesmerized by the long lines of her graceful body, the gentle flare of her hips, and the perfection of her ass encased in those expensive jeans. As she moved, her hips swayed seductively, her long, lustrous red hair hanging board straight down her back, grazing the waistband of those low-slung jeans.

He wanted to run his fingers through her hair, wrap the thick silk around his fist before pulling her head back and exploring her mouth with his tongue.

"It'll work. You'll give me a tour of the club, we'll print — with Luke's approval, of course — and my readers will go nuts. Susan won't have any more ammunition for the press. We'll be able to tell people what goes on behind those doors without revealing a single member."

Tag met her eyes when she stopped abruptly, standing much closer than he expected. For a brief moment, there was silence in the room; the only sound was each breath they took, growing more and more labored as they remained motionless, brought on by whatever chemical reaction occurred between them when they were in the same room. A response so potent that, should they give in to it, Tag feared it could very well rock him to his core.

Turning away, he stood once again, and it was now his turn to pace. He certainly liked where she was going with this, but that didn't matter.

It wasn't his call.

HOW WAS IT possible to be so infatuated with a man like Tag Murphy? Even with all of the things she knew about him and, more importantly, knew about herself, McKenna didn't understand the attraction she felt.

A few weeks ago, she'd have blamed it on simple lust. The kind inspired by the sight of a hot, sexy man by a woman who hadn't had sex in longer than she cared to admit. This ... this ... whatever you wanted to call it was beginning to border on obsession. So much so, McKenna was stuttering her thoughts.

There was just something about this particular man, with his compelling good looks and sophisticated, dominating presence, that caught her attention. Maybe it was those eyes that changed from the color of cool crystalline to that of deep, glistening emeralds. Or perhaps it was that he was so tall, although she couldn't pinpoint a measurement, but he was quite a bit taller than her own five feet seven inches. Not so tall that she wouldn't be able to slide her hands up his neck and explore his beautiful bald head with her fingertips.

Oh, God, it could very well be his shaved head, because Tag pulled it off so effortlessly. The man was the epitome of male perfection.

Even more impressive than his height or his inquisitive eyes or that sexy head was the thick, ropey muscle that she sensed beneath those fancy suits he wore. She'd felt his solid, well-muscled thigh between her legs just minutes ago, and she'd had to quell the urge to grind against him because he was just that damn hot. She wondered, albeit briefly, how thick other parts of him were.

McKenna knew, as much as she admired his physical perfection, that generally wasn't what drew her to a man, and as much as she tried to pretend that was the case now, she knew she was drawn to him by something more than his eye-pleasing appearance. Tag Murphy was also successful and intelligent — two highly appealing qualities when she considered her history.

Remembering where she was and what she was trying to do, McKenna unglued her eyes from his shapely ass and waited until he turned around. "You know it'll work."

"It's not a bad idea." He paused, glancing around the room before a smile tipped his lips. "But you know it's not my call. I'll have to talk to the McCoys and get back to you."

McKenna watched as he turned to go, suddenly wishing she could keep him there for just a little while longer. There were so many things that intrigued her about this man, so many things that she wanted...

A sigh threatened to escape, but she held it in, waiting for him to say something.

"In the meantime, don't write any more fucking articles."

Well, that wasn't what she wanted to hear.

"I'll try." She returned his smile. "You've got twenty-four hours to get back to me. If I don't hear from you by then, one way or the other, I'm launching my next one. And this one is guaranteed to raise some eyebrows."

For the rest of the day, McKenna and Whisper, along with two other part-time employees, worked to try and keep up with the staggering response to the article on Tag.

Pictures of him were flying all over cyberspace, women intent on knowing more about the hunky attorney who seemed to have a dark side, a side that apparently more women than just McKenna wanted to explore.

She found it both amusing and a little irritating. Jealousy wasn't a good color for her, but McKenna was learning that she had developed some sort of possessive gene when it came to Tag. She'd be smart to figuratively pull that little emotion straight out of her brain, wad it up, and throw it in the trash. Then set the can on fire. Twice.

She didn't have time to play games with Tag, or anyone else, for that matter. Even if she was enjoying it to some degree, she knew better. McKenna was in no way the type of woman Tag would want on his arm. Or even in his bed. She wasn't the typical submissive he seemed to be interested in, nor did she play in threes.

No, McKenna had her own dominating personality that she knew would conflict directly with Tag's. She might fantasize about what it would be like in Tag's arms, but McKenna knew it would never work. And she wasn't in the market for a temporary sex partner.

"Well, I'm outta here, Mac," Whisper called from the doorway of McKenna's office, successfully breaking her from her thoughts.

"You got a hot date tonight?" she asked, glancing up from the image of Tag still laid out before her. She was preparing tomorrow's article, although she had a sneaking suspicion she would hear from him.

That was why she was preparing *two* articles.

Her readers would get something they'd all been waiting a long time to hear about, only she hoped she'd get a quick tour from him, and she could share some of the much-anticipated details about the infamous Club Destiny.

"Of course." Whisper laughed, although from where she sat, McKenna couldn't detect a trace of humor reflected in Whisper's warm brown eyes.

"Why're you laughing?" McKenna asked, suddenly a little concerned for her friend.

"Seriously? Honey, when you've been together as long as we have, you're lucky to get fast food for a date."

"What do you do for fun?" McKenna knew that Whisper and Anna had been together for at least four years now, so maybe their hot dates had dwindled to the occasional date night, but still. There had to be some spontaneity in their relationship.

"We start by eating dinner, followed by dishes, chased by several hours of whatever is the hot show on television. The most excitement might be a quick laugh over something one of us saw on Facebook."

"Well, if you want my advice…" McKenna grinned — like her advice had worked for her in the past. "You need to take that woman out sometime."

"I hear ya."

The look that passed over Whisper's pretty, round face had McKenna wanting to ask more questions, but she knew her friend, and she knew now was not the time to press. Instead, she just smiled. "Have a good night. I'll see you in the morning."

"Back atcha, boss lady. See you tomorrow."

With that, Whisper was out the door, and she was once again alone in the office.

Two hours later, McKenna was sitting back admiring her handiwork. Two articles about Tag finished and ready to go to the editors. Once they approved them, hopefully before morning, she'd be ready to share something with her readers.

Stretching her tight back muscles, McKenna damn near fell out of her chair when her cell phone rang, startling her. Fumbling, she managed to grip it before hitting the green button to connect the call.

"McKenna Thorne," she greeted the caller. Not many people knew her cell phone number, so she didn't bother checking to see who it was.

"Dinner. Tonight." The gruff Texas drawl belonged to none other than the man she'd been thinking about for the last few hours.

Because of work, of course.

Her heart beat double time against her ribs, and McKenna kept her butt in her chair, not trusting her legs to hold her upright. "Where were you thinking?"

Okay, so yes, she was seriously considering this.

"Does it matter?"

The cockiness in his response sent a chill down her spine. The good kind. Did she care where they went? No, not really. Would she let him know that? Ummm…no.

"I don't go out to dinner with strange men."

"Well, darlin', I assure you, I'm not all that strange."

McKenna couldn't help herself. She giggled. *Fucking giggled.* Good grief, what the hell was wrong with her?

"When?"

"Right now. I'm downstairs."

Holy shit.

McKenna launched herself up from her chair and moved over to the window, pulling the curtain back and peering down into the parking lot. Sure enough, there was Tag's undeniable black Maserati Quattroporte Sport GT S parked near the entrance. No, she didn't even actually know what that was, but she'd been researching the man… It'd come up.

"Five minutes," she told him and hung up the phone without listening for a response. She rushed into the private bathroom in her office, praying five minutes would be enough time to at least feel presentable.

"You weren't wearing that when I was here earlier today," Tag commented as she slid into the sleek, sexy car.

No, she had been wearing jeans, which she rarely wore, and the instant Tag had stormed into her office, she'd felt entirely underdressed to be in his presence. The man didn't do casual. He was the epitome of the business professional, always wearing an expensive suit that was obviously tailored for his massive body.

"You don't like it?" she taunted him, buckling her seat belt and trying to pretend he didn't affect her as much as he did.

"I didn't say that," he growled as he put the car in gear and pulled out of the parking lot.

McKenna had a closet full of power outfits. She preferred skirts and dresses of all types, from floor-length to micromini, she wasn't picky. If it was soft and flowing, she usually snatched it up.

Tonight, she hadn't gone for demure. No, when she'd rapidly flipped through her closet in her office, where she kept a couple of emergency outfits, she'd been searching for something to strengthen her resolve. The knee-length A-line skirt paired with a white silk blouse and her favorite Louboutins — the black ones with the red leather open toe — had been the perfect combination.

Apparently Tag appreciated her choice.

McKenna relaxed into the luxury seat, keeping her eyes focused on the passing scenery as she inhaled the delectable scent of Tag. Likely expensive cologne, if she had to guess. Whatever it was, it worked for him. And her.

She didn't ask where they were going, because she figured, at this point, it honestly didn't matter. Allowing herself a couple of minutes to acclimate to being in such close proximity to the man who made her breath choppy and her palms sweat, McKenna let the soft music playing through the car's interior calm her. As much as anything was going to calm her at this point anyway.

By the time they reached the restaurant, she was feeling almost in control of her disobedient hormones.

That was until Tag took her hand.

Chapter *Three*

TAG HANDED THE key to the valet as he exited the car, moving slowly around to the passenger side and waving off another attendant who had started toward them. He opened the door and offered McKenna his hand.

He would question that move for the next ten minutes, he knew. The second their fingers touched, there was an influx of warmth that penetrated his bloodstream. Her soft, smooth fingers fit perfectly in his palm, and despite his better judgment, he didn't let go of her hand as they made their way into the restaurant.

"Mr. Murphy," the hostess greeted him as they approached. He returned her polite smile before she turned and led them to a small table in the back.

"Nice choice," McKenna whispered as he stood back, placing his hand on her lower back, allowing her to take her seat first. When he sat in the chair beside her, rather than across from her, he noticed the slight tilt of her eyebrow and the small smile on her perfect, full lips.

"So, tell me a little about you," Tag said a few minutes later after the waiter had successfully taken their order and brought the wine.

"What do you want to know?"

Everything. Tag thought it but didn't say it. "What made you want to be a journalist?"

"I'm not sure that I've ever *wanted* to be a journalist" — McKenna's smile brightened her entire face — "but I wanted to own something of my own. I didn't want to work for someone else after watching what my father went through." She paused, looked away before returning to meet his gaze. "I think it was my senior year in high school, when I helped with the school newspaper, that I first found an interest in sharing other people's stories. Then when I started college, I had no idea what I wanted to do. *No idea.*"

Tag wanted to ask about her father but decided that question would have to wait. She didn't look interested in going there at the moment.

"What did you major in?"

"Marketing." McKenna's musical laugh made Tag smile. "I have no idea why, but it seemed easy enough. I was halfway through my junior year when I started a blog. It was innocent, for the most part, and lasted all of a year before I ventured out and started Sensations, Inc. It's been going strong for four years now."

Tag did the math in his head, and if he figured it correctly, McKenna was twenty-five years old. That put her just seven years younger than him. Starting her own business at twenty-one was pretty impressive, but Tag was finding there were several things about her that impressed him. Her intelligence and drive definitely ranked at the top of the list.

"And you make money writing about sex?" he asked bluntly, distracted by the way her lips touched the glass as she sipped her wine.

"I do." Setting her glass back on the cloth-covered table, McKenna seemed to be watching him. "It's no different than what the McCoy brothers do."

There was a substantial difference, but Tag wasn't about to explain the two. He merely cocked his eyebrow, waiting for her to continue.

"Okay, so maybe there's a slight difference. But yes, to answer your question, I do make money talking about sex. I give people what they want."

"And people want to know about whether I keep toys in my dungeon?" He still had a hard time believing that one.

"Women lust after sexy, successful men. And you fit that profile, so yes. They want to know your dirty secrets."

"It doesn't bother you to share people's personal information with the world?"

"Well, technically, my reach isn't quite that far. And it's not as if I share all of the information I receive."

"No?"

"No," McKenna stated firmly but didn't elaborate.

They were interrupted by the waiter stopping by to refill the wine and let them know the food would be out shortly. He got the feeling McKenna was a little defensive about her career choice, and Tag's goal was not to piss her off on their first date.

First date? What the fuck? Had he just pulled that out of his ass or what? This damn sure wasn't a first date.

Obviously Tag was quiet for too long, because McKenna took the opportunity to throw out a question of her own. "And what about you? What made you want to be a lawyer?"

"My father's a lawyer. It seemed like an easy path to take, to make him happy."

"Did you spend your life trying to make him happy?"

Okay, so apparently he needed to carefully word his answers from here on out because he'd clearly given her too much information in just that one sentence.

"Not necessarily, no. My father didn't have it easy, and I realized at an early age that he gave everything he had to raise me on his own. I figured this was an easy way to give back to him for all he gave up for me."

Again, his mouth was clearly not getting the signals from his brain.

"What about your mother?"

"My mother passed away when I was in high school." This was a conversation Tag had no intention of having with her, so he quickly changed directions. "What do your parents think about what you do?"

"They pretend not to notice." McKenna grinned. "They both know exactly what I do, and if they enjoy it, they don't tell me. But they aren't against it, either. My parents have always been extremely supportive of me and my sister."

"Is your sister older or younger?"

"Older."

When the waiter approached, bringing their food, the conversation slowed, and they managed to eat while talking about much less personal topics. He found it relatively easy to talk to her, which was another thing that surprised him. She was smart, witty, and just as aggressive with her quest for knowledge as he expected her to be. For some reason, that didn't bother him like it normally did.

Once they finished their meal, they ordered dessert and shared another glass of wine while they waited.

"What happened to your father that made you not want to work for anyone else?" Tag asked the question he had put off earlier.

The way she shifted her jaw as she stared back at him, he knew she was debating on whether she was going to answer him.

"So that's how this is going to go?" she questioned.

"What? I'm interested in you, McKenna. Is that too hard to believe?"

"Yes. It is."

Tag knew she was deflecting, but he wasn't going to let her get away with it. "You know more about me than I do about you, so I figure it's only fair."

McKenna paused for a moment, sipping her wine as she stared back at him. Just when he thought she was going to blow off the question entirely, she answered, "Let's just say my father hasn't been dealt a promising hand throughout his career.

"He's one of those men who can sell ice cubes to an Eskimo, but due to his salary, he was always one of the first to be let go when a company decided to cut back. He'd already done what they needed him to do, so as far as they were concerned, he was expendable."

McKenna took another sip of her wine before continuing, "I didn't want to be that person. I didn't want to bust my ass to make my employer money only to be tossed out if they needed to make budget cuts."

Tag wasn't about to question her logic. As far as he was concerned, she made perfect sense. And by owning her own company, she knew what she was getting into and what she would get out of it day after day.

"While we're getting personal…" McKenna smiled as the waiter set their desserts down in front of them. "Why do you choose to give so much money to charity?"

The question caught him by surprise, although he knew it shouldn't have. If McKenna had been digging for information on him, she would've found the couple of mentions related to his sizable charity donations. "I don't need the money," he stated simply.

"Not good enough," she countered as she lifted her spoon to her mouth.

Tag smiled, his insides twisted with anticipation because he found so much enjoyment in watching her eat. Everything she did was sinfully erotic, even eating, and he wanted to sit there and watch her.

"It's my way of giving back. I've been blessed, I won't deny it, and as far as I'm concerned, if I don't need it, there are some very deserving people who do."

Realizing he had somehow led them back into a personal territory neither of them seemed comfortable with, Tag decided on a much more appropriate question. "Since you're so interested in what's in my closet, I've got a question of my own," he said as he watched her take another bite of crème brûlée.

"Only if you let me see what's in your closet," McKenna teased.

"From where I sit, it won't be long before you have a personal tour."

To his satisfaction, McKenna blushed, her freckle-dotted cheeks turning a pretty pink.

"What's your question?" she asked, obviously trying to distract him from watching her.

"If the police were to pull you over tonight, what's the most interesting thing they would find in your car?"

Tag knew the question was absurd, and based on the way she laughed, she knew it, too. He didn't find it much different than the one she had thrown out to her readers in her last article, though, so he waited patiently for her to answer.

"You're serious?" she asked.

"Very."

"Why would you think I have anything out of the ordinary in my car?" she questioned, still smiling.

"I don't know. Why would you think I have anything out of the ordinary in my closet?"

"Touché."

"Okay, forget that question. I've got a better one for you," Tag said seriously. "How many dates am I going to have to take you on before I get to know what color your bed sheets are?"

ON THE DRIVE back to her office, McKenna suddenly realized she wasn't ready for the night to end. She also realized it was in her best interest to get over that little disappointment, but she couldn't seem to help herself.

When Tag stopped the car in front of her office building, McKenna fumbled with her seat belt. It'd been a long time since she'd gone on a date, especially one that had gone as seamlessly as this one had, and she wasn't sure what she was supposed to do now.

"Thanks for dinner." She could at least thank him. That was a start.

When his warm hand touched her arm, McKenna stilled. It was totally insane of her to want something from this man, but when he touched her, even so innocently, she had a sudden craving for so much more. Getting to know him on a much more intimate level had done the exact opposite of helping her to stop thinking about him.

Glancing down, she noticed a drastic difference between his bronzed fingers against her pale wrist, and that led to much more inquisitive thoughts. Like what the rest of him would look like against her.

"I had a good time," he said, but his voice wasn't laced with the confidence or the arrogance she was used to. No, there was something much hungrier in his tone.

Knowing she shouldn't, McKenna turned slightly, glancing over at Tag's handsome face, her eyes grazing over his angular jaw, his perfect nose, and then to his eyes and the incredibly thick, dark lashes that would make most women jealous. Then she made the mistake of looking at his luscious lips. She had successfully avoided looking at his mouth for the better part of the evening, because when she did, she found herself fantasizing about what exquisite pleasure she might find in those lips.

When his hand came up, his fingers tilting her chin so that she faced him more directly, McKenna was transfixed on the way he moved closer to her. She held her breath, waiting, desperately hoping he would kiss her while praying he wouldn't, because she wasn't sure she was strong enough to resist a man like Tag. And she should resist him. She knew she should.

Oh, God.

When his soft, firm lips met hers in the sweetest, gentlest of kisses, she had to hold back the urge to crawl over the center console and settle into his lap.

He didn't push for more, nor did she, but their lips lingered for long seconds before he pulled back. "I'll see you tomorrow."

McKenna nodded, her fingers instinctively going to her mouth as though she were trying to hold on to the feel of him. She wasn't sure what to say, so she didn't say anything at all. As gracefully as she could manage, she opened the passenger door and escaped the tight confines of Tag's extravagant car. She hurried to her own car, never looking back.

As it turned out, walking away from him was the hardest thing she'd done all day.

Chapter *Four*

"I'M NOT SAYING it's a bad idea, but you know I'm going to have to talk to Luke," Logan told Tag after he'd spent the last half hour explaining McKenna's request.

"That's where I'm headed next," Tag replied coolly, leaning back in his chair.

After leaving McKenna a short while ago at her office, Tag had called Logan asking if he could stop by to talk. Because he knew what Logan was likely expecting, he'd been sure to be very detailed in his reason for needing to come by. Despite Logan's disappointed tone, he had agreed.

Ever since his arrival, he and Logan had been sitting on the back porch hashing out McKenna's request. As always, Logan was playing the devil's advocate, but he did seem sincerely interested in the idea. In Tag's opinion, McKenna's suggestion was a win-win for them, but no matter what he said, it would never be up to him. And yes, Tag fully intended to talk to Luke himself, but he'd wanted to run it by Logan first. Just to get a feel for what he thought.

"It's a good plan," Tag restated, taking a long pull on his beer and admiring the view of the pool from where they sat.

The view brought back pleasant memories of times he'd spent at their house in previous months — specifically images of Samantha.

Tag was grateful that Sam had been engrossed in work ever since he'd arrived, which meant she was paying him absolutely no mind. Considering he wasn't interested in answering the questions he knew were plaguing both Logan and Sam, it couldn't have worked out better. From where he sat, he could see Sam just inside the house, feverishly typing on her laptop, never once looking up.

He felt a little awkward not explaining himself, but since neither of them had asked, he hadn't offered. Tag could sense the question lingering between him and Logan, but it was never mentioned, and since they hadn't gotten together in the last month for any of their late-night trysts, he figured it was clear that it likely wouldn't be happening anymore.

When he thought back to his dinner with McKenna and the interest he found himself having in her, Tag didn't doubt that his relationship with Logan and Samantha had come to an abrupt end. All three of them had insisted they maintain exclusivity for the duration of their time together, and Tag knew he couldn't promise that any longer. He didn't quite know what the hell he was doing with McKenna, but he felt it was best to avoid any lascivious activities with the two of them for the foreseeable future.

"I don't disagree with you there," Logan said after a moment of silence. "I'm not sure how Luke will feel about it, though."

Tag wasn't too worried about Luke. The man was having a hard enough time dealing with the overbearing members who were suddenly worried their identities would be leaked. That's all they seemed to be worried about. As far as Tag was concerned, they were a bunch of self-righteous assholes who didn't care about anything other than themselves, especially not what might potentially happen to Luke and Logan should Susan Toulmin continue on her tirade. Even with his sudden distaste for their reactions, in a way, he did understand their concern, which was partly why he liked McKenna's idea.

He figured some insight into the club would likely deflect some of the interest. With so many people wanting to know more, it was only a matter of time before information got out that they didn't want to. As far as the member list, Luke wasn't worried, and neither was Tag. That list was highly confidential, and there were only three people who even knew the contents of the entire list — Luke, Logan, and Tag.

Had Tag not insisted, in order to represent them successfully, he'd likely be in the dark, as well. Not that he cared who was on the list, but at least he had some idea of what the impact would be should Susan actually find someone to listen to her. And that was only a matter of time, Tag knew.

"Are you interested in her?" Logan's abrupt, serious tone had Tag turning back to face his friend.

He didn't quite know how to answer the question, or possibly, he just didn't know how to explain what it was he felt for McKenna at this point. He was interested in her, yes. That was undeniable. But how far that interest would take him was yet to be seen. "There's something there," he admitted calmly, leaning forward in his chair and resting his forearms on the table.

So much for getting out of there without an inquisition.

When Tag thought Logan would ask another question, he surprised him by pausing to stare out at the pool. The door behind them clicked as it opened, and Tag knew that Sam was coming to join them.

"Is something wrong?" she asked sweetly, walking over to Logan as he leaned back in his chair, allowing her to sit on his lap.

"Nothing's wrong, baby." Logan smiled, and Tag saw the mix of admiration and longing on Logan's face that was always there when he looked at his wife.

"Are you sure?" she asked again, her eyes darting back and forth between the two of them. There were a few seconds of silence as Sam got comfortable.

"I don't know her," Sam began when it was clear no one else was going to speak, turning her attention to Tag, "but I think she's exactly what you need."

The statement was so far out of left field Tag felt blindsided by it. He didn't know what to say, or whether he was supposed to say anything at all. "Look, Sam, I'm sorry."

"Sorry?" To his surprise, Sam smiled knowingly. "You don't have anything to be sorry about, Tag."

"I know you two are looking for someone…" He wasn't sure what he was trying to say at this point, so he stared down at his beer bottle, tearing at the label.

"Tag." Sam's stern tone forced him to meet her gaze. "Please don't ever worry about me and Logan. We have each other, and that's honestly all we will ever need."

Tag watched as Logan wrapped his arms around her waist, holding her tight and resting his forehead against her arm. It was a sweet gesture, and it effectively made Tag feel like the outsider he had been all along.

"I care about you," Sam clarified. "How can I not? What we've had these last few months has been amazing. I'll always care about you, which is why I understand that this isn't permanent. We would never expect that from you just as you didn't expect it from us."

No, Tag hadn't expected a permanent relationship with Logan and Sam, which was why he had opted to be with them in the first place. His relationships were always temporary, and he enjoyed them that way. He wasn't sure what he wanted from McKenna, but for some reason, maybe he was just plain crazy, he felt there was something else between them. Whatever it was, he knew he had to at least pursue it to find out.

"Trust me, Tag," Sam said as she wrapped her arm loosely around Logan's head, holding him closer to her. "Logan has taught me so many things about myself, I still feel like I'm evolving. You never have to worry about me or him, for that matter. When it comes down to it, we know what the other one needs, and I can assure you, we'll figure out how to satisfy all of the cravings one day." Her smile was sweet and gentle, so much like the woman herself.

Tag would never forget the time they'd had together, but he also knew that, as far as long term, it wouldn't have worked for much longer anyway. The sex was phenomenal, and there wasn't a single time that he hadn't found exactly what he was looking for from the two of them, but he knew something was missing.

Truthfully, he didn't want to feel as though anything was missing, but he felt it nonetheless. When he looked at McKenna, he felt something more than the intense physical attraction, and it might just be a figment of his imagination or some misplaced desire to have what the others around him had obviously found. No matter what it was or what it wasn't, Tag had to take this chance. For his own sanity, if nothing else.

"She's a lucky woman," Sam grinned. "And I think she might just be what you need."

Tag wasn't sure about all that, but he smiled anyway.

"Thanks, Sam. Well, I need to get going." Tag had to get over to the club and talk to Luke as soon as possible. He needed to have an answer for McKenna by morning or risk some more shit being broadcast worldwide.

"I'll call Luke and let him know what I think. That way, when you talk to him, it won't be a surprise," Logan said, looking up from where he sat still holding Sam.

With a nod and a smile, Tag walked away.

MCKENNA HAD ONLY been home for a few minutes before she found herself pacing the floor. After checking her emails, hoping mostly for her editors to return both of her potential articles for tomorrow, she'd been disappointed not to find anything from either of them in her inbox.

This left her with precisely nothing to do except get on her own nerves.

In order to avoid that, she found herself back in her car, heading downtown. Figuring that the lesser of two evils would be to get out of the house, it had been an easy decision to head over to Club Destiny for a drink. Except now, as she drove through the darkened streets, McKenna was beginning to wonder whether her masochistic side was making another appearance.

Ever since she'd exited Tag's car back at her office, she couldn't help but think about that mind-blowing kiss. It hadn't been anything more than a meeting of lips, but it was somehow more explosive than some of the down-and-dirty, tongue-action kisses from her past.

Most of them, actually.

The only thing about it that bothered her was the easy way Tag had seemed to drive away afterward. How could he not have been affected by that? She had been nearly knocked right out of her gorgeous designer shoes.

So, in order to avoid pacing back and forth, or worse…cleaning her entire house from top to bottom, McKenna was pulling into the parking garage of one place she was pretty much guaranteed to run into Tag.

Hell, she was a lost cause — there was no denying it.

After pulling into one of the few spaces left in a garage that was already full on a Thursday night, McKenna shut off the engine and gripped the steering wheel.

She got the strange feeling that all of the times she had encountered Tag in the past were only leading up to something more. After each meeting, she found herself more and more affected by him, but she couldn't pinpoint what that meant. The only thing she knew for sure, their relationship was slowly morphing into something entirely unexpected. Whatever it was that they continued to dance around couldn't be ignored forever.

Nor did she want it to.

No matter how much she tried to convince her overactive imagination that this was strictly business and nothing more, she knew that wasn't the case. Yes, she wanted a tour of the club, and she wasn't about to pretend otherwise. She wanted to walk the halls, talk to the owners, and get a good understanding of what went on there. Her readers expected her to have the lowdown on anything and everything erotic. Club Destiny fit that description.

Except she found herself thinking more about Tag than she did about anything else. She still wanted to do all of those things, but it seemed she had a more selfish motive now. One that involved bringing her closer to a man who exuded so much … masculinity. He was distinguished and reserved, yet approachable and so intensely male; and above all else, he pulled it all together and still exuded that laid-back southern charm that she found so damn hot.

There was something else she'd managed to pick up from her conversations with him. He wasn't interested in relationships. He hadn't admitted as much, but she could sense how much of himself that he kept in reserve, reluctant to share with others. And maybe it was just because she was a journalist that he wasn't interested in talking about himself, but she didn't think so.

McKenna would never downplay her abilities, and one of them included pretending with the best of them. Since she knew whatever was happening between her and Tag would be temporary at best, she would just have to convince him that she wasn't interested in anything other than an exclusive on the club. While she was at it, she was going to try to convince herself of the same thing. Any interaction with Tag Murphy was safer that way.

She didn't figure their dinner date would lead to anything more because McKenna was still convinced she was way too outspoken and forward for a man like him. But stranger things had happened, and she knew never to expect anything less than the unexpected.

Slowly exiting her car, she tried to force the thoughts away, because no matter what little hope she had left, she knew Tag was clearly out of her reach in any way that might matter outside of their business relationship.

"Damn it," McKenna muttered as her heels echoed on the concrete floor as she made her way to the back entrance to the club.

"Such dirty words coming from such a pretty mouth." The deep, sultry southern twang echoed around her, and McKenna fought the urge to stop.

"What do you want, Murphy? You have an answer for me yet?" she asked in her cool, professional tone, remembering the path her thoughts had been leading down for the last few minutes.

"I've got plenty of answers for you, baby," Tag growled softly, nodding his head toward the bouncer standing near the back door. The man nodded back, stepping out of the way so Tag could open the door, allowing her to walk in ahead of him.

Such a gentleman.

It would seem she had memory problems, because instead of remembering why she didn't want to like this man, she suddenly wanted to know what he would be like in bed. Was he the same southern gentleman? The one with the soft, sweet kisses? Or would that rough, intimidating dark side of his come out? *Shit.* Now she wanted to know.

Once inside, Tag put his hand on the small of her back, and McKenna damn near stumbled in her three-inch heels. The warmth of his hand seared her spine and had a direct effect on the sensitive, apparently needy place between her thighs. Unsure where he was leading her, McKenna continued walking until they reached the bar.

"Kane," Tag greeted the familiar bartender whose name McKenna hadn't known until now.

"What's up, T?" The devilishly handsome, if not intimidating, man greeted. "What can I get you?"

"Get my friend anything she wants and put it on my tab."

Damn him. She was half tempted to glare at him and tell him that she didn't need anything from him other than an answer to her request from earlier in the day. She didn't, though.

"I'll be back in a few minutes," Tag whispered in her ear, the rough, gravelly words sounding more like a promise than just to inform her.

"Take your time." McKenna tried to play it cool, tried to pretend like she didn't care one way or the other what he did, but the truth was, despite knowing better, she still wanted to know more about the intensely sexy attorney.

But she wouldn't be doing that now. Tag was gone.

A second later, she saw him emerge from the crowd as he ascended the stairs to the second floor. Her eyes were glued to him, unable to detect the stunning physique she knew was beneath that expensive suit.

She continued watching him as he punched in that secret code that would lead him to the kink and depravity that existed in that other world she wanted to know so much about.

Shaking off the thought, McKenna thanked Kane for her drink and then went in search of an empty table a little farther from the crowd. As much as she would prefer to stand, or even walk around, she couldn't bring herself to do it. The restless energy made it difficult, but there was no way she was going to let Tag know how tight he wound her. She had no idea whether he could see her from where he was, but on the off chance that was possible, she wasn't going to give him anything to use against her later.

She settled for a table that allowed a view of the dance floor and sat down. She watched several of the gyrating couples, wondering whether they even knew what was on the other side of that door on the second floor. She certainly wondered.

Most of these people were probably too excited about a night out with friends even to care. With the music blaring and people trying to speak over it, McKenna managed to get lost in the chaos of the club rather than wondering what Tag was doing at that very moment.

If she was lucky, he was talking to Luke about the exclusive, but she tried not to get her hopes up. He'd seemed to allude to that fact, but knowing Tag, he would never out-and-out tell her exactly what she wanted to know. She had thought about reminding him of her threat to disclose more information, but she wasn't naive enough to believe Tag was swayed in any way by threats. No, the man was probably impossible to rattle with his abundance of confidence and his *I don't give a fuck* attitude.

"McKenna? McKenna Thorne?" An unfamiliar voice caught her attention, and she slowly turned to look at the man standing just a few inches to her left.

She didn't immediately recognize the sexy cowboy, but she rummaged through as many mental images as possible to try to figure out whether she knew him. She figured she didn't based on the way he questioned whether she was really the person he thought she was.

"That's me," she replied to the tall, handsome stranger with the black Stetson pulled low over his eyes, throwing his face in just enough shadow that she had a hard time identifying him anyway.

"Travis Walker," the man introduced himself, taking off the black Stetson and holding it to his side momentarily.

As soon as she got a better look at those sinful blue-gray eyes, she recognized him. "Mr. Walker, nice to actually meet you in person."

McKenna had not been introduced to any of the Walker brothers up to this point because she had been unable to attend the groundbreaking of the new Alluring Indulgence resort down in Austin, despite having made every effort. Due to other, more pressing matters, she had regretfully declined the invitation she'd received.

Without asking, Travis took the seat beside her, setting his cowboy hat back on his head and pinning her with a wickedly sexy grin.

McKenna tried to pretend she wasn't on the edge of her seat, ready to rapid-fire questions at this man because, aside from the Club Destiny story, the Walkers' new resort was fast becoming the talk of the media. At least in her circles it was. She was impatiently ready to learn everything there was to know about this new erotic retreat that was making headlines faster than they were building.

"What brings you to Dallas?" she questioned him, watching as he took a long pull on his beer.

She had to agree with the other erotic newsfeeds that she kept her eye on these days; this man was undeniably as intensely attractive as everyone claimed. With his smoldering eyes, that rugged stubbly jaw, those dazzling white teeth, and yes, even his slightly crooked nose, Travis Walker was definitely swoon worthy.

"Business."

And he was also extremely vague.

She had heard that about him.

Apparently, according to the rumors, he wasn't much for talking, but when he did open his mouth, people usually dropped what they were doing to listen. She would probably drop everything just to listen to the deep rumble of his voice and that mouthwatering Texas drawl.

"Investors, right?"

Travis questioned her with a glance, cocking one eyebrow as he watched her.

"You're here looking for an investor for the new resort?"

He still didn't answer, but he smiled, and she was taken aback by his rugged masculinity. Those tall, dark, and devastatingly handsome men seemed to do that to her.

"Are you interested in doing an exclusive on the resort?" he asked, cutting right to the point.

McKenna bit her lip, fighting the urge to jump up and down in excitement. She managed to hide her enthusiasm. Instead, looking at him skeptically, she asked, "An exclusive?"

Another thing she had perfected...playing hard to get.

"If you're not interested, I'd hate to waste your time." The beginnings of another smile tipped his perfect lips, and McKenna had a hard time listening to the words coming out of his mouth. She wondered if this was what happened to all women who came face-to-face with this man.

But, as much as she admired a pretty face, there was still only one man who had managed to intrigue her to the point of distraction in recent months. Travis Walker was definitely panty-melting hot, but fortunately for her, her panties were fire retardant where he was concerned. Tag, on the other hand, was an entirely different story.

"I'm interested," she said softly but loud enough for him to hear. "In an exclusive," she added for good measure, because the way his eyes swept down to her mouth spoke of things better left unexplored. "Did you have a time frame in mind? From what I remember, you just recently broke ground."

"Building is underway. As far as I'm concerned, the hard part is behind us. Let me buy you a drink, and we can work out the details."

McKenna smiled at the sexy cowboy. How in the world could she resist that?

Chapter *Five*

"*AN EXCLUSIVE*? WHAT the hell is that?" Luke's face was a mask of confusion, but Tag saw the smile pulling at the edge of the other man's mouth. Luke knew exactly what Tag was referring to, probably thanks to a conversation he'd had with his twin, Logan, moments before Tag had arrived.

"She wants to do an article, or a series of them, on the club. Sensations, Inc. would have the privilege of using the information she obtains first for her online magazine."

"So, what? She comes in here, walks through the halls, and peeks in the rooms?" Luke looked serious now, and Tag knew the question he wasn't asking.

"Yes. In a sense. I would restrict her to the private area on the second floor," he said, feeling the need to clarify. If McKenna Thorne thought he was going to reveal all of their secrets, she was sadly mistaken.

"And I assume you'll be the one taking her on this guided tour?" That hint of a smile was back, and this time it unnerved Tag slightly.

"I will." Tag was all for taking her on the tour, but he had an entirely different idea for how this was going to work than he figured McKenna did.

It was an idea that he had given considerable thought to, as a matter of fact.

Tag leaned back in his chair, watching while Luke pondered the information he had just been given. He seemed sincerely torn on whether or not he wanted to do this, which only made sense. Granted, had Tag come in here and suggested this to Luke McCoy a few months ago, he'd have been laughed right out the office, followed by a string of obscenities that would probably make his ears bleed. That was before Luke's entire personality had an overhaul. He knew the credit for that miraculous feat went to Tag's step-brother, Cole, and their lover, Sierra Sellers.

These days, it took quite a bit more to get the hard-ass Luke McCoy riled up, although it was guaranteed to happen if anyone said anything cross about either Sierra or Cole. Luke was protective of those he loved, and even more so about his two lovers.

"Considering Susan is chomping at the bit to try and get someone to listen to her, I think that allowing McKenna to write a few respectable articles about the club would be in your best interest."

"My best interest?" Luke grinned. "Why do I get this feeling that you're getting something out of this deal?"

Well, there was that.

Tag smiled knowingly and continued, "She's looking to get enough information to provide legitimate, factual details to her readers. I figure what better way than to introduce her to some of the idiosyncrasies of some of the members. Namely me."

Tag had come up with the idea after leaving McKenna's office earlier in the day. Of course, his reasons might be a little selfish, but he didn't need to tell Luke that. It was obvious by his expression that he knew exactly what Tag was after.

For the next fifteen minutes, Tag offered Luke a glimpse of his perspective on how this exclusive would work. By the time he was finished, Luke was smiling. "And I get to preview and approve any story that goes out, right?"

"That's the agreement." McKenna had already volunteered that detail, but Tag was going to ensure it was firmly stated in the fine print.

"I say go for it, bro. I don't see that it could make things any worse," Luke stated before pausing briefly, then smiling. "But one more thing."

Tag didn't like the sound of that.

"Good luck." Luke laughed unabashedly. "I've read some things on McKenna Thorne. You're a braver man than me, Murph. Braver man than me."

Tag grinned. When it came to McKenna, he was ready for the challenge.

As Tag descended the stairs, he scanned the crowded bar, hoping like hell McKenna hadn't left yet. He wasn't sure how well he liked that feeling, but nonetheless, it was there. It wasn't often that he found himself hopeful for anything, much less a woman.

Considering he had been in Luke's office for close to an hour, it was possible she had given up and gone home. He doubted it, though. He couldn't think of a single reason she would show up at the club unless she was hoping to get an answer from him tonight. She wasn't a regular. He would've known if she were, because McKenna was the type of woman who attracted attention, especially from men. Even if she didn't intend to. If he was right, she was planted somewhere close, probably watching him right now as he looked for her.

His mind was scanning through the images he'd conjured up while he'd been sharing his plan with Luke, and at this point, he was damn ready to show McKenna exactly what he had in store for her.

That's when he saw her.

Her back was to him, and he recognized all of that crimson silk flowing down her back even from halfway across the room. He could only see her in profile, but he could tell she was laughing, her smile practically lighting up the entire room as she regarded the man sitting beside her.

A man who might be damn lucky if he was allowed to walk out of the bar with both legs intact.

Taking a deep breath and a quick detour by the bar, Tag tried to calm himself. As he waited for Kane to pour the bourbon, he continued to watch McKenna and the cowboy sitting across from her. Thankfully, before he went over and made a complete jackass out of himself, he recognized exactly whom she was talking to.

Travis Walker.

Infatuation

Tag hadn't even known the guy was in town. Not that he should have, but he figured Luke or Logan would've filled him in. As part of the agreement between the men, Travis had applied to become a member of the club. Last Tag had heard, he'd been approved but hadn't come back to sign on the dotted line.

Maybe that's why he was there tonight.

Tag retrieved his drink from the bar and headed in McKenna's direction. She was so engrossed in her conversation with Travis she didn't see him approach, which was more than fine with him. He came up from behind, set his glass on the table, and then leaned down until his lips brushed the soft outer edge of her ear. "Miss me?"

He felt the shiver that ran through McKenna at his words, but other than that, she did a good job of hiding her reaction.

"Travis." Tag greeted the man sitting across from McKenna, holding his hand out until Travis gripped it firmly and returned the handshake. "Good to see you again."

"Murphy," Travis acknowledged. "Looks like we both might just want the same thing from Ms. Thorne."

Tag clamped his teeth together but never changed his expression from one of indifference as he glanced back and forth between the pair. The jealousy that coursed through his bloodstream was growing all the more annoying each time he felt it, but he'd be damned if he knew what he was supposed to do to stop it.

"Is that right?" he questioned.

McKenna finally looked over at him briefly, and if he wasn't mistaken, there was a rosy tint to her pale cheeks that he hadn't seen earlier.

"An exclusive," she said, smirking as though she found his reaction humorous.

"Well, I'm not sure Club Destiny is necessarily pursuing Ms. Thorne; however, it is a discussion we're currently having."

Had Travis been anyone else, Tag would've been irritated that he seemed to know about the club's personal business.

"I better get going," Travis stated as he stood. "I've got a meeting with Luke shortly."

54

"How's your brother?" Tag asked as Travis stood. Tag had been keeping tabs on Zane ever since the groundbreaking ceremony for Alluring Indulgence, but he hadn't heard anything in the last few days.

"Better." Something in Travis' eyes told Tag there was more to it than his simple answer, but true to form, the man wasn't going to elaborate.

Hell, Tag was surprised he'd said as much as he had in the last few minutes. Aside from business, which this could probably be categorized as, Travis wasn't known for his long-windedness.

"Glad to hear it. And it was good to see you again." Tag pulled out the chair on the other side of McKenna, watching Travis intently. He couldn't help but wonder whether Travis Walker had more interest in McKenna than just a story on his upcoming resort. He also couldn't help but wonder why he actually gave a damn. But he did.

"You, too. And as for you, Ms. Thorne, I look forward to seeing you again soon."

When the cowboy walked away, Tag turned his attention to the beautiful woman now staring intently at him. He knew what she wanted. And as much as he'd like to think it was him that she was after, he knew better. The sexy journalist was after the tidbit of information he'd garnered from Luke McCoy earlier.

As much as he wanted to tell her the answer right here and end her suspense, he wasn't going to. Where was the fun in that? Not to mention, this wasn't the place to do it. Figuring that taking her up to his private room would give away more information than he was willing to at this point, he decided on a different tack.

"What time can I meet you at your office in the morning?" he asked, sipping his bourbon.

"Tomorrow?" The single word dripped with disappointment, but he had to give her credit; he didn't detect a hint of it on her stunning features.

A smile threatened as Tag kept his eyes on her, watching for the telltale sign of her anxiety. She wanted this exclusive; he knew she did. But if he wasn't mistaken, McKenna wanted something else, as well.

"Yes. Tomorrow. Unless you won't have time to see me."

Her lengthy pause, as she regarded him, intrigued Tag.

"No. Tomorrow's fine. I get to the office around six, and I should be there for most of the morning."

"Six? You're out a little late for a woman who gets up so early."

"Don't worry about me, Mr. Murphy. I'm quite capable of deciding when is too late," she retorted before pushing her chair back.

He'd successfully pissed her off. He hadn't necessarily been trying to, but the back-and-forth between them led him to believe it was what she expected. She was still wary of his intentions even after dinner and that little tease of a kiss that still made his dick stir when he thought about it.

"I'll see you in the morning then," he told her and then turned away as though brushing her off.

"What time?" she asked, and he heard the exasperation in her voice. McKenna was used to controlling the situation, making those she interacted with bend to her will, but she would soon learn Tag wasn't the type of man she normally did business with. Nor was he the man who would bow at her pretty little feet and give her everything she demanded.

"What time what?" he asked, pretending not to know what she was talking about.

"What time will you be at my office?"

"I'm not sure. I guess it depends on what I do tonight. Don't worry, I'll be there."

McKenna glared at him and then stormed off. Tag enjoyed watching her walk away, but he'd have much preferred to see her on her knees before him.

If he had anything to say about it, she'd be doing more of the latter real soon.

Chapter *Six*

MCKENNA WAS IN her office promptly at six o'clock the next morning, armed with a large coffee and an even larger dose of frustration. She was still pissed at Tag for leading her on the night before, insinuating she would get the answer she wanted before the night was out. He hadn't actually committed to giving her an answer, but yes, she had assumed. Shame on her.

Now, she was expecting him to show up, at his leisure, to give her an answer.

Well, she'd be ready for him.

That morning, when she'd crawled out of bed and into the shower, she'd decided it was time to don the power outfit. The one that made her feel as though she could conquer the world. Every woman had one, and hers happened to be a tight black miniskirt, a sheer black shirt, and a black camisole beneath it. To top off the ensemble, she had on her favorite platform-heel, thigh-high boots because she was a woman on a mission.

She'd pulled her hair up on top of her head, clipped it in stylish disarray, and that was that. As always, she didn't use a lot of makeup, but this time, she'd accentuated her eyes, knowing that men seemed to salivate when they got a good look at her eyes. Exotic, people called them.

Pulling her chair up to her desk, she opened her laptop and began prepping today's article. She'd finally received the edits, and she just needed to make a couple of tweaks to get it prepared for publishing. McKenna was going to be prepared for Tag no matter what time he decided to show up.

"*Depends on what I do tonight,*" McKenna mocked him out loud, her fingers digging into the keyboard.

The audacity of that man.

With her fingers flying across the keyboard, McKenna managed to immerse herself in the juicy details that she would be posting later that day. Obviously so engrossed in what she was doing, she hadn't realized what time it was until there was a knock on her office door.

Glancing at the clock on the computer, she saw that it was after nine, which meant Whisper was somewhere in the office.

"Come in," she called out but didn't get up from her chair, nor did she look up from what she was doing. McKenna knew who it was, because if it were her assistant, she wouldn't have knocked. She'd be damned if she were going to appear eager for this conversation.

Truth be told, it was killing her.

"Morning," Tag said in that overly charming twang of his, which she had to admit caught her attention, and she slowly allowed her gaze to slide from the computer screen to the man standing just inside the door of her office.

Oh, Lord! Have mercy.

Tag Murphy was a powerful, confident man when he was sporting one of those fancy, expensive suits, but what she saw before her nearly had her eyes bugging out of her head.

Gone was the buttoned-up attorney, and in his place was the intimidating, mouthwatering man wearing a pair of faded, well-worn jeans and a long-sleeve, black button-down shirt. She wasn't surprised to see he was wearing long sleeves, because now that she thought about it, she'd never seen Tag wear anything else.

"Morning," she whispered, still staring at him with renewed interest. Gone was all of the animosity she'd built up overnight, and in its place was scorching-hot lust.

When Tag closed the door behind him, then engaged the lock, McKenna bit her bottom lip.

"Did you come with an answer for me?" she asked, not feeling nearly as poised as she had hoped to be when he arrived.

"I might have," he drawled out slowly. "But first, we need to get a few things cleared up."

She couldn't agree more.

Standing, McKenna forced the starch back into her legs as she moved around to the front of her desk and leaned against the edge. She could exude the powerful executive every bit as much as he could; only she could do it in four-inch heels. She crossed her arms over her chest, her legs at her ankles, and waited for him to proceed.

The way his gaze lingered on her legs for longer than was appropriate in a business setting made her smile.

"That outfit normally work on men?" Tag asked, sounding just as cocky as he had the night before.

"I don't see you complaining," she retorted, straightening her back just slightly.

"Oh, honey, I'm not complaining, but I can tell you what you'd be wearing if it were up to me."

McKenna didn't even want to go there. She had a good idea.

"Cut to it, Tag. Are Luke and Logan interested in my offer or not?"

She watched him, feeling the intensity in those forest-green eyes. He might've shed the power suit, but he hadn't shed the dominant alpha male that was obviously a part of his chemical makeup.

"There are some rules to this endeavor, so before you get excited, you might want to read the fine print."

The fine print?

Had he seriously drawn up a contract? *Oh, fuck.* No sooner had she thought it than Tag pulled a folded piece of paper out of his back pocket.

"Want me to read it to you? Or do you prefer to do that yourself?" Tag asked as he moved closer. His gaze was predatory in nature, and she felt like a gazelle that had just been cornered by a hungry lion.

"I can read it, thank you." That should've come out a little bit more firmly, but McKenna was suddenly having a hard time focusing on anything except the warm, hard male body standing mere centimeters away. The rich, musky scent of his cologne tickled her senses, and it was like a starburst of lust had been set off in her bloodstream. It was a heady thing, his smell.

He was holding the paper, and she had to unfold her arms from her chest in order to take it. The downside was the move also allowed Tag to see how her nipples had puckered — her body's apparent approval.

She knew she should move, should return to her chair and read the contract word by word, but she couldn't seem to get her legs to cooperate.

"Here, let me help." Tag's voice caressed her nerve endings while his breath grazed her cheek. He was leaning in closer, bending his head down so that his lips were close to her ear, and from this proximity, she could feel the warmth of his body like an electric blanket set on high.

She didn't want his help. At least, not for reading the contract. She'd be happy to accept it, though, if he were offering to help her in other ways … namely to sate the maelstrom of lust that was raging like a wildfire in her veins.

She unfolded the paper, turning it right side up and then glancing at the first line.

Her breath caught in her chest.

"Is this even legal?" she asked, her gaze darting to his as he moved back slightly.

"Every word," he assured her, but she doubted it.

"Length of contract is seven days?"

"That's just for the exclusive. There's another clause at the bottom. Be sure to read that."

She wasn't even close to the bottom, and she could barely breathe, her body no longer willing to hold herself up as she read all of the raunchy, libidinous things that he intended to "introduce" her to. Nowhere in the contract did it state that she would have to participate, but she had a sneaking suspicion that part was assumed. The funny thing, her body was totally on board.

"You have to be kidding." The words spilled out on the breath she'd managed to hold in.

"Never." Tag was even closer than before, this time the hard plane of his chest brushing against her fingers where she held the paper in front of her. "You play by my rules for the next seven days, and I promise you won't be disappointed."

A week? McKenna wasn't so sure she'd last seven minutes with this man, let alone seven days. "I don't understand."

"What's not to understand?" Tag took the paper from her hand, placing it on the desk behind her, then tilted her chin up with the tips of his fingers until their eyes met.

And held.

"You want something that I can give you, and in return, I want something from you," he explained, his voice low and calm, the opposite of everything churning within her as he stood so very close.

"And what do you want?" McKenna asked, trying to eliminate the tremble in her voice.

"You."

It was then that the room faded. The only thing McKenna noticed was the warmth of Tag's chest against her breasts, the rigid length of his erection pressing intimately between her thighs, the sultry, intoxicating scent that was so unique to him, and the mesmerizing heat swirling in his green eyes.

The answer should've been easy. The exclusive would likely launch Sensations, Inc. into another dimension, and the passion in Tag's beautiful eyes promised so many things McKenna wrote about for her readers' benefit. Now she had the opportunity to experience them with Tag.

Even with the experience she had in the lifestyle, she was still hesitant.

Promiscuous McKenna wasn't. Prone to heartache ... that was more like it. In fact, she knew that this wild ride Tag would take her on would likely result in another devastating broken heart because she couldn't resist being pulled into his orbit.

There was no doubt about it — McKenna wouldn't survive this with her heart intact.

TAG HAD BEEN hell-bent on walking into McKenna's office, handing her a contract, and all but throwing her down on the desk and fucking her blind. But standing here, so close to her, inhaling her sweet, fresh scent, and watching the confusion linger in her exotically beautiful eyes had him pausing.

For a woman who exuded such confidence, such drive, he felt the tension course through her veins as easily as he felt the warmth of her body pressed into his. She wasn't pushing him away, but she might as well have been by the way she looked at him.

Uncertainty.

That's what he saw when he looked at her. And that dark, possessive beast that lurked just beneath the surface roared loudly, insisting that this was one opportunity he'd been searching for. The chance he couldn't let pass him by. Because no matter what happened a week from now, Tag had the next seven days to show this woman exactly how hot the fire between them could be stoked.

"Say yes, McKenna." His fingers lightly brushed down the soft, smooth skin of her jaw, then trailed along the long, sleek column of her neck, soaking up the baby-soft feel of her skin.

He wanted to put his mouth there, to kiss a path over her warm, fragrant skin as he removed every stitch of her clothing until she stood before him completely vulnerable.

"One week, that's all I ask." He couldn't resist trying to persuade her. Honestly, he thought convincing her would be the easy part, but Tag was beginning to realize there wasn't anything easy about McKenna Thorne.

"One week. It's that simple?" she asked, her eyes still locked with his.

Simple? Tag knew this would be anything but simple. Yet he needed her to say yes.

He slid his finger back up the long, perfect column of her neck until he reached the bottom of her chin, and he tilted her head just slightly, offering him better access to those soft pink lips that beckoned him. Ensuring she knew what he was after, Tag glanced down at her lips, then back to her eyes. When her tongue darted out, swiping over her bottom lip before she pulled it in between her teeth, he groaned.

And then he kissed her.

Only this wasn't a regular, run-of-the-mill kiss. This was passion and fury laced with carnal desires as their mouths met and sought everything the other was willing to give.

McKenna's arms came up to circle around his neck, and Tag pulled her closer, lifting her easily off of the floor and setting her gently on the desk behind her. Cupping her cheeks, he held her mouth to his, ensuring she wouldn't get away, although she was kissing him back, seemingly just as invested in this wild, uninhibited kiss as he was.

Her soft, sweet moans had his cock jerking as he pressed between her thighs, his hips rocking against hers causing that damn short skirt to ride up. In less than five seconds, he'd been reduced to a horny teenager thanks to the smoking-hot woman in his arms.

"McKenna." Tag managed to break the kiss, both of them panting yet neither of them pulling away. "If we keep this up, you'll be naked in less than a minute."

The seductive little smirk that tipped her kiss-swollen lips nearly pushed Tag to his limits. Instead of sinking to his knees and burying his head between her luscious thighs, he pulled away, taking two steps back. If he'd had hair, he would've thrust his hands through it at that point. Instead, he simply stood there, staring at the one woman who single-handedly stole every ounce of his common sense with just a kiss.

"I'm in." McKenna grinned, standing up and adjusting her skirt, although it didn't cover much more when it was in place than it had when he'd pushed it farther up on her hips.

"Seven days," he reminded her.

"I'm pretty sure I can handle you, Tag," she said with another cocky smile. "But I've got a couple of amendments to the contract that I'll be sending your way this afternoon. If you're still interested, call me and let me know."

Tag didn't think for one second that she could say anything that would change his mind. For some reason, he had a feeling McKenna was way more experienced in his world than he'd given her credit for, and he was beginning to wonder whether or not he could handle *her*.

With a not-so-subtle adjustment, Tag resituated himself before turning his back on her and heading to the door.

"Starting tomorrow morning," he informed her, "you'll meet me at the club at eight o'clock sharp. Be sure to finish reading the contract so you know everything to expect." It was his turn to smile. "And I'll be waiting for those amendments."

Chapter *Seven*

MCKENNA WAS UP with the sun the following morning, eager and anxiously awaiting the limousine that would be coming to pick her up. After she had amended the contract to suit her better, she'd sent it to Tag and received an email response. Not a phone call like she'd expected. That had made her smile.

According to the information in the contract, she would be taking a full leave of absence for the next week and had to be prepared to do so. That included packing her clothes and other necessities, which she had done the night before.

As soon as she'd received Tag's agreement to the additional terms, McKenna had called Whisper into her office and shared the details that she was allowed, having to make sure someone would handle Sensations, Inc. while she was away. To her delight, Whisper was eager to be in charge, and since McKenna trusted her with her life, there weren't any issues.

Well, except one tiny one.

The seven days she'd be spending with Tag Murphy.

As soon as she'd read the fine print in the documents he'd provided her, she'd known he'd set her up. But little did he know, she was up for the challenge. Even if it would be the biggest one of her life thus far.

Being under Tag's thumb for one whole week was going to be both exciting and nerve racking at the same time. Considering the instructions he had included in his email response, she didn't doubt Tag was out to see how far he would be able to push her.

As she stood in her kitchen, sipping coffee and watching out the front windows, McKenna let her mind drift back to the day before and the kiss they had shared. The full-on mating of mouths was more than any kiss she'd ever experienced, and the thought of it still left her flustered.

Lord, have mercy, the man could kiss. The instant their mouths had fused together, his exquisite taste had annihilated her brain cells, which only went to prove that she was crazy for agreeing to do this. Considering the sheer velocity of a chemical reaction that ignited when they were in the same room together, McKenna knew it was only a matter of time before they gave in to it.

McKenna knew she would've given in to him yesterday had he just said the word. She knew she should proceed with caution, but her body didn't seem to understand the limits her brain normally tried to implement. Having known what his body felt like pressed against hers, the only thing she wanted more was to see him naked while he rubbed up against her.

What McKenna didn't understand was why these feelings of intense lust and desire seemed to be morphing into something else. Did she want something more? With Tag? Hell, with anyone? She didn't know how to answer the question, because until the day she'd come face-to-face with him, McKenna had been satisfied with her life — lack of sex and all. She had a vibrator. What more could she possibly need?

Ever since she'd met him, McKenna found that the more she learned, the more she wanted him. Her physical attraction to him was insane; she realized that. She couldn't help but wonder whether this was more than merely physical. He made her hot, and he made her want things she hadn't wanted in a long time; that was clear.

Of course, most of the things he made her ache for did relate to sex in some manner, but there was something else, too. She respected him. Of all the things she had learned about Tag in recent months, all of them were things that made her like him that much more. And she got the impression he respected her too.

With her coffee mug to her lips, her attention was drawn to the long, sleek, black limo that pulled down her street and in front of her house. Maybe for the next few minutes, she would be able to distract herself from the astonishing thoughts of Tag.

After dumping the rest of her coffee in the sink, McKenna rinsed the cup and placed it in the dishwasher. With her heels clicking on the hardwood floor, she made a beeline for the front door, not wanting to keep the limo driver waiting. She reached the door at the same time the doorbell rang, and McKenna quickly pulled it open and smiled at the handsome man before her.

"Ms. Thorne?"

"That's me," she greeted, trying not to smile too much. It seemed the grin had been permanent ever since her libido had awakened the day before, and quite frankly, she knew she looked like an idiot, but she couldn't seem to help it.

Taking a step back, McKenna let the driver in so he could help with her things. When she went to pick up one of the suitcases, he immediately stopped her with a gentle hand on her arm.

"No, ma'am. I'll get those."

"I'll be happy to help," she insisted, reaching once again for the bag.

"I've been informed not to allow you to lift one pretty little finger."

With that, the driver easily moved all four of her bags onto the front porch, allowing McKenna to lock the door behind her.

"Please, follow me," he instructed, hefting one bag under each arm.

She felt a little silly not assisting him with her things, because they could've easily accomplished it in one trip if she had, but she wasn't about to argue with him, either.

Once they reached the car, the driver opened the rear door and allowed her to climb in, quickly shutting it behind her as soon as she was situated.

"Hello, McKenna." Tag's deep voice rumbled through the car's interior, and McKenna's heart nearly pounded out of her chest.

He wasn't supposed to be there, yet he was.

Sitting comfortably on one side with his ankle resting on the opposite knee, one arm reaching across the back of the seat, he looked as calm as ever. She wasn't faring nearly as well. Her palms were suddenly clammy, and she had to ignore the urge to fidget as she stared back into those glistening emerald eyes.

"Good morning," she managed to say with more confidence than she felt. It was one thing to feel off center around him; it was an entirely different thing to let him know she felt that way. "I wasn't expecting to see you so soon."

"I wanted to greet you personally."

Was it just her or was his voice extra smooth today? The rich cadence of his tone was like a physical caress, her tummy immediately tumbling as though she were on the downward curve on a roller coaster.

She managed to nod as though she understood his reasoning, not breaking eye contact. She wasn't sure what she was supposed to say, but she knew no matter what, she couldn't let him see how much he affected her.

"Champagne?"

Her eyes wavered from his briefly as she glanced over at the bottle sitting in a built-in ice bucket. A small dose of liquid courage might be just what the doctor ordered. "It's a little early, don't you think?"

"I can mix it with orange juice if that makes you feel better." That sinfully sexy grin tipped his tantalizing mouth, and McKenna couldn't resist smiling back.

"Deal. Then we can call it breakfast."

"I was thinking about something else entirely for breakfast," Tag mumbled, and McKenna bit her lip.

It was then that she realized all bets were off when it came to Tag Murphy.

TAG RETRIEVED ONE of the glasses from the overhead rack and poured the champagne and orange juice before handing the glass over to McKenna. When their fingers brushed as the glass changed hands, he felt the residual spark from yesterday's breath-stealing encounter. The one that'd had him tossing and turning half the night.

Unfortunately, he'd resisted the urge to waylay the throb between his legs because he was anticipating a much more impressive interaction soon. He was tempted to see just how far McKenna was willing to go and whether or not she had actually read the contract in its entirety the night before.

He knew she had — the woman was nothing if not thorough, he had learned — but he was still anxious to test her.

"I see you're dressed for comfort," he commented, allowing his eyes to rake over her long, smooth legs as he spoke.

"If I remember correctly, that was the instruction." She smirked, sipping the mimosa.

He knew what she was referring to, and he realized he never should've doubted McKenna or her desire to push him as much as he was pushing her. "What are you wearing beneath that skirt?"

"I read every single word of the fine print," she assured him, and Tag's body immediately took notice of what she was revealing.

Now if only she would actually reveal more.

"Show me." Pinning his eyes on hers, Tag watched every nuance of her response to his demand.

"Do you always get right to the point?" she asked, setting the now empty glass in one of the wooden cup holders.

"Only when it benefits me."

"How does this benefit you?" McKenna asked.

Tag noticed she wasn't making any effort to do as he'd told her. The little vixen was going to learn soon enough that he expected full and total compliance because he wasn't much for asking a second time. Instead of responding, he narrowed his gaze on her.

When she squirmed, albeit it very slightly, he knew he had won this round.

"Show me, McKenna." He lowered his voice just a notch. "I won't tell you again."

Those exotic eyes widened, but there wasn't a hint of fear in her penetrating gaze. No, what he saw there was more of a dare than anything else. But then she took the hem of her skirt and slowly inched it up over her creamy thighs, then higher. Until Tag got a glimpse of the bare, smooth skin of her mound.

"All the way," he ordered. "Either lift it up completely or take it off. Your choice."

The limo finally began to move, and Tag knew it was only a matter of time before they would be pulling up to the club. Although James had been instructed not to open the back doors for any reason, McKenna didn't know that. So, technically, Tag had all the time in the world.

McKenna's breath hitched audibly, but she did as he'd instructed, lifting her skirt up over her hips and baring her beautiful pussy to his gaze. She appeared unfazed by his request for her not to wear anything underneath her clothes, but the slight tremor in her hands was a telltale sign that she was just as affected by her peepshow as he was.

He was prepared for her, though. While tossing and turning for half the night, Tag had come up with a few ideas on how to break down some of her resistance, and little did she know, although a major turn-on, her dominant nature was going to be put to the test.

She didn't have to worry. Tag had made a vow not to touch the enticing vixen, which was going to be a test of his own willpower, because the woman tempted him in ways he didn't understand. As he watched her teeth chewing on her bottom lip while her hands shook slightly, he wondered why the hell he was torturing himself that way. The thought of touching her, tasting her, had all but consumed him ever since he'd kissed her the day before and felt how responsive she was to his touch.

"So fucking pretty," he growled, his hunger undisguised. Not that he could've hidden how much he wanted her, because as each day passed, Tag found he wanted her that much more.

It was still a little surreal to know that, for the next seven days, Tag was going to get to know her in ways he hadn't honestly expected but wouldn't deny wanting. He figured that turnabout was fair play. If she was going to get insight into what it meant to be a member of the club, he was going to know everything there was to know about this woman. Not only how explosive her kisses were and how damned sexy she looked without clothes on, but Tag wanted to know the real woman.

During the night, while he had been lying in his bed thinking about McKenna and all of the naughty things he wanted to do to her, he had also committed himself to learning every nuance, every little smirk, every tiny detail of this fascinating woman who seemed to have no inhibitions.

And in order to do that, he would make damn sure she understood how hot she made him burn. If he was going to bring her on board, show her the ropes — pun intended — then he fully expected her to get a feel for what it was like to reap the full benefits of the lifestyle. And he was going to give himself over to the experience completely. For at least the next seven days, Tag refused to hold back, because he knew for a fact this opportunity wasn't going to come around more than once in his lifetime. This woman was unique; he knew that much about her already.

"Are you sure you're ready for this?" he asked, returning his gaze to her eyes. "You can put your skirt down now."

McKenna adjusted the flimsy material, allowing it to cover her thoroughly before meeting his eyes once again. "I can handle anything you can dish out."

Tag was beginning to believe that was true. Not only was she stunningly beautiful, she was intelligent and witty and … fun. And not in the way he was used to finding women entertaining. As much as he ached to bury himself inside of her, Tag had an unfamiliar desire to figure her out, to get inside of her head and see how she thought because he was just so damned intrigued by her.

So, for the next seven days, Tag was giving himself over to this woman, and he only hoped when it was over, he would walk away unscathed.

Twenty minutes later, they were pulling up to the club, both of them barely noticing that they had arrived.

Surprisingly, McKenna had prompted a casual conversation, and Tag found himself laughing and enjoying her company for more than just the sheer pleasure of looking at her. She was so easy to talk to, and her interest in life made him yearn to see it through her eyes. That idea was outside of his comfort zone on so many levels.

Tag would admit to being successful, but by no means had it come easily. It wasn't due to a bad childhood, because his childhood couldn't be classified as either good or bad. He was just there. His parents loved each other immensely, and considering he was a side effect of that love, they cared about him, but they'd never doted on him or encouraged him. They'd simply subsisted with him. And what he told McKenna about why he'd become a lawyer was the sad truth. His father had worked his ass off in order to ensure that he and his mother were provided for, but Jackson Murphy had existed solely for his wife and no one else. And when Tag's mother had passed away when he was barely a teenager, he hadn't been sure his father would survive there for a while.

Over time, his father managed to pull himself up by his bootstraps and go through the motions of life until one day, by some strange coincidence, Jackson had met Cole's mother and fallen head over heels for her.

Tag didn't begrudge his father having met Victoria, but he'd soon learned that he was once again a byproduct of his father's first love, and he'd been pushed by the wayside yet again. So, call him a hard-ass, call him selfish, call him anything, but Tag never wanted to experience the type of relationship that would allow him to push all of the people who were supposed to be important to him away. Never.

And he had never feared that would happen, because Tag kept himself at a distance from those he interacted with. He made his life about his job and the few mutually exclusive relationships that he ventured into — most of them where he was the third because it was what he knew, what he was comfortable with. No one expected anything from him, because he wasn't the glue that held it together, which was more than fine by him.

Until McKenna.

For some reason, Tag wanted to experience this through her eyes, to know what it was like to be the focus of someone else's attention, and this was his chance. For the next seven days, McKenna belonged to him and he to her. Now, he just had to keep reminding himself that, just like every other relationship, this one was temporary.

It wasn't like he had any crazy notions running through his head, but he would admit to experiencing a little anticipation a time or two. Did it make him crazy to think that McKenna could possibly be what he needed, as Sam had suggested?

He'd never had thoughts like that running through his mind, until recently. Granted, he wouldn't deny the underlying need was related to the intensity of the attraction between them. If only that attraction were based on pure and simple lust, he'd be much more confident in his own judgment.

McKenna challenged him. She was smart and so damn beautiful he wondered at times just what she was doing with him. She was also confident and poised under pressure, and he admired that about her. He had no idea whether he was truly looking for something more than sex, but he had to consider it, because, before McKenna, he'd never had a concern. If Tag was lucky, temporary would be all she had to offer him. At least then he wouldn't have to worry about anything more. Especially anything that his lust-filled brain might be overanalyzing.

McKenna wasn't like the usual women he involved himself with. First of all, he got the impression that she was more familiar with his lifestyle than she was letting on. Judging by the straightforward demand she'd included in their contract, he had proof that she wasn't just writing her articles based on secondhand experience. This woman had ventured down some of the same paths he had. Another reason he was looking forward to the next few days with her.

As he helped her out of the car, watching while she glanced around as though seeing the club for the very first time, he remembered the single line she'd insisted was added to the contract.

Tag Murphy, for a twenty-four-hour period to be determined by him, will belong to McKenna Thorne, and during this time, he will relinquish all rights to make any decisions whatsoever and follow, without interruption, all instructions laid forth by her.

He still smiled at the wording, because it was in no way written in the same legal jargon that he was familiar with, but he easily understood her point. Admittedly, Tag had never been on the receiving end of a dominating woman, but looking at McKenna now, seeing the natural confidence in her every step, he was interested in learning something from her in return.

Taking her hand, Tag led her into the building and then through the back stairwell that would take them to the second floor. After two coded security locks, they were entering the vast hallway that would lead to his private room.

He didn't rush her along, and he wondered whether she truly thought this was what everyone sought when joining the club. It was entertaining to meet new members and see their excitement about being led down the luxuriously decorated hallway with its light brown faux leather walls and the random sconce dotting the otherwise bare walls. The floor was tiled with dark gray and brown slate, and in Tag's opinion, it wasn't much different than a five-star hotel. Yet watching the intrigue on a new member's face could've led him to believe they were peering into the rooms themselves, seeing whatever went on behind closed doors.

That wasn't the case in this section of the club. However, Luke had found a way to play it up as though this were the most exciting feature available for a new member. And quite frankly, for a short time period while they were being evaluated, it really was.

He also knew that on the other side of the doors were simple, relatively small, nothing-fancy apartments that members had the option of renting. Originally when Tag had joined the club, he had taken one of the only vacant rooms, and it'd worked for him for the times that he used it. However, once one of the larger suites had become available, he'd immediately requested to move, and Luke had been generous in obliging him.

Another coded security lock had to be disarmed before they made their way into his private domain, and once inside, Tag gave McKenna a brief tour while James brought her luggage up.

Once her bags were delivered, Tag gave James a generous tip and then locked the door when he left. Turning to McKenna, he found her standing at the floor-to-ceiling windows, staring out at the glimpse of the Dallas skyline. Downtown Dallas was definitely not an attractive area to look at during the day, but at night, with the dirt and grime of the city swallowed by the cover of darkness, Tag would admit it was a sight to see.

Luke and Logan had taken over the club at a time when the only thing that the building offered was a minimal amount of security. Throughout the renovations to the building, they had also worked with the city to revitalize the area surrounding the club, which, in the long run, seemed to work in their favor. Club Destiny was interestingly enough one of the most sought-after nightclubs in the area.

After watching her for a few minutes, Tag couldn't resist the urge to move behind McKenna, placing his arms around her and glancing through the crystal-clear glass as he worked to see the city from her perspective. He had a hard time focusing on anything other than the way she fit against him, nestled up to his chest while her head rested beneath his chin. There was a peculiar comfort that holding her afforded him, one he wasn't expecting but oddly didn't shy away from.

"What do you think?"

"I was expecting red velvet and black lights." McKenna laughed, and the light, sultry sound soothed the beast pacing inside of him.

"Sorry to disappoint." He laughed with her.

"This is nice," McKenna stated a few minutes later. Tag wasn't sure whether she was talking about the view or his apartment or even his arms being wrapped around her, but either way, he had to agree. This was nice.

"Do all of the rooms look like this?" McKenna asked, pulling away from him as she wandered through the living room.

"They're very similar, some are just smaller," he answered, his eyes tracking her movements.

The woman was feminine grace in its classiest form. With her long, glossy fiery-red hair hanging down her back in waves and the smoothness of her pale skin, Tag couldn't take his eyes off of her.

Infatuation

"It's not as big as I expected it to be," she commented as she fingered the intricate glass pieces sitting on the wood beam mantle.

"The club or the apartment?"

Another provocative laugh had Tag's entire body going rigid. He wanted to see her naked. He wanted to explore every inch of the beautiful woman with his tongue.

Chapter *Eight*

MCKENNA MADE HER way along the ornate wooden mantel, admiring the little pieces of Tag she glimpsed in the small, intricate glass figurines and wooden sculptures that decorated the top. Although she knew this wasn't where he lived, she was impressed by the aesthetic detail that had been put into decorating the space. It was warm and inviting, almost the complete opposite of what she'd originally expected.

"Both, actually," McKenna clarified her statement. "I envisioned something bigger. With more … toys." Now she was just teasing him, and his answering laugh told her that he knew it.

"I've got toys, darlin. I'll show them to you as soon as you're ready."

McKenna didn't doubt that for a second.

For a few minutes, she had allowed herself to see the man for who he really was, not for who Tag allowed the world to see. She was enjoying being able to glimpse this aspect of him, though she was pretty sure most people didn't take the time to notice. Either that or he didn't allow them the chance.

She was intrigued.

It wasn't the apartment that captivated her, because quite frankly, it was just an apartment. Sure, the floors were a dark cherry mahogany wood, the walls were a faux leather buttercream that must've taken some serious time to finish, and the furniture was obviously expensive. But it was the little things that made up the man standing just a few short feet away from her that captured her interest.

She continued to walk through the open living space, glancing throughout, simply trying to pass the time and rein in some of the anxiety that had infused her from the moment Tag had put his arms around her. For a few minutes, while they had stood staring out at the dingy city, McKenna had almost forgotten why she was there.

It was easy to pretend that this wasn't what it actually was. A business arrangement. In her world, business was sex, although she wasn't normally engaged in it but rather writing or talking about it. This was undeniably different from that, but she could feel the sexual tension pulling at her, beckoning her. That's exactly what she expected when she was near Tag. It was his appeal.

Pure, carnal sex.

And here she was, day one of seven, about to go on a journey into the infamous world of Club Destiny to see what made it, and the man who had bravely offered to show her, tick.

She turned to see Tag still standing by the window, backlit by the morning sun, looking so damn delicious she wanted to jump right into the sex part, because quite frankly, it had been a damn long time for her.

Not that she was going to tell him that.

Her hormones were in flux, her nerves rioting, and she was ready to get on with whatever it was he had in store for her for the next few days, although she figured they probably needed to talk about it first.

"About the contract," she said as she made her way to the large leather sofa.

"What about it?" Tag asked, moving around to the overstuffed chair sitting off to the side.

"I want to share my journey with my readers." She'd given it some thought, and the contract hadn't stated how she would handle the article, only that Luke had to approve prior to publishing. McKenna was fine with that, but she wasn't about to lose a solid week without giving her readers some juicy details.

"I'm good with that." He grinned. "Luke has to approve, but then you can post whatever you want."

Whatever she wanted? It was her turn to grin.

"And since this is day one, let's make sure to give your readers something to talk about." Tag lowered himself carefully into the chair, resting one ankle on the opposite knee and looking so damn sexy, again McKenna nearly forgot why she was there.

She wondered what he had in mind. Truthfully, she was ready to jump into her twenty-four hours of being in charge, but she knew Tag wasn't going to go for that just yet. She was still surprised he'd accepted it as an amendment to the contract. He was a prime alpha male, used to being in control, not being controlled, which meant McKenna would have to bide her time.

"And just what did you have in mind?"

"Naked." The single word jarred McKenna, her eyes flying to Tag's, waiting to hear what he would say next. She hadn't misunderstood, but she wasn't about to jump at the first word out of his mouth. Although she wanted to.

Her heart was pounding like a bass drum against her ribs, her pulse beating furiously in her neck, but she fought to control her excitement.

"You heard me, McKenna." Tag's rich, dark voice washed over her, making her legs tremble and her tummy quiver.

Yep, he was saying what she thought he was saying.

"Here?" Wow, and that was a stupid question.

"Have another preference?" he asked with a smoldering look on his ruggedly handsome face.

She wasn't about to tell him all of the images that had been playing through her mind for the last couple of days. But in her fantasies, Tag was the one naked and she was the one in control. The thought made her smile.

"Start with the shoes," Tag told her, looking as laid-back and relaxed as she'd ever seen him.

Shoes were the easy part. And yes, McKenna knew what to expect, and being naked was likely going to be the easiest part of the next week with Tag. Not that it was going to be easy at all, but she was sure it was just the tip of the iceberg.

According to the contract, which McKenna still thought was a fictitious load of bullshit, Tag had promised a number of wickedly delightful ways of making her come. The terms did not state that she had to be willing or participate in any way, but he had offered her the full experience of Club Destiny, with him as her personal guide. There was no way she could've refused.

With smooth, controlled movements, McKenna fought back the nerves jangling in her tummy and reached down, unbuckling one sandal and sliding it off. It didn't take long for the other one to follow. The gentle thud as the second shoe hit the floor had her heart rate accelerating.

"Now the shirt," Tag insisted, his eyes never moving from hers.

McKenna could feel the warmth in that hot green gaze, and she decided she'd push him a little. Standing, she slowly slid each tiny button from its loop, allowing the material to gape open as she went along. No, she wasn't wearing anything beneath it, because that had been his instruction, and although she'd laughed when she'd read it, there hadn't been a trace of humor in the sound.

Just simple, hard-core lust.

Her nipples pebbled beneath the heat of Tag's stare along with the cool air that caressed her now exposed skin as she allowed the blouse to slide down her arms and pool on the cushion of the sofa just behind her.

Tag simply nodded his head, evidently directing her to remove the skirt, and thankfully, that didn't require much effort, because McKenna's hands were shaking. With trembling fingers, she managed to unhook the clasp, allowing her skirt to fall to the floor and land at her feet.

Standing before this man she knew so much and so little about, McKenna expected to be nervous. And she was. But there was something that had transpired between the two of them in recent days that made it easier than she'd expected. Granted, being naked didn't bother her in the least. It never had, which explained some of her past decisions, but this wasn't like that. This was just between the two of them, and although she knew what the intent of this was, McKenna couldn't help but hope for more.

"Beautiful."

Despite his attempt to hide his reaction, McKenna heard the gruffness in the single word and caught the small smile that tipped his lips, revealing one sexy-as-hell dimple in his right cheek.

"Happy?" she asked, feeling entirely too exposed but not at all uncomfortable.

"Very."

Holding her breath, McKenna waited patiently for his instruction, wondering exactly what his intentions were. If she had her say, he'd be touching her, but she wasn't getting the impression he was looking to go that direction.

"I read something about you." Tag didn't move from his chair, looking totally at ease, but the fire burning in the magnetic green depths of his eyes told a different story.

"What did you read?" McKenna wanted to know what he had discovered about her, but just knowing he had been researching made her body warm another degree.

"I read that you like to be in control."

Well, that wasn't all that surprising. She owned a magazine geared toward libidinous carnality and erotic lifestyles. There were a lot of things she enjoyed, and yes, dominating an uber-sexy male was part of the package. In fact, McKenna had never been on the receiving end, so not only was this an opportunity for her to find the true story behind one of Dallas's most salacious swingers clubs, but this was her chance to take a step back. To relinquish that hard-won control.

"True," she replied, still standing completely nude in front of Tag and fighting the urge to fidget. She would not give him the benefit of seeing her squirm, though.

"Come here," Tag ordered, and McKenna's entire body shivered.

Taking the few short steps to close the distance between them was pure torture, but somehow she managed. She would have run if Tag had committed to putting his hands on her, but since he still hadn't moved, aside from the outline of his erection tenting his slacks, she wouldn't have known she was affecting him in any way.

"On your knees."

Her immediate thought was to question him, to ask what he was going to do, but then McKenna thought of her own sessions with the few submissives she'd been with in her past. Their frequent disobedience resulted in hours of riveting punishment, but McKenna wasn't exactly ready for that yet.

Or maybe she was.

Slowly kneeling before him, McKenna kept her eyes trained on him, waiting to see what he would do.

"You're going to make this easy on me," Tag stated, leaning forward in his seat, watching her before him.

"That's what you think." She couldn't resist pushing him just a little.

MCKENNA THORNE KNEELING at his feet was one of the hottest things Tag had ever seen. Naked was even better. It was also one of the hardest things he'd ever done. He didn't have the slightest clue what it was about this woman, but she intrigued him. Maybe it was because she pushed back when he was normally used to remarkably little resistance. Whatever it was, he liked it.

Tag wasn't a Dom in the formal sense of the word, nor did he dabble in the true world of BDSM. He didn't get off on having a woman at his feet, kneeling before him, naked and ready to please him. Although he didn't begrudge anyone, or their lifestyles, it just wasn't his thing. However, as he took in the sensual beauty before him, he wondered whether that would all change with her.

With McKenna, he wanted to push the envelope, to play with her until there was the slightest crack in that cool, confident exterior. He had no interest in trying to break her, by any means. He just wanted to push until she pushed back. He wanted nothing more than to feel those sweet, succulent lips on his throbbing cock or immerse himself in the soft warmth of her body for hours on end, but that wasn't what today was about. Today was the introduction. And McKenna was naked.

"Hungry?" Tag didn't take his eyes off of her, nor did he pretend not to notice the soft, smooth curves she was putting on full display for him.

"Do I have to eat while I'm naked?" There was the slightest glimpse of uncertainty in the swirling colors of her eyes.

"Honey, you have to do everything naked today."

Her eyes never left his, and Tag was suddenly the one feeling a little uncertain. Not of what he had planned but of how much credit he gave himself when it came to his control.

"Then, yes. I'm starving." McKenna never moved from her kneeling position before him, and Tag was hard-pressed to get up from his seat. Thankfully he'd thought ahead as far as food was concerned, and he was expecting a call any minute.

Since Club Destiny was limited to members only, well, with the exception of McKenna, he wouldn't be able to have the food delivered to a private room unless he asked one of the security guards to bring it up. Until McKenna, there had never been a non-member through the security-coded doors. That was to ensure the identity of their members was kept completely secure, which at times turned out to be inconvenient for various reasons, such as restricting members from inviting anyone who was not already a member.

It was also something they were working on for the Walkers' new resort — Alluring Indulgence. Although it would be an invitation-only resort, they would allow exclusive membership should one of the invited guests choose to join. However, since the overall concept was significantly different from Club Destiny, they were working to determine how to allow the *plus ones* — or *plus many* in certain cases — without risking the confidentiality they were determined to maintain.

That wasn't an option at Club Destiny, and the members were informed of that prior to committing. And due to the fact that they had invited McKenna, an email blast had been sent out to all members advising of her presence. Had Tag not insisted on a very rigid confidentiality clause in the contract she'd signed, he would've been a little worried. Even if he did trust her. Although, he wasn't quite sure yet why that was.

"The food should be here any minute." Tag stood, holding out his hand for McKenna, helping her up from the floor.

Having a beautiful naked woman in front of him was not a foreign concept to Tag, but not touching her was. And in this case, this particular woman was making it damn difficult to remember the stipulations he had insisted upon.

The subtle sound of his phone ringing broke the intimacy lingering between them, and Tag reached into his pocket and retrieved it.

"Murphy," he answered, recognizing the number of the club. "Thanks. I'll be right down."

The food was there.

"Give me a few minutes to go down and get the food, then we'll eat and talk." He forced a smile when what he actually wanted to do was feast on McKenna.

A simple nod was all he received, but she still didn't break eye contact. She was certainly good at this game.

Several hours later, Tag excused himself and headed downstairs to the main floor to take an urgent phone call. He didn't want to leave McKenna, but he was finding it more and more difficult to keep his hands off of her as she sat naked before him. He needed a breather before he broke his own contract.

When he was finished talking to Xavier Thomas, he took a minute to catch his breath. No, the conversation with the president and CEO of XTX wasn't what had him feeling a little out of sorts. That could only be attributed to the red-haired vixen still naked in his private room.

Naked.

Fuck.

Admittedly, Tag had been trying to throw McKenna off-balance by insisting she be naked for the first day, but the woman was as confident and composed as though she were fully dressed. He, on the other hand, wasn't handling the sight of her exquisite nudity nearly as well.

They ate, they talked casually, and Tag helped her to unpack her things. Never did McKenna act as though being stark naked was an issue for her. Granted, maybe that *wasn't* a problem for her. After all, she had…

His thoughts were immediately interrupted as Luke McCoy approached with a sly grin on his face. "How's it going?"

"Depends on who you ask," Tag retorted.

"I'm not going to say I told you so." Luke laughed. "At least not yet."

When Luke turned, his eyes roaming the room, Tag allowed his gaze to follow, wondering whom he was meeting. Not that it was any of his business, but he welcomed the distraction.

"Meeting someone?" Tag finally asked when he didn't see anyone he recognized.

"Travis Walker."

"Did he ever sign on the dotted line?" Tag never had heard the final outcome of that last meeting.

"He did. He's coming by today to get the keys to his private room."

That wasn't surprising. Considering Travis lived in the Austin area, driving up to Dallas would normally be a one-day trip.

"Is he planning to come here often?" Tag wasn't sure why he was so curious, but after last night, he found himself taking an interest in the man.

Luke turned to face Tag more fully, and he felt the impact of the club owner's scrutiny. It wasn't like him to ask a million questions, so he fully understood Luke's sudden concern.

"Something I should know?" Luke asked.

Tag shook his head and turned away as casually as he could muster. He didn't have a problem with Travis Walker, but he couldn't deny being curious as to his interest in McKenna. If he thought the man was only interested in her in a professional capacity, he wouldn't be having this conversation now.

"Are you interested in…?" Luke let his words die off, but Tag knew how to finish the sentence.

"No." He was surprised by his own adamant response, but Tag knew without a doubt, at least at this point, he had no interest in sharing McKenna. With anyone.

That was a complete turnaround from Tag's normal M.O., he knew, but he wasn't questioning himself just yet. There were plenty of things he intended to experience with the sexy redhead, but sharing her was not in the plans.

"He was asking about you and McKenna the other night," Luke added, and Tag could sense he was still staring at him.

"He seems to have an interest in her," Tag said, the words escaping before he had a chance to stop them.

"He did ask whether you two were exclusive."

"He just out-and-out asked?" Tag jerked his gaze back to Luke's face. He didn't believe for a minute that the quiet cowboy would've broached a subject like that with Luke. Or with anyone, for that matter.

"Not specifically, no."

Tag noticed the mischievous look in Luke's eyes. The man was a lot of things, but a matchmaker he could never be. That didn't mean he wasn't interfering.

It wasn't a secret that Tag generally preferred threesomes. Both Cole and Luke were well aware of that, but what did surprise him was Travis's interest. He didn't know much about the man, and as far as he could tell, Travis preferred it that way.

There was a rumor that Travis was bisexual. Now, he had no idea who'd started that rumor, nor did he actually care about Travis's personal preferences, but it was another reason Tag questioned his interest. Tag wasn't bisexual, nor had he ever been.

"Then how exactly did it come up?" Tag asked when Luke didn't offer more.

"Let's just say he's open to playing."

Tag cocked an eyebrow. *What did that mean?*

"But he swings both ways."

Tag kept any expression off of his face. He still didn't believe that this conversation had just happened. Something had prompted it, and Luke was now confirming the rumor that Travis Walker was bisexual, as well.

"He's interested if you guys are," Luke finally bit out, sounding oddly frustrated as he stormed off.

Tag had to admit, there was a bit of satisfaction in getting Luke riled up.

Tag followed Luke with his eyes, but the instant that the damn cowboy came into his peripheral vision, Tag no longer cared about Club Destiny's owner.

His gaze locked with Travis's, and he suddenly felt like puffing out his chest and proving which of them was the bigger man. Tag felt a strange sense of insecurity where McKenna and Travis were concerned. Even more so than his sudden and strange infatuation with McKenna, Tag did not like this jealous reaction one damn bit.

Without another thought, Tag turned and headed for the stairs.

Chapter *Nine*

MCKENNA SCROLLED THROUGH her email on her iPhone, checking to see if there was anything urgent she needed to handle. From the look of it, Whisper had everything under control, and the only thing left for McKenna to do was sit back and enjoy this one-of-a-kind experience.

She just wished she could enjoy it while wearing clothes.

Unfortunately, Tag had left a short while ago to take a phone call — or so he'd said. Despite being left to her own devices, she managed to ignore the curiosity that had sparked the second she was alone. Instead, she was sitting motionless on the sofa, still clad in nothing whatsoever as she tried to keep herself occupied.

What the hell was taking Tag so long?

She should've been relieved not to have his intensely hot glare glued to her nude body. Acting was obviously not her strong suit, but she had put on the performance of a lifetime for the last few hours. Pretending not to be intimidated or more than a little uncomfortable at being naked in front of a man she barely knew and profoundly lusted after was harder than it looked.

Now, she felt like a guitar string that had been turned one revolution too many — another subtle notch and she would break in two. So she honestly should be grateful that Tag was taking his time, but for some reason, she wasn't.

Maybe because she'd been enjoying seeing the discomfort on his face.

He was undeniably affected by her nudity, although he was pretending otherwise. He didn't appear to be as good of an actor as she was, though. She'd even heard him groan on one occasion, and she'd fought off the urge to smile, but she had certainly been grinning on the inside.

It hadn't taken long for her to realize exactly what he was hoping for, but McKenna hadn't given Tag what he expected. Rather than giving in to his manipulations, she opted to grin and bear it. Actually, *bare* would be a more accurate term.

She continued to remind herself that she would have her turn. He had agreed to her amended contract, which meant at some point in the next few days, she would be in charge, and she was already preparing a mental list of things she would do to the man to get him back for this.

Although, he did have a little bit of time before that happened, and McKenna didn't have a clue what was in store for her. She only prayed he didn't expect her to leave the private room naked, because then she might just have to speak up.

When the door opened, McKenna steeled herself for his reappearance and turned her head as though sparing him a glance. With butterflies staging an all-out riot in her belly, she went back to thumbing through the emails on her phone. Or pretending to, anyway.

"Sorry it took me so long," Tag said as he put his cell phone and wallet on the small breakfast counter before making his way over to the chair he had planted himself in earlier.

"Mmm hmm." Pretending to dismiss his comment, McKenna couldn't tear her eyes away from the phone although she didn't see a damn thing on the screen. All of the letters had blurred together, her mind wandering to other things immediately.

Like what he planned to do next.

Or what she *wanted* him to do next.

"Are you doing okay?" he asked after he'd situated himself into that casual pose of his.

"Fine. Why?" she asked, looking up at him for the first time.

"Just making sure you're still willing to go through with this."

Crossing her arms over her breasts would only have him giving her that questioning stare as if she was trying to cover herself, so McKenna chose to put her hands down to her sides. With more brazenness than she'd thought she had, she managed to uncross and then cross her legs again while she was at it, noting the way his eyes lingered between her thighs a little longer than expected. "There isn't anything that you can do that'll have me changing my mind."

Nothing.

Had she known his intentions originally, she might have given this more thought. Now that she was here, she fully intended to fulfill her end of the contract, even if it killed her. The sexual tension was thick between them, and honestly, she wanted to see where it led them more than she wanted to back out from this small dose of humiliation.

"Be careful what you wish for, darlin'." Tag's dark, sultry tone sent a torrent of sensation flowing through her bloodstream, instantly making her nipples harden.

She wanted to challenge him to push her, but she got the feeling he was about to do so anyway. The harder she pushed, the harder he would push back, and right now, McKenna didn't trust herself not to go a little too far.

There was no way she could deny wanting him. She'd been enthralled since the very first day she'd seen him and overcome with a bad case of lust ever since. So, honestly, this opportunity gave her a chance to get closer to what she truly wanted.

Tag Murphy in her bed.

Or his.

"I'm game for whatever you can dish out, *darlin'*." Mocking his choice of endearments, she curled her fingers into her palm, praying he didn't see just how nervous she was.

"Spread your legs," Tag insisted, and the room immediately heated several degrees. This wasn't the laid-back country boy she'd been privy to earlier. This man was dead serious.

God, she loved watching him lose control.

She didn't move a muscle, nor did she smile. She was unable to do anything except breathe. The intensity in his gaze spoke of hot, lustful promises, and McKenna wasn't so sure she wouldn't beg him to touch her if he kept this up. Controlling him was going to be as impossible as controlling her own hormones where he was concerned. Pushing him, on the other hand, was a given.

"I'm not going to tell you again." Only his mouth moved. Not his hands, not his head. He was sitting in that chair, stone still, yet McKenna could feel the tension coming off of him in waves.

Slowly she uncrossed her legs, and she was instantly wet. It took several seconds before she managed to spread her knees apart, her clit throbbing with anticipation. If he would only touch her, they stood a chance of making it through the rest of the day before one of them lost it.

A battle of wills was what this was. Two dominating personalities, both intending to push the other to the breaking point, did nothing except promise a firestorm that was likely to blaze out of control.

"Touch yourself, McKenna." Back was that laid-back Texas drawl, but his voice belied the stiff way he held himself.

She pondered his instruction for a moment, wondering whether she could actually go through with it. At least if she did, she could relieve the tormenting ache that had taken up residence between her thighs.

Dropping her cell phone onto the cushion, McKenna eased her hand between her legs, making sure he could see everything she was doing.

TAG HAD THE hard-on of the century, and the self-inflicted pain was damn near more than he could handle. He couldn't pull his eyes away from McKenna's long, graceful fingers as they separated the soft folds of her pussy, sliding between her labia. *Fuck.* He wanted to throw himself to his knees before her and bury his face between her legs, licking her clit until she screamed his fucking name.

She was tormenting him, and she knew it, but he couldn't seem to stop himself. When McKenna began to moan softly, Tag knew he was in for it.

"Don't come yet," he demanded, his voice thick with the desperation flooding his veins. "I want to watch you."

Her eyes flew open, and a flash of something dark and dangerous dashed through the eerie colors.

Tag stood, moving to the small table between them and lowering himself onto it. This allowed for a front-row view, close enough he could see the slick juices now coating her index finger. He bit his tongue.

McKenna slowly pushed one finger inside, using her other hand to rub circles around her clit, those dick-teasing moans increasing along with her breathing. She was so fucking hot he wondered whether the smoke detectors would go off.

"That's it, baby." Lowering his voice, he kept his tone even, hopefully not revealing just how worked up he was by the live porn right there in his living room. "Do you like to fuck yourself?"

"Yes." Her tone was bold and brazen, her eyes closed once again as she continued to finger herself, her head leaning back against the headrest of the sofa. "God, yes."

Fuck.

"Don't you dare come, McKenna." The words came out strangled and harsh, but Tag couldn't stop them.

"Make me come, Tag." McKenna opened her eyes, and he could see the determination in them.

"I can't touch you, darlin'," he growled, wondering why the fuck he had come up with that idea in the first place.

"*Can't?* Or *won't?*"

92

"Stipulation of the contract, remember? No touching for twenty-four hours." Yep, he only had himself to blame for that dumb-ass inclusion.

"Then watch while I make myself come."

Self-assured and shameless, that's what McKenna was. And he fucking loved that about her. "Show me."

His cock was throbbing insistently, begging for attention, even if by his own hand. Tag refused to give in. He might have fucking blue balls by morning, but he was not going to let her win. Not this time.

His eyes returned to where she was now thrusting two fingers deep inside her cunt, the fingers on her other hand pressing against her clit but no longer moving. "Come for me, McKenna. Fucking come for me, baby."

That was all it took.

McKenna's head thrashed back against the couch; her fingers thrust one final time before her legs closed, trapping her hands between them as her body spasmed. It was the sexiest fucking thing Tag had ever seen. And what he wouldn't give to climb on top of her and ram his iron-hard cock between those soft, supple thighs...

Sucking in a harsh breath, he managed to stand up, despite the discomfort.

By the time night rolled around, Tag had finally managed to coax his body back to normal or as close as he was going to get. It was difficult, but he managed.

McKenna had been engrossed in her laptop for the last hour, allowing him to focus on other things. Like his job. Now that he'd taken care of the few fires, he was left with nothing else to focus on except her.

"Where am I sleeping tonight?" McKenna called from the sofa, not turning to look at him.

"My bed," he answered easily. She'd have company, too, because there was no damned way his big body was going to fit on that little couch. "With me."

The subtle hitch in her breathing made him smile. At least until he remembered that he'd vowed not to touch her. Granted, after eight o'clock tomorrow morning, all bets were off.

"Well, I think I'm going to turn in now if that's okay with you."

There wasn't a chance in hell he'd be able to fall asleep, not after having his hormones scrambled and then fried for the better part of the day, but he was willing to try.

It was late, and they had a busy day tomorrow.

Until then, he was just going to suffer.

Chapter *Ten*

Article number one, as approved by Luke McCoy:

The Sinful in Seven Series:
Day 1: Pushing Limits

Ever wonder just how far you can be pushed?

It's funny because I never thought I'd go this far, but here I am. At the hands of Club Destiny's very own Tag Murphy. Yes, ladies, you heard me correctly. The one and only uber-sexy attorney for Club Destiny has agreed to give me a personal tour of the place we've all fantasized about belonging to.

So, what did Day One entail? Multiple orgasms? Debauchery? Wild, out-of-control orgies? Well, I'm disappointed to say that up to this point, Club Destiny has not lived up to its notorious reputation, but I'm still holding out hope that it will take an interesting turn.

I'd like to thank Luke and Logan McCoy for being so generous by allowing me to walk the halls and share my interactions with those who just want a tiny morsel of detail to savor.

So, sit back, hold on tight, and let's enjoy the journey together!

-McKenna Thorne

Chapter *Eleven*

MCKENNA WOKE THE following morning to a warm body pressed up against her back. She knew where she was, and she knew who was with her, which explained the way her body tingled just from his touch.

Tag was breathing softly, and McKenna suspected that he was awake, but for just a few minutes, she wanted to cuddle in his warmth, to forget the reason she was here, and to pretend for as long as she could that this was her reality.

Considering McKenna didn't do relationships, nor did she usually do mornings after, to be held in the arms of a man was foreign yet incredibly comforting at the same time. Somehow, through the course of her life, sex had become an intimate interaction that was based on pleasure rather than affection, and McKenna suddenly missed the sweet companionship that could be found by waking up next to someone.

Not that she had ever wanted it. Well, not since the one relationship that had left her heartbroken and jaded. She found she didn't need the companionship because it came at a price. A price she wasn't willing to pay ever again.

With Tag, she didn't feel like she had to worry about that. There was a combustible energy that consumed them when they were in the same room, but there wasn't the risk of it turning into something more. Tag was not that man; she knew that much about him.

Considering what little she did know about him, McKenna was still highly aware of the unspoken connection that she felt between them, which spoke volumes about what they were doing here. She didn't go to sleep with strangers, didn't wake up with their warmth penetrating every molecule of her being, yet here she was. This was new for her. An adventure she'd signed up for and one she was anxious to explore because that's what Tag did to her. He had a magnetic pull on her, and McKenna couldn't fight it. She didn't *want* to fight it.

When Tag's arm moved, his warm hand slipping down to cup her naked breast, McKenna kept her eyes closed and sucked in a breath. One hand enveloped her entire breast, and she was surprised by the roughened skin of his palm as it sensually scraped over her sensitive nipple, bringing it to life. She had expected Tag's hands to be polished and smooth, just like his personality, but she should've known better. He seemed like the type of man to live life to its fullest, getting his hands dirty while he was at it.

A breathy moan escaped her lips as she pressed into the hard length of his erection prodding her bottom. She was naked, but he was not, which had relief and disappointment warring inside of her.

McKenna didn't know what she wanted, other than to feel the heat of his hands on her skin, the firm warmth of his mouth on hers. She'd dreamed about it for weeks now, wishing for an opportunity such as this to present itself, because whatever this attraction between them was, it was definitely based on sex and carnal satisfaction, which she was fully on board with.

Yet she felt the distance he was purposely keeping between them. That was the only way to explain his need to have her naked in front of him but refuse to touch her. He knew what he was doing, building the flames until a wildfire raged out of control, burning through her veins and making her body come alive with need. She sensed that was something he was familiar with, the end goal with his lovers.

She wanted to be his lover. Even if for such a short time.

When his lips met the sensitive spot at the base of her skull, trailing downward, McKenna's body went rigid as another vicious jolt of lust consumed her.

"Tag." She could barely speak his name, but the plea on her lips was what she needed him to hear. She needed him to relieve the ache that had been building ever since she'd laid eyes on him, ever since his mouth had begun tempting her with that very first kiss.

"I'm here, darlin'."

That husky Texas twang did strange things to her insides. "Touch me, Tag. Please touch me." McKenna wouldn't hesitate in telling him what she wanted. It was the way she was made. When it came to sex, or physical gratification, she was overzealous.

"Tell me." The insistence in his tone sent a chill racing down her spine.

This was what she longed for in her lovers. She longed for the alpha male who would dominate her, take her in every way possible. That's not usually how it ended up, because McKenna found that the men she came in contact with were looking for *her* dominance. They wanted to be mastered. Although she had enjoyed that aspect of sex previously, McKenna secretly wanted to be on the other side, so to speak.

Placing her right hand over his, the same hand covering her breast, McKenna squeezed firmly. "Harder. Like this." She manipulated his fingers beneath hers until they were pinching her nipple, sending sparks of pleasure-pain bolting straight to her clit. "Harder."

It still wasn't enough. She needed more.

Tag apparently got the message, because his callused hand began forcefully rubbing her breast, pinching her nipple between his index finger and thumb as he pulled her closer against him.

When his other arm worked its way around her, McKenna found herself on her back, on top of him, both of his well-muscled arms wrapped around her, both hands massaging her breasts almost violently as she ground her ass against his cock, wanting to feel him inside of her.

"You're going to make me come, Tag," she moaned. "Just by touching me." *Oh, God.* His touch was forceful and turbulent, but in no way was it painful. It was the exact opposite.

"Come for me, McKenna," he growled, his hands only on her breasts, nowhere else, but she could feel every part of him infusing her as though she had just taken him inside of her body.

"Oh, God, yes!" Her body imploded, her orgasm a welcome burst of fiery sensation blasting through her and leaving her sated and limp in his arms.

"That was so fucking sexy." Tag's voice grumbled in her ear, the rich, dark tone soothing the frazzled nerves that were still sparking.

"Do I get a turn?" She couldn't help but ask the question, still lying on top of him, her back to his front, her head turned to the side, her cheek brushing against his as he held her in place. "Please tell me that I get a turn." The last came out as a whispered plea.

"You will. I promise."

Not what she wanted to hear, but somehow what she'd expected. He was keeping himself from her, refusing her yet again, and she was beginning to hate this game.

Long minutes later, Tag rolled her gently off of him and eased out of the bed, leaving her to watch him as he rose, and when she got a good look at his body, her jaw dropped.

As he stood before her, clad in a pair of black boxer briefs and nothing else, McKenna was stunned by the sight of all that ink. His wide back, his well-muscled arms, his broad chest...almost entirely covered in intricate artwork that had her riveted.

It had clearly taken some time to do all of that. Her eyes grazed on his thick, sinewy arms, admiring the hours of work someone had put in to accentuate an already-perfect form.

He was beautiful.

As she watched him walk away, she didn't peel her eyes from him, watching the way the muscles beneath the ink moved gracefully.

Oh, fuck.

She was in serious, serious trouble.

TAG'S MIND WAS still reeling, remembering the feel of McKenna's lithe, slender body sprawled out on top of him, her tits in his hands, her ass grinding against his steel-hard cock. He wanted her with a desperation he could taste.

And to have her come apart in his arms from just his touch, Tag had been beside himself for the last couple of hours. He had taken her to breakfast at one of the small, hole-in-the-wall places he frequented, and as they sat in near silence, Tag watched as McKenna ate, never noticing what was going on around her.

The waiter was barely able to walk without tripping over himself every time he passed by their table, his eyes glued to the most beautiful woman in the place. McKenna didn't seem to notice.

Men did double and sometimes triple takes from where they sat, drinking their coffee, shoveling eggs and bacon while they admired her from afar. Even women were watching her, obviously enthralled by her sensual beauty. Never once did he see anything other than admiration in the faces of those around them.

McKenna was by far the most beautiful woman Tag had ever laid eyes on. To the point of distraction.

Today she was wearing a sleeveless silk shirt and hip-hugging black slacks that caressed every slender curve. But it was her hair — the fiery, crimson silk that flowed down her back, over her shoulder. She hadn't contained it the way she normally did with some delicate-looking clip. Today it was like a satin curtain hanging down, touching the top of her perfect, heart-shaped ass.

When her eyes finally met his, Tag couldn't help but smile. She seemed so oblivious to the envy that was pulsing in the air around her. He just knew that if any of her admirers got close enough to see those striking, unusual eyes, they'd be just as infatuated with her as he found himself to be.

"What?" Even her voice was mesmerizing.

"Nothing. How's breakfast?" Tag had long since finished his meal, now left to sip his coffee and observe everything about this woman who somehow intrigued him beyond explanation.

"Great." Glancing around, McKenna smiled when she looked back at him. "I've never been here before, but I'm definitely going to give it some press on my blog. Very impressed."

"It's not much to look at." Tag didn't usually come for the decor, though. The food was enough to keep the seats filled and a line out the door. Especially for breakfast.

"The best places usually aren't. With food like this, I don't care if I'm sitting in the back alley." Her husky laugh had his blood taking an unexpected detour farther south. He wasn't opposed to taking her to the back alley, either.

"So, what's the plan for the rest of the day?" McKenna locked her eyes with his as she pushed her plate away and delicately wiped her mouth with her napkin before placing it beside the half-empty plate.

Tag eyed the remaining bacon on her plate, and without asking, he reached over and stole the last piece. When she smiled, he felt like he'd just opened his eyes to stare directly into the sun.

Fuck. This woman was doing something to his head. Both of them, actually.

"I'd like to introduce you to Luke this morning. He'll be at the club with my brother and their wife." He waited to see if McKenna would have any sort of reaction to the way he described the threesome.

"I hear congratulations are in order. The three of them must be so happy." McKenna smiled, glancing up at the waiter when he stopped to collect their plates and hand Tag the bill.

"How'd you hear about that?" He didn't think they were trying to keep their blessed baby news a secret, but as far as Tag knew, the information hadn't been shared outside of a handful of people.

"I have my sources."

Of course she did.

"I guess that will make you an uncle, huh?"

"That it will," he replied, subtly hitting the waiter with the small book that held the bill and his credit card. The man couldn't seem to take his eyes off of McKenna, and Tag was about ready to pry them from his fucking head if he didn't move on.

"Sorry. I'll be right back," the man stuttered before shuffling off.

"So, what'll we do after I meet the three of them?"

"We have a members-only meeting this afternoon that I want to take you to. Travis Walker will be there to provide Club Destiny's members with an introduction to the resort. He's looking for some interest in his venture, and Logan and Luke thought their members might just provide what he's looking for."

He could see the enthusiasm in her eyes. This would be her first glimpse at the members. "Don't be surprised if attendance is low." Tag felt it necessary to warn her. "They've been informed of your presence, so I wouldn't be shocked if no one shows up."

"Understood." She smiled again, acknowledging the waiter when he returned a few seconds later.

Tag signed the credit card receipt and tossed the pen on the table. "Ready?"

"As I'll ever be."

Chapter *Twelve*

MCKENNA HAD SEEN the man standing just two feet from her before, but for some reason, she'd never noticed how incredibly big Luke McCoy was. Nor did she realize how very small Sierra was.

And Cole ... well, he was an entirely different specimen altogether. That man was obscenely attractive.

"Nice to meet you, McKenna," Sierra said sweetly, extending her hand.

McKenna quickly returned the gesture, shaking the proffered hand before doing the same with Luke and Cole.

"So, I hear you're doing an exclusive on the club," Sierra mentioned, unabashed enthusiasm flashing in her eyes. "Have you met Samantha McCoy yet?"

McKenna wasn't sure what the two had to do with one another, but she shook her head and then answered with a quick no.

"Well, I'm sure she'll be at the meeting this afternoon. She'll be ecstatic to meet you. Sam is always talking about your magazine or something you posted somewhere."

McKenna could feel the intensity of Cole's and Luke's gazes as she stood before them. She wasn't sure what they were sizing her up for, but she could clearly sense their hesitation. Trying to ignore them, she smiled at Sierra. "I'm looking forward to meeting her."

"I presume Tag's taking good care of you?" There was a hint of mischief in Luke's penetrating gaze.

"He is." Not quite as good as she would've liked, but that was more her hormones speaking than anything else. "Would you mind if I asked you a few questions, Mr. McCoy?"

McKenna couldn't get over the fact that she was actually face-to-face with the owner of Club Destiny. Nor could she allow this opportunity to pass her by.

"Tomorrow," Tag interjected. "I've scheduled some time for you and Luke to meet. He's agreed to answer any questions you may have."

Luke grinned and McKenna's body flushed. Apparently he didn't have any illusions about who she was or what she was after in this case.

"Be gentle with him." Cole laughed. "He's a virgin when it comes to interviews."

Luke McCoy and virgin in the same sentence? That made McKenna laugh, and everyone else, for that matter. "I promise to go easy on him."

"You look so familiar," Sierra commented, making McKenna feel a tad bit uncomfortable. "It's like I know you from somewhere."

Yes, well, McKenna was pretty sure where Sierra knew her from, but she wasn't going to be the one to say it out loud. "Maybe from my website? Or my magazine?"

"I guess…" Sierra still didn't seem convinced, and McKenna hoped no one else said anything.

Tag's eyes narrowed on her, and McKenna saw the recognition in his eyes. She wasn't embarrassed by her past, but had she been old enough to know better, she was fairly certain she wouldn't have made the decision to pose nude. But that was back then, and she was a different person now, having explored her sexuality in various ways, including posing nude for one of the nation's most highly rated men's magazines. She had learned to ignore the constant stares and frequent double takes, because more often than not, that was how she was recognized.

"Do you mind if I steal McKenna for a bit?" Tag asked, obviously assisting to divert the conversation.

"Not at all. I hope to talk to you more this afternoon." Sierra smiled sweetly. "And I'll have to introduce you to Sam. She's going to love you."

The comment caught McKenna off guard, but she managed to conceal it easily. "I'm looking forward to it."

"I'll take you home," McKenna heard Cole say to Sierra as they walked away, and the soothing sound of his voice as he spoke to the woman he loved had McKenna wishing for something she'd never wanted before.

Maybe it was the man standing beside her, the one who took her hand in his as they walked up the steps leading to the second floor and the private rooms of Club Destiny.

Once on the other side of the doors, McKenna was stunned when she was suddenly pushed up against the wall, Tag's hard body pressed intimately against her. She barely had time to catch her breath before his mouth descended on hers, their hands instantly groping one another as though they'd been forced to be apart for the last couple of hours rather than by choice.

When he finally pulled back, she was reluctant to let him go, but McKenna opened her eyes and got lost in eyes the color of the forest after a spring rain. "What was that for?" She was still breathless, but she was at least coherent. She wasn't so sure she had been when she'd given herself over to the most passionate kiss she'd ever known.

Well, aside from the one in her office.

"I'm having a damn hard time keeping my hands off of you," he growled, nipping her ear with his sharp teeth.

"Well, whose fault is that?" she whispered as she tilted her head to the side, hoping he'd use those teeth on her skin.

"I don't know what it is about you, McKenna..." Tag trailed hot, wet kisses down her neck, sending shards of pleasure ricocheting through her body like she'd been hooked up directly to an electrical current. She didn't know what it was, either, but whatever it was, she did not want it to end.

Taking her hand, Tag quickly pulled her down the hall, her heels clicking on the slate tile floor, echoing through the long, narrow corridor. When they passed Tag's private room door, she bit her bottom lip. She hadn't ventured anywhere other than his room, and she was torn between wanting to see what else went on behind those secured doors and wanting Tag to strip her naked and have his wicked way with her.

When they approached a large, open room at the end of the hall, Tag slowed. Walking in the room, McKenna noticed that there was no one else in there other than the two of them.

"Playroom." His words rang in her ear as she glanced around, noticing the elegant decor and expensive furniture.

"What do you do in the playroom?" she dared to ask.

"Anything you want."

"So others can come in here at any time?" The thought intrigued her, but for some reason, McKenna had conjured up more of a wicked image of Club Destiny than just this.

"They do."

"Is this the only room?" She wondered what all of the fuss was about if this was the only playroom they had.

"They don't have themed rooms here," Tag commented, staring down at her. "And trust me; this room sees plenty of action."

"It doesn't seem to be seeing anything at the moment," she responded, still trying to wrap her mind around it.

"Oh, darlin', that's where you're wrong." Tag's mouth was once again closing in, and McKenna welcomed the persistent press of his warm, firm lips on hers. Sliding her arms around him, she pulled him closer and then gripped the back of his sexy bald head. God, she loved his beautiful, smooth head.

Within seconds, the air crackled with ignitable heat as Tag devoured her, his tongue insistently pressing into her mouth, dueling with hers while he held her body as close as physically possible. When he broke the kiss long minutes later, they were both out of breath.

"I want to see your mouth on my cock, McKenna."

The words weren't a request, and she knew it. She couldn't help but revel in the intensity of his tone, the demand in those striking, all-knowing eyes, and the zing his words inflicted deep down low.

He was going to let her touch him, and McKenna damn sure wasn't about to let the opportunity pass her by.

TAG WASN'T SURE why he'd tortured himself for so long. The sweetness of McKenna's mouth was like a drug, the feel of her skin beneath his fingertips like an addiction he had no chance of kicking. He wanted her.

Right here.

Right now.

The playroom was empty, but that didn't make a damn bit of difference to him. It could've been filled wall to wall with people and he would still want to see her on her knees with his cock between her soft lips as she sucked him. Taking her hand, he led her to a black leather sofa, putting his hand firmly on her shoulder and pushing her until she was sitting before him.

With his eyes locked on her expressive face, he eased the button on his slacks from its mooring before sliding down the zipper.

"Take what you want from me, McKenna," he ordered her, ensuring she heard the command in his tone.

Tag could see the passion in her eyes, the need to be dominated, the need to be forced to do something out of character for her. He might be selfish in his abrupt pursuit of her, but he was going to ensure she got what she needed, as well.

When her deft fingers slipped inside the waistband of his slacks, Tag had to hold his breath. She gently scraped her fingernails along the sensitive skin of his lower abdomen as she easily lowered his pants until they were at mid-thigh. From the second she freed his cock, Tag knew this was going to require more willpower than he'd ever had to muster.

With his eyes fixated on her fingers, he watched as her nails raked along the spot where his leg met his torso, then lower until she was gently gliding over his balls, causing his cock to throb as it stood at full mast between them. He wanted her fucking mouth on him, wanted to watch while she blew him until he came with a vengeance.

There wasn't a thing she could do that would make him last longer than a few minutes, but he fully intended to enjoy every single second. One perfect fingernail trailed along the underside of his cock, then teased the flared head before moving back up his shaft.

Pure fucking torture.

He'd already insisted that she take what she wanted, so he couldn't very well tell her to wrap her mouth around his dick, but shit, he wanted to. Instead, he kept his mouth closed, his teeth clamped firmly together as he watched her pale fingers torment his swollen cock.

When her eyes darted up, meeting his, Tag saw the hunger reflected in them, and he swore he'd never seen that much want in his entire life. It was a fucking turn-on like no other to see the unobstructed lust in her eyes and to know that McKenna didn't make excuses for what she wanted.

Her eyes returned to her task, her fingers wrapping around his cock, gripping him tightly and slowly sliding down, then back up, her tongue darting out and swiping the oversensitive head of his cock.

Fuck.

There was no denying how fucking hot she made him, but this was out-of-this-world erotic. She wasn't rushing, and she wasn't doing this solely for his pleasure. McKenna was giving him the hand job of the century, and Tag was never going to forget this moment.

One hand eased between his thighs, cupping his balls before kneading them with just enough pressure to have the breath lodging in his throat. He exhaled on a groan, wondering whether it was possible to die from too much pleasure.

Then, she used the flat side of her tongue to ease along the hypersensitive underside of his cock, her head tilted to ensure he had a perfect view of every move she made. He groaned, unable to control himself, because holy fuck, he was going to come before she ever took him into her mouth.

Sweet fucking ecstasy was what it was.

By the time she slid her lips around his cock, Tag was sweating and on the verge of losing control. She tortured him with her tongue, sucking him fully into her mouth, wrapping his dick in velvet warmth.

"Fucking suck me, McKenna." Tag was on the verge of being rendered completely incompetent by the paralyzing pleasure, and he knew he couldn't take much more. "That's it, baby. Let me fuck your mouth."

Gripping her hair, Tag began thrusting forcefully past her lips, the vibration of her soft moans ricocheting straight through his balls until he was damn near blind with the need to come down her throat.

"Fuck," he growled, unable to slow his pace, her fingers gently caressing his balls as her mouth bathed him in moist heat. "Aw, fuck, baby. I'm gonna come. Fuck yes!"

It was all he could do to remain standing as his orgasm ripped through him, shattering his mind in the process and leaving him feeling…something.

Something he was pretty damn sure he didn't want to feel.

Chapter *Thirteen*

BY THE TIME the afternoon meeting rolled around, McKenna was feeling a little off-kilter. Not because of what had happened earlier that morning while they were still in Tag's bed, or even while they were in the playroom. No, McKenna felt a little deprived of that something more she was hoping for. Did it make her a nympho to be lusting after one man every second of the day?

Considering she hadn't had sex in almost an entire year, McKenna did feel a little unsatisfied, but only because she couldn't get her mind off of Tag and the things she wanted to do to him and him to her.

But now, as they sat in the largest of the three conference rooms, a little larger than the playroom but no less sophisticated or stylish, McKenna suddenly wanted nothing more than to sneak out with Tag and go back to his private room. For some reason, she was letting herself get carried away by her hormones when she should've been focusing on why she was actually there. This meeting, for instance.

"Thanks for coming," Logan McCoy greeted the room.

McKenna had been blindsided when Logan McCoy and his wife, Samantha, had walked into the room. The man was devastatingly handsome just like his mirror image, Luke, only he was a more refined version. She could tell by the way he spoke that he was used to being in control. Even if he was just a silent partner in the club, no one would've known by the way that he addressed each member personally.

"As many of you already know," Logan continued, standing in front of the group of at least forty people, "Luke and I are currently in the process of another business venture that we feel will only enhance Club Destiny and be mutually beneficial to its members."

This was the part McKenna was interested in.

"I'd like to introduce you to Travis Walker, co-owner of Walker Inc., and the brilliance behind Alluring Indulgence Resort."

There was a small round of applause that broke out, followed by the sexiest cowboy McKenna had ever met walking before the crowd of people. Looking relatively the same as he had the last time she'd seen him, Travis wore a long-sleeved, button-down black shirt tucked into those sexy-as-hell dark Wranglers and a belt buckle, but it was that black Stetson pulled low over his ruggedly handsome face that attracted so much attention. He was a mystery.

For the next half hour, McKenna forced herself to pay more attention to Travis's speech and less to his sexy southern drawl, although she was pretty sure some of the other women in the room had a more difficult time than she did. Watching the presentation flashing by on the screen outlining the overall concept of this mega resort that was currently in the construction phase was definitely worth her attention. The grand opening was going to be spectacular, he told them, and McKenna was bound and determined to be invited.

Glancing around the room, McKenna's gaze landed on the sexiest man in the room standing toward the back, talking to Luke and Cole. It wasn't the first time in the last thirty minutes she'd sought him out, either. Her body was like a heat-seeking missile, and Tag was the intended target.

Everything about him seemed to catch her eye — from his hard body encased in that expensive charcoal-gray suit to that sheepish grin of his. And especially the way his eyes met hers across the room and that subtle nod of acknowledgement followed by that heart-stopping smile he seemed to have only for her.

They were now nearly two days into the seven-day exclusive, yet McKenna was more interested in seeing Tag naked and making him lose control than she was in learning more about the club that she was supposed to be scouting.

One playroom. *Really?*

McKenna had been an invited guest to several of the swingers clubs in the area. She didn't turn down the opportunities, from a research-only perspective, and a number of them made this one look like a child's clubhouse. There had to be something about Club Destiny that had these people forking over big bucks just to be exclusive members. She knew damn well they didn't spend exorbitant amounts of money for a public space to congregate and have sex. Hell, they could find that in their own living rooms.

Nope, she was missing something.

She had yet to see the rest of the club, and she wondered when Tag was going to take her on the grand tour. From what she'd seen already, McKenna knew the front area was reserved for the general public club and bar that saw a vast number of people on any given night. Then there was the second floor, which housed the handful of private rooms, one large playroom, a couple of meeting rooms that she was privy to today, as well as what appeared to be the club's private office. But she wasn't naive enough to believe that she'd seen all of it yet. For one, McKenna happened to know that there was something downstairs, beneath the private wing reserved for members only.

There weren't any doors leading to the area from the main club that she knew of, nor did she think it was the kitchen area, because it would've been too large for what they catered to.

No, there was undoubtedly something beneath the floor they were currently on, and heaven help her, McKenna wanted to know what it was. But when her eyes met Tag's, once again her mind went blank, and the only thought that flittered through was one that involved smoking-hot sex and two naked bodies.

McKenna managed a subtle smile, but her attention was suddenly diverted to the three women who'd caught her eye. Several others in the room were paying careful attention to them, as well, but to her dismay, the three beauties that attracted so much male attention looked intent on something, and McKenna realized they were clearly moving in her direction.

"McKenna, meet Samantha McCoy and Ashleigh Thomas," Sierra said by way of introduction. "Sam, Ashleigh, this is McKenna Thorne."

Ashleigh was the first to hold out her hand, her grip gentle as they shook. "I know you."

McKenna forced a smile, wondering exactly what would come out of Ashleigh's mouth next. This was how it always was whenever she met or was introduced to someone new. They knew her, but they didn't know from where. Most of the time, to her relief, they knew her because they were a fan of her magazine, but sometimes, it was because of the other magazine her image had been imbedded in.

"You're the owner of Sensations, Inc." Ashleigh smiled brightly. "I am absolutely addicted to your magazine."

"Thank you." McKenna managed to speak, though she felt the intense interest coming from Samantha, and it made her just a tad uncomfortable.

"I meant to congratulate you earlier today, Sierra." Hoping to deflect the three women, McKenna focused on Sierra and the baby news. "The three of you must be ecstatic."

"Well, I am, I can tell you that much." Sierra laughed. "I'm not sure Luke and Cole are going to survive the pregnancy, though. They've become so overprotective I barely get a chance to take a shower by myself."

Samantha laughed, and McKenna felt the tension ease between them. "Honey, you being pregnant has nothing to do with the three of you being in the shower, unless you consider that's probably where the baby was conceived."

Sierra blushed prettily.

Samantha attracted her attention once again, and McKenna smiled, meeting her head on. There was no time like the present to get this out of the way. She could tell by the look in her eyes the woman knew who she was and how she recognized her.

"I have to agree with Ashleigh," Sam grinned, "I'm definitely a fan of your work. Your blog is the first thing I review each morning, especially since you began pursuing Tag."

"He's definitely catching the attention of my readers," McKenna offered. "After that first post, my website blew up with interest. Just want to give the readers what they want."

"So how is the exclusive coming along?" Samantha asked, her gaze still firmly planted. "Is Tag showing you anything you didn't already know?"

McKenna sensed a double entendre in Samantha's comment, and she suddenly felt like she was in an interrogation room, the heat of the overhead lamps making her sweat. If she wasn't mistaken, Samantha harbored a little resentment toward her. She just didn't know what could be the cause.

"It's been interesting."

Samantha briefly glanced across the room, and McKenna followed her gaze. When she noticed Tag was the intended recipient of Samantha's attention, she realized instantly what was upsetting the other woman.

Being that McKenna's job entailed knowing the dirty little secrets of the city's most prominent residents, she was well aware of Logan McCoy's intense fascination with threesomes and sharing his wife with other men. Though Logan was entirely too discreet for her to find out exactly which man was his current third, his wife didn't have quite the same level of conservative control as he did. The way Samantha was looking at Tag now told McKenna everything she didn't want to know.

It also explained why Tag was hell-bent on taking things so slowly.

Heat suffused her as she thought back to that morning and their early dawn foreplay — the only time Tag had actually put his hands on her since she'd been there.

"Are you and Tag…?" McKenna fought the urge to slam her hand over her mouth as the words spewed forth, unable to be stopped.

"We were." Sam nodded, a sad smile on her face. "I think his interest has been successfully diverted."

McKenna didn't know what to say to that. A flurry of emotions coursed through her, one being a powerful, black rage that pounded through her veins, followed by overwhelming nausea that threatened to erupt violently. If Tag was currently in a relationship with Logan and Sam, what the fuck was he…?

Shaking off the thought, McKenna realized both Sierra and Ashleigh were staring at her like she had grown three heads, and they were currently snapping their teeth. "I'm sorry. Had I known…"

What the hell was *she* apologizing for? Tag was the one who should be pleading his case, not her.

"No, no." Samantha locked those glowing green eyes on her. "It's not like that, McKenna, and I apologize if that's what you thought." Although Samantha seemed sincere, McKenna's heart didn't quite believe the words coming out of her mouth. "What Tag does is his business, and I assure you, I was well aware of his interest before he even talked to Logan about this exclusive. He's not that type of guy."

Sam's assurance didn't do anything to ease the anger pulsing like a bad tooth.

"Is it safe to assume we're going to get some more juicy stories about Tag?" Sierra asked, looking a tad uncomfortable as she glanced back and forth between Samantha and McKenna.

"Oh, yes. You'll get all you can handle." McKenna bit the words out. "I'm sorry, I need to go. It was great to meet you all." She met Samantha's eyes once again before she abruptly turned and found the closest exit, never once looking back as she hastily made her way out of the room and down the hall.

Despite the anger that made her ears ring, McKenna was totally consumed by a mortifying sense of loss, which made positively no sense.

What the hell had she been thinking?

TAG HAD BEEN watching the four women from the moment Samantha had made her way over to McKenna. Since he never took his eyes off of them, he was also privy to the look Samantha had sent his way, followed by McKenna's knowing stare.

Infatuation

As soon as McKenna separated herself from the other three women, Tag didn't need to guess what had transpired between them, although he had no idea what Sam could've said to piss McKenna off to the point she was fleeing like an injured animal. Or why Sam would've said anything in the first place.

Excusing himself from the conversation he was having with Travis Walker, Tag calmly followed her out of the room although she was walking at a much faster clip than he was.

Just when she would have swung the door leading down to the main club open, Tag planted his hand firmly against the steel, effectively stopping her. She might be pissed, but Tag's own ire was increasing as rapidly as she'd been trying to get away, especially after she had ignored him when he'd called her name.

Crowding her between the door and him, Tag waited for her to turn around. She was eerily still for two beats of his heart before she turned and leveled him with those exotic eyes. What he saw reflecting back at him was so unexpected he took a step back.

"What the fuck is wrong with you?" she questioned. "How the fuck could you do that to me?"

Okay. McKenna was obviously pissed. If he hadn't known by the way she'd stormed out, he would've figured it out, because he wasn't sure he'd ever heard her say the F word so many times in one breath.

"What did I do, McKenna?" Tag had never been one to play games, and he wasn't about to start now. If she was pissed, he was sure she had a reason, but he wasn't going to play the guessing game and try to figure out what had made her that way.

"You're fucking Samantha McCoy and you had the balls to—"

Tag stopped McKenna short, pushing her up against the wall. Her sharp intake of breath told him that he'd startled her, but the anger in her eyes didn't let up.

"First of all" — he moved in close, their mouths nearly touching — "my personal life is my business. Not to be shared with anyone. Got that?"

She didn't nod her understanding, but Tag knew she heard the underlying message loud and clear.

116

"Second of all, I don't play games, McKenna. If I was fucking anyone, I wouldn't have had my dick in your mouth a few hours ago."

Tag might not have permanent relationships, but he didn't play around with multiple partners at one time. Not outside of any multiple partner situations, anyway.

"Sam told me that you and she were…"

The words died on her lips, and Tag saw the understanding in her eyes, followed by a raging inferno of heat. She certainly understood.

Tag had ended his relationship with Logan and Samantha after the last interlude because of McKenna Thorne. And no, he didn't know what the hell was going on between the two of them, nor did he expect it would be anything lasting, but Tag wasn't about to let the opportunity pass him by.

"Past tense," he assured her in case there was any question.

"Oh."

Tag wouldn't have heard her whispered response had he not been pressed against her, his mouth hovering a breath away hers. The heat of the moment had passion igniting instantaneously between them. He wanted to taste her sweetness, to inhale her into his lungs, but he couldn't. Not right now, because right now he was supposed to be back in that meeting room, not out in the hall fucking around.

"Now, let's go back into that room," he said sternly. "There are some people I need to talk to. Not to mention, you're looking for an invite from Travis Walker, aren't you?"

He knew what she was looking to gain from this adventure they were on, and as much as he knew the attraction between them was mutual, neither of them could afford to lose sight of what they were there for. "He's in there and now's your chance."

McKenna nodded as he backed away, taking her hand. She seemed slightly reluctant to go with him, but he couldn't do anything about that. Not right now.

Once they were back in his room, he would certainly show her what it meant to let her anger get the best of her. Tag had learned years ago not to be led around by either his dick or his emotions, and that lesson had come in handy more times than he could count.

Tag was just about to excuse himself so he could meet up with McKenna and Travis, who had been talking for the better part of the last hour, when he was approached by one of Club Destiny's newest members.

Ever since Tag and McKenna had returned to the meeting room, he'd been involved in a multitude of discussions with the attending members. Most of them wanted his personal assurance that their identities would not be revealed in any one of McKenna's stories. They were all well aware of who she was and what she did, and though they all praised her magazine, not one of them actually wanted to be in it.

So, when Stephen Crawford approached, Tag fully expected more of the same questions.

"Crawford," Tag greeted the man, offering his hand.

"Seems you're the man of the hour." Stephen shook Tag's hand, and when their palms touched, there was a disturbing tingle at the back of his neck that he couldn't seem to shake.

"Not sure about that. I think Travis Walker has drawn quite a bit of interest from folks here."

"Oh, I won't disagree with you about that. I'm definitely interested in learning more about AI and what it'll cost me to get an invite."

Tag knew that there wasn't any amount of money that would secure an invite to the exclusive resort once it opened, but he wasn't going to tell Stephen that. Tag didn't know the man all that well, but what he did know, he wasn't so sure he liked. Why Luke had decided to allow the man to join the club was beyond him, but it wasn't his place to question Luke's decisions.

"What can I do for you, Crawford?" Tag glanced over at McKenna, noticing the way she was laughing with Travis, the other man staying close to her at all times.

As much as Tag wished it weren't true, he had come to acknowledge, although not fully accept, the lingering jealousy that was glimmering in the dark recesses of his soul when it came to McKenna. He was almost certain he had nothing to worry about when it came to Travis, but he wasn't thrilled to see them so close together.

"I heard you were bringing a journalist, but I didn't realize you were bringing McKenna."

Tag got the impression Stephen was hinting that he knew McKenna personally. "And?"

"You do realize who she is and what she does, don't you?"

Tag straightened, giving himself about four inches on Stephen Crawford, and he pierced him with a look. "I know exactly who she is. McKenna Thorne is an award-winning journalist and a successful business owner who's interested in doing a series on Club Destiny, and I invited her to explore so we could get a tasteful story about the club."

"Right." Stephen's snide remark had Tag's hands fisting at his sides. "I figured you brought her here so you can share her with the rest of us. I've heard she's interested in that rough shit. You know, maybe a gang bang on Tuesday."

Tag was unable to control himself, and before he knew it, he had Stephen Crawford pinned to the wall, his forearm across the other man's throat. He leaned in close. "I'm not making a request here, let me make that abundantly clear. One more word out of your mouth about McKenna, you won't like me. Understand?"

Tag instantly backed off, doing his best not to draw attention but still pinning Stephen with a glare. He could tolerate a lot of things, but he realized immediately that he couldn't tolerate anything being said about McKenna.

By anyone.

Much less, the snobby little bastard standing before him.

"Sorry, man. Didn't realize you got all possessive about your little fuck buddies. It's a little difficult to figure out exactly who you're nailing these days, what with all the action you've been seeing lately."

Infatuation

Tag had absolutely no idea what Crawford was referring to, but rather than question him, he bit his tongue. It took a tremendous amount of willpower not to pummel the little shit until he was unrecognizable.

Taking a deep breath, he walked away.

Fuck.

He needed a drink.

Chapter *Fourteen*

MCKENNA DIDN'T HAVE the slightest idea what had gotten into Tag, but by the time the meeting was officially adjourned, he was in a serious state of pissed off.

Her own anger had subsided, more so from Tag's explanation than anything else, but her conversation with Travis Walker hadn't hurt her mood, either. There was something about that dark, brooding cowboy that got to her. It was a different feeling than the one that she had when Tag looked at her, but McKenna felt a spark of something hot and wild in Travis's intense blue-gray eyes. She just didn't connect with that spark the way she did with Tag.

She liked being in Travis's company, and as long as she was talking business, the man seemed to open up more than she expected. Especially when she prompted him to give her a few details on the new resort they were all anxiously waiting for.

Now she was sort of wishing for Travis's presence, because she was certain Tag wasn't going to be the best dinner companion considering he hadn't said more than two words since they'd left the club. When he'd offered dinner, she realized she hadn't eaten since breakfast, but when she'd agreed, Tag's reluctance was evident.

However, here they were sitting at a quaint little Italian restaurant that smelled like heaven. It wasn't the kind of place she expected Tag to take her to, but even the hostess had known his name, which meant he likely frequented the place.

"Have you met Travis's six brothers?" McKenna asked after they had received their wine and placed their orders with the cute waitress who was giving Tag that lustful eye she had seen on so many women's faces.

Tag's eyebrows drew downward into a frown, and if she wasn't mistaken, he wasn't particularly thrilled about talking about Travis. Considering he wasn't offering titillating conversation of his own, she couldn't think of anything better.

"Yes," he grumbled, picking up his wineglass and downing half of it in one swallow.

"Are they all as involved with the resort as Travis?"

"Not all of them," Tag commented with less of a huff than before. "Sawyer and Kaleb contribute the most, but I figure by the time the doors open, the rest of them will be in it up to their elbows."

She waited a heartbeat, to see if he was going to continue, but when she realized he had said all he intended to, McKenna asked the most obvious question. "Is something wrong?"

"No, why?"

Liar.

"Because you've been quiet since we left the club. I saw you talking to Stephen Crawford earlier." McKenna knew Stephen, and she didn't care much for him. She'd been surprised when she'd seen him at the meeting, wondering what the hell the McCoys were thinking allowing him to join.

He was a little on the creepy side, always calling Sensations and requesting that they do an article on him. Apparently, being a wealthy playboy meant people were interested in his jet-setting lifestyle — or so he informed her. Even if she were down to her last reader, McKenna wasn't so sure she'd subject them to anything about Crawford.

At first, McKenna had declined his offer, letting him know that their articles were already mapped out for the foreseeable future. Not that it was true, but she wasn't about to tell him that she'd think about it. And ever since that day, with every rejection she'd given him since, he continued to be just as persistent. To the point that he'd showed up at her office insisting he be allowed to speak with her in person just last week. According to him, he had some information that he knew she would find appealing. Thankfully, Whisper had better sense than that, and she'd told him that they'd get back to him.

Since then, they'd been inundated with nasty comments posted on their blog ranging from rude remarks about her magazine to downright disgusting accusations about her personally. Luckily, Whisper always managed to take them down before they did too much damage.

"He's a jackass," Tag mumbled before turning away from her, seemingly interested in what others were doing in the restaurant.

"I'm pretty sure he's harmless," McKenna said while she stared at his profile. "He's just a pompous ass."

Tag jerked his gaze back to hers, the muscle in his jaw flexing violently. "I want you to stay away from him," he demanded.

Before McKenna could comment, the waitress arrived with their food, setting the plates in front of them. She graciously waited for her to leave before she addressed Tag. "Why is that?"

"He seems to think he knows you, that's all."

"Well, I assure you he doesn't. And you don't have to worry about me. I'm a big girl; I can take care of myself."

"I mean it, McKenna. Stay away from him." Tag sat forward in his chair, paying no mind to the food in front of him.

His gaze was focused on her, and McKenna fought the urge to react and tell him exactly what she thought about his domineering attitude. Instead, she kept her cool and settled for a soft, pleasing, "Understood."

She could play the demure, easily controlled woman when she needed to, but in no way did she like it. It wasn't like Tag was going to be around long enough to worry about whether Crawford continued to harass her.

Focusing on her food, McKenna ate slowly until her appetite returned thanks to the delectable meal. She was beginning to wonder whether Tag was some sort of food connoisseur, because each restaurant he took her to seemed to be better than the last.

It didn't take long before the anger that had been bubbling in her stomach disappeared, and she lost herself in the excellent cuisine, which more than made up for her grumpy dinner companion.

TAG FULLY EXPECTED McKenna to bite his head off for that last comment, so he was completely taken aback to see her fully engrossed in her meal. It hadn't taken long for her pleasant mood to turn to tolerant thanks to his shitty attitude, but he couldn't seem to shake it.

Yes, his insistence that she stay away from Crawford may have seemed a tad over the top, but there was something about the man Tag didn't like. And that was aside from his disrespect for McKenna.

As soon as he had a chance, he fully intended to have a long conversation with Luke and Logan about how the hell Crawford had been approved for membership. They didn't have to tell him anything, but he had some serious concerns about the man's mental stability.

Forcing himself to eat, Tag did his best to pretend he wasn't strung as tight as a virgin's ass. Between his confrontation with Stephen and the intense sexual tension between him and McKenna that no amount of anger could stifle, he wasn't much in the mood to eat.

Along with Crawford's crude comments, Tag had also allowed the casual conversation he had witnessed between McKenna and Travis to rub him the wrong way. He knew he could save himself a lot of heartburn if he just didn't give a shit, but for some reason, it wasn't that easy. Nor did he know how to address it, which only pissed him off more.

It wasn't like he could tell Walker to back off, because McKenna didn't belong to Tag, so who was he to interfere in her life? Although for now, at least for the next five days, he had the ability to control whom she did see. If he didn't think it would piss her off, he would insist she stay away from the man. But that wouldn't be very conducive to business, because she was interested in an exclusive on the resort as much as she was on Club Destiny, and truth be told, Tag only wanted her to be successful.

An hour later, Tag was leading McKenna back into his private room. Neither of them had spoken much ever since she'd deceitfully conceded to his insistence that she stay away from Crawford. He didn't know everything about her, but Tag damn sure knew McKenna wasn't one to take orders well.

"I'm going to take a shower," McKenna stated firmly as she walked into his bedroom, leaving him standing in the small, open kitchen. Since they'd left the restaurant, she hadn't spoken more than a couple of words, and when she had, it'd generally been a polite response to something he'd done, like opening the door for her.

He'd effectively pissed her off.

Well, she was about to get over it.

Following her, Tag made no attempt to be discreet about his intentions. He stood in the doorway of the bathroom, leaning casually against the jam. With his arms crossed over his chest, he stared back at the woman who ignited more than heat and flames inside of him.

She didn't look nervous, nor did she look happy.

"You gonna watch?"

"Yes." Amongst other things, but he didn't say that out loud. And watch he did.

McKenna slowly undressed, every movement apparently choreographed for his viewing pleasure. She took her time, removing each article of clothing, piece by piece, until she was standing before him the same way she had been the day before. Completely and beautifully naked.

Those curves should be illegal. All of that red silk flowing down her back, teasing the top of her creamy ass. Tag wanted to worship every inch of her. And the look she gave him dared him to.

He tracked every move she made as she entered the oversized shower, turning on the water and standing back while she waited for it to heat. For the last two days, his dick had been in a constant state of turmoil, needing to be buried inside of her heat. Hell, for the last couple of months, she'd tormented his thoughts with her simple existence. And here they were.

Tag removed his shirt, unbuttoning each button, never taking his eyes off of her. He unhooked his cuffs and then let his shirt slide down his arms until it fell to the floor at his feet. Thinking ahead, he'd discarded the jacket and tie before he'd followed her from the kitchen. His shoes were the next to go, followed by his slacks, underwear, and socks, until he stood just as naked as she was.

When McKenna's eyes drifted up over his torso, down his arms, he wondered what she thought. That morning, when he had slipped out of the bed, he'd felt her eyes on him, but she hadn't said anything. Reading her every expression, Tag knew that wasn't disdain he saw in those inquisitive eyes. That was lust.

The artwork that marked so much of his skin had taken years to do, and each individual tattoo meant something to Tag. And yes, there wasn't much of his upper body that wasn't tattooed — one of the main reasons he insisted on long-sleeve dress shirts as his wardrobe of choice.

He was a reputable attorney, and he'd represented some very influential people in this town. The problem, he knew, was that not everyone was as open-minded as he would want. But standing before McKenna, he didn't care what anyone *else* thought of him … only her.

When her tongue darted out to moisten her lips, his stomach tightened. Fond memories of earlier that day when she'd given him that wicked-ass blow job infiltrated the lusty haze. It was his turn to return the favor, and the thought made his hands fist.

He couldn't wait to put them on her.

"Are you going to stand there all day? Or would you like to join me?"

Tag didn't detect an ounce of sweetness in her tone, but by the way her nipples puckered as she stared at him, he knew she wanted this as much as he did.

His legs ate up the space between them until he was in the shower with her, beneath the warm spray. He didn't touch her. At least not with his hands. His eyes were another story. He let them drift over her wet, smooth skin, lingering briefly on her rosy pink nipples, then roaming farther.

McKenna continued with her shower as though he weren't there, lathering her hair and then rinsing, never taking her eyes off of him. Tag liked the way she looked at him; his body hardened even more from the passion swirling in her expressive eyes.

By the time she was finished soaping her body, he was slowly stroking his cock. That little show she'd just put on was enough to have him coming in his hand, but he fought the urge.

"Put your hands on me," McKenna insisted, and the hint of dominance he detected in her sultry tone had him releasing his rock-hard dick and taking another step closer to her.

He felt like he was looking at a naked woman for the first time. Like this was his first chance to touch such a beautiful, exquisite form.

He cupped her neck with both hands, tipping her head up with his thumbs beneath her chin as he absorbed the soft, silky feel of her. When her lips parted, he couldn't resist the urge to press his mouth to hers.

The kiss was gentle at first. An exploration of tongues as he paid close attention to the sweet taste of her, the soft warmth of her lips as she slowly licked him, delving deeper but never pushing to take the kiss any further.

Slowly, he swept his lips over the corner of her mouth, then on to that sexy dimple in her chin before venturing down the sleek line of her neck. Still holding her, he tilted her head back as he nibbled slowly, tasting the salty sweetness of her skin before letting his mouth rest briefly on the rapid pulse beating there.

As he moved to her collarbone, he let his hands slide down her shoulders, her arms, until his hands met hers, and he twined their fingers together. Pulling back, he lifted her arms until they were over her head and then turned her so her back was up against the tiled wall.

He liked the way she kept her eyes locked with his as if she were trying to see something more inside of him. More than the fiery embers sparking between them, slowly building into something that threatened to burn them both alive.

With one hand, he secured both of hers above her head against the wall and let his other hand return to her chest. Flattening his palm, he spread his fingers wide, nearly spanning the entire width of her small frame. Tag liked that she was tall, but he got off on how fragile she seemed in comparison to him. She was feminine grace, meant for a man to hold, to touch, to love…

Slowly sliding his hand downward, he allowed his fingers to stroke gently over her hardened nipples, stopping long enough to cup one full breast, kneading it gently as she closed her eyes. Watching her pleasure was the equivalent of stroking his own cock; the mere sight brought him closer and closer to the edge.

Squeezing more firmly, he listened to her sharp intake of breath. He used his thumb and index finger to tweak her nipple hard, meeting her eyes when they flew open wide. Her chest was rising and falling with every labored breath she took, and it was intoxicating to watch. She wanted him as much as he wanted her.

"Keep your hands there," he instructed, letting go of her wrists and using both hands to knead her breasts, pulling her nipples between his fingers. His cock was rock hard between them, throbbing with the urgent need to bury himself inside of her.

Ignoring his own body, Tag lifted her breasts and teased the pebbled tip with his tongue, swirling around her nipple. The vibrations from her soft moans shocked his senses and had his cock pulsing. She was so damn responsive, and Tag loved the way she gave herself over to the sensations, never trying to rush him, just simply enjoying his touch.

It was a damn good thing he was such a patient man.

Chapter *Fifteen*

MCKENNA WASN'T SURE whether her legs were going to hold her up much longer. Controlling the need to touch Tag, to taste him, was harder than she thought. But the feel of his warm mouth on her skin was sensual torture in the most pleasant form.

For some reason, she'd expected this from him. Never rushing, always savoring. That's the impression she'd had of him since the very first time their eyes had met. Oh, she didn't doubt that he could get down and dirty, but this was something deeper.

She would do her heart a gigantic favor if she would just remember that this was all about pleasure and nothing more. But something in the way he touched her, looked at her, felt like more than just two bodies coming together for the sake of it.

She forced her eyes to remain open so she could watch as his mouth devoured her breasts, one at a time, gently laving her sensitive nipples with his tongue before sucking hard, sending spasms of need to her clit. McKenna watched as his tongue traced down the center of her tummy, then teased her navel as he lowered himself to one knee, propping the other up and then lifting her foot until it rested on his hard thigh.

Peering down the length of her body, she moaned when his fingers separated her labia, one thick finger grazing her clit as his eyes shot up and met hers.

There were no words, but they weren't necessary. Their bodies were communicating in ways McKenna wasn't familiar with but wanted more of. When his tongue slid through her slit, her body spasmed, and she had to focus on keeping her knees locked or sliding to the floor in a puddle.

Exquisite. Fucking. Torture.

Tag's hot tongue invaded her, slowly tracing her folds, gently lapping at her clit, and then slowly sliding inside of her repeatedly.

"Tag!" She couldn't take much more of this. She was hanging by a frayed thread, her orgasm within reach.

For several long minutes, Tag teased her with his tongue, his lips, never allowing her to reach the pinnacle. When he stood abruptly, McKenna wanted to scream, but she settled on a groan. Then his mouth met hers, and Tag took from her as she gave everything in return. She tasted herself on his lips, reveled in the intoxicating feel of his body pressed against hers.

"Turn around," he whispered as he continued to pepper her mouth with soft kisses.

She didn't hesitate as she turned around, planting her hands on the wall only to have her entire body pressed closer until her breasts were crushed against the cold slate, her hands trapped.

When Tag began the same sensual torture from the back of her neck down to her bottom, McKenna just knew she was going to explode. The gentle scrape from the stubble on his chin down her spine sent chills into her hair, another moan escaping.

"Please, Tag." She wasn't sure what it was she wanted, but she needed more.

His finger trailed from the base of her spine, down in the crack of her ass until he easily spread her legs and speared her pussy with two fingers. She did scream then, her body instinctively rocking against the intrusion as she felt him rise to his full height once again. She prayed he wouldn't stop what he was doing because she was so close…

"That's it, baby." Tag's gruff voice rumbled in her ear, and she turned her head.

He gripped her neck with one large hand, sinking his teeth into her bottom lip as he thrust his fingers into her pussy over and over until she lost it. Her knees threatened to buckle as her orgasm ricocheted like stray bullets through her insides, her stomach muscles clenching painfully.

When Tag turned her, pulling her flush against his chest and backing them both under the hot water, McKenna leaned into him. It was all she could do to wrap her arms around his narrow waist, digging her fingernails into the rigid muscles of his back as she was assaulted repeatedly by the mini detonations that one orgasm had set off inside of her.

A few minutes later, Tag was helping her out of the shower, slowly drying her skin with a warm towel before using it to dry himself. McKenna was speechless as she watched Tag's corded muscles bunch and flex with every movement. When he took her hand and led her back to the bedroom, she suddenly wished for sleep, because she was exhausted from that one explosive release, but she wanted more.

He stopped and then turned her so the backs of her knees met the mattress, his warm, callused hands once again sending chills over her skin as he caressed her sweetly. Her mind was getting mixed signals from his touch, and she repeatedly reminded herself this was about sex. He was just showing her how sensual it could be when they came together, even without the rough, hard fucking they were both more accustomed to.

Before she knew what had happened, McKenna was flat on her back, Tag's sexy body coming down over her, his cock sheathed with a condom as he settled between her thighs.

When had he done that?

Her brain was fuzzy with desire to the point that she wasn't paying attention to much of anything except the feel of his hard body beneath her fingers or the warmth of his mouth as he kissed her once more, long and deep this time.

When she felt the head of his cock pushing against her entrance, McKenna threw her arms around his neck, pulling him closer until their torsos were touching completely, the warm, heavy weight of him a welcome distraction to the thick penetration of his cock inside of her. He was big, she'd already known that much, but as he pushed deeper, filling her perfectly, McKenna tried to relax in order to take him inside of her fully.

There was a small bite of pain, quickly absorbed by the intense pleasure. She wanted to rock her hips, to increase the friction, as nerve endings she hadn't realized she had were suddenly begging for attention.

"Fuck." Tag's tortured groan tickled her ear. "You're so fucking tight."

Her body lit up from his words, and she tried to move once more, only to be held down by his body weight. To her delight, Tag began moving, just pushing deep, then pulling back as he continued to torment her.

"Please," she begged, pulling his head to hers. "Please, Tag. I need to feel you." Something about the way he looked at her had tears pricking her eyes, and McKenna was scared of what it meant. She was becoming attached to him, and she knew it. He made it too easy for her to want things she'd sworn she would never have.

"Feel me, baby." Tag touched her cheek with the backs of his fingers as he flexed his hips, pushing deeper. "Your pussy's so damn hot."

McKenna closed her eyes briefly as she focused on the place where they were joined, the pulse of his cock inside of her, and the overabundance of sensation as her body acclimated.

When the bed shifted, his weight suddenly disappearing, McKenna opened her eyes and stared up at him. He was kneeling between her thighs, still buried to the hilt. Long, painful seconds ticked by before the gentle glide of his erection through the delicate tissue had her gasping for breath.

"Watch, McKenna," Tag demanded. "Watch me fuck you."

Biting her lip, McKenna focused on the pain she caused herself. That or she was going to come right then and there before he began moving.

He didn't make her wait for long. Her eyes locked on the place where his body was joined with hers, and when he lifted her legs over his arms, she was treated to short, shallow thrusts of his hips, followed by longer, harder ones until he was fucking her hard and fast. She latched her fingers onto his thighs, trying to pull herself against him as he pounded into her over and over.

"Come for me, McKenna." The words sounded as though they had been ripped from his chest, and when she looked up at his face, she noticed the sweat beading on his forehead.

The welcome tingle started deep inside of her, only to blossom into a full-blown assault on her senses as another orgasm ripped through her, his name tumbling from her lips as she fought to hold on to him, scared if she let go, she'd never be the same again.

Chapter *Sixteen*

Article number two, as approved by Luke McCoy *and* Travis Walker:

The Sinful in Seven Series:
Day 2: Business As Usual

Is it true that Club Destiny might have a little competition?

I find it fascinating that with all the hushed whispers and absurd rumors, Club Destiny still functions as a normal business on a day-to-day basis. It's true, though, the club may be a little out of the norm, but when all is said and done, business is business.

One of the items on the agenda at a member's meeting held today was the introduction of another upcoming attraction that has been hitting the headlines. Today, I had the pleasure of listening to Travis Walker, co-owner of Walker, Inc. and the brain behind the Alluring Indulgence Resort, explain in detail some of the exclusive amenities that will be available to future guests. I am happy to clear up one of the rumors that we've all been curious about... Luke and Logan McCoy have invested an undisclosed amount of money in the new resort.

What does this mean for Club Destiny?

According to Luke McCoy, nothing. Club Destiny will continue as it has for the last five years under his watchful eye.

-McKenna Thorne

Chapter *Seventeen*

AS HE LAY in the dark, Tag held McKenna against him, her head resting on his chest as he continued to rub his fingers down her back. Her soft, even breaths told him that she was asleep, but no matter what he did, he was unable to do so himself.

Something had happened between them when their bodies had come together, and he couldn't get the remembered feel of it out of his brain. As much as he wanted to deny it, Tag realized this was different. Whatever was going on between him and McKenna, no amount of excuses about sex for the sake of sex was going to change that.

He wouldn't go so far as to label it, but he could openly admit — to himself, anyway — that he'd never felt it before. It was as though she'd penetrated his soul. What had happened between them wasn't only about two bodies colliding, it was much deeper, and quite frankly, Tag wasn't sure how he felt about that.

He couldn't seem to let her go from his arms, and that spoke volumes. Sex for the sheer pleasure of it wasn't a foreign concept to Tag. As a matter of fact, he'd been involved in a number of relationships where that was the only thing he wanted. And now that he was nestled against McKenna's body, he had a hard time remembering what that was supposed to feel like. Not like this, he knew.

But he had to remember why she was here. She wasn't here to fall in love with him, and he wasn't supposed to be entertaining those thoughts, either. This was supposed to be a lesson. Teaching her about the carnal side of his lifestyle, introducing her to kink and debauchery. Not complicating his life with things like feelings.

McKenna knew more about his lifestyle than she was letting on, and he was almost certain that she was aware of how much he knew about her. Still, it didn't change anything, because this was where he wanted to be. At least for a little while longer.

Fuck.

How in the hell had he let this get so damn complicated? The last thing he needed at this point in his life was a damn woman who plagued every waking thought. So how the fuck did he explain this?

By the time dawn arrived, Tag had managed a few hours of sleep. Barely. He would've still been asleep if the cushiony warmth he'd been pressed against hadn't moved.

"Where're you going?" he mumbled, still groggy from sleep but aware that McKenna was getting out of bed.

She didn't answer him, but he managed to catch her eye as she walked across the room.

Hmmm... The woman was thinking too much. He could sense it. And yes, he might've let his mind get away with some irrational thoughts in the early-morning hours, but he knew he was over it now.

Shit, he hoped he was.

He turned onto his back, putting his hands behind his head and kicking the sheet off of him. He waited patiently for McKenna to emerge from the bathroom, which she did a few minutes later.

"Where are you going?" He eyed her as she made a beeline for the door.

"I need to go ... out."

Tag didn't respond, he just nodded. What was he going to do? Chase her down?

Not this time, no.

He'd let her go. Give her a little time to clear her head. Lord knew he needed a little space of his own.

After she left, he forced himself out of the bed, into the shower, and then down to meet Logan in the club. He hadn't expected his day to go this way, but the urgent voice mail from Logan changed any plans he might've had.

"Morning," Logan greeted when Tag approached. There wasn't an ounce of "good" in his tone, which was why he apparently left the word out.

"Mornin'." Tag took the seat across from Logan, noticing the newspaper sitting on the table between them. Even with a passing glance, he saw the huge picture and the caption across the front page.

Shit.

"I take it you haven't seen this yet?"

As he watched Logan sip the coffee he'd been smart enough to bring with him, Tag wished like hell he'd thought to make some before coming down. Unfortunately, he was running on nothing, and since there wasn't a soul behind the bar that early in the morning, he knew he wasn't likely going to get his fix anytime soon.

"I haven't." No, Tag had been too consumed by one red-haired vixen to know what the hell was going on. If he wasn't careful, that might become a problem.

Taking a minute, he skimmed the article printed beside the huge picture of Susan Toulmin. It was one of her better shots, obviously taken before she'd lost her mind.

Admittedly, the woman was attractive, and if they weren't careful, she might just grab someone's attention. Like the reporter who'd obviously felt the need to print this article.

"She doesn't seem swayed by the judge's insistence that she keep her mouth shut," Logan bit out.

There was no doubt that Logan was frustrated, but Tag could only imagine how friendly Luke was going to be after reading this.

"Son of a motherfucking bitch!"

Okay, he didn't need to imagine. Luke came stomping down the stairs from his office, a litany of additional curse words trailing him.

Fuck. It was too damn early to have to deal with the McCoy twins without having his damn coffee.

And just like that, in walked the red-haired vixen carrying not one but two large paper cups of coffee, and she was heading straight toward him. A small smile tipped her lips as she handed over one cup, their fingers brushing one another.

From the looks of it, the few minutes McKenna had spent out that morning had done wonders for her mood. He wasn't sure what she was thinking or what she was feeling, but he could definitely sense she'd calmed down some.

"Thank you." Tag held on to the last word — *baby* — before it could come out.

"You're welcome." McKenna started to walk away, but Tag put his hand on hers, stopping her.

"Wait. Join us, please." He needed her at the moment. Not only because he didn't want her to walk away, but she just might have some suggestions on how they could handle this new issue.

MCKENNA GLANCED BACK and forth between the other two men sitting at the table before her attention was redirected to the newspaper lying in front of Tag. Susan Toulmin's big head filled up the majority of it, along with the caption, *"How many is too many?"*

Instead of reading the filth she knew she would find, McKenna looked up at the three men now focused on her.

"What do you think?" Logan asked.

"About what?" She hadn't read the article, so she didn't know what it said exactly, but she had a pretty good idea. No matter what, it wasn't going to douse Club Destiny in rainbows and sunshine.

"I don't care what anyone thinks. I want to know what the hell we can do about it," Luke growled.

"Unfortunately, she's not violating any request by the judge because she's not talking about the trial. And she hasn't released any names." Tag didn't sound all that confident.

Infatuation

"I suggest we fight fire with fire." Backing down had never been McKenna's style, and despite the fact that she didn't have a horse in this particular race, something about Susan just rubbed McKenna the wrong way. And, yes, maybe there was a bit of defensiveness she felt for the men at the table.

"We'll start with a series of articles." McKenna knew her next recommendation was not going to go over well. "We need to make the readers want to like the people behind the club. Once we can do that, defending the club won't be necessary, because you'll have more people in your corner than you know what to do with."

"The people behind the club?" Logan looked skeptical. "As in *me and Luke*?"

"To start, yes." McKenna could practically hear Luke's teeth grinding together. "It's not like we'll provide your social security numbers or your addresses, but we need to let people know just how real the two of you are. Since you" — McKenna focused on Luke — "are the face of Club Destiny, it only makes sense that we share a little bit about you."

"You want to share the details of my private life?"

McKenna knew he didn't like the idea, but it made sense. "Are you ashamed of your life, Luke?"

"Fuck no, but I don't think it's anyone's fucking business."

The vehemence in Luke's tone was crystal clear, but so was the smile that tipped Logan's lips. Maybe, just maybe, she had someone in her corner. She was surprised that Tag hadn't weighed in at all, but she knew just what to say to rectify that. "And you." She glanced at Tag. "The amount of interest I garnered from one single article was ridiculous. People want to know more about you. At least this way, we'll take the focus off of the other members and redirect everyone's attention toward the three of you."

"Are you fucking serious?" Luke again.

"Very much so." McKenna stopped talking and watched all three of the men as they contemplated what she was suggesting.

"What's in it for you?" Tag finally asked.

McKenna smiled. He knew her better than she'd thought.

"I'll write up the articles, I'll get each of you to bless them, and I'll even get the first one out today." She paused for a moment. "In return, I want to see why people spend outrageous amounts of money to be members here." Leaning in closer, McKenna lowered her voice. "And if any of you try to tell me that they're willing to spend it on an absurdly boring playroom and a miniscule apartment, I call bullshit. I want the real reason. And I want a tour."

There, at least it was out there.

When Luke smiled, looking directly at Tag, McKenna knew she'd pegged it. Club Destiny wasn't about the second floor or the sleek, gray slate floors, or the open play area that might draw a few people from time to time. Shit, these people didn't need to pay the kind of money Club Destiny charged; they could get the same thing for a hell of a lot cheaper down the street. There was something that no one was telling her.

"What do you think?" Luke asked Logan.

"I think it's not a bad idea." He, too, was smiling. "What about you? Anything we need to watch out for?" Logan turned to Tag.

"As long as she doesn't talk about the lawsuit, you're good as far as I'm concerned." Tag didn't sound thrilled about the idea, but he wasn't turning her away, either.

"And the tour?" Luke asked Tag directly, all three of them pretending she wasn't sitting right there.

"I'll do the tour. Friday night."

Friday? McKenna wondered why he wanted to wait so long and on her last night there, to boot. It was only Sunday, which meant she had to wait all freaking week.

Instead of pouting, McKenna smiled and then asked, "Which one of you wants to go first?"

Logan and Luke immediately pointed to the other, and Tag just sat back, sipping his coffee. She could feel his eyes on her, but she didn't look at him.

"You're the face of the club." Logan laughed, talking to Luke.

"We have the same fucking face," Luke barked, but he followed it with a smile. "I guess I'll go first."

Intimidating — the first word that came to mind as McKenna sat down in an empty chair in Luke's office. Luckily for her, she hid her emotions well, because when he sat down behind his desk, he didn't look at all friendly.

"Interview away, Ms. Thorne." His gruff voice told McKenna the next hour was not going to be a pleasant one if she didn't do something about it now.

"Please, call me McKenna," she told him as she tried to get comfortable in the hardback chair. It wasn't happening. "Do you mind if we move over to those chairs?" Tilting her head in the direction of a small seating area on the other side of the room, she waited for his response.

Without saying a word, he simply stood, then waited for her to do the same.

Why was she so damn nervous? It wasn't like Luke McCoy was famous or something. But there was something about him that made her … apprehensive.

By the time they were seated and she was a fraction more comfortable, McKenna could see the tension in his strong jaw had only intensified.

"I don't bite."

Apparently, her outburst helped to relax Luke a little, at least if his smile was anything to go by.

"I'm just going to ask some simple questions, and feel free to respond however you want. Do you mind if I record this? It's only for my notes. I promise, I won't publish the recording in any way."

Luke nodded his head but kept his eyes trained on her.

"Have you ever done an interview before?" McKenna was pretty sure she knew the answer, but she really was hoping to get Luke to loosen up a little.

"What do you think?" he replied smartly.

"Okay. For the record, your answer is no." McKenna didn't need to record that, but she hoped it would make Luke lighten up.

It didn't. Reaching into her memory banks, she tried to remember some of the funniest interview questions she'd heard or asked before.

"How many pairs of shoes do you own?" McKenna kept a straight face as she asked the question, even when Luke tilted one eyebrow and looked at her questioningly.

"You want to know about my shoes?"

"Me personally? No, not really."

Finally. Luke cracked a smile. A genuine one. It was then that McKenna truly understood what Sierra and Cole saw in the man. He was beautiful. Especially when he wasn't brooding.

"Okay, now on to the serious questions." McKenna clicked on her recorder and focused every ounce of her energy on Luke.

Chapter *Eighteen*

TAG HIT THE end button on his phone at the same time McKenna walked through the door. Turning in his chair at a small desk, he looked up at her and was surprised to see a smile on her face.

"The interview went well?" Not that he hadn't expected it to, but Tag was well aware of how hard Luke could be on people. He definitely wasn't the most sociable, but ever since he'd fallen in love with Sierra and Cole, he had changed. Not that he would admit it.

"It did." Making a beeline for her computer, she barely spared him a glance, which bothered him for some reason.

He knew she was probably going to work on her article, but he had at least been hoping for a minute of her attention. Didn't look like he was going to get even a few seconds.

Turning back to his computer screen, Tag tried to pretend that her shrug off didn't bother him. That didn't work, so he opened his instant messenger and found her name in his contact list.

He typed, *Know what happens when I get ignored?* And hit enter.

No, what? Was the reply a few seconds later.

I get a sudden urge to … pull out my toys.

Thought you didn't have any toys.

I never said that.

You implied it.

Want to see my toys?

Yes.

Tag honestly didn't expect that answer, so as he looked at the three small letters glaring back at him from the screen, he had to readjust his slacks.

Don't tease me, McKenna.

Or what?

The woman was going to kill him.

That's it.

Tag didn't wait for a response. He stood abruptly and stormed over to the sofa, where McKenna was sitting. He easily removed her laptop from her grasp and set it on the coffee table behind him before taking her hand and helping her to stand. The moment she was on her feet, he tossed her over his shoulder and carried her to his bedroom.

Her laughter made his cock throb harder. And the way she pinched his butt made him laugh.

Putting her back on her feet, Tag pulled McKenna close and pressed his lips to hers. He'd been thinking about this all day, and now that she was back, he was ready to give her a brief introduction to a couple of his toys.

"Don't move."

McKenna's body went rigid, and the smile disappeared from her beautiful mouth, but Tag could see the passion reflected in the multicolors of her eyes. She was instantly turned on, which only made him want her more.

Tag retreated to the other side of the room and the armoire where he kept his clothes. Among other things.

After rummaging around for a couple of minutes, more for effect than anything, he returned to her side, not bothering to hide what he had retrieved. "Turn around."

McKenna turned but not before Tag saw the hint of another smile at the corners of her mouth.

He set the items on the bed in front of her while he slowly removed her clothes, placing kisses on her smooth skin as he went along. Hell, he would've been happy to do that for hours, but he could feel the tension in her well-sculpted muscles.

They were standing at the end of the four-poster bed, which was perfect for what he had in mind. Keeping her facing toward the mattress and away from him, Tag took one of her hands and attached a soft, leather cuff to her wrist before attaching the clip on the other end to the hook at the top of the post. He continued to do the same with her other arm, then he used another set of cuffs to fasten her ankles to the hooks at the bottom of each post.

He took a step back and admired his handy work. Truly, standing before him was the sexiest woman he'd ever laid his eyes on. With her red hair still clipped at the back of her head, he was able to admire the graceful column of her neck, the smooth contour of her shoulders, and the slender curve of her waist. Not to mention her delectable ass.

"Are you shaking?" Tag asked when he noticed her trembling slightly.

"No." She didn't sound very convincing, but Tag heard the humor in the one word.

"Have you ever been tied up, McKenna?"

"No." That did sound convincing.

"Are you nervous?"

"Nervous, no. Anxious, yes."

Tag moved closer, removing the clip and allowing all of that glorious red silk to fall around her shoulders, down her back.

"What are you anxious for?"

"You to touch me."

Tag liked that McKenna didn't hesitate in answering his questions. She wasn't shy when it came to what she wanted, and she obviously had enough experience to know that she'd get exactly what she wanted if she played along.

Using the tip of his finger, he followed the curve of her waist, over her hip, then beneath the luscious curve of her ass. He didn't go any farther, just simply reversed the motion until he reached the gentle swell of her breast. His other hand followed suit, performing the same motion on the opposite side until he had both hands cupping her breasts, and his chest was pressed against her back.

"You're so damn beautiful," he whispered in her ear, licking her earlobe as he kneaded her breasts.

Glancing down at the bed, he took stock of the items he'd placed there earlier, figuring he'd give her a choice. Tag didn't doubt that she was all too familiar with each item, but he knew for a fact she'd never been on the receiving end of one.

"Do you have a preference?" he asked.

It took a few seconds before she forced out her answer, but that was likely because he was pinching her nipples between his fingers, none too gently.

"Crop."

"Why that one?" Tag had had an idea she would pick it, although he wouldn't have cared which one.

Truth be told, he didn't use these toys much. He wasn't into hard-core BDSM, nor did he experiment with it regularly. He used them for what they were...toys. They heightened the sexual experience, but it wasn't something he had to have.

"I like it."

"To be used on you? Or to use on someone else?"

"I've never had it used on me." McKenna's voice was just a whisper, and Tag detected a hint of excitement in her tone. He was beginning to think McKenna might just be his equal in more ways than one.

What he didn't know was what that actually meant.

MCKENNA TRIED TO focus on the cool air caressing her skin, but that wasn't working. Her mind was ablaze with images of what might be next in Tag's game. And she had no doubt this was a game. She'd known it the second he'd tossed her over his shoulder so easily and when he'd secured her wrists and ankles to the bedpost.

Maybe she should feel a little concern as far as the bondage went, but she didn't. If anything, she trusted Tag. Why? The way he held her, touched her, and even that possessive tone she detected — all of those things contributed to the level of trust they had already developed between them, even if unknowingly.

She found it interesting the way he put the toys down in front of her, obviously to intimidate her. She wasn't. No, she was turned on like hell, but in no way was she intimidated.

She didn't know anything about Tag's reputation at the club, but she knew of the reputations of several Doms in the area, and he wasn't one of them. That was because he wasn't a Dom. He didn't indulge in that lifestyle, although he obviously found some interest in it based on the toys on the bed in front of her.

A riding crop. A small paddle. A suede flogger.

She had several of each in her toy box, although she hadn't used them in quite some time. These didn't look to be cheap toys, which didn't surprise her. Tag didn't seem like the kind to go cheap on anything, much less pleasure.

But the riding crop, well, in her experience, it would be the least painful, at least when used by a novice.

As Tag retrieved the riding crop, McKenna bit her lip. Okay, so now she was getting a little nervous. Here she was, spread eagle and secured firmly with the leather restraints, which offered her barely any room to move. There was no way she was going to get away from the pain he would likely deliver.

When she felt the cool steel tip of the handle slide down her spine, she shivered involuntarily. He was going to tease her first, apparently. She smiled. His mouth followed; the warmth of his lips trailing down her naked back had her pussy dripping and her nipples hardening painfully.

The anticipation was as exciting as the act. She knew that much. When Tag's hands gripped her hips, his mouth going lower, spreading teasing kisses over her bottom, McKenna fought the urge to wiggle away from him. Or maybe she wanted to get closer. Either way, she forced herself to remain still, letting the pleasure encompass her.

Just as she was getting used to the soft, light kisses, a sharp sting assaulted her ass, and she flinched. Barely. Okay, so the riding crop definitely hurt, but it was an exquisite pain that overtook her entire body. When he used his big hand to rub the sting away, she pushed her bottom against him, wanting to feel his hands on the rest of her body.

That's not what she got.

Another biting sting landed on her left butt cheek, and she moaned. Oh, yes, she definitely liked it.

Who would've thought?

For the next few minutes, Tag continued to tease her, chasing the pain away with his tongue and his lips, his fingers and his palms, only to deliver another crisp, sharp sting followed by several more. By the time he was finished, McKenna was biting her tongue, trying to keep from crying out. The tears streaming down her face were involuntary as was the throbbing need that had taken up residence between her legs.

"I didn't think your ass could get any prettier." Tag's warm breath heated the skin of her neck as he whispered close to her ear. "I was wrong."

The riding crop suddenly appeared before her, back on the bed where it had been originally, and she felt Tag's big body shift behind her. His broad shoulders maneuvered between her legs, and when she looked down her body toward the floor, she could see the top of his head moments before her body was accosted by ethereal pleasure.

His tongue began stroking her clit fiercely, showing absolutely no mercy until she was begging and pleading for him to let her come.

Instinct had her holding back, mainly because that was what she would've expected from her playmate had the situation been reversed. Another jolt shook her body, making her limbs weak as Tag thrust two fingers deep inside of her, curling them until he was skillfully manipulating her G-spot.

"Tag!" She wouldn't be able to hold on much longer; she knew that much. "Please, Tag! Let me come!"

"Come for me, baby," he growled from between her thighs, his tongue quickly returning to her clit, his fingers doing wondrous things to her until she...

Exploded. That's exactly what she did when her orgasm ripped its way through her, shaking her to her very core. She was weak and barely able to keep her legs beneath her as he slowed his manipulations, still keeping his fingers deep in her pussy, his tongue gently stroking her clit. Using care, he held her legs so she didn't collapse, but he didn't stop the sexual torment.

"So fucking sexy." His voice pierced her hazy brain as did his movements.

Before she knew what he was doing, her arms were released from the restraints, as were her legs.

"Put your hands on the bed." The insistence in his tone said he was hanging by a thread, and McKenna couldn't help but smile. With ease, she massaged her wrists before bending at the waist, and placing her palms flat on the mattress, her legs still spread.

Tag wasted no time before sliding his cock into her pussy from behind, gripping her hips firmly and giving himself over to the same pleasure he'd given her just moments before. McKenna somehow found the strength to stiffen her legs, keeping her body rigid as he pounded inside of her, stroking each nerve ending back to life instantly.

He wasn't gentle, but McKenna didn't want gentle. She wanted to feel him inside of her, to make him lose control the same way he made her without even trying.

"McKenna. Baby," Tag groaned from behind her, his fingers digging painfully into the tender skin at her hips as he thrust several more times. And as if he knew exactly what it took to send her over, Tag stilled at the same time another orgasm detonated inside of her, her release apparently triggering his.

Chapter *Nineteen*

Article number three, as approved by Luke McCoy (albeit reluctantly):

The Sinful in Seven Series:
Day 3: Putting Sex in Sexy

Did I hear you correctly?

I have to admit, it takes a lot to intimidate me, yet Luke McCoy managed to do just that with a look. During a very candid interview with the owner of Club Destiny, I had a firsthand look into the infamous sex club owner's life — that's right, we said it. Let me tell you, what I learned today was not what I expected. I'll say one thing: Luke McCoy puts the "sex" in sexy.

Although you'll get to see the full interview in the future, I'm happy to share some very exciting news. Luke and the loves of his life, Sierra and Cole, are expecting a baby! That's right. The threesome announced recently that they are expecting their first child in just a few months, and they have promised to keep us apprised when the blessed day arrives.

Congratulations Luke, Sierra, and Cole!

-McKenna Thorne

Chapter *Twenty*

Article number four, as approved by Luke McCoy:

The Sinful in Seven Series:
Day 4: Interesting Is Putting It
Mildly

Be careful what you ask for…

After the first three days, I find myself wondering what all of the fuss is about. I've met Luke… I've met Logan … and as you know, I've spent countless hours with my tour guide, Tag Murphy. I've met their significant others, yet I'm still searching for all of the lewd and repulsive acts that I keep hearing about. I'm hoping for lewd and repulsive because that's what you are looking for, right?

Well, I'm sorry to say that, up to this point, everything appears a little too normal for my taste. I mean, seriously, I've yet to find a single whip or chain, much less a sinfully delicious orgy to get involved in.

But, I promise you … I will keep looking.

-McKenna Thorne

Chapter *Twenty-One*

DAY FIVE. TAG wasn't sure he was going to last three more minutes, much less three more full days. The sun was just beginning to peak through the vertical blinds in his room, wrapping McKenna's naked body in a warm glow that mesmerized him.

They were exhausted from the day before, when they had both been working diligently to put out the fires caused by Susan Toulmin. Of course, their frequent breaks throughout the day, during which they'd attempted to sate the hunger that couldn't seem to be alleviated, probably hadn't helped, either.

McKenna had worked to get Luke's interview from Sunday into an article that would captivate her audience as well as get some readers on his side, versus the crazy interest in what Susan had to say. Based on what they'd seen on her blog last night, it was working. Today she intended to speak to Logan and get his article drawn up. Tag admired her persistence, but he couldn't help trying to distract her a little.

Like right now.

He was distracting himself as well, which wasn't necessarily a bad thing. Considering all of the things that continued to plague his mind, mainly where this woman was concerned, he welcomed anything to sway his thoughts.

"Mmmm," McKenna moaned sleepily when Tag moved her hair off of her neck so he could kiss the sweet spot that always made her moan. He found that he really liked to nuzzle against her pulse, and she seemed to enjoy it, as well.

When her hand slipped between them, gently gripping his dick, Tag sucked in a breath. She was gentle, but her soft fingers against the throbbing shaft sent a chill darting down his spine.

"My turn," she whispered as she turned over to face him, and Tag rolled onto his back, allowing her to move closer.

"Your turn to what?"

"To play with you."

"Brilliant idea." He grinned as she peeked at him through lowered lids.

Her body was warm from sleep as she continued to stroke him with her hand while pressing her perky tits against his chest. Trailing his hand up and down her spine as she began teasing his nipple with her sharp little teeth, Tag closed his eyes and let himself get lost in the pleasure.

"What's this one for?" McKenna's words broke his sensual trance, and Tag opened his eyes to see her placing small kisses over the tattoo just beneath his collarbone.

"It's a symbol," he answered, unsure whether he really wanted to get into the whys and hows of his body art. Yes, he had numerous tattoos, and yes, they meant something to him. Every single one.

"A symbol for what?"

Tag met her eyes, detecting only interest from her. And it wasn't because she wanted to share his story with the world, he could tell. She was genuinely interested in him.

"Everlasting love."

Her eyes widened at his admission, and he wondered what her immediate assumption was.

"Did you get it because of someone?"

When she turned her attention back to kissing his chest, teasing his nipple, he could tell she was trying to appear disinterested. She wanted to know, but it was obvious she was fearful of what his answer was going to be. That spoke volumes about this woman, the one he found himself drawn to more than any woman from his past.

Truthfully, none of his tattoos was in any way related to a woman from his past.

"No." His simple answer had the result he'd thought it would. McKenna stilled, just briefly, before returning to her quest to make him crazy with lust.

By the time she made her way to the one place he wanted her right then, Tag was damn near sweating and shaking from the need consuming him. She didn't ask any more questions, and for that he was grateful. Explaining his tattoos wasn't something he enjoyed doing, mainly because they were his and his alone, as far as he was concerned. To others, it was art, to him, it was his life mapped out on his body.

"Oh, hell yes," he hissed when McKenna's sweet mouth enveloped his cock, her tongue curling around the hard shaft. Closing his eyes again, Tag got lost in the sensations.

Gripping the sheets in his hands, he fought the urge to slide his fingers through her hair and hold her to him. He didn't need to, because she wasn't going anywhere, but fuck, he wasn't sure he could take much more. Without the control, he was nothing, and this woman stripped him bare with just a look, and her touch reduced him to nothing.

"McKenna." Fuck, he was going to come; there was no holding back. "If you don't stop, I'm going to come in your mouth," he warned her, in case she expected more from him.

She didn't move, just began sucking and stroking that much faster, that much harder, until Tag couldn't hold on any longer.

"What did you think of the article on Luke?" Tag asked Cole several hours later when they met for lunch.

"I'm impressed, I've got to say. That woman managed to make him seem much nicer than he really is." Cole laughed, but Tag saw the love reflected in his stepbrother's eyes.

"That's for damn sure." Tag had been quite impressed himself after reading McKenna's article before she'd given it to Luke for his blessing. After reading it, Tag had known damn well there was no way this couldn't at least help their cause.

"How is she doing, anyway?" Cole asked.

"With what?"

"The exclusive. Luke told me that she figured you guys out and insisted she be given the real tour."

Infatuation

That she had. And although Tag wasn't keen on the idea, he knew he had no choice. She was correct to assume there was something more than the brief introduction she'd received to the private quarters of Club Destiny. And that's all they really were. The real action was, in fact, in the second club that still had never been mentioned in the media.

Luke and Logan had been brilliant to come up with a general admission club that would receive the interest of the general public, and they had never denied the additional area sanctioned off for members only above the club. However, the second club, the one without a distinguishable entrance, had never been mentioned.

Until now.

McKenna Thorne was too smart for her own good, as far as he was concerned. While the issue wasn't showing her the second club, subjecting her to what went on there was something he wasn't quite comfortable with. Yet. Not to mention, Samantha, Sierra, and Ashleigh didn't even know about the second club, and the men they were with had worked diligently to keep it from them.

The men weren't prone to keeping secrets, but there was a sense of possessiveness that came along with their relationships, and from what Tag knew, Luke, Logan, Cole, and Alex weren't interested in sharing them the way it would be expected if they were to show up there.

Now Tag had been backed into a corner.

"I'm not sure how I'm going to work that one out yet," Tag told Cole as they waited for their food.

"Well, you better come up with something soon."

"How's Sierra doing?" Tag redirected the conversation.

"Amazing as always."

Again, Tag saw the love in Cole's eyes when he talked about his lover. "I know you aren't sharing it with anyone, but do you know who the baby's father is?"

He wasn't sure why he asked the question, but he had wondered about it ever since Luke and Sierra had announced the pregnancy at dinner with the Walker brothers not too long ago.

Cole didn't look happy with the question, but to Tag's surprise, he answered. "We do."

Unsure where to go from there, Tag glanced around trying to think of something that would be neutral ground for both of them. To his surprise, Cole continued.

"Do you think Sierra should marry the baby's father?"

Tag noticed that his brother wasn't sharing who the father was.

"Why?" Tag didn't understand what the benefit would be, but he understood Cole's insecurity.

"Shit, I don't know."

"Have the three of you discussed it?"

"Not in depth, no. I mentioned it last week, and Sierra got pissed at me."

"Do you want her to marry the baby's father?" Tag didn't care which one of them was the father, because as far as he was concerned, their baby would be more than loved by the three of them. And even if they didn't have a traditional family, that didn't mean it was wrong.

"Not necessarily."

"What's really going on, Cole?" Tag hadn't grown up with Cole, nor had they ever been close like real brothers, but they had become friends over the years, and he knew him. There was something truly bothering him.

"I guess I'm just having a hard time figuring out how it's all supposed to work. Who does the baby call daddy?"

"Both of you?" That was the logical answer to Tag.

"Does it work like that?"

"Why wouldn't it? Same-sex couples have children all the time. This wouldn't be much different. Regardless of who the birth father is, that doesn't make either of you less than the other."

Cole became instantly fascinated with his beer bottle, and Tag left it at that. He might be able to dish out advice, but admittedly, he didn't have the first clue what it would actually feel like to be in a relationship as complicated as theirs.

The only thing he did know, they loved each other. That was clear. And from Tag's interaction with the trio, he never got the impression that any one of them loved one person more than the other. And as long as they were happy, what the fuck did it matter, anyway?

"I heard you're meeting with Travis this afternoon," Cole said when his eyes met Tag's once more. Shit, at this rate, he was going to have whiplash trying to keep up.

"Three o'clock," Tag confirmed. "We're talking about the resort."

"He's been talking to a couple of the members over the last couple of days."

Tag was curious as to which ones, but he didn't ask. Questioning Cole wasn't going to get him the answers he needed, nor did he want the McCoys to think he was trying to find out inadvertently.

"That's what I hear. Sounds like he's got a couple of additional investors."

"Looks like it. I don't know who they are, but I do know he turned down Stephen Crawford after the man approached him."

Tag hadn't heard that. He'd fully expected Crawford to approach Travis, but he was a little surprised to learn he'd turned the interest away.

"How did he become a member?" Tag heard himself ask the question before he could stop it. He'd expected to have this conversation with Logan and Luke, not Cole, but now it was out there, and there was no way he could take it back.

"Fuck if I know," Cole huffed. "Luke won't tell me shit, and when I asked Logan, he wouldn't say, either. Something's going on there, I can feel it. I just don't know what it is."

For the remainder of their lunch, Cole's comment stuck with Tag, and he made a mental note to talk to Luke and Logan as soon as his meeting with Travis was finished.

MCKENNA WAS SITTING at an empty table in the club working on her laptop and waiting for Tag to finish his meeting with Travis. Her interview with Logan had gone well. Better than well, actually. He had invited his wife, and after spending an hour talking to the two of them, McKenna felt as though she had an insider's view into their lives. It was fascinating, to say the least.

What surprised her most was Sam's keen interest in everything. The woman's appetite for knowledge was insatiable, and for part of the interview, McKenna had found herself answering more questions than Logan. All in all, it'd worked out well, and her article was almost finished.

If she would just focus on what was in front of her and not her curiosity about what Tag and Travis were discussing behind closed doors, she might just finish it. No matter how hard she tried, McKenna's brain was set on replay, and the video was of the past few days she'd spent with Tag. Apparently her brain was on sexual overload.

Maybe it was due to the interview she'd had with Luke earlier in the week and the way the man had openly answered one of her more personal questions as it related to sex. Admittedly, ever since that discussion, she'd had a difficult time not imagining what it was like to be Sierra in the middle of that fantastically hot man sandwich.

Ménage.

Not a foreign concept for McKenna, although she would admit to experiencing at least one in her entire life. But again, McKenna had done some serious experimenting for a few years, and she'd found many different sexual scenarios that had struck her fancy. A threesome was definitely one of them. At the time.

But for some reason, it didn't interest her right now. Granted, it wasn't like she hadn't given it a fleeting thought or two in recent days. Especially when she had been talking with Tag and Travis, but what red-blooded woman wouldn't at least fantasize about that kind of orgasmic bliss? She was guilty of the passing thought.

Now ... well, McKenna had developed a very personal, very possessive fondness for Tag Murphy. The idea of sharing him or him sharing her didn't do much for her, which, in all honesty, really surprised her. Not that he would feel the same, but McKenna knew that anything more than what they were doing now just wasn't going to happen.

She knew from experience and from the stories her readers had told her that it wasn't about quantity but rather quality. So, no, she didn't venture into sexual situations often with a man she didn't know well. She could admit that her experience was vast; however, the number of partners she had had in her life was not.

She had questioned herself recently as it pertained to Tag, but McKenna realized she knew a lot more about him than she gave herself credit for. They had shared a few informal discussions prior to their first interlude, and one of those times had been a visit he'd made to her office, before her article referring to his dungeon. Aside from that, it just felt like there was a connection between the two of them. Something that was possibly even stronger than they were.

Sometimes she forgot about that meeting because it had been so normal. She wasn't sure why he'd showed up that day, but he had. If she thought about it now, she figured he was just trying to get an idea of what he might be able to expect from her as far as the media were concerned. Up until that point, she hadn't written anything over the top about him or the McCoys, but she had made a few references on her blog.

That meeting had been normal in comparison to the meetings that had followed for sure. Especially every time they'd come in contact with one another after that first very brief kiss in his car. Okay, so maybe she was dreaming or perhaps even delusional. She honestly didn't know how Tag felt about her, aside from the heat she saw in his eyes when they were together. But she did feel something in his touch, in his kiss, that she was pretty sure she had never felt before.

As her thoughts continued to drift, McKenna was vaguely aware of both Tag and Travis approaching the table where she sat.

"I hope it's me you're thinking about." Tag's resonant southern drawl invaded the sexual haze she was encroached in.

McKenna realized she was smiling, which was probably what he was referring to. "Maybe. How did your meeting go?" She immediately changed the subject.

"Very well," Travis answered. "And now I've got to get back to Austin to take care of a few things." As he extended his hand to Tag, McKenna watched the two shake hands. "Thanks. And you'll be hearing from me soon."

When Travis turned and extended his hand to her, McKenna gently gripped it in return and smiled. "If you don't mind, one of these days when you have a few extra minutes, I'd really like to interview you."

"Yes, ma'am." Travis's thick Texas drawl made McKenna realize one of the many reasons women must flock to this man.

With that, Travis headed for the main doors, stopping to talk to Luke on his way out.

"Are you hungry?" Tag asked as he watched her.

She wasn't sure what it was, but he seemed oddly intense at the moment, but she let it go.

"I could eat."

Chapter *Twenty-Two*

Article number five, as approved by Logan McCoy:

The Sinful in Seven Series:
Day 5: Interviewer or
Interviewee?

Who's asking the questions here?

Did I say that Luke McCoy put the "sex" in sexy? Well, I meant Logan McCoy. No, wait. I meant Luke. Hell, they both did — with a capital S-E-X.

Today I was honored with the opportunity to interview Logan McCoy and his beautiful wife, Samantha. Let me just say, I'm not sure who was really asking the questions. The one thing I know for sure, if there were ever any doubts, there definitely aren't anymore. These two are very much in love.

Needless to say, Mr. and Mrs. Logan McCoy are two very passionate, practical, and exceptionally powerful people. I assure you, I will definitely think twice before deciding to cross either one of them.

I promise a glimpse into their interview in the future, so hold tight!

-McKenna Thorne

Chapter *Twenty-Three*

Article number six, as approved by Tag Murphy (and yes, he got a kick out of this one):

The Sinful in Seven Series:
Day 6: Hanging In

Is it hot in here to you?

Well, if not, then I think I'm having a hot flash.

-McKenna Thorne

Chapter *Twenty-Four*

TAG COULD'VE SWORN it was Thursday and not Monday.

At the rate the day was going, he'd be hard-pressed not to drink himself into a blind stupor by sundown, and the sad part about it … it was only ten o'clock in the morning.

He admired McKenna for how she managed to juggle so many things at one time and still remain the cool professional that she was. In fact, things had gotten so out of hand they'd opted to go to the Sensations, Inc. offices so she could handle a few issues that had arisen during the few days she'd been absent. Although, based on what he saw, Whisper Durant was doing a fine job of handling them, but she was the one who had requested McKenna's presence.

The articles on Luke and Logan had lit up the phone lines at Sensations, Inc., and although they had called in every additional person they had, it still seemed the influx of interest was too much. Not for McKenna, though. She was amazingly cool under pressure, and Tag found himself just watching her.

She was currently sitting at her desk, her fingers flying over her keyboard as she did whatever it was that she did. Answering a ton of questions, he was sure.

"Mac?" Whisper's voice came from down the hall long before she approached, and she wasn't any quieter when she walked through the door.

Tag fought the urge to laugh. *Whisper.* The woman was so incredibly loud he wondered whether her parents had known what they were getting themselves into.

He sat on the sofa in McKenna's office, his laptop in front of him, and watched the exchange between the two women. They couldn't have been any more different from each other. McKenna was tall, slender, with porcelain skin and vibrant red hair, while Whisper was cute, short, with bronze skin and a short, white-blond bob. They were an interesting pair. Tag couldn't help but notice how well they worked together and how much they knew what the other was about to say.

He was still entranced by watching McKenna when his phone rang, startling him and causing the two women to look his way. Glancing down at it, he saw that it was Logan, and as he quickly hit the talk button, he snuck out into the hall.

"What's up?"

"Where the hell are you?"

Damn. Why was it that Logan seemed to be the McCoy twin losing his cool these days? For all the time Tag had known him, he was never rattled, but something about this entire situation was definitely making the man nervous.

"Sensations offices. Why?"

"I need you to meet me. At XTX."

XTX? Tag had just been by there that morning for a meeting with Xavier Thomas. To his surprise, the meeting had gone exceptionally well, but that was probably because there wasn't a lot of drama there.

Unlike Club Destiny.

"When?" Tag conceded, pacing back and forth down the hall.

"Now would be perfect."

Of course it would.

"Give me a few minutes," Tag told Logan before hanging up.

As he turned to enter McKenna's office again, he passed Whisper, who smiled up at him. Tag smiled back although he got the feeling she was up to something.

"I need to head over to XTX. Logan's ass is on fire, and he wants me to come by."

McKenna laughed, and the pleasant, sultry sound made Tag wish he could lock the door and strip her naked. It was like his dick had radar set to acknowledge her every sound.

"I can have Whisper take me to the club when I'm finished here," she said, barely sparing him a glance.

"No. I'll come back by. It shouldn't take too long." Tag had no idea how long it would actually take, but he couldn't imagine Logan McCoy going off on a tangent for too long.

But shit, what did he know?

Half an hour later, Tag was walking into the luxurious front entrance of XTX, a place he frequented at least once a day. Being that he was now their lead attorney, thanks to some apparently stellar references, he found that he thoroughly enjoyed representing the company.

Maybe that was because there weren't too many issues at the moment. Not to mention, he had a team of four additional lawyers who managed everything from trademarks to the infrequent lawsuit against the company for whatever reason. Most of his time was spent ensuring the cases were being handled appropriately, and they were pushing back when necessary.

And then there were days like today when he felt as though everything was mission critical for one person or another, and today was obviously Logan's day.

Taking the stairs, Tag kept his pace casual. He wasn't in a rush, because from the sound of Logan on the phone, the man wasn't in any mood to just shoot the shit. He was in rare form, and likely Tag was going to get the brunt of it.

He was beginning to wonder if he truly was that disconnected to what was going on. He couldn't imagine that he was, because seriously, even though he and McKenna were spending twenty-four hours a day together, they were still living life as normally as they could. Which was funny, because to Tag, it felt a little too normal. Something he definitely wasn't familiar with and found himself starting to question repeatedly.

Granted, they weren't at his house, they were at the club, but still…waking up to McKenna each morning was strangely nice. Especially considering he wasn't usually the type to spend the night with a woman, and he definitely wasn't the type to play house with one. Even to this degree.

When he approached Logan's door, he greeted Deanna, Logan's assistant and the woman responsible for keeping the man on track. At least at work. Sam was ultimately responsible for keeping him on his toes, though.

"Afternoon," Tag greeted as he glanced down at his watch, realizing it was already after twelve.

"Sit," Logan barked, and Tag couldn't help but cock his eyebrow. He was all for dropping everything he had going on to take the time to meet with Logan, but he damn sure wasn't up to being commanded.

"Shit. Sorry," Logan said, appearing somewhat apologetic.

Tag closed the door behind him and then took the chair opposite Logan's huge desk.

"What's up?"

"This is what's up." Logan thrust a newspaper at him from across the desk, and Tag reached forward, retrieving it and skimming the headline.

Shit.

"Why the fuck did you let that little bastard into the club?" Tag asked directly.

Staring back at him in black and white was the image of Stephen Crawford and Susan Toulmin. Apparently — according to the first paragraph in the news article — Stephen and Susan were teaming up to share some intimate details of what they knew about the club.

"We didn't *let* him in," Logan sighed. "He's blackmailing Luke."

What the fuck?

"What the hell does he have on Luke?" And why the fuck didn't he already know about this? Tag might not be a joint owner in the club, but he was expected to represent them and to ensure that the club and its members were legally safeguarded from shit like this.

"It's complicated."

Tag peered back at Logan, waiting to hear the complicated version. Shit, he didn't care which version he received, but damn it, he deserved one of them. And fast.

"What do you mean, 'it's complicated'? How fucking complicated could it be?"

"It's about Sam."

What the hell? Tag was thoroughly confused at this point, but he waited as patiently as he could for the rest.

"Luke is taking the brunt of it all, but actually, this bastard has pictures of Sam." Logan sighed in defeat. "From one of our visits to the playroom at the club."

"How the hell did that happen?" Was he in the fucking Twilight Zone? Tag was so damned confused that his head was beginning to hurt. "I thought the club was secure. How the hell did someone get a camera in there?"

Logan leaned back in his chair as he ran his hand through his thick, dark hair. The man definitely didn't look like he had been sleeping lately. Tag could imagine why. If pictures of Sam were to get out, that could be a huge hit to a lot of people. Including XTX, where Sam currently contracted, as well as CISS and definitely Club Destiny.

"We don't know who is responsible, but we do know that Stephen Crawford paid the person off. Apparently money goes a long way these days."

"And he's not blackmailing Luke for money?"

"No. The little fucker is insisting that he be allowed to join the club. After several repeat denials of his application, apparently Crawford wasn't willing to give up."

Tag wasn't happy about the situation in general, but at least there was a method to the McCoys' madness. For the life of him, he never could understand how Crawford was allowed in.

"Does he know about…?" Tag didn't finish his statement, but he knew he didn't need to.

"No. And thankfully neither does Susan Toulmin. Neither of them was ever trusted enough to be invited to *The Club*."

Well, at least they had that going for them.

"According to that article, they're going to start sharing names. The good thing — not that any of this is good — is they only have the names of the few people they might've met along the way. Unfortunately, some of those are very influential."

Which meant Club Destiny was in a world of hurt at the moment.

Neither man spoke for several long minutes as Tag scanned the article in front of him. The only thing he knew for a fact was that Susan and Stephen together were a recipe for disaster.

"Does Travis know about this?" Tag had no idea why he would, but with their newest venture also on the line, he wondered whether they had shared it with him.

Logan nodded but didn't say a word.

"And why the fuck did I not know about this before now?" Tag was furious, and he was more than a little offended that the brothers wouldn't have sought his help in the matter.

"Shit. I don't know," Logan exhaled. "This is Sam's reputation we're talking about. And you know I'll go to any length to protect her."

Tag understood the message. Logan meant that he would go to lengths outside of the law in order to protect the woman he loved.

He didn't like it, but somehow, Tag understood.

BY THE TIME Tag returned to the office, McKenna was just finishing up. He'd been gone longer than she'd thought he would, but he had been thoughtful enough to send a text message telling her that he would be delayed.

Five hours was one hell of a delay.

Since she hadn't talked to him, she didn't know what had called him away for so long, nor was she sure she wanted to ask. Not with the way he was looking at her now.

Her day had been a long, stressful one, and at the moment, she wanted nothing more than to sit in a dark room and sip a glass of wine. It was that bad of a day. It hadn't started out that way, but ever since she'd received that nasty email from Stephen Crawford, things had gone downhill rapidly.

Infatuation

To pass the last few minutes, McKenna had been glancing at today's newspaper articles online and had run across one in the *Dallas Morning News* that caught her attention and was probably the reason Tag had run out on her earlier in the day.

"You ready?" he grumbled as he stood in the doorway.

McKenna contemplated his mood for a moment, trying to determine whether he was mellow or angry. Those seemed to be the only two settings he had these days, and quite frankly, she didn't know which to expect most of the time.

Either way, as she looked him over, taking in his overall appearance, she couldn't help but find him sexy, regardless of how he was acting. He was impeccably dressed, and even at the end of the day, his brilliant white button-down shirt was wrinkle free, and the shiny forest-green tie he had selected that morning still hung perfectly straight, accentuating his beautiful dark eyes. His suit jacket was open, his hands thrust into his pockets, and he looked like a damn model posing for the camera.

She felt his dark, brooding eyes on her now as he seemed to wait for her answer. "Ready," she replied, undocking her laptop and sliding it into her bag.

When they reached the car, Tag opened the passenger door for her and waited patiently while she got situated before shutting it. McKenna could feel the tension in his rigid body, see the strain on his normally relaxed face.

Questioning him to share would have been her usual way of handling a situation like this, but McKenna managed to choke down the litany of questions that hung on the tip of her tongue. If Tag wanted to share, she figured he would. And if he didn't, well, that would sting just a little, but what could she do?

They were halfway to the club when Tag suddenly veered off the highway onto the feeder road. McKenna didn't ask him where he was going, and holding back damn near killed her. She was inquisitive by nature, but she was also smart. Tag didn't want to talk; that was abundantly clear.

When they pulled into a small clearing, one that looked out over the beautiful display of downtown Dallas's finest, all lit up against the inky backdrop of night, McKenna suddenly didn't feel like talking, either. As she took in the white lights flashing on the Reunion Tower sphere that sat high above the other buildings and the clean, green lines outlining the Bank of America Plaza building, she managed to relax, letting all of the other stresses from the day go.

The gentle hum of the motor in Tag's seat as he moved the chair backward broke the tranquil silence, and McKenna glanced over to see him looking at her.

"Come here."

The thick, southern drawl and the dark, rich tenor of his voice sent a chill racing down her spine. McKenna didn't delay before releasing the seat belt buckle and maneuvering over the center console until she was straddling Tag's thighs. He eased the steering wheel up, putting more space between him and it, allowing McKenna to ease down onto him more comfortably.

When he cupped her face, the gentle way he touched her wasn't lost on her. His dark eyelashes framed his all-seeing, all-knowing eyes, and McKenna nearly drowned in the passion that took up residence there. When they traced her face, landing on her mouth, she had the urge to kiss him, to lock their mouths together and feed off of his hunger. Only she wasn't sure she needed more, because she was consumed by it already.

McKenna could still sense the tension, but it was changing, melding into something much more discernible. She knew it hadn't been a particularly easy day for either one of them, but then again, she wondered whether many of them were. It wasn't like they had jobs free of stress, but she didn't know if those even existed in the first place. Whatever was on Tag's mind, McKenna knew that, for just a little while, when they came together, he'd be able to forget.

"I need you," he whispered in the dark.

"I need you, too." She wasn't sure why she said the words, but she felt as though he needed to hear them. This need she had acquired for him still shocked her, because for all intents and purposes, there was so much about Tag that she felt she didn't know.

Right now, it didn't matter, because as far as what she felt for him, McKenna knew everything that was important. After the day she'd had, nothing sounded better than getting lost in this man, his touch, his kiss. He was the equivalent of a bottle of wine — able to soothe her frazzled nerves with just a taste.

"Kiss me, McKenna."

She let her gaze roam his face, stopping on his mouth, then back to his eyes before she leaned in and gently swiped her tongue over his bottom lip. He didn't rush her, but his hands left her face, easing down between their bodies. By the way he moved, she knew he was releasing the thick, firm erection she felt pressing between her thighs.

That's when she kissed him.

Unleashing all of her pent-up desire on him, McKenna licked into his mouth, tasting him, breathing him in as he slowly kissed her back, using his tongue to explore her the same way. Finally, their mouths were fused together, his breath was her breath, and hers was his as they fed on one another, taking what they both needed.

She lifted her hips when his hands pressed between her thighs, giving him more room, allowing him to slide her panties out of the way beneath the wispy skirt she wore until she felt the thick head of his penis pressing against her entrance.

He captured her moan with his mouth as he slid deeper inside of her, filling her completely. And in that instant, she was aware of the difference, aware of the heat of him without the barrier of latex. He wasn't using a condom.

He pulled his mouth from hers and looked up into her eyes, obviously asking the vital question without words. They didn't need words because somewhere in the last week, they'd developed a trust between them, one that was unspoken, and so foreign to her that tears threatened behind her eyelids.

"I'm clean," he whispered, "I've never…"

McKenna knew what he was trying to say, and she assured him that she was, as well. Without speaking, she nodded her head, letting him know they were safe. She was on the pill, and she trusted him implicitly.

Tag gripped her hips firmly and pulled her down on him, his hard length driving into her as once again he crushed his mouth to hers, stealing the moan that she couldn't hold in. Even in the tight confines of the car, he managed to move inside of her, brushing against inflamed nerve endings that were screaming for his touch. Their bodies moved in sync until they were both panting, and McKenna had to break the kiss just to breathe.

Glancing down at him, she continued to raise and lower on his cock, as fast as she could manage as he assisted by lifting her bottom. She was lost in the sensation, relishing the feel of his hard length relentlessly tunneling through sensitive tissue.

She didn't feel the need to tell him that she was about to come because she sensed he could feel it. Her body was gripping him, pulling him deeper, trying to hold him inside of her even as he retreated over and over. Faster. Harder.

"Mine."

The word was barely recognizable, and she wondered whether Tag even meant to say it, but that didn't matter because it was then that her breath lodged in her throat, and her orgasm took her, shaking her to her very core as he followed her over.

Chapter *Twenty-Five*

FRIDAY MORNING CAME way too early, in Tag's opinion. Even after he woke McKenna by sliding into her wet, warm heat, taking her without haste, he'd still been reluctant to get out of bed.

That was three hours ago, and here he was, sitting in Luke's office with McKenna by his side. He hadn't yet shared the new information he had learned yesterday with her, but for some reason, he needed to have her there with him.

Maybe it was because it felt as though the world as they knew it was about to come crumbling down around them, and over the course of the last seven days, somewhere along the way, McKenna had become an anchor in the sea of chaos that allowed him to remain grounded. She calmed him in ways he'd never expected, while, at the same time, she set fire to his blood.

She hadn't asked questions last night, although he'd fully expected her to because that was her nature. And maybe that was the other reason he felt the need to keep her close. She understood him in ways he didn't even understand himself.

"Good morning," Luke greeted when he walked into the room minutes later.

Tag looked up at him, questioning him with just his eyebrows. There was nothing good about that morning, he knew. He wondered whether Logan had spoken to his brother and explained their conversation from yesterday.

Still watching Luke closely, he noticed the way the man's eyes darted back and forth between him and McKenna before he finally shut the door to his office and took a seat at his desk.

"Logan talked to you." It wasn't a question, and the frustration on Luke's face said more than words ever could.

McKenna glanced back and forth between him and Luke; the fact that she didn't know what was going on was apparent.

"McKenna doesn't know, so I'd appreciate if you could give us your side of the story."

Luke sighed, leaned back in his chair, and propped one ankle on the opposite knee, his hands steepled in his lap. For long seconds, he didn't say a word, but finally, with a rush of air, he began, "Stephen Crawford is blackmailing me. Or rather, he's blackmailing Club Destiny at Samantha's expense."

McKenna's sharp intake of breath was the only sound in the room after Luke's statement.

"He's using pictures of Sam as leverage, and he demanded admission to the club, which obviously I made the decision to do just to buy some time."

"According to Logan, he hasn't been given full privileges, though, correct?" Tag questioned.

"Correct," Luke confirmed. "And since Susan never did have full membership, either, they lack some information that could truly take down the club."

"Take it down?" McKenna's concern rang loudly in the otherwise quiet space.

Luke glanced at her before answering. "If Susan and Stephen release the information I'm sure they have, which is a list of certain members, all hell is going to break loose."

That was an understatement, in Tag's opinion, although they still didn't know which members might've come into contact with either of them. Other than those who were in attendance at the last member meeting, where Travis Walker had shared some insight into his new resort.

"If either of you read the article yesterday," Luke continued, "then you know they're gearing up and using all of this publicity to their advantage. At this point, winning a lawsuit isn't going to prove a damn thing, because even if we can keep Susan from talking, we're going to have a hard time with Stephen."

"Did he sign a confidentiality agreement?" McKenna asked.

"He did."

When her attention turned to him, Tag shook his head. "We've got about the same leverage against him as we do Susan. But in either case, with the blackmail, it isn't going to make a damn bit of difference. If they decide to release the pictures of Sam, it isn't going to be good for anyone, including XTX and CISS."

McKenna seemed to contemplate that for a second. "What if we have something on him?"

"On who? Crawford?" Luke asked.

"Yes."

"Like what?" It was Tag's turn to question her. What the hell could she possibly have on Stephen Crawford?

"As I mentioned before, for the last few months, Stephen has been adamant that we do an article on him, but to this point, we've refused, mainly because the guy creeps me out." McKenna shifted her gaze between both of them, and Tag watched every expression. "Since we haven't agreed, he's resorted to threats." McKenna held up her hand, stopping him from saying a word.

"No, I don't have concrete proof they are coming from him; however, I do have an IP address, and that should be easily traceable. And" — she paused momentarily — "I hired a friend of mine to track him for the last few weeks, which has offered me a little bit of damning evidence, although I'm not sure how much it's going to help."

Tag noticed Luke was no longer leaning back in his chair but rather resting his forearms on the desk and hanging on McKenna's every word.

"What sort of evidence?"

"I don't know for sure because there are hours of video, but I'd be happy to let you have a look at them."

Tag heard every word they were saying, but his brain was still hung up on McKenna's original statement — Stephen Crawford was threatening her.

"If you don't mind," Luke said, "I'd like to get the videos over to Alex at CISS and have him take a look at them. And if you get the emails over to Dylan or Cole, they'll be able to track the IP address."

McKenna glanced at Tag, but he still couldn't say a word. What was there to say? Despite all of this, he wasn't sure anything was going to help.

What they really needed to do was talk to Samantha McCoy and see what her take on the situation was.

Except there was one problem...she didn't know about the pictures.

MCKENNA WOULD'VE PREFERRED to keep the upper hand and not share the information she had, but that was before she knew what Stephen and Susan were planning to do. If McKenna was going to help, she needed to know exactly what ammunition the two of them had. For now, she wasn't going to question her own intentions, because no matter what her ulterior motive might be, she felt as though this were the right thing to do.

"You mentioned pictures. What are they of?" She had a fairly good idea, but in her line of work, she did her best not to assume anything.

"The club has a monthly... How do I put it?" Luke looked as though he were searching for just the right word. "Get-together. It takes place in the playroom."

McKenna figured Luke thought that said it all.

"Who attends these get-togethers?" she asked, for his benefit.

"Anyone. Everyone. It's a free-for-all in every respect, and a few months ago, Sam was itching to be a part of it, so Logan relented. And Sierra was also in attendance."

McKenna was watching Luke and noticed the sudden worry line that appeared in his forehead.

"Does Stephen have anything on Sierra?" She couldn't help but ask the obvious question.

"If he does, he hasn't brought it to my attention. However, he claims that he does have pictures of me and Cole."

McKenna didn't need to ask what that meant. If there were images of Cole and Luke while they were intimate, and she assumed that's why everyone was worried, it was likely Sierra was included. She only wondered why Luke wasn't as concerned about those.

"Does Cole know about this?" Tag asked, obviously just as surprised by Luke's admission as she was.

"He does now. I told him last night. And I'm having a hard time convincing him to let this go for now." There was a sudden smirk on Luke's handsome face, and McKenna wanted to know what he was thinking.

"Fuck." Tag exhaled and then stood abruptly from his chair before pacing back and forth.

Luke obviously read the question on McKenna's face, because he continued, "Let's just say my temper is child's play in comparison to Cole. He just has a much better grip on his anger issues."

Tag growled in response, and McKenna was fixated on him as he continued to walk back and forth. She'd only thought there was tension before, but now she could feel it pulsing in the air. Almost like a beast trying to break free, and yet Tag insisted he keep it under control.

"Okay, so let me get this straight." McKenna tore her eyes from Tag and returned them to Luke. "Stephen Crawford is blackmailing you with pictures of Samantha McCoy, and probably pictures of Sierra, as well. His demand is to be given admission to the club, which you have already done. Although you mentioned that he hasn't been given full access. What does that mean?"

Tag immediately stopped pacing and stared at Luke as though waiting for what he would say next. McKenna didn't know which one of them to look at. Considering Tag didn't look like he was ready to share anything more, she turned her attention back on Luke.

"The other club," he responded, not looking over at Tag once. "The *real* club."

"That's the tour I'm supposed to get tonight, correct?" McKenna glanced up at Tag, and the anticipation that suddenly ignited in her belly was enough to make her heart flutter.

If she was going to get a tour of the real club, as Luke referred to it, and they opened it to only certain members, not all of them, she wanted to know just what the hell went on there.

"And you said Susan didn't have admission to this part of the club, either, correct?" McKenna felt the need to clarify all of the details. It would only help them to figure out what to do next. This was the part of her job that she loved. The investigative process, because you couldn't just rely on what people told you most of the time. It was worth the time and effort to research a claim before publishing anything. It was professional, not to mention, it ensured that she wasn't made to look like a fool.

"No, she didn't have access." Luke leaned back in his chair once again, his eyes resting on the desk in front of him. "I never trusted her enough."

Luke's distrust of most people was obviously a good thing for them all.

"So, where do we go from here?" she asked Tag directly.

"Let's start by getting the video and the emails over to CISS," Tag stated as he stood just a few feet away, "then we'll go from there. I have to agree, I don't want to file a lawsuit against Stephen, because that's only going to put him on the defensive, and he's going to retaliate."

McKenna waited to see if Luke would say anything, and when he didn't, she did. "I think we need to at least respond to them in some way. It's what they want. They're trying to get a rise out of Luke and maybe Logan, too. If we sit back and pretend to ignore them, it's only going to piss them off."

Both men paused momentarily, hopefully considering her statement. They shared a look between them before Tag turned back to her. "What do you suggest?"

McKenna smiled.

She had just the thing.

Chapter *Twenty-Six*

TAG PRAYED LIKE hell that this was going to work. He had serious doubts after looking at all of the faces staring back at him in the large meeting room, but he had to admit, it was worth a shot. Aside from outing Samantha on their own and taking a direct hit that they would probably never recover from, he wasn't sure they had much of a choice anyhow.

He was mostly there for support and to show the members that he was on their side. No matter their final decision, he would ensure their interests were protected to the best of his ability.

Tag's eyes were glued to the woman now standing in front of the entire room. She was dressed to reflect the immaculate professional that she was, and he knew he wasn't the only person riveted by how incredibly stunning she looked in gray pinstriped slacks that accentuated her tiny waist and her curvy hips while the crisp white button-down shirt hinted at her impressive cleavage, although she wasn't doing anything specific to draw attention to her body.

"Thanks for coming here today," McKenna addressed the entire room after Luke took his seat beside Cole. "I know most of you probably know who I am, and I hope by the end of this meeting, I can erase some of the fear I see in your eyes."

Uncomfortable laughter rattled through the room.

Behind McKenna, on the projector screen, was an enlarged image of the front-page article from the *Dallas Morning News.*

"As many of you know, I'm here doing an exclusive on Club Destiny, and before you panic any more than you already have, I want to tell you that your anonymity is my first and foremost priority. I will, in no way, offer any names in any of my articles on this club."

Tag might've imagined it, but he thought he heard several sighs of relief.

"However, from where I stand, I'm not the enemy that you need to watch out for." McKenna pointed behind her to the screen. "Most of you have probably already read the article and understand the intentions of Stephen Crawford and Susan Toulmin, which is why we have invited each of you here today.

"You'll notice amongst you there are several familiar faces not in attendance today. If you stop and think about who is not here, you will also note where you normally see those people."

Tag held his breath, waiting for McKenna to get to the point.

"I've learned in recent days exactly how far Luke and Logan McCoy will go to protect the members of their club. And this may upset you at first, but if you think long and hard on their reasoning, you'll understand that their methods have always been in your best interest.

"Each one of you is considered a full member of Club Destiny." McKenna paused, and Tag waited to see if anyone would say anything. When they didn't, she continued. "What does that mean? Well, it means that you have full access to the entire club, while some members are restricted to certain areas, including the private wing.

"This may seem a little underhanded if you think about it, but again, every decision that Luke and Logan have made was in your best interest. Due to the nature of the club and certain activities that go on, each new member is put on a probation period in which they are observed, and more importantly, trust is established. That means that not every member you see within these walls is allowed to venture into *the club.*"

McKenna emphasized the last words, referring mainly to the real Club Destiny, which not many people even knew about. Every person in that room had at one time or another been to the other club, although they probably hadn't thought anything of it at the time.

"The two people that you see on the screen behind me were never granted full membership." McKenna smiled. "Now I'm going to tell you why I am here today, and why you're hearing this from me and not from the owners."

This was the part Tag worried about. McKenna did a fine job providing the backstory per se, but this was the point where it was going to get a little touchy.

"Most of you have been worried about how much Susan Toulmin knows. If you've ever interacted with her in any capacity, then you've worried your name may be on this mysterious list she keeps referring to. Well, it very well may be. It may very well be on Stephen Crawford's list.

"Thanks to CISS, Luke and Logan have compiled their own list of people in attendance at one or more of the nightly events in which Stephen or Susan were present. Don't worry; there is no video evidence of any of this, as far as we know. Your visits are captured via the security codes that you enter upon entry and exit to this floor. That also doesn't mean that every one of you is on that list. It does mean it's a possibility, and Luke and Logan wanted you to be aware of what was going on. That is why your presence was insisted upon."

McKenna stopped once again. This time when her eyes met his, he smiled. She was doing a phenomenal job. She hadn't wanted to be the bearer of bad news, but she'd agreed because she wanted to assure everyone that she was not the enemy. Tag respected her for that.

"Now I'll tell you why we brought you here today. It wasn't just to inform you of the growing concern, which most of you already knew about. It's to ask for your help, but let me preface this by saying you are in no way expected to react or agree to anything we suggest. In fact, we are open to your suggestions, as well."

Tag stood, knowing it was his turn to address the room. As much as he wished McKenna could keep talking because she was doing such a remarkable job, he wasn't about to let her take the brunt of what they were about to unleash on them.

"Many of you know me, mainly because my face has been all over the news as it relates to Club Destiny and the current lawsuit against Ms. Susan Toulmin. For those who do not, my name is Tag Murphy, and I am Club Destiny's legal counsel. My job is to represent the best interest of this club and, therefore, of its members.

"In light of the lawsuit, it has come to our attention that there are some other things going on that are affecting you as members as well as the owners of this club. These are serious matters, and I want to make sure you understand that your anonymity is not the only thing on the line here."

Tag continued to explain in brief detail what Stephen Crawford was doing and what he was using as blackmail against Luke and Logan. That did not go over well, because, rightfully so, the members felt as though they had been unnecessarily dragged into the middle of this mess by Crawford's admission into the club. They were accurate in that regard, but when Tag continued to explain, there was a measure of understanding amongst them. Although, that didn't mean they weren't angry.

"Why doesn't Samantha just suck it up? She's the one they're after," one of the members asked.

The growl that erupted from the back of the room, coming from Logan's direction, was predatory in nature.

"I'm sure that explains it clearly," Tag said, referring to Logan's reaction, "but I'm going to reiterate that Logan and Luke are working to ensure that your membership to this club is kept strictly confidential. But I can also tell you that, without your cooperation, our hands are tied."

That settled the room down some. It was clear from his comment that, at this point, their identities were going to be released if Susan or Stephen had anything to say about it. Tag didn't fault Logan for wanting to protect Sam. Hell, he wanted to protect Sam. But the only thing he could think about was if McKenna was in this same situation and what he would do.

As much as it concerned him to think that way, he knew he'd go to any length necessary to protect her.

ONCE THE SPEECHES were concluded, McKenna stood at the back of the room with Tag, watching while Logan and Luke addressed the crowd of people. It was still a civil conversation, but it was hanging by a thread. If anyone ever doubted how protective the twins were of their lovers, they had no question about it now.

And yes, there was an idiot in every crowd. Today was no exception. There was one who continued to insist that Samantha be responsible for her own actions. When Tag told her that the particular idiot was a state senator, McKenna sighed. Of course he was. Hypocritical bastard.

By the time the meeting was adjourned, Luke and Logan looked about ready to spit fire, and McKenna couldn't say that she blamed them. After they'd reasoned with the members, the members insisted that they were in no way supportive of their names being released. They didn't care that Logan and Luke were willing to waive their membership fee for the following year if they allowed McKenna to use their name in an article on the club.

"What the fuck are we going to do now?" Luke barked as he approached them when the room had completely cleared of everyone except the McCoy twins, Cole, and Alex McDermott — whom McKenna learned was the head of CISS and Ashleigh Thomas's soon-to-be husband.

"When is the next *free-for-all?*" McKenna asked, trying to keep a straight face. She didn't find any of this amusing, but the fact that these guys couldn't come up with a better reference still tickled her.

"Next week."

"Hmm…"

"What does that mean?" Tag asked, standing straight and tall at her side.

"I was just wondering." She didn't really know why she wanted to know, but she was thinking that maybe if she knew what went on there, she could give it a sexy twist that her readers wouldn't be offended by. Not everyone was into public displays or group sex of any kind, so it would be a risk either way.

"Well, I need to get back to the office," Logan said. "And tomorrow I plan to talk to Sam. She deserves to know what's going on."

McKenna couldn't argue there. In her opinion, Sam deserved to know a long time ago. However, she understood Logan was only trying to protect her as best he knew how, even if she didn't think he was going about it the right way.

"I'm going to put something together, and I'll let you all read it and let me know what you think," McKenna explained. "With your approval, we'll publish a brief article and see what type of response we get."

"Were you able to figure out where the emails to McKenna came from?" Tag interrupted, speaking to Alex.

"Dylan's working on it as we speak. He'll have more in a little while. I'm heading back to the office now to check out the video. Hopefully, we'll get something that might help."

Alex didn't look at all hopeful, and McKenna was beginning to understand how dire this situation was. Club Destiny was going to take a hit, and based on today's meeting, if the members' identities got out, there very well might not be a Club Destiny in the future. She couldn't imagine what must be going through Luke's head right now.

Two hours later, McKenna was putting the finishing touches on the story she'd prepared. It wasn't going to be anything radical, nor would it probably get a lot of attention, but it was the answer to the threat that the newspaper article had implied.

"Will you read over this?" she asked Tag when he reappeared in the living room. He had disappeared with the excuse that he was taking a shower as soon as they'd made it back to his room. Now it was McKenna's turn to shower, because, in just a little while, they would be doing the official tour of the underground club that no one seemed to know about.

She wondered whether attendance would be low tonight considering the meeting and the topic of discussion. However, she also wondered whether it might have the opposite effect. Some people got off on the anticipation that they just might get caught doing something taboo. She suspected that many of Club Destiny's members were, in fact, kinky like that.

"Sure." Tag glanced down at the laptop before walking around to sit on the cushion beside her.

"If you don't mind, I'm going to take a shower now."

"You could've joined me." Tag grinned for what seemed like the first time that day.

"I could have. But I figured you'd need all of your energy for tonight."

As if she had thrown ice water on him, Tag's smile disappeared, and he turned his attention to the computer screen. McKenna headed into the bathroom, unable to stop thinking about what his reaction actually meant.

Chapter *Twenty-Seven*

IT WAS PROBABLY easier to get into the White House, McKenna thought to herself as they continued down a narrow corridor that would lead to The Club @ Club Destiny. Yes, she'd learned earlier that this risqué, off-the-grid place had been dubbed The Club by the members. And if they would ever actually get in there, she might be a little more excited.

So, after the first security-coded entrance — which she quickly learned was manned by an armed security guard and required each person to enter their own assigned code — there were two additional doors that required more codes, but these were tricky ones because they were assigned based on the member's application, and the questions were random. McKenna had filled out all of the necessary paperwork with Luke earlier, which allowed her this one-time-only entry.

By the time they finally arrived at the secret club's main entrance, they were required to show ID, which was scrutinized more by the club's security than even the TSA at the airport.

Once McKenna stepped inside, she immediately realized what all the fuss was about. And yes, this was definitely what these members paid for. From where she stood, it appeared to be one open room, probably close to four thousand square feet if she had to guess.

To her immediate right and left, there were bars, but these weren't just any bars. The front and top were made of glass, outlined in neon LED lights — one pink and the other blue. Behind the bar, the wall was one solid mirror with short, glowing glass shelves the same color as the respective bar, randomly placed holding three liquor bottles on each shelf. And if that wasn't enough to catch someone's attention, the bartenders at each bar definitely would.

The bar on the left — outlined in blue LED lights — was obviously for the men, or at least for the men who were seeking women. The bartenders — two of them — were wearing bras that were anything but. They were made out of slinky chains, and they wrapped around the full naked breasts of each woman. Through the glass, McKenna could see that each woman also wore thigh-high black boots and the tiniest scrap of lace in the form of a G-string.

As for the bar on the right — outlined in pink LED lights — there were two men who either lived in the gym when they weren't working or were just blessed with amazingly good genes. To her surprise, they were wearing more than the women. Both wore a pair of faded, well-worn blue jeans that rode low on their lean hips. Of course, they were shirtless, but each man had a collar around his neck. And not like the Chippendales collars. No, these were leather dog collars.

McKenna couldn't stop herself from staring at any of them. The women were exotically beautiful, and the men were mouthwateringly scrumptious. She should've known.

There was barely enough light in the entire space to see much of what was going on, and with the concrete floors that appeared to be painted black and the walls that sported the same dark color, McKenna's eyes had to adjust, especially after having been drawn to the bright LEDs.

When Tag took her hand, she turned her attention to him, realizing he was staring at her. She smiled up into his handsome face, suddenly thankful for his presence as it brought her a sense of security she hadn't realized she would need.

"Ready?" he asked.

She wasn't sure whether she knew the answer to that question. Suddenly she was feeling a little bowled over by everything she was going to find here. Instead of answering, she nodded her head in agreement and then followed him as he led her on a tour of the spacious club.

Above her, McKenna noticed there were rooms made of glass on walkways that outlined the perimeter of the club on two additional levels. On the ground floor, there were two large rooms at each of the back corners made entirely of glass. From the looks of it, there was absolutely no privacy whatsoever to be found within the space. She hadn't really expected any.

Scattered throughout were black leather chairs, sofas, and even what appeared to be round futons made of the same dark fabric. Not that she could see much of the furniture for the multitude of bodies that were everywhere.

Down the center, four steel poles went from floor to ceiling, holding two metal cages on each — one above the other. In those cages were both men and women, with only one person in each and every single one of the occupants completely naked. A couple of them were dancing to the erotic music that pulsed throughout the club, a few were pacing back and forth, and a couple of them even appeared to be masturbating, but they were all doing something to entertain the crowd below them.

Tag didn't seem to be interested in explaining anything to her, or maybe he just figured that it was self-explanatory. Either way, he kept his hand in hers and held her close to his side as they walked around the perimeter of the main floor.

Once they arrived at one of the large glass rooms at the back, McKenna realized the reason for most of the security. Inside the room was a beautiful woman. No, maybe that wasn't an apt description. She was more stunning than anything else. Thigh-high boots with at least five-inch heels, a leather halter, a skimpy G-string that was held together by chains, and a wicked-looking leather whip made up her outfit, and the woman did not look like one to mess with. Her hair was long, straight, and jet-black, while her skin was like creamy alabaster. Severely cut bangs covered her forehead, while her lips were painted a vivid, glossy red. The woman looked ... untouchable.

Standing before her was another woman, completely nude and chained to hooks that were hanging from the ceiling and sticking up from the floor. Her arms were directly above her head, but her legs were spread wide. Her back was to the crowd and her bottom was lined with bright red whelps. In front of her, where the audience could see clearly, there was a naked man on his knees, his hands behind his back and his tongue between the woman's thighs.

McKenna would admit that the scene was intensely graphic and more than a little arousing. She couldn't tear her eyes away, and when the obvious Dominatrix lifted the whip and struck the other woman again, McKenna didn't even flinch.

Tag either didn't find the scene appealing or he was more interested in showing her the rest. McKenna followed behind him when he tugged on her arm, successfully breaking her concentration on the sexually stimulating group behind the glass.

When they approached the other glass room, McKenna found herself equally drawn to it. Before her were two well-built, extremely handsome men and one female. This one resembled normal, everyday porn, except the reactions of the participants were much more…unscripted.

"Are these actors?" she asked Tag.

"No. These are members," he replied, looking down at her. "They can reserve the rooms, and these two are actually booked out for months."

McKenna could understand that. This was a fetish club. The members were here for one reason only, and that was to experience the sexual gratification that they longed for. It was intense, intriguing, and downright sexy as hell.

Turning her attention back to the two men in the glass room, McKenna watched as one man rammed his cock into the other man's ass, his hands gripping the other man's shoulders as he continued to thrust hard and fast while the woman sat at the top of the bed, watching, masturbating. McKenna wondered whether the woman was the wife of one of them, and the man was living out his fantasy.

Either way, it was hot.

TAG GLIMPSED THE scene before him, noticing that it was one of the many he'd seen before. Considering he'd been involved with Sam and Logan for the past few months, he hadn't come to The Club recently, but standing here now, he realized that he might very well be a little desensitized when it came to this place.

Not that the sight before him wasn't erotic as hell, and he knew the people were fulfilling one or many fantasies all at the same time, but he just wasn't interested. Now, McKenna, on the other hand, appeared to be riveted to the threesome before her, just as she had been to Mistress Serena in the other room.

He wasn't into it tonight, and maybe that was because of the confusing urge to lock McKenna up and keep her for himself that had taken him by surprise just a short while ago.

Possessive? Yes, he appeared to have developed a sudden longing to ensure no other man — or woman — ever took part in the pleasure that only McKenna could bestow upon them. He wanted her all to himself.

And wasn't that just fucked up crazy?

Tag had always been the dominant partner, yet with McKenna, he had met his match. She was in no way submissive, and in many ways he figured she could give him a run for his money. And it fucking turned him on.

Now that didn't mean he'd lost every kinky desire he'd ever harbored, because truth be told, he wouldn't have any problem taking her to one of the rooms upstairs, slowly removing every last stitch of clothing she had on, and ravishing her while others watched. That's one kink he doubted he would ever get over.

But sharing her with another person was not going to happen. Not tonight. Maybe not ever.

When she looked up at him, he could damn near taste the lust pulsating through her veins. This turned her on. Was it the voyeuristic aspect? Or did she fantasize about herself inside of one of those rooms living out her deepest, darkest fantasies?

Tag didn't know the answer to any of the questions that plagued him, but he did know that before he took McKenna to view the upstairs rooms, he wanted to introduce her to Mistress Serena — the woman in charge of The Club. While they waited for her to be finished with her subs, Tag took McKenna back to the bar.

"What would you like?" he asked, realizing he wasn't sure whether she drank anything more than wine.

"Vodka and Seven please," McKenna told the bartender when she approached.

The music was loud but not so loud that they couldn't have a civil conversation, so as they waited, Tag turned to her. "What do you think so far?"

"It's…interesting." Her smile had the ability to make his blood boil.

"Just interesting?"

"Do you want my professional opinion or my personal one?"

"What's the difference?"

"If I look through my professional lens, I could describe every nuance and detail down to what the women and men in the cages are doing right at this very moment. Or even the group settled on a large round sofa in the center of the room. If I look through my personal lens, I'd tell you that it's interesting in a fetish club sort of way."

"So, are you saying this doesn't turn you on?" he asked, taking the two drinks the bartender set in front of him and slipping her a twenty-dollar bill as a tip. The drinks were free in the club, but the tips were appreciated.

"It absolutely turns me on," she clarified. "But that doesn't mean it's something that appeals to me right now."

"Do you like being watched?"

That was part of the intrigue of the club, he knew. The voyeuristic aspect — the watching and being watched — was what most people really sought when they came to a place like this. There were the hard-core masochistic types, and before the night was through, he was sure they'd see some things that would damn near blow her mind.

Because it was dark, Tag couldn't tell whether his question made McKenna blush or not, but he could see from the look in her eyes that she was hesitant in answering him.

"Do you?" he asked again.

"Yes."

Tag fought the urge to pull her against him right then and there and do to her the things he'd dreamed about since the day he'd met her. Instead, he kept his distance, leaving the few inches between them as he glanced back at the first room, noticing Mistress Serena was, in fact, coming out of the room.

And walking directly toward them.

Tag saw McKenna's eyes widen as Mistress Serena approached, holding a stainless steel whipping rod in her hand.

"Mr. Murphy, I see you brought your guest." Mistress Serena's sultry voice was surprisingly calmer than he was used to, and he noticed she seemed more fixated on McKenna. Tag wondered whether it was the immensely dominating personalities that both women exhibited.

Did Mistress Serena see McKenna as a threat? The thought intrigued him.

"McKenna Thorne, meet Mistress Serena. She's in charge of The Club."

"Nice to meet you," McKenna replied, not holding her hand out or moving in any way.

Tag watched in amazement as McKenna kept her eyes up and locked with the Dommes. Most people, it didn't matter whether it was a man or a woman, seemed to lower their eyes when Mistress Serena scrutinized them.

Tag glanced over, witnessing the small smile on Mistress Serena's lips and the way she held the whipping rod close to her chest as though fearful she might just use it unexpectedly.

"Will the two of you require a room this evening?" Mistress Serena asked, not directing the question to either one of them specifically.

"Yes," Tag replied. He wasn't completely sure they would be using it, but he was definitely going to show McKenna one of the rooms at a minimum.

Infatuation

If he had anything to say about it, she might just become familiar with it while they were there.

Chapter *Twenty-Eight*

MCKENNA WATCHED MISTRESS Serena as she walked away. Never once did she lower her eyes from the intimidating woman, wanting to ensure her that she was in no way a submissive, nor was she here to play. Having been in the dominating role before, McKenna had no desire to be dominated by a woman like her.

"She manages the club?" McKenna asked when Mistress Serena was out of earshot.

"With an iron fist. She's the official club manager, *and* she's a Domme. Whether because of one or the other, she allows absolutely no room for bullshit," Tag explained. "She ensures the safety of every club member, with the help of two of her submissives who make the rounds frequently if Mistress Serena is otherwise engaged."

McKenna was happy to hear that. From experience, she knew that BDSM was not something that should be experimented with without extreme caution. Especially when it came to punishment the likes of which she'd seen Mistress Serena dishing out. There was too much room for mistakes or for people who were doing it for the wrong reason.

"So you reserved us a room?" McKenna couldn't help but ask the question as she looked up into Tag's piercing green eyes.

"I wanted to ensure you received a full tour," he told her. "Whether we use the room is entirely up to you."

McKenna's belly fluttered with excitement. It could have been the atmosphere in which they were enveloped, or just the man standing a few inches away from her, but whatever it was, she was highly aroused, and if she had her say, they'd definitely be putting that room to good use. However, before she could commit to something like that, she wanted to see the rest of the place.

"If the people in the rooms aren't actors, are the ones in the cages?" McKenna referred to the eight cages suspended above the crowd.

"No, they aren't actors, either. They're members. There aren't any actors here. The only employees are the bartenders, and as you'll notice, there are armed security guards at either end of the bar."

McKenna turned, and that's when she saw two big, burly men standing at opposite ends of the bar. When she looked at the other side of the room, she noticed two more.

"There aren't any waitresses, either. Luke and Logan didn't want to take the chance of one of the waitresses being subjected to something they didn't want to be subjected to."

Interesting.

McKenna completely agreed. Although these people paid high dollars to be members of the club, and no matter how thorough a background check was done on them, you couldn't predict what a human being might do. And with sexual stimulation of this nature, there was bound to be at least one person who didn't know how to control him or herself.

She had to admit she was highly impressed with how well thought out this club was. This wasn't your run-of-the-mill sex club, and it clearly wasn't an anything-goes kind of place, either.

"So what's upstairs?" she finally asked.

"Let me show you." Tag took her empty glass and returned it to the bar before taking her hand and leading her to a large metal staircase that led up to the second-floor landing.

When they reached the first of the two floors, McKenna heard the sounds coming from every direction before she actually saw anything. On all four sides, there were glass rooms, about five on each wall, made entirely of glass on three sides while butting up against the exposed brick wall of the exterior. For all intents and purposes, they were exact replicas of the rooms on the ground floor, just significantly smaller.

Guarding each wall were security guards who stood watch over the people who were both inside the rooms as well as those who were seated just outside in the chairs lined up in front of them. It was a live porn show for anyone who wanted to view, and from what McKenna could tell, it catered to almost every kinky fetish.

The number of people in each room varied about as much as what they were doing. It was a fascinating mishmash of assorted fetishes, ranging from the standard woman/man or woman/woman or man/man intimate encounter to people wearing blindfolds and being treated to oral pleasure of different types, to a room with six women in a daisy chain. For some reason, it seemed as though these rooms were relatively tame.

"Is there a difference between this floor and the next?" she questioned Tag as they made their way back to the staircase.

"Yes." Tag turned and looked down at her. "Since everyone has to stop at this floor, they only allow certain activities here. The hard-core scenes are upstairs. They figure that not everyone is into some of the things these people come up with, and this allows members an opportunity to decide for themselves just how much they can handle."

"But what about the rooms downstairs?" McKenna knew that at least one of the scenes downstairs was not for the faint of heart.

"A member has to submit in writing what they intend to use the room for as well as everything that they could engage in while they are there. Mistress Serena reviews every application and decides whether she's willing to allow it on the ground level or not."

"But what makes her a good judge on what's appropriate? She's a Domme," McKenna retorted.

"Trust me; she doesn't let anyone get out of hand." Tag grinned and then took her hand, leading her up the second flight of stairs. "Are you sure you're ready for this?"

"Yes." McKenna was curious to see what exactly they considered hard-core.

On the third floor, as they made their way around the perimeter, she found it almost impossible to look into each of the rooms. She didn't have much of a choice because all of the walls on this floor were made of glass as well, and surprisingly, there were even more people sitting in the viewing rows than the other floor.

She saw everything from a man licking a woman's shoes to a man wearing a diaper while a woman spoon fed him something and varying degrees of other, less attractive things going on.

"Okay, I think I'm good," McKenna told Tag as they neared the stairs once again. She was ready to get back to one of the other floors. Either that or perhaps rip her own eyeballs out.

Thankfully, Tag descended the stairs until they were back on the ground floor, where he led her back to the bar and ordered more drinks. Once they were served, he took a step back, gesturing with his hand for her to lead the way. She appreciated that he was allowing her a few minutes to get acquainted with her surroundings. Not that she hadn't seen everything before in some form or fashion, but this was the real reason she was here.

Considering for the last few days, McKenna had been playing house with a man she continued to find more and more compelling the longer she was around him, she knew this was what she had worked so hard to get to. Being with Tag was a bonus, one that she was pretty sure would only last as long as the contract specified. So, being the savvy businesswoman she prided herself on being, McKenna set about the room, attempting to log everything into her memory for use later.

Surprisingly, there were two different scenes from the ones earlier when they'd arrived. She was just grateful they were much more sexually stimulating than where they had just been on the third floor.

Now, if the alcohol would only help to erase what she'd just witnessed up there, McKenna might just be able to get on with their night.

FOR THE LAST few minutes, Tag had followed closely behind McKenna, doing his best not to disturb her as he watched in amazement the way she mentally archived every little detail of the club into that brilliant mind of hers.

He was glad for this diversion also because it allowed him to forget the few things they had just witnessed on the third floor of the club. There was a reason he didn't go up there. He was a staunch supporter of the phrase "to each his own," but he also knew better than to subject himself to that type of activity. It did absolutely nothing for him.

To his relief, McKenna didn't seem to be bothered by it one way or the other, aside from her enthusiastic agreement to leave. Now that they were back on the ground floor, surrounded by writhing, thrusting bodies in various stages of undress, she seemed to be once again focused on the most intriguing aspect of the club.

When she stopped to linger in front of one of the glass rooms again, Tag moved closer, taking her empty glass from her hand and depositing it on a table near them along with his. Pulling her up against him, Tag pressed his chest against her back, wrapping his arms around her waist as the fresh, sexy scent of her hair lingered in front of him.

He glanced at the room McKenna was fixated on, seeing Mistress Serena once again, but this time she had two men with her, one of them on his knees before her with his tongue buried in her pussy. Tag recognized the one licking her cunt as one of her submissives while the other was a regular member of the club who repeatedly requested Mistress Serena's company.

Holding McKenna close to him, Tag felt her chest begin to rise and fall more rapidly as the scene played out before them, and he knew, without hearing, that her breathing was becoming a little more labored. Her arousal was proof that she had all but forgotten about what had transpired on the third floor, and he was grateful.

As she leaned into him, Tag slid his hands beneath the hem of her shirt, caressing the smooth skin he found there. Sweeping her silky hair out of the way, Tag tilted his head down and gently sucked on her neck until she was pressing against him. He wondered if she even realized she was doing it. In fact, she seemed so focused on the scene in front of her, he wondered whether she even knew he was touching her.

When she turned in his arms and pulled his head down to hers, crushing her mouth to his, he got his answer. She apparently liked it.

Kissing her back was the hardest thing he'd done in a long time because he was trying to keep himself under control. With several people hanging around, their eyes just as easily roaming the two of them as the trio in the room, he wanted to ensure McKenna knew exactly what she was doing.

When she pulled back and those exotic eyes locked with his, he held his breath. He didn't care what she said next as long as the result was going to be him buried inside of her in the very near future.

"You were going to show me that room, weren't you?"

It was his turn to be speechless as he nodded his head and took her hand, damn near dragging her back to the stairs. He managed to slow down as they ascended, but how, he wasn't sure. He just needed to put his hands on her. All over her. Everywhere.

He wanted to drown out all of the chaos in his brain, and the only way he found that was possible was to lose himself in McKenna. Ever since that very first kiss in his car, Tag noticed that the noise in his head quieted when he touched her. The only thing he couldn't seem to get past was the place.

The club didn't bother him; in fact, he had frequented it on many occasions, reaping its full benefits, but with McKenna, it just felt different. For the first time in his life, he questioned whether or not he wanted strangers witnessing the ecstasy he managed to find in McKenna's arms. Maybe it was the vulnerability he felt when she unraveled him with just her eyes or the barest of touches.

As they approached the second floor, Tag realized it was too late to think about it now. The only option he had was to continue until one or both of them firmly decided otherwise.

Approaching the security guard, Tag typed his code into a small, portable keypad the man held out in front of him. The guard glanced down at the screen before turning it back for Tag to see. On the screen were three red numbers that corresponded to the room they'd been assigned. Nodding his head, he walked as slowly as his long legs would allow with McKenna in tow.

Once at the room, he had to scan his club key in order for the doors to open. Tag pushed open the heavy glass panel door, then stood back and allowed McKenna to precede him into the room. The door closed behind them with a whoosh, the lock clicking loudly in the small space.

"The McCoys spared no expense, did they?" McKenna asked as she began moving about the small space.

"They're concerned about safety," he told her. "Can you blame them?"

McKenna smiled back at him, and he once again was lost in her beauty. Good God, he was turning into a fucking sap.

"After seeing that floor," McKenna nodded her chin upward, "I can't say that I do."

Tag couldn't agree more. He had never been fond of the third floor, but that's because his own kinks leaned more toward bondage, the occasional spanking, and being watched. He didn't even get a great thrill out of watching.

Tag stood back, allowing McKenna to look around the ten-by-ten room. There wasn't much to see, really. The back wall was made of exposed brick while the other three, including the only door, were made of glass. Still to this day, Tag had no clue how Mistress Serena managed to keep all of the glass so clean and clear, but somehow she did.

He knew the rooms were sterilized after each person left, and for sanitary purposes, they used only a fitted white sheet on a small mattress in the room. That's also why the room reeked of bleach and disinfectant. The floor was tiled with white marble, and the only other piece of furniture was a small bedside table with a single drawer in it.

McKenna pulled open the drawer while Tag watched, and he knew what she would find. Condoms. That's all. And there weren't that many, because again, Mistress Serena was concerned with safety, so she had them restocked after every use to ensure they hadn't been tampered with, which Tag explained to McKenna as she eyed them.

"It's definitely not an upscale hotel room." McKenna smiled.

"That it's not," he agreed.

"Do you do this often?"

Her question shouldn't have surprised him, but he suddenly wasn't sure he wanted to answer her. Why, he didn't know. "Not as often as you think," he finally replied.

As she walked the perimeter of the room once more, Tag followed her with his eyes. "Come here."

McKenna's gaze met his as she slowly turned and approached him. Mixed with the heat he saw churning in the brilliant colors, he also saw something else.

Nervousness.

"We don't have to do this, you know," he explained as he took her hands in his and pulled her close until her breasts were pressing against his chest.

"I know."

"I'll be more than happy to take you back to my room and tie you up again," Tag said lightly.

That damn smile of hers lit him up from the inside out yet again.

"I might just take you up on that offer." McKenna's hands roamed up over his chest before cupping his neck. "After."

After?

Tag couldn't get a single word out of his mouth, but then again, he was fixated on her soft, full lips. Unable to stop himself, he leaned down and pressed his mouth to hers, sliding his tongue over her bottom lip. "This is your show, baby," he whispered.

He caught the faint nod of her head before she pulled him closer and crushed her mouth to his, and he let her take all she needed from him.

And just like that, the room disappeared, as did anything and everything other than this woman in his arms.

Chapter *Twenty-Nine*

MCKENNA INHALED TAG'S intoxicating scent, his delicious taste, and the spectacular feel of his warm, needy hands on her body. It was almost enough to make her forget where they were. Almost. She could still smell the pungent, bitter scent of disinfectant even over the warm, spicy scent of Tag. She could sense the brutal, blinding fluorescent lights that beamed down on them from the ceiling. And she could hear the muffled throb of the music from outside of the glass walls.

But none of it seemed to matter as long as she was right here with this man. She was aroused. The images of the scenes that played out on the ground floor were burned into her brain, reminding her of all the things she wanted to do to him. All of the ways she wanted to show him just how good it felt to lose that hard-earned control.

But this wasn't the place for that. A couple of years ago, this might've been the place for a lot of her fantasies, but right now, there was only one thing on her mind.

Gripping the waistband of Tag's slacks, McKenna moved backward, closer to the lone mattress sitting in the middle of the room. Gently lowering herself until her bottom rested on the edge, she looked up into those intimidating green eyes and the lust and passion that swirled there. He knew what she was doing just as well as she knew.

Breaking the eye contact, she returned her attention to his belt, deftly unhooking it before releasing the button and lowering the zipper of his slacks. Once she bared the velvety length of his erection, she pushed his shirt out of the way and pressed a kiss to his lower abdomen, the muscles taut and toned beneath her tongue.

This man's body was honed to perfection. There was no doubt in her mind that he took care of himself. He was lean, with just the right amount of muscle to make her want to use her tongue to trace every single valley between each well-defined plane.

Without further hesitation, McKenna caught his gaze once more before she pulled the thick head of his cock into her mouth. She used her tongue to tease the crest and then sucked. Hard.

She didn't stop watching him, and when his eyes closed, the look on his face could only be described as euphoria. McKenna continued to tease and torment him with her lips and tongue, using her teeth on occasion to gently scrape the sensitive underside.

"McKenna," Tag growled. "Baby."

She loved when he said her name. She loved when he fought to maintain some semblance of control. And she loved how she was able to push him closer and closer to the edge, even if he didn't want to be there.

His hands gripped her hair roughly, sending jolts of pleasure through her, making her muscles clench with excitement.

"Come for me," McKenna said, using her tongue to lap at him as she watched the instant his eyes opened, meeting hers. He was forcing himself to hang on, when the only thing she wanted was for him to lose control. "Come for me, Tag," she demanded before she sucked him fully into her mouth, gripping his shaft with one hand and stroking him in sync with the movement of her mouth down the length of him.

She didn't let up, simply taking him deeper, stroking him faster until the pull in her hair intensified and the pain lanced all the way down her spine. Then he exploded in her mouth, her name from his lips the only sound in the room.

After saying a formal good-bye to Mistress Serena, McKenna and Tag returned to his private room, where she sincerely hoped they were going to pick up where they'd left off at the club. It was apparent while they were there that neither one of them had any desire to explore any more than they already had.

Not that the public display hadn't turned her on, because, well … it had. But not the way she'd expected. Not in a way that made her crave more, because quite frankly, she lost control of all thought processes when Tag touched her, and being out in public could prove to be a risk she wasn't willing to take. Regardless of how well secured the place was.

McKenna would admit that the club was stellar in every aspect. She was highly impressed and secretly envious of the members who had the opportunity to go when the urge called. But something told her that The Club wasn't a place Tag frequented. She didn't care either way. She didn't. Okay, maybe she did. Just a little. But he didn't seem all that interested in it the way she would've assumed.

The man was very … sensual.

She knew from experience that didn't necessarily mean he was into some of the risqué aspects of sex. Although, she sensed he liked to explore. There were so many questions she wanted to ask him, so many things she wanted to know. Like what turned him on. Or what turned him off. What he hadn't done and what he had.

Except when he touched her like he was doing now, all of those inquiries no longer mattered. She only wanted to live in the moment, to feel what he was feeling, to see what he was seeing with those all-knowing eyes.

"Turn around," Tag instructed, his hands on her shoulders.

McKenna turned around, away from him. They were standing in his bedroom, and she was now in front of a large, frameless mirror leaning against the wall. It looked like it weighed a ton and cost a fortune and had been selected just as much for decor as for practical use. Standing in front of him, with Tag at her back, McKenna watched every movement he made behind her.

"I want you to watch," he explained as his hands slid around her waist, slowly lifting her shirt until he managed to pull it over her head.

Her hair tumbled back down around her shoulders, over her breasts and down her back as the skin of her belly was revealed, looking even paler against the midnight-blue color of her bra.

Tag easily unclasped the front closure of her bra and then released her breasts before cupping them with both hands. The warmth of his palms against her nipples sent a shiver down her spine. In the reflection, she noticed the drastic difference in their skin tone, his much darker than hers, accentuated by the bold ink colors along his forearms. Somewhere along the way, he had removed his shirt, allowing her to admire the intricate artwork that detailed almost every inch of exposed skin.

When he hefted her breasts in his hands, spreading his fingers to expose her pink, puckered nipples, McKenna was fixated on the sight before her. This was as erotic, if not more so, as watching other human beings engaged in the same thing. Only this was better because this stimulated more than just one of her senses. He was touching her, which was what it all boiled down to. She needed his touch. Ached for it.

His fingers closed, her nipples trapped between his index finger and his middle finger, sending shards of pleasure-pain darting from her nipples to her clit. He repeated the action several times, her body temperature rising with each bolt that ripped through her.

"Put your hands on your breasts," Tag instructed as he slowly moved his away.

McKenna quickly did as he instructed, noticing the difference between when she touched them and when he did. She much preferred his rougher touch to her softer one, but seeing him behind her heightened the sensitivity in her breasts.

His hands slid down her torso, over her stomach before reaching for the zipper on the side of her skirt. With smooth, easy movements, he had her skirt sliding down her legs and pooling at her feet, leaving her clad in only a midnight-blue thong that matched the bra he'd discarded earlier. And her boots.

"So beautiful."

The gruff sound of his voice scraped over her senses the same way his callused palms had against her breasts, making her nipples pucker beneath her fingers once again.

He didn't hesitate before removing her panties, as well, leaving her standing before the mirror in only her boots while his hands slowly slid up her thighs, stopping at the place she wanted to feel him most.

It was as though she was watching this happening to someone else, except for the exquisite feel of Tag's hands against her flesh, his fingertips gently separating her wet folds before the roughened tip of his finger swept over her clit, making her inhale sharply.

"I'll never get enough, McKenna," Tag whispered.

McKenna's eyes flew up to meet his.

Was it just her or was there something in the way he said those words? Something that said he didn't want to get enough of her?

When he pressed his lips to her neck, breaking eye contact, she wondered if she'd only imagined it. Returning her gaze to where he was currently sliding one finger inside of her, McKenna exhaled on a moan and leaned farther into him.

She needed more. More of him in every way, but she couldn't find the words to tell him, so she simply held on to the last vestiges of her sanity as he began thrusting his finger inside of her. She could feel the telltale tingle of her orgasm as it took root deep inside, the need to come overpowered her, and when Tag nipped the sensitive skin where her shoulder and neck met, she gave in.

TAG WATCHED AS McKenna came apart in his arms, her head falling back onto his shoulder, her body spasming around his finger still buried deep inside of her and those sexy-as-hell moans of hers like an electric current right to his dick.

She was the sexiest damn woman he'd ever laid eyes on. With her standing before him completely exposed and vulnerable, he couldn't resist making her watch. He had the pleasure of watching her come every time, but he knew she wasn't aware of how intensely erotic it was to watch her. Now she knew.

Even after she'd so exquisitely pried his release from him earlier, Tag couldn't wait to fuck her again. Gently maneuvering her until they were closer to the wall, he reluctantly removed his finger from her sweet, warm pussy and turned her in his arms until she was backed against the wall.

Taking a step back, he slowly removed the rest of his clothes, keeping his eyes on her and enjoying the feel of her gaze as she followed every movement. There was something powerful about the way she looked at him, something reassuring in the way she bit her bottom lip as he easily released his swollen, stiff cock, stroking it firmly as he stepped out of his slacks.

As soon as he was naked, he closed the gap between them once more, lifting her right leg and positioning the throbbing head at her opening before thrusting one time, without warning, deep inside of her. He had to have her, and he couldn't wait another second to feel her wet heat wrapped around his aching cock.

Sucking in a breath, he held her leg higher, pistoning his hips as he drove his cock deeper and harder into the tight, wet depths of her pussy over and over until he was consumed by the intense friction.

As much as he was scared to admit it, Tag had never felt this way in the arms of any woman. He wasn't prepared to give himself fully to her or anyone else, but he feared his choice was being ripped out of his grasp each and every time he touched her.

Using his free hand, he tilted her chin until their eyes met, never slowing his hips as he pounded inside of her over and over, harder and faster. "Come for me, McKenna."

He was on the verge of exploding, but he refused to do so until she was right there with him. The connection was made between their bodies, but as he stared into her eyes, Tag knew there was a deeper connection than that. Whatever was consuming him was consuming her, as well.

"Come for me!" he growled, barely holding on as her sweet heat pulsed around him. "Fucking come for me."

Her eyes closed, and she moaned, her pussy throbbing and pulsing around his dick as he followed her over, free-falling into something that scared the shit out of him.

No rest for the weary.

Tag was beginning to realize that was McKenna's motto.

Saturday morning, officially their time together should've been over, but he couldn't bring himself to question her or him at the moment. Instead, Tag found himself being rushed by the red-haired vixen insisting that he shower and get dressed because she needed to meet with the McCoys.

All of them.

Apparently Samantha McCoy had called and left McKenna a message directly, insisting that she meet with her as soon as possible. According to McKenna's explanation of the voice mail, Sam didn't sound all that happy. Tag figured Logan must've shared the dreadful news with her.

Now they were driving to the restaurant that Sam had requested they meet at for lunch.

"Did she say anything else?" Tag was curious to know exactly what he was walking into. He'd never known Samantha to panic, yet he couldn't very well blame her in this case if she did.

"No. She was surprisingly calm but asked that I meet with her and Logan. She mentioned Luke would be there, as well."

Well, this was bound to be loads of fucking fun.

By the time they reached the restaurant, McKenna was drumming her fingers on her thigh, and Tag found her anxiety a little amusing. Not that he would tell her as much. Nor was he going to reassure her that things were going to be fine, because honestly, he didn't know whether that was true or not.

Stephen Crawford currently had Logan and Luke by the balls, and unless either of them was willing to give in, Tag didn't see how this was going to work out in anyone's best interest. Although, he had a good time watching McKenna try to come up with a way that wouldn't hurt anyone in the long run.

As much as he liked her positive attitude, he was beginning to wonder about her naïvety at the same time.

Granted, he also liked that he was out of the hot seat for the time being. Being the lawyer, everyone generally looked to him to fix the problem. He didn't have a quick fix for this one, and if he had to guess, although no one had mentioned it yet, Tag was almost certain he was in those pictures, as well.

That thought gave him pause. He wasn't sure whether anyone intended to show McKenna those photos, but he was suddenly worried that they would. The relationship he'd shared previously with Samantha and Logan was between the three of them, and he didn't regret a single minute he'd spent with them, but he wasn't sure McKenna would be as open-minded as he was if she saw them. He remembered the way she had run out of the meeting room after speaking to Sam for the first time. However she had learned about his relationship with them, she hadn't been happy about it.

Several minutes later, they were seated at a table in one of the sectioned-off areas at Sam's favorite restaurant. They had a private room, which was definitely a plus, because the conversation he was sure would be had shouldn't be heard by others. Considering there were more than just a few people at the table, it was guaranteed not to be a quiet conversation, either.

Tag waited for McKenna to take a seat before sitting in the chair beside her. As expected, the entire group was there: Sam, Logan, Luke, Sierra, Cole, Alex, and Ashleigh — pretty much everyone who had something to lose if Stephen and Susan followed through on their threats.

"Thanks for meeting with us," Sam greeted. "The least we could do was buy you both lunch."

Tag noticed the misery shining in both Logan's and Luke's eyes.

"No need," McKenna responded, pulling her napkin from the table and into her lap.

Tag fully expected to see her squirm under the scrutiny of the fourteen eyes that were resting on her at the moment, but she didn't. She was as poised and calm as he'd ever seen her.

"I'm going to start out by apologizing to everyone at this table," Sam said in a desperate tone. "Had I known about this, I can assure you, I would've tried to come up with a way where no one else could've gotten hurt by my actions."

Sierra immediately reached over and took Sam's hand. "Honey, I think I should be apologizing. I'm the one Susan retaliated against. I'm just so sorry you had to get dragged into this mess."

Tag fought the urge to roll his eyes. He knew how close these women were and how overprotective Luke and Logan were, but shit, they could sit here all day and wish this away, but it wasn't going to make a damn bit of difference.

There was a brief lull in conversation as the waitress took their orders before disappearing once more and shutting the door behind her.

"I'm sure I don't need to fill anyone in on what we're looking at, although I'm still disappointed that my husband felt the need to keep me in the dark," Sam said, addressing the entire table.

Logan didn't move, nor did he look at Sam. The hard line of his mouth said it all. He wasn't at all sorry he'd kept this from her, and if Tag had to guess, he wished at this point he'd never said anything.

"Does anyone have any suggestions on how we can fix this?" Alex asked, looking none too happy about being there.

Although Alex wouldn't be directly affected, his company would. Not to mention, XTX was going to get a lot of heat should this hit the front-page headlines. Xavier Thomas was not going to be a happy man, nor would any of the other clients who had originally been looking to hire Sam in the future. And that meant Alex and Ashleigh both would be in the line of fire, even if inadvertently.

"I'm sure Logan and Luke informed you that we addressed the members, but we got nowhere with them. They aren't willing to help even though this is going to affect them just as much as it will you," McKenna spoke up. "I'm not sure that really sank in with them at the time."

"Oh, they knew exactly what the hell we were talking about," Luke barked. "They're just a bunch of selfish bastards who think they're above everyone else." Luke's anger was palpable.

"Were you able to find anything on the videos that might help?" McKenna asked Alex.

"Nothing that we didn't already know and nothing the media wouldn't expect from a lowlife playboy like Stephen Crawford."

"His credibility is highly questionable," Logan said. "But that isn't going to make a difference once this gets out. The press will forget him and Susan in an instant, but they'll be all over us immediately."

"I think it's best if I just come clean and accept responsibility for my actions," Sam declared, glancing back and forth at all the faces focused on her. "You don't know how truly sorry I am that there isn't anything I can do to slow this runaway train, but I would if I could."

"You know," Ashleigh interrupted, "I've always believed in telling the truth, but what if we head this off by reporting that those are fakes. You know, altered to suit the needs of those two?"

Everyone at the table stopped and turned toward Ashleigh. Tag fought to keep from laughing when Alex's mouth dropped open as he stared at his future wife.

"Ashleigh Marie!" Sierra scolded with a laugh. "You've been spending way too much time with us."

That had the table erupting in laughter.

Well, everyone except for McKenna.

"You know, that might just work," she stated, glancing around the table. "I'm not saying we have to out-and-out lie about it, but what if we spin a story that gets people questioning them even more than they already are?"

"Like what?" Luke asked.

"I don't know." McKenna shook her head briefly. "I haven't thought it completely through yet. But I think it's time we take some of the attention off of them and put it back where it belongs."

"Didn't you already try that with the interviews?" Tag asked.

Infatuation

It was a good idea, provided they could stay within the realms of the truth as much as possible, because the last thing they needed was to make this fucked up situation any worse.

He just feared they were already heading down that path.

Chapter *Thirty*

"WHAT DO YOU mean, it won't work?" McKenna asked as she and Tag walked into his private room. Lunch had lasted longer than they'd expected, but neither of them had anything else pressing to do. Well, except try to divert a disaster waiting to happen.

"That's exactly what I mean, McKenna," Tag retorted angrily.

She wasn't quite sure when he'd stopped supporting the cause, but as soon as they'd gotten into his car, he had torn into her about spearheading this little clusterfuck. His words, not hers.

"Well, I think it will work," she answered, making sure he heard the irritation she was currently strangled by.

Throughout all of the conversations at lunch, he hadn't said much, and when he had, he hadn't contributed either way. Now she knew why.

"Of course you do."

"What the hell is that supposed to mean?" She immediately turned to face him, not even stopping to set her purse down.

"You've got stars in your eyes, darlin'. You think everything is going to work out when you should be stepping back and asking yourself why you even care. This doesn't affect you, but for some reason, you're sticking your pretty little neck out when it'd be in your best interest to keep your mouth shut."

McKenna flinched like he had just slapped her. And she felt as though he had. She was too dumbfounded to come up with a retort. What was he trying to say? She didn't belong here? These people didn't deserve her help? Or was he just worried she was getting too involved, and it might just infringe on his life once she walked out, which she should have done first thing that morning, but she hadn't.

That thought had her stomach churning.

Staring back at him, McKenna realized that's exactly what he was saying. She was getting too close, and he wasn't comfortable with it. Somewhere along the way, in the last seven days, McKenna had started believing that Tag might actually care about her. And what a fucking mistake that had been.

How could she have been so naïve?

Taking a detour over to the couch, McKenna picked up her laptop and then went straight to the door. She was leaving. She didn't have to put up with this shit from him, and as far as the contract was concerned, they had both fulfilled their end of the deal. With the exception of her amendment. But looking at Tag now, she didn't give a shit about that anymore.

"Where are you going?" Tag growled.

"Anywhere but here."

"You can't just leave," he argued, but he didn't sound very convincing.

"The hell I can't. I don't need to wait around while you try to come up with some bullshit reason to push me away. You can twist it however you want, but it doesn't change a damn thing." McKenna was doing her damnedest to rein in her temper, to not let him see how angry she was at what he was doing.

"There's nothing to twist."

"The hell there's not. You feel something, damn it. I don't care if you're too stubborn to admit it or not. You feel it just like I do," she yelled.

"That's where you're wrong." Tag's tone cooled significantly, and McKenna braced herself for the impact of what would come next. "It's about sex, darlin'. That's all it has ever been about."

She couldn't have steeled herself for that if she'd wanted to. His words stung, but more importantly, they pissed her off.

Taking a deep breath, she swallowed the pain and anger as best she could. "Thanks for the tour, Tag. Don't worry, I know the terms of our agreement. I'll make sure I get Luke's blessing before I write my final article," she said through clenched teeth. "*If* I write anything at all."

With that, she calmly opened the door and gently shut it behind her, resisting the urge to slam it and fighting the tears that threatened to fall.

Stupid tears.

By the time McKenna got home, she was over the hurt, and she was on her way to a good pissed off. During the cab ride home, she'd had plenty of time to think. Maybe not plan like she wanted, but more than enough time to realize exactly where she had gone wrong.

Once inside her house, McKenna dropped her purse on the table in the foyer and put her laptop down on the kitchen counter before venturing to the cabinet, where she retrieved a wineglass.

If she weren't so worried about doing something incredibly stupid, she would bust out the vodka. But she knew better than to immerse herself in hard liquor when it came to drowning her sorrow. Instead, she would settle on a glass of her favorite red and a phone call to the one woman who would know how to make it all better.

"McKenna?" Whisper greeted when she answered the phone. "Is everything all right?"

"No." That was the only answer she had for that question. No, everything was not all right. Nor was she sure it ever would be again.

"Where are you?"

"At home," McKenna answered reluctantly.

"I'm coming over. Don't move a muscle until I get there," Whisper said quickly.

"Wait." That wasn't why McKenna had called. She didn't want to pull Whisper away from whatever she was doing.

"Nope, no waiting. I'm on my way."

The phone disconnected, and McKenna stared down at the screen that showed her the call had, in fact, ended.

True to her word, ten minutes later, Whisper was banging on the front door, and McKenna was running to answer it. The second she opened it, her friend walked right in bearing gifts in the form of two more bottles of wine. McKenna grinned. Leave it to Whisper to make sure she was taken care of.

"Where's Anna?" McKenna asked as she trailed behind Whisper on the way to the kitchen.

"She's … out." Whisper's curt answer was her way of saying she didn't want to talk about it.

Without asking, which McKenna totally expected, Whisper pulled out another wineglass, filled it, and then refilled McKenna's before hopping up onto the center island counter and turning the full brunt of her attention on McKenna.

"I want every last detail, and if you leave anything out, I'll know."

McKenna smiled. She couldn't help herself.

Pulling out one of the barstools, she plopped down and proceeded to tell Whisper — minus a few minor details — exactly what had happened over the last week. By the time she was finished, Whisper was staring back at her with her mouth hanging open.

"What?"

"You fell for him." It wasn't a question, and McKenna knew she didn't need to answer, either.

It was *that* obvious.

But she lied anyway. "I did not fall for him."

"Bullshit. You went off and fell in love with dreamy lawyer man. What were you thinking?" Whisper was laughing, but that didn't make McKenna feel any better.

What *had* she been thinking?

"It's not like that," McKenna stated firmly, pushing her empty wineglass toward her friend so she could refill it.

"It is *so* like that."

"No, it's not. It's just a job."

That got Whisper to laughing so hard McKenna thought she might just fall off the countertop.

"Honey, sex is never a job for you. No matter how you try to spin it or what you tell yourself."

Okay, so maybe that was true. McKenna had experience; she'd even done some crazy shit in her lifetime, but no, when it came to sex, she didn't do it casually. Ever.

Which was why she was so surprised she had gone and given in to Tag. Okay, and maybe surprised wasn't the right word for it, either. From the moment she'd laid eyes on the sexy, laid-back lawyer, McKenna had wanted him with a ferocity that she didn't even recognize.

Ever since the rat bastard who'd broken her heart sixteen months earlier, she had sworn off men. But she could pretend with the best of them. Her readers thought she was worldly when it came to sex, except she knew better. Sure, she knew what she wanted, and she had lived out some of those fantasies with Tag because her stupid, naïve heart had convinced her much more cautious brain that it was okay.

It was definitely *not* okay.

"He's scared." Whisper's words broke through her thoughts and pulled her back to the present.

"Nothing scares that man," she explained to her friend. "He got what he wanted, and he must've realized I was falling too fast, which he likely knew would happen."

"You give him way too much credit," Whisper commented as she refilled her own glass. "He's only human, and honey, there ain't no man — or woman, for that matter — who wouldn't fall for you if given half a chance."

It was McKenna's turn to laugh. "They're just curious to find out whether those pictures were airbrushed or not."

When she looked up at Whisper, she noticed her friend was no longer smiling. Preparing herself for the tongue-lashing she was about to receive, McKenna focused on her wineglass, turning it slowly on the granite countertop.

"Boss lady, I don't know what happened to you, but I can assure you, when the world looks your way, they don't see the mistakes of that young, naïve eighteen-year-old girl. Hell, that was so long ago I doubt anyone even remembers it."

Right. McKenna knew people remembered because she received emails day in and day out from men asking whether she was going to bare all in her magazine any time soon.

They remembered.

"Dreamy lawyer man is not like that," Whisper added.

"He is so like that. His life revolves around sex. From the toys in his private room to the raunchy club he's a member of, Tag lives and breathes sex."

When McKenna looked up, Whisper was looking at her skeptically.

"You need to talk to him."

McKenna broke eye contact and went back to twirling her glass. "I'm done talking. I'm done trying to help. He made it abundantly clear that he doesn't need nor does he want my help."

"He might not, but the McCoys do," Whisper argued. "They trust you, Mac. They've proven that. And you'd be smart not to let them or yourself down by letting one man's insecurities drag you down."

McKenna didn't believe Tag had a single insecure bone in his entire body. He exuded confidence and self-assurance to the point she could practically taste it when she was around him. And truth be told, she had tried to inhale it at every opportunity, hoping like hell he could infuse her with just a fraction of his hard-won control.

She'd failed.

"So, what's next? Do we write an article to counter Stephen and Susan's threat? Or do we sit back and let Samantha McCoy take a beating for being the woman she wants to be?"

McKenna didn't like the idea of anyone hurting Samantha. Or any one of the people she had come to know over the last week. She didn't want to turn her back on them, even if she risked having her heart smashed and smeared. She wasn't that woman. She was stronger than that.

"No, I'm not going to let her take the fall. But I'm going to need your help."

Whisper clapped her hands like a little girl, grinning from ear to ear. "Gladly."

Chapter *Thirty-One*

TAG WAS AN asshole. A stubborn asshole at that.

He knew it, and now McKenna knew it, too.

Two incredibly long weeks had crawled by, and Tag hadn't heard from her at all. Not that he had tried to contact her, either. Because, well … because he was a jackass.

The worst part about it all was that he couldn't stop thinking about her. Day, night, it didn't matter. She constantly plagued his thoughts. On top of that, she was working diligently to help Sam and Logan out of the current situation they were in, although no one seemed to be making any headway.

Everyone was moving stoically forward while Tag felt like he was just sitting still. He had frequent meetings with both Sam and Logan, yet neither of them mentioned McKenna at all. He knew they were talking to her because he read the articles that came out each day. In fact, that was the first thing he did every morning. With a cup of coffee and his tablet computer, he sat at his kitchen table and consumed his caffeine almost as quickly as he consumed whatever she wrote.

It was making him fucking crazy.

And still he had no intentions of doing anything about it.

What the hell could he do? Grovel? Plead? Beg? Sure, maybe. But that wasn't in his nature. And he absolutely refused to turn into his father. He would never let any one woman own him to the point he didn't care about even himself anymore. That was probably his biggest fear of all.

After Tag had James return all of McKenna's personal things she had left with her abrupt departure, he hadn't even returned to his private room at the club. Nor had he gone to the club.

His life now revolved around work, trying to figure out a way to get Sam and Logan out of this mess without taking everyone else down with them. Thankfully, Stephen Crawford appeared to have gone into hiding. They weren't that lucky as far as Susan went. The woman was at it each and every day, talking foolish nonsense to whoever would listen to her, yet not a single name or even a hint of a picture had been mentioned.

As Tag sat at the table now, powering up his tablet, he waited patiently to see what McKenna had been up to the day before. He knew the articles she published would share as much insight as he was going to get as to what was going on in her life, and he had settled for at least knowing she was okay.

With a couple of touches to the screen, he pulled up her magazine's website and scrolled to the last post, which had been at nine o'clock the previous night. Glancing at his watch, he noticed it was already eight.

When I Say No,
That's What I Mean

Dear Mr. Stephen Crawford,

I debated for days on how I should address your insistent, constant requests, and last night, it finally came to me. A public apology seemed to be in order. So, I'm writing this for you — and the rest of my readers — because I felt it was critically important to ensure you received the message.

First of all, I appreciate your daily emails, and yes, I read each and every one. Including those that don't contain your signature. You know, the ones that are a little harsh — the belligerent threats to my safety and the safety of my staff.

Yes, those are the ones.

Glad you remember.

So, here, for everyone to see, I want to make a public apology, because apparently I have not made myself clear. No, I am not interested in sharing any information about you with my readers. No, I am not interested in helping you manipulate my friends or those I care about. No, I am not interested in... Insert all of those cruel, nasty comments you made here.

I am just not interested. *And I want to apologize if, in any way, my repeated use of the words* no, no thank you, absolutely not, and please do not send any more requests *weren't clear enough for you to understand.*

Thank you,
McKenna Thorne

By the time Tag finished reading the article, his vision was blurry from the red haze that had consumed him. That little fucking weasel was still harassing McKenna. Not only that, she hadn't bothered to tell him about it.

Why would she? Oh, right, she wasn't speaking to him, so the last part actually made sense.

Leaving his coffee cup and his tablet on the table, Tag grabbed his car keys, his phone, and his wallet and was out the door. It was long past time for him to pay someone a visit.

Two minutes into his drive, Tag's cell phone rang, and he hit the button to activate the Bluetooth. "Murphy."

"Where are you?" Logan's deep voice filled the interior of the car.

Why did the man always start a conversation with that question?

"In my car," he said vaguely.

"I need you to meet me at XTX."

"Sorry, can't do it. I've got somewhere I need to be," Tag responded.

"Meet me at XTX in fifteen minutes, Murph. No excuses."

The call ended, and Tag slammed his hands against the steering wheel. His temper was getting the best of him these days, and he was pretty sure he knew why. Those damn McCoy twins were starting to piss him off. But it wasn't like he had much of a choice, so he pulled over, made an abrupt illegal U-turn, and headed toward the XTX offices.

This better be good, that's all he knew.

MCKENNA HADN'T KNOWN where else to turn, and somehow she'd ended up at XTX, requesting to speak to Samantha McCoy. To her surprise, not five minutes later, Logan had showed up, but Sam was nowhere to be found.

Now she was sitting in an empty conference room, a glass of water on the table in front of her and her nerves in a serious state of uproar.

It wasn't like she didn't know who was responsible for tearing up the Sensations, Inc. offices. Seriously, Stephen Crawford made it way too easy. That didn't make what he'd done any easier to swallow.

From the moment she'd reached the main door of her office, McKenna had known something was wrong. Seriously wrong. The fact that the door was unlocked and standing open was her first clue.

Instead of turning around and walking back out to her car, McKenna had morphed into the girl in the scary movies who proceeds into the unknown, despite knowing better. The only difference between her and that naïve young girl was that McKenna had pulled her handgun from her purse before she'd entered the office. Maybe not the smartest move ever, but she knew how to use it, so she at least wasn't walking into the unknown ill-prepared.

What she'd seen before her stole her breath.

The entire office had been ransacked. Completely. Everything in there was trashed. *Everything.* All of the desks, phones, chairs, computers, filing cabinets … everything had been overturned, and some of them had even been thrown through walls. *Through.* The. Wall.

After a quick assessment, McKenna had debated on what to do. The only thing she'd known to do was to call Whisper. After briefly informing her assistant of what had happened, she'd instructed her to call all of the employees and tell them not to come in. From there, she'd locked the main door, practically run to her car, and begun driving until she was pulling into the parking lot of XTX.

Once Logan came down to talk to her, she managed to explain to him what was going on. He interrupted her briefly to make a phone call, and she heard him telling Alex McDermott the details before instructing him to have someone sent over to Sensations, Inc.

She didn't know what good that was going to do now. The damage was done. The only good thing was that he had decided to take out his rage on her office equipment rather than her employees. *He* being Stephen Crawford. There was no doubt in McKenna's mind that he was the bastard responsible.

When the door opened, McKenna looked up from watching her fingers fidget nervously, fully expecting to see Logan standing there, but to her surprise, he wasn't the man staring back at her. Suddenly, as though he'd jump-started her heart, she was overcome by an uncomfortable pounding in her chest.

"Where's Logan?" How she managed to produce words, she didn't know.

"He's talking to Sam," Tag explained as he shut the door behind him. "They'll be here in a minute."

McKenna nodded her head. She would wait for them then. She had absolutely nothing to say to Tag. Not one thing.

So maybe she had a million things to say to Tag.

But she wouldn't.

"Why are you here?" *Or maybe she would.*

Her brain was fuzzy, her palms were suddenly damp, and her heart was still pounding. All from the mere sight of Tag Murphy in all of his sexy glory.

Not that she had forgotten how incredibly attractive he was or how intense his presence could be. No, she'd thought about him each and every day for the last two weeks, secretly hoping he would call. He never had.

"Why didn't you call me?" Tag questioned her as he sat down in the chair beside her.

He was way too close. Close enough for her to inhale the spicy scent of his cologne mixed with the heady scent that was unique to Tag.

Instinctively, her eyebrows darted down into a frown, her head cocked just slightly, and she stared back at him. Why hadn't she called *him*? Was there something wrong with this man?

"*Today*, McKenna. Why didn't you call me *today*?" Tag clarified.

She knew exactly what he meant, but she played along, masking her emotions but never taking her eyes off of his. "I didn't feel as though this were any of your business," she told him.

And that was the truth.

For the last two weeks, McKenna had been racked with a multitude of emotions ranging from heart-wrenching pain to blood-boiling anger. None of which she particularly cared for. And yet here he was, sitting beside her as though nothing had transpired between them. Acting as though her first reaction should have been to call the one man who had deliberately, and hurtfully, pushed her away.

The door opened, and Logan and Sam walked into the room, saving her from having to answer Tag's questions. That didn't stop him from continuing to pin her with his unhappy gaze.

"McKenna." Sam approached quickly. "I'm so sorry this happened."

The despair in Sam's brilliant green eyes had a lump forming in McKenna's throat. This was the exact reason she shouldn't have come here. In no way would she ever blame Sam for anything that had happened. Sam wasn't going to be that easy on herself, though.

"It's not your fault," McKenna stated around the knot that threatened to choke her.

"But it is—" she began, but thankfully Logan stopped her by interrupting.

"Cole is on his way over to your office. I gave him the key you gave me," he explained as he pulled a chair out for Sam to sit in. "Alex and Luke will be here in a few minutes."

McKenna glanced around at the three of them, but her eyes landed on Tag. He had an expression on his face that she didn't recognize. She couldn't tell whether it was disbelief or disdain. Regardless, Tag didn't look happy to be there, and more importantly, he didn't look happy with her.

"Do you have security cameras at your office?"

Security cameras?

It took a second to figure out what Tag was talking about, because she was apparently way too wrapped up in trying to figure him out. *Oh, God.* How had she forgotten she had security cameras?

Since this was a good thing, McKenna wondered why Tag looked a little out of sorts.

Chapter *Thirty-Two*

ALEX AND LUKE walked in as Tag was asking a question, but he didn't spare either of them a glance. The way McKenna's eyes widened, obviously in realization, he knew the answer before she said anything.

"I do," she replied, her eyes darting between the five people staring back at her.

The answer was a good one as far as Tag was concerned, but there were two things they needed to consider. One: her security cameras had been destroyed along with the rest of her office. Or two: they were still intact, and they now had something to hold against Stephen Crawford. Although he hoped it was the second, Tag knew that it was in his best interest — as their lawyer — not to listen to the rest of the conversation. But he couldn't seem to convince his legs to get up and walk out of the room.

"Where are they?" Alex asked, standing off to the side with his arms crossed over his chest.

"They are recorded via a web feed. I had them installed a few years ago after our first break-in," McKenna explained.

First break-in? How many had the woman had?

"They're hidden really well for this exact reason," she continued.

"Someone bring her a laptop." Tag instructed, not looking at anyone else in the room except for McKenna.

From the moment he'd walked in, she had seemed to be holding up fairly well, even though he'd noticed the slight tremble in her hands that she was working to keep hidden.

As soon as their eyes had met when he'd walked through the door, Tag had witnessed that invisible mask sliding into place, effectively hiding any emotion she might be feeling. Her pride was a tangible thing, he knew.

"I've got a meeting to go to, but if there is anything I can do, let me know," Samantha stated suddenly, her voice disturbing the heavy silence that hung in the room. "McKenna, again, I'm so very sorry—"

This time McKenna was the one to cut her off. "Sam, this isn't your fault. None of it is. I'm insured, so everything's covered, although I'm sure my insurance company isn't going to be too happy with me this time."

Tag couldn't seem to get past McKenna's comments that this was a reoccurring event.

Sam nodded her head and turned to walk out of the room but not before Tag saw the sheen of tears in her eyes. He didn't blame her.

All of a sudden, it seemed as though everything was beginning to crash down around them. Even with a renewed hope that they had evidence of Stephen Crawford doing this, which they might be able to hold against him, they still weren't out of the woods yet.

Tag knew from a legal perspective, countering the blackmail wasn't going to be the best avenue to pursue, but he also knew he wouldn't be able to convince Logan or Luke of that. No matter what they did at this point, these pictures were going to get out, and honestly, every attempt they made to stop it only bought them time.

After McKenna had found the website where she could access the security camera feed, the laptop was handed off to Alex. While the rest of them waited patiently to see if there was anything they could garner from it, Tag opted to interrogate McKenna a little, although he could see how unhappy she was to answer his questions.

"How many times has this happened?" he asked. "Or better yet, when is the last time this happened?"

"Not in a long time up until recently, but never to this magnitude," she answered, glancing back and forth between him, Logan, and Luke.

Realizing he was changing the subject, Tag moved on to the other question bothering him. "What prompted you to write that article?"

"I don't know." McKenna shook her head and looked down at her hands. "I think his last email just pushed me too far."

"I want to see that email," Tag demanded, knowing his tone wasn't in the least bit polite.

"I'd like to see it, too," Logan chimed in.

McKenna pulled out her cell phone, scrolled through what appeared to be her email, and then typed in something. A second later, Tag's phone beeped along with Logan's with an incoming email. He didn't hesitate before reading it.

It was then that he was grateful for his overabundance of patience, because what he read infused him with a blinding rage so violent he damn near crushed his phone with his bare hands.

"Did you give this to the police?" he managed to ask, though he could feel the muscles in his neck straining as he fought the urge to lash out at someone for allowing this to happen to her.

McKenna shook her head. "How would that help? It would only bring light to this situation, and until Luke and Logan figure out what they want to do, I wasn't about to be the one to raise any more interest."

Tag didn't like the answer. Not one fucking bit.

Based on the shit Crawford was spewing, McKenna very well could be in danger, and as much as he liked and respected Sam and Logan, Tag wasn't capable of sitting back and allowing this to go further. If Crawford was the one who'd torn McKenna's office apart the way she'd described, the man was on the edge. And if they weren't careful, he was about to go over.

"I want to drop the lawsuit against Susan." Luke spoke for the first time since he'd walked into the room.

Tag jerked his head toward him. "What?"

"You heard me. I want to drop it. Sierra won hers, so there really isn't any more we can do. As we all know, nothing is going to stop her from getting what she wants."

"And what does she want?" McKenna asked.

"Fuck if I know," Luke growled, his disgruntled tone letting everyone in the room know what he thought of the situation.

"She feels as though she was jilted by Luke and Cole, right?" McKenna asked no one in particular. "And if I had to guess, no one has approached her civilly because of the way she's acting out, am I right?"

Tag glanced back at Logan and Luke. McKenna had nailed it, because Luke and Cole both had tried to talk to Susan, but Tag knew without a doubt there hadn't been anything civil about the conversations.

Since the day Luke had called him, advising him to file a lawsuit for breach of contract, he'd been irrational any time her name was mentioned. Even Logan had tried reasoning with Luke, but he'd failed just like the rest of them. So, Tag had done what he'd been hired to do.

And yes, Sierra had won the lawsuit Susan had filed against her accusing her of misrepresentation, and Tag had sat back watching the entire thing play out. He hadn't been Sierra's legal counsel, because he was a corporate attorney, but the man she had hired was one of the best Tag knew.

Granted, it hadn't hurt that Susan really was batshit crazy. He was surprised the judge was able to keep a straight face anytime the woman showed up in court. He certainly hadn't been able to.

"What are you suggesting?" It was Logan's turn to ask.

"I don't know." McKenna dropped her head into her hands.

And there lay the problem. They continued to circle back to the same answer every time. No one knew what to do, how to handle it, or even what the next step might be.

It was beginning to piss Tag off, because quite frankly, the group surrounding him was some of the smartest people he knew, and not a single one of them, himself included, had made it this far in life by not solving problems. There was some way they could get out of this, maybe not entirely unscathed, but there had to be some way.

Tag was just worried that the McCoy brothers were going to take matters into their own hands after this. And there lay the other problem.

They were going to have to beat Tag to it.

Chapter *Thirty-Three*

MCKENNA MANAGED TO get out of the XTX building without having to talk to Tag one-on-one. Unfortunately, she knew her good luck had run out the moment she pulled into her driveway. His car was parked on the street, and he was standing beside it. Not sitting in it, but standing beside it.

She was tempted to hit the button to close the automatic garage door once she pulled safely inside, but she knew that would be childish. Not that she really cared.

She didn't.

She took her time gathering her things before slowly exiting the car. Taking her time didn't help to strengthen her resolve any. Now she was standing just outside of her car, staring at the provocative man who still looked intensely sexy even with that grim look on his face. As she stood in front of him, McKenna realized her spacious two-car garage had never felt smaller than it did right then.

Fine. If he wanted to talk, they could have it out right here because she was *not* letting him into her house. She watched as he turned his back on her and went to the entry door that led into the house.

Shit. She was letting him into her house.

McKenna had no choice except to follow because he was standing at the open door waiting for her. She refused to act like a petulant child, although she felt she was more than entitled.

Once inside, she set her purse down on the bar before turning to face him. Only she had to take a step back, which put her dangerously close to him and the hard countertop pressing into her back. She could barely breathe for how close he was to her.

It wasn't like her house was small and he didn't have plenty of square footage to take up, so she didn't understand why he insisted on being quite this close. If she could find her voice, she might just ask him.

Nope, voice had definitely gone on hiatus.

Shit.

And now he was touching her. The warmth of his rough fingers slid over her cheekbone, then traced her jaw until he was gripping her chin and tilting her head back even more. When she met his eyes, she realized he was fixated on her. More importantly, he was fixated on her mouth, and damn her traitorous body for doing a sudden and intense preheat.

Still no voice.

Instead, she licked her lips.

Mistake.

Tag leaned in closer, his fingertips still tilting her chin, his mouth hovering dangerously close to hers as she inhaled the unique, dangerous scent of him into her lungs. And wouldn't you know it, the man didn't even have bad breath, so she was hard-pressed to find any reason to try to break away from him.

Closing her eyes, McKenna tried to focus on breathing, but the only thing she managed to do was absorb the warmth of his chest through her clothes and into her skin. He wasn't quite touching her physically anywhere except for his fingers on her chin, but she felt like he was wrapped around her completely.

God, she'd missed this, the security that blanketed her by his mere presence. The way he swamped her senses with his nearness. If it weren't for that persistent reminder flashing brightly in the far recesses of her brain, McKenna might very well have given in to him right then and there.

"What do you want, Murphy?" McKenna deliberately called him by his last name, trying to prove to him as much as herself that he wasn't going to get away with intimidating her or whatever it was he was trying to do.

"You."

McKenna's eyes jerked open, meeting his, and she noticed he had moved a fraction of an inch back, allowing her to see his face clearly in front of her.

"Me?" she laughed. "You want *me*? Well, you have a damn funny way of showing it."

That got him moving. She inhaled desperately as he walked away, pacing back and forth just a few feet from her but enough that she could refill her lungs with much-needed oxygen.

She waited for him to speak, but he didn't. He began walking through her house from one room to the next looking at everything in detail. Gripping the countertop, she forced her feet to remain planted firmly where she was. She would not follow him. She would not. Eventually, he would have to come back to the kitchen, and if she was lucky, he would leave.

No, *she didn't want him to leave*.

Yes, damn it; she *did* want him to leave.

Inhaling slowly through her nose and exhaling even more slowly through her mouth, McKenna tried to figure out what the hell she did want. How could she possibly let him walk in here and treat her as though nothing had happened when she deserved an apology at the very least?

Two weeks, damn it. Two long weeks he hadn't called or emailed or texted. Nothing. Not a single word and all of a sudden she ended up face-to-face with him, and he suddenly wanted her again.

McKenna heard the sound of his footsteps as he came back into the kitchen, and she calmed herself enough to let go of the counter and turn to face him. Only this time, when she turned around, she was gifted with the sight of his back … as he walked out the door to the garage, closing it quietly behind him.

What the fuck?

TAG KNEW HE shouldn't have come. He knew that he in no way deserved any of McKenna's attention, yet the second he'd seen her at XTX, he hadn't been able to stop himself from needing to know she was okay.

Well, goddammit, now he knew.

He kept moving, his feet eating up the sidewalk as he made his way back to his car, hoping like hell he would be able to get in it and drive away before he did something as stupid as turning around, going back inside, and pushing McKenna against the wall and taking her with the intensity that he felt coursing through his entire body.

He was just stepping into the street when he heard a door slam behind him, her heels clicking on the concrete, and then her voice when she screamed at him. *Screamed.*

"What the fuck are you doing, Tag Murphy?"

He smiled but kept his back to her. Now she was calling him by his full name.

Debating on whether he should turn around, he stopped where he was. Her heels clicked furiously on the pavement as she walked toward him. The woman was fast.

When she appeared in front of him, he straightened. McKenna got to him in ways he damn sure wasn't comfortable with. It wasn't until he had been perusing through the knickknacks and pictures, getting a better glimpse of who she really was, that Tag realized that. Or rather *remembered* that.

It was the main reason he had pushed her away so forcefully that day in his private room at the club. He was scared shitless about what she made him feel. *That* she made him feel. He didn't want to feel anything, because he had gotten so damned used to not feeling at all that it bothered him more than he cared to admit.

"You're leaving? Just like that?" Her eyes pierced his, and from this far away, all of the colors merged together, but it was the brilliant blue that sparkled like a gas flame. She was furious, and he'd be damned if it didn't make her just that much fucking hotter.

"I shouldn't have come," he finally said when she didn't stop looking at him.

"No, you shouldn't have. But, damn it, you owe me an apology."

Tag saw the moment ˚she realized she had said too much. She was right, though. He did owe her an apology. Hell, he owed her more than that, but he couldn't figure out a way to tell her without giving too much of himself away. He refused to fall for this woman.

Absolutely fucking refused.

"I'm sorry," he muttered halfheartedly.

Yes, he was a world-class asshole, but he didn't know what else to do except try to piss her off to the point that she pretended that this had never happened. Same as he was. Tag didn't want to feel more for her, didn't want to lose himself in one woman, because that would only lead to him losing himself somewhere along the way.

He wanted to go back to the two weeks where he'd managed to stay as far away from her as possible because it made things easier.

And he was a fucking liar.

"Fuck you, Murphy," McKenna screamed before storming back up the driveway.

Fuck him? Why the hell did he let her get to him like that? He knew he should keep moving toward his car, but damn his legs, they turned and did the exact opposite of the instructions from his brain.

By the time he caught up with her, McKenna was back inside her house, and he managed to stop the door just when it would've slammed in his face. Pushing it open, he let it crash into the wall before reversing the motion and slamming it closed.

When she turned on him, fire smoldering in those brilliant multicolored irises, he lost every last ounce of his control. Stalking her, he managed to control himself long enough to slam her into the wall without hurting her before he crushed his mouth to hers, letting the intoxicatingly sweet taste of her kiss burn through him like wildfire.

Maintaining a small semblance of sanity wasn't an easy feat, but Tag waited to see whether she would shove him away. But she didn't.

No, McKenna Thorne stole his breath when she pulled his head roughly, crushing her mouth to his in a tangle of lips and teeth and tongues. They battled for control of that one sweltering kiss for long minutes until they were both panting as they fought to suck in air.

He lifted her, pressing her against the wall none too gently when she began to climb his body, their mouths fused together, ragged groans being torn from both of them as the fury raged into a conflagration of lust and need.

Tag couldn't get enough of her, and he figured she felt the same when she began thrusting her pelvis against his raging hard-on, grinding against him until he was furiously working to release his slacks at the same time he was trying to hold her. It wasn't that she was heavy, but there was so much movement, her hands snaking between them trying desperately to remove his shirt. When it was apparent she wasn't having any luck, he heard the sound of buttons snapping, popping off, and flying against the wall behind her.

By the time he freed his cock, she was clawing his back with her sharp nails as he slid his hand between their bodies, lifting her skirt and ripping her panties. As soon as he had access to her wet, warm pussy, Tag slammed his cock into her repeatedly.

Here they stood, her against the wall, his hands holding her ass as he plowed deeper with ferocious need while she continued to claw him, holding him to her as their mouths sought everything they'd denied themselves for the last two weeks.

It wasn't gentle or sweet or any of those romantic words that would describe two bodies coming together. This was an all-out fucking, and they were both intent on more. Their bodies were coated in perspiration by the time McKenna whimpered, breaking her mouth from his and dropping her head against the wall, screaming his name as she came in his arms.

Tag had no choice but to follow when her internal muscles clamped down on him painfully, his orgasm ripping him damn near in two, leaving him absolutely and infuriatingly altered down to his very soul.

Chapter *Thirty-Four*

MCKENNA HADN'T BEEN positive her legs would hold her once Tag put her feet back on the ground, but somehow she managed. The relentless way they had gone at each other left her feeling just a tad dizzy. Never, not one time in all of her life, had she ever done that. That type of up-against-the-wall, take-it-because-you-want-it, soul-shattering sex was foreign to her.

Now that she'd had it, she knew she was going to want it again.

With Tag.

Which didn't help her cause any.

Damn it.

She managed to readjust her skirt — although her panties were a lost cause — as Tag was pulling his pants back over his hips and buttoning them. His shirt was about as long gone as her panties thanks to her need to rip it clean off of him.

Now, as they stood facing one another, their breathing coming back to the realm of normal, McKenna had no idea what to say to him. The silence was strained and more than a little awkward, which only made McKenna want to fidget. She forced herself not to.

She couldn't help but ask herself the obvious question: Was this makeup sex? Or was it just I-can't-get-you-out-of-my-system-but-I'm-damn-sure-gonna-try sex?

She knew which one she wanted it to be, but she also knew that what she wanted and what he wanted were two entirely different things.

"McKenna," Tag said gruffly.

That was all it took to break whatever small bubble of hope had swelled up in her chest for all of a minute. The way he said her name was the equivalent of slamming her head against a brick wall, and everyone knew you could only do that so many times before there was permanent brain damage.

She turned and walked away. She didn't run, and she didn't even walk very fast, but she did move with purpose. Straight to her bedroom, where she grabbed clothes from her dresser before heading into the bathroom. She was going to take a shower, and when she got out, she could only hope Tag would be gone.

Twenty minutes later, she emerged from the bathroom at least calmer than when she'd gone in. She needed to eat something, and then she was going to head over to Sensations, Inc. to see if she could assess the damage a little more with a clear head.

As she walked through the living room, she clutched her chest in shock because seeing Tag sitting there was more than she'd expected, and honestly, it'd scared the shit out of her. Along with the brief flash of terror from not expecting him to be there, another emotion surfaced, one she didn't want to even consider.

As he had his head in his hands, she wasn't even sure he knew she was there. She was almost certain he didn't, because this was Tag, and he would never allow anyone to witness him looking so ... vulnerable.

Her heart pounded harder, but this time it wasn't from fear. Once again, it was that damn hope surging out of the blue and threatening to make her look like an idiot one more time.

Did she say something? Should she clear her throat and let him know she was standing there?

"Come sit down," he said before she could string together enough words to make a coherent sentence.

Reluctantly, McKenna moved closer to him, but she didn't sit beside him on the sofa. She chose to sit on the edge of the chaise lounge she much preferred. Once she was seated, she waited to hear what he would say next.

God, she hoped it wasn't an apology, because based on what she'd witnessed outside, he really sucked at those.

"Will you come stay with me for a few days?"

His question couldn't have been more unexpected if he had asked her to marry him and have his babies. She couldn't mutter a single word, because her heart was suddenly ten times larger than only seconds before. Was he asking her because he realized that there was something more between them than just intense, blinding lust?

"Or I could stay here with you," he continued, looking up at her now.

There was an influx of nerves that rioted in her tummy, likely from a horde of tap-dancing butterflies, but McKenna still couldn't form a sentence. She was smiling, too. Smiling because she just couldn't believe this was the same Tag she knew so intimately.

"And if not, let me hire a bodyguard for a few days."

The bottom dropped completely out of her stomach, and McKenna suddenly felt … nauseous.

"A … bodyguard?" Damn her stupid, *stupid* heart for thinking that this man was capable of feeling a damn thing.

"Yes. I'm worried about what Crawford might do next," he explained as though he hadn't just ripped her heart into a zillion tiny pieces before grinding them into the hardwood like dust.

McKenna swallowed. Hard. Then she stood. Once she was sure she wouldn't either fall over or go after him with the closest sharp object, she turned toward the kitchen and didn't stop until she was no longer in the same room.

Stopping at the counter, she had to take a deep breath to keep the tears at bay. She would not cry. No matter what, she would *not* cry. Not in front of him.

Damn it! She wanted to scream from the pain that had ripped through her from her own stupidity.

"McKenna," Tag called from behind her. "Are you okay?"

No, dammit, she was not okay. She would never be okay again because the idiot that she was had mistakenly given her heart to this man knowing that he didn't want it. She suddenly whirled on him.

"I want it back!" she cried out, tears streaming from her eyes no matter how hard she tried to hold them back.

"Want what back?" Tag looked confused, and she wanted to laugh and cry at the same time.

"My heart," she told him with as much conviction as she could. "I want it all back. Every single minute I spent with you, every single kiss I shared with you. I want them all back. You don't deserve them."

Tag didn't move, and McKenna felt like an overemotional lunatic, but she couldn't seem to stop herself.

"You need to go." *Finally, something that made sense.* "You need to leave, and I don't want your help. I can take care of myself."

She turned away from him, sobbing like a baby with her face in her hands. When she heard the door click shut behind him, McKenna crumbled to the floor.

TAG SAT IN his car, staring at his house. He couldn't bring himself to get out of the car just yet because he still wasn't sure why he was here. He was half tempted to turn around, go back to McKenna's, pull her into his arms, and tell her all of the things he knew she wanted to hear.

Watching her heart break because of him was the worst thing he could have possibly imagined. And the worst part of it all, he did care about her. Hell, he would almost venture to say he had fallen for her, but he didn't quite believe it.

How? How could he possibly have fallen for her?

What they had was nothing more than an extremely passionate case of lust. That's all it was. He hadn't known her long enough for it to be anything more. Right?

There was no such thing as love at first sight, and he wasn't capable of giving a woman all of the things his father had given. His entire life. His happiness, his sense of self. All of those things his father had given his mother, and the day that she'd died, Tag had watched his father damn near die right along with her.

Infatuation

He wasn't the man who would be able to give to one woman, because then there would be nothing left for anyone else. Just like how his parents were. He knew they loved him because he was their son. But the love they had for one another blinded them to anyone and everyone else.

It might have taken years, but his father had somehow found another woman that he would devote his entire life to, which, in the long run, left Tag without. Cole had never understood Tag's issues, because his mother still, to this day, doted on him and loved him the way a mother should, even if their relationship was rocky.

Tag didn't have it in him. He couldn't give everything away. Where would that leave him? Who would that make him? He would no longer be the man he had worked so hard to be.

Instead, he would be nothing.

Except, when he thought about McKenna, he sensed that there was something he was missing. When it came to her, even in the short amount of time he had known her, he knew that she had changed him. And instead of losing himself, he seemed to understand more what he was capable of.

Putting his forehead against the steering wheel, Tag wanted to curse himself for being such a jackass. He could come up with more excuses, but it only went to prove one thing.

McKenna Thorne scared the shit out of him.

Why? Because he felt too damn much for her.

Ever since their eyes had met that very first time, he'd known there was something about her. And each and every encounter since then had only proved that she was the one woman who could so easily take his heart and smash it like glass beneath a jackhammer.

He couldn't afford to care for someone like McKenna. She was too outspoken, too ornery, too funny and cute and smart. She was too everything that he wanted but didn't know whether he could actually have.

Tag wished like hell he had a sad story to tell, one that would explain why he feared commitment the way he did, but from the outside looking in, even his parents' love for one another didn't seem like a sad story. Since Tag had refused to ever allow a lover to get close, he couldn't even blame a broken heart for the fear that consumed him.

Forcing himself out of his car, Tag went inside his house, heading right for the shower. It was high time he got his act together, because this was not the man he was. And he didn't have time to contemplate love.

Because he had already decided … it wasn't for him.

Tag walked into the club a short time later, wanting nothing more than a couple of hours where he didn't have to think about anyone or anything. The second he spotted Luke, he knew he'd come to the wrong place.

"What's up?" Luke greeted with a handshake when he approached.

"Hopefully nothing," he said, quickly shaking his hand and then brushing past him.

Relief flooded him when Luke shrugged him off and walked the other way, which allowed Tag to take a seat at the bar and order a Jack and Coke. "Go light on the Coke," Tag told Kane.

"Rough day?" Kane asked as he grabbed the bottle from behind him.

Kane's comment conjured up an image of when McKenna had been wrapped around him like a damn blanket just a few short hours ago. Rough. Literally. And damn, he wanted more of her right now.

Tag didn't answer Kane; he just nodded his head. The last thing he wanted to do was talk. He preferred to sit right there, drown his thoughts in whiskey and the unruly chaos happening around him. Unfortunately, the crowd seemed a little subdued tonight, and Tag found himself glancing around to see what was different.

Nothing, really. Not as far as he could see anyway. The club was packed like usual with people laughing, talking, and having a good time while some were dancing. Even the tables were all full. Not much different than any other night, he supposed.

That's when he saw her.

Just when he was turning back around in his seat, Tag's eyes landed on McKenna, sitting across the bar from him.

With Travis Walker.

A wave of jealousy so powerful swept through him Tag wasn't sure how he hadn't fallen off the fucking barstool. The professional in him wouldn't allow himself to stalk across the room and take her by the arm, pulling her away from that damn cowboy.

The alpha in him told the professional to go fuck himself.

Tag emerged from his seat, downing the last of his whiskey before slamming the glass back on the bar top. He could hear his heart pounding in his ears, feel his hands balled into fists at his sides as he moved around to the opposite end, where the two of them were talking.

"Murphy," Travis greeted, eyeing him suspiciously when he approached.

"Walker."

McKenna didn't even spare him a glance, but that didn't stop Tag from interrupting.

"Didn't know you were in town," he told the man sitting beside McKenna, drinking a beer, and watching him closely.

"Didn't know I had to get permission." Travis smirked.

Why was it that he suddenly felt like a foolish teenager trying to prove his own worth? He was reduced to childish machismo standing here, practically facing off with Travis Walker when it was apparent the two of them were only talking. Hell, they weren't even sitting that close to one another, but Tag still didn't like it. At all.

There were two words that came to mind, but no matter how hard he tried, Tag couldn't seem to spit them out. Instead, he allowed his arm to gently brush McKenna's, wondering if there was a chance in hell that she felt exactly how sorry he was.

Chapter *Thirty-Five*

MCKENNA MADE IT into the office a little after seven the following morning. That was later than usual, but she hadn't been able to fall asleep until close to three, and she felt like death warmed over. She was sure she looked like it, too.

Her office didn't look much better.

By the time she arrived, Whisper was already there, along with two security guards that Alex McDermott had placed on twenty-four-hour watch.

"Hey," Whisper greeted when McKenna walked through the main doors.

The place looked a million times better than it had even the night before when she'd stopped by after Tag left her house. Seeing everything she'd worked so hard to build in such disarray had caused her to go to the club for a drink, where she'd run into Travis Walker.

They'd shared a beer, but it hadn't taken long for her to remember he wasn't much of a conversationalist, or maybe he just didn't find her interesting. Either way, after Tag had come and gone, she'd called it a night. Only that wasn't when her night had ended.

Unfortunately, she'd spent the better part of it replaying every scene from every time she had been near Tag for the last couple of months only to make herself hurt that much more.

"Did you call the insurance company?" Whisper was standing in front of her now as she stared at the mess around them.

"Not yet," she told her. "That's the first thing I'm doing this morning, though."

That was the plan anyway. Just as soon as she docked her computer and figured out whether there was anything pressing to take care of. She wasn't sure how anything would take more priority over getting everything in the office replaced or having the walls repaired, but for some reason, McKenna had a hard time dealing with it all right then.

When she made it to her office door, she slowly pushed it open, remembering what she had seen the night before.

And there it was.

In brilliant red paint sprayed across the wall was the word *whore* in bold, capital letters. If she'd had any doubt who had done this, she definitely didn't now. Surprisingly, there hadn't been a single printed article the day before about Club Destiny or the McCoys by any newspaper or blog that she knew of, so at least something good had come out of it all.

"Are you okay?" Whisper's voice startled her, and McKenna spun around to see her friend standing in the doorway.

"I will be," McKenna said, hoping Whisper assumed she was talking about the mess that Crawford had made. What she was really referring to was the devastation that had currently taken up residence in her heart.

That thought immediately invoked memories from the night before when Tag had stood beside her chair, his eyes boring holes into her skin as he'd spoken to Travis. She'd never said a word, and she'd never looked at him. Mostly because if she had, she would've broken down in tears, and she was tired of crying. In fact, she was pretty sure her tear ducts had dried up.

"Have you talked to him?" Whisper asked in an unusually soothing voice.

"Who?"

That prompted Whisper to put her hands on her hips and stare back at her like she had lost her mind. "Okay, woman. I'll let you play this game for a few more minutes, but that's all you get. Ten minutes, tops. Then I'm coming back in here, and there better be a damn smile on your face, or I'm going to put one there myself."

Whisper's outrage made McKenna smile. She couldn't help it. Her friend had the ability to make her laugh even when she didn't want to. She was such a drama queen.

"See, I knew it wouldn't take ten minutes," Whisper retorted before turning and walking back down the hall to her office near the front.

McKenna was tempted to call Whisper back in, because the moment she was out of sight, her smile disappeared. As much as she wanted to wish away all of the hurt, the anger, the confusion that riddled her body, she was unable to do it because thoughts of Tag were constantly running through her mind.

The night before, she had come up with a million ideas on how she could've handled the entire situation differently, but she always came back to the same thing. She should've never laid eyes on him, because that was when it had all started.

From the moment she'd seen him for the very first time, McKenna had been fixated on him. Something in the confident way that he moved, the assured way he spoke, and the sensual way he made her feel with just a slow, gentle caress of his eyes over her skin made her want him. And now that she had, she wasn't sure how she was going to go on without him.

If she had to compare what she felt for Tag to any man she had ever known, there was absolutely nothing that came close. It hadn't mattered how much she'd warned herself ahead of time, McKenna's heart had been his from that very first kiss when he'd stolen her breath with the gentle press of his lips. And each and every subsequent time he'd touched her from that moment on, he had taken another piece of her soul without her permission.

She might very well be able to live with it if she didn't feel cheated. As if she'd never had a chance in the first place. But that was how Tag made her feel. He'd closed himself off, and although she knew without a doubt that he wanted her, he was refusing to give himself to her.

For whatever reason, the stubborn man would close himself off from her indefinitely.

Shaking her head to try and get rid of the depressing and unchangeable truth, McKenna pulled her laptop from her bag and docked it on her desk. As she waited for it to boot and her monitor to come to life, she willed her hands to stop shaking.

Ever since he'd walked out of her house, an unshakeable chill had taken up residence in her soul, and no matter what she did, she couldn't get warm.

As soon as her computer was up and running, she immediately opened her email, hoping to lose herself in work for a few hours. She glimpsed through the headings of the emails filling up her inbox, trying to decipher which might be more important, when she came across one titled *YOU THINK YOU'RE BETTER THAN ME.* All caps definitely attracted her attention, and McKenna clicked on it to open the email fully.

The image on the screen shocked her to the point she swore her heart stopped beating.

"MURPHY," TAG ANSWERED when the unfamiliar number registered on the screen.

"Mr. Murphy, this is Whisper," the soft voice said, confusing him.

Whisper?

"Is something wrong?" he asked, immediately getting to his feet.

He began pacing the floor of his office as his heart raced like he had just run a marathon.

"I think you need to come over here," she said, sounding as though she were trying to keep her voice low.

"Where?" he asked as he headed to the hook on the wall to retrieve his coat. He knew there was only one reason Whisper would be calling him, and he didn't care where she told him to go, he would be there within minutes.

"Sensations office."

Tag locked the door as he exited before heading down the main corridor that would lead him outside. He had come to his official law office because that was the one and only place that it seemed didn't remind him of McKenna. Even his own house reminded him of her, and she had never been there.

"What's wrong?" he questioned but didn't stop as he hurried to his car, tossing his jacket on the passenger seat and folding himself inside before starting it.

"I was going through the emails, and…"

When Whisper didn't continue, Tag squeezed the phone, impatiently wanting to rip the answer from her but knowing he needed to relax. Shit, he didn't even know what the problem *was.*

"I'm the only other person who sees the general email, other than McKenna, but there are pictures…"

Fuck.

Tag drove, doing his best to abide by the traffic laws as much as possible but not really seeing much of anything around him.

"I'm less than five minutes away," he told Whisper before disconnecting and dropping his phone into the center console.

Tag didn't even need to ask what pictures they were because he had a pretty good idea. By now, there was no chance that McKenna hadn't seen them, and surprisingly he was more worried about how she would react to them than how anyone else would.

Almost exactly five minutes later, Tag was strolling through the main door of Sensations, Inc., and he didn't stop to greet Whisper when she headed his way. His feet wouldn't allow him to stop, so he headed right for McKenna's office, tapped on the door once before opening it.

All concern for the pictures immediately dissolved as a blind, maddening rage ignited from within when he saw the word written in bold red ink behind where McKenna sat. That son of a bitch!

Pulling out his phone, Tag pulled up Cole's contact card and hit the button. "I want someone over to McKenna's office to paint. Today," he told his stepbrother harshly. "I don't give a fuck how much it costs or who you find, just get them over here now."

Tag disconnected the call as soon as Cole agreed. He knew he wouldn't need to explain because Cole had already been to McKenna's office, and he wasn't sure why anyone else hadn't done the same thing. She should not be subjected to that filth.

"Tag." McKenna was standing at her desk, staring at him like he was breathing fire, and he wondered if he possibly was. He was so angry his head was beginning to throb.

"I want to see the email," he told her when he managed enough self-control not to bark the demand at her. To his surprise, she simply stepped back from her desk, holding her hand out as though telling him to have at it.

Tag moved around behind the screen and peered down at the image staring back at him. *Oh, fuck.* He scrolled through the email, looking at image after image of the very first day Samantha and Sierra had gone to the club's monthly get-together. Someone had probably filmed the entire thing, because there was image after graphic image that included every single one of them in various positions, doing things to one another that never should have made it to a camera lens.

Glancing up at McKenna, Tag suddenly didn't know what to say. She looked physically ill, and he could only imagine. When he took a step toward her, she took two steps back.

"McKenna." Tag had no idea what to say, but he knew he needed to say something.

Anything that would take the look of complete and total rejection off of her beautiful face.

"Don't," she whispered, wrapping her arms around herself. "I don't want to hear a word. Those were taken before I even knew you, and I don't need any explanations. They pretty well speak for themselves."

Tag wished like hell he could've prevented her from seeing him so intimate with Sam, but this was outside of his control.

As a matter of fact, all of this was outside of his control. He couldn't stop Stephen Crawford from wanting whatever he thought he deserved; he couldn't stop Susan Toulmin from wearing her emotions on her sleeve and expressing them in a very peculiar way; he couldn't stop Logan and Luke from trying to protect the women they loved, and more importantly, Tag couldn't stop himself from falling in love with McKenna Thorne.

All of those things had already taken place, and no amount of denial or rejection was going to change the way people chose to react, but there was one thing he might have a chance at.

"I'm sorry," he whispered, feeling every emotional wall he'd ever erected crumbling down around him as he stood staring at the best thing that had happened to him. "No, wait," Tag told McKenna when she started to talk over him, "just listen to what I have to say.

"I'm sorry you had to see the pictures," he began, noticing how she glared back at him, "I'm sorry that you were somehow dragged into this mess, but above all, I'm sorry that I don't know how to express what I feel for you.

"This has never happened to me before. I didn't *want* it to happen to me, yet here I find myself ready to go to my knees and beg for forgiveness because you are exactly what I didn't want.

"You're the woman I want to put first above everyone else, the woman I want to have beside me through times like this when it seems as though nothing is going the way that it should, the one I could see myself going batshit crazy over, and the *only* woman who has ever had me considering the possibility that there is more ... more for me."

Tag held his breath, knowing that he sucked at apologies, but he had laid his heart on the line with that one.

McKenna was still standing just out of reach, but he was scared to move closer, suddenly terrified that she was going to send him on his way. That was likely what he deserved, but he wasn't sure he'd survive it if she decided he wasn't what she wanted.

Chapter *Thirty-Six*

MCKENNA HEARD EVERY single word that passed Tag's lips. In fact, her heart had woken up somewhere after "go to my knees" and hadn't stopped listening until he was finished. Now, as she searched for the words, all of the things she wanted to say to him died somewhere between her brain and her lips.

For days, she had mentally prepared speech after speech, outlining every single emotion line by line, hoping she would have the chance to tell him exactly how she felt. She'd also wanted to tell him exactly how he made her feel, including the heart-wrenching pain he'd inflicted without a second thought.

Except, seeing him there, more vulnerable than she had ever seen him, McKenna knew he had had a second thought. Or maybe even more.

"I ... I don't know what to say," she said, that anxious, desperate ache once again starting deep in the center of her chest.

"You don't have to say anything, McKenna. Just believe me." His voice, gruff and uneven, was woven with uncertainty.

"I believe you," she told him. She hadn't expected those words to come out, but as soon as she said them, it wasn't like she wanted to take them back.

Tag's eyebrows rose as he considered her, but when he didn't move closer, she closed the gap between them, throwing her arms around his neck and pulling him down to her.

"Wait." Tag's urgent plea had her pulling back slightly. "About the pictures…"

McKenna needed to tell him the truth, to let him know how sick those pictures made her, but that was because she couldn't bear to think of him with another woman. Not in the past, not in the present, and definitely not in the future. No woman except her. "Have you been with another woman since you were with me?"

"Never."

"Do you plan to be with another woman after me?" she asked, trying to force the grin that she could feel tugging at the corners of her mouth.

"I don't want there to *be* an after," Tag whispered, his mouth hovering just above hers.

"Then we can work it out." McKenna pulled his head back down to hers, and this time she didn't let him go.

She couldn't help herself as she tried to climb his body, sucking his tongue into her mouth, holding the back of his head to her as though he would escape given half a chance. Then, when he started to pull back, gripping her hips and still holding her close, McKenna opened her eyes and peered deep into those seductive eyes.

"Not here," Tag told her, cupping her face in both hands. "Get your things. You're going home with me."

Pulling back, she debated, but only for a fraction of a second before she grabbed her laptop and her purse and followed him out of her office. She watched with wide-eyed fascination when Tag stopped at Whisper's office.

"When the painters get here, go home. The security guard will stay with them," he instructed, waiting for Whisper to nod her head in understanding.

A small smile passed Whisper's lips as she and McKenna made eye contact. It was a look she had seen before on her assistant's face, usually after she'd done something mischievous. And now that she thought about it, McKenna did find it fairly coincidental that Tag had showed up all of a sudden on the same day they'd received the photos.

"I'll take care of everything. Go," Whisper said, her grin spreading across her entire face.

There was no time to respond because Tag took her hand in his, leading her directly from the building to his car. When he opened the door for her, McKenna moved to climb in, but before she could, Tag pulled her against him, his lips pressing against her forehead in a gesture so sweet the tears she thought had dried up threatened to fall.

When he released her, McKenna looked up at him and asked, "What was that for?"

"Because I haven't done it nearly enough."

That was all she needed to hear.

When Tag pulled his car up to his house a short while later, McKenna had to fight to keep her jaw from unhinging. She had seen some nice houses in wealthy neighborhoods in her lifetime, but she wasn't sure whether she had ever seen anything of this magnitude.

The house, if that was what it could be called, was a monstrosity. From the front, once past the expanse of lush green grass, the multitude of stout oak trees, and the well-groomed shrubbery, was a red brick colonial house that was significantly wider than it was tall. With two stories and more windows than McKenna had ever dreamed of having, the house was a head turner.

Tag pulled the car down a side driveway, bypassing the huge circular drive that bisected the front lawn, and into one of the bays in a four-car garage, each with individual garage doors. From the outside, McKenna noticed the same setup on the other end of the house, and she wondered whether there was another garage on the other side or if it was just designed that way to balance the layout.

As the garage door closed behind them, McKenna was suddenly anxious to have a look at the inside. Knowing Tag, she figured the house would be as immaculately put together as he was, and she was excited to get a better feel for how he lived. So much could be learned of a person by looking at how they lived.

McKenna waited patiently for Tag to open her door for her since that was what he seemed to want to do, and once they were inside the house, her awe of him only intensified.

Coming in through the garage door, they didn't step directly into the kitchen like the floor plan of her home. No, she wasn't greeted by a refrigerator, rather a washer and dryer and enough square footage to house a full Laundromat.

For the next half hour, McKenna allowed Tag to take her on a brief tour of the house, admiring the warm, soothing tones of the walls, the large, masculine furniture that filled each room, and the artwork that was just as unique as the artwork on his body.

"Would you like some wine?" Tag asked as they stood in the master bedroom.

"Yes," she told him, but still holding his hand, she stopped him before he would have led her out of the room. "But not right now."

McKenna wasn't sure she wanted anything more than him. As far as she was concerned, they had wasted more time than they should have in recent days and weeks.

For now, he was all that she needed.

EVER SINCE HE had laid himself bare in McKenna's office, Tag felt slightly off-kilter. Except for the times when McKenna looked at him the way she was looking at him right now. With her heart in her eyes, he sensed that she felt everything he'd somehow found the strength to say.

Only she hadn't said much of anything since.

When her hands went around his neck, pulling him close, he growled involuntarily and easily swept her up off of her feet and carried her over to his bed. Once he deposited her on the mattress, McKenna surprised him when she rose to her knees, gripping his tie in her hands and pulling him toward her. Hard.

"Remember that amendment to our contract?" she asked sweetly, but the intensity in her eyes belied her tone.

"I remember." *How could he forget?*

"Well, I think this might just be the perfect place for me to exact my revenge."

Tag instinctively went rigid, his body hardened by her tone and the anticipation that suddenly circulated through his veins. He'd never been dominated by a woman. Although he had a feeling this wouldn't work out quite the way she anticipated, he was more than willing to let her have her way with him if it made her happy.

"I'm all yours, darlin'." Tag held his hands out to his sides as a sign of surrender, allowing McKenna to pull him closer, still gripping his tie in her fist.

"The first thing we need to do is to get you out of these clothes," she informed him, stepping down from the bed, allowing her body to brush down the front of his.

As she eased around behind him, slowly pulling his suit jacket off of his shoulders, Tag remained unmoving, waiting for her instruction.

"Lose the tie," she instructed in a firm, crisp tone that had his fists clenching at his sides.

Doing as she said, he easily unknotted the tie, then pulled it out from under his collar before tossing it on the floor beside them. She had been kind enough to lay his jacket on the chair beside his bed, but as far as he was concerned, there was no need. At this point, he was ready to rip his own clothes off, not giving a damn whether he was wearing a five-thousand-dollar suit or not.

"Turn around."

Tag turned to face her, his back now to the bed as he looked down at the sexy, red-haired vixen who had somewhere along the way weaved herself into his heart and ensured she stayed twined there for the duration. No matter how much he had tried to push her away, in the end, it had been him who had given in out of sheer fear that if he tried to live another day without her, he might not make it through.

McKenna's small hand easily slipped each tiny disk on his shirt from its mooring as she watched him with a wickedly sexy grin on her face.

"Take off the belt," she instructed, and Tag didn't falter as he unhooked the black leather from the chrome buckle before pulling it from the loops and letting it fall to the floor beside the tie.

"Now the pants." McKenna was still unbuttoning his shirt, letting her fingers graze his chest as she went, clearly knowing exactly what she was doing to him.

With quick, easy movements, he rid himself of his slacks, letting them fall to the floor at his feet. He still had his shoes on, so there wasn't much more he could do at the moment, so he waited patiently as she continued.

Then the temptress went and damn near blew his mind, lowering herself to her knees, trailing her tongue from the middle of his chest all the way down in one torturous lick. When she brushed the head of his cock through his boxer briefs, Tag grunted.

"Don't worry," McKenna crooned. "You'll get yours soon enough."

Tag didn't want his. Well, he did, but he wanted to lay her out on the floor right there and feast on her for hours on end in ways he hadn't had the chance to yet.

While on her knees, McKenna untied his shoes, allowing him to toe them off, then removed his socks, which offered him the chance to step out of his slacks. Standing before her, clad in his boxer briefs and his shirt, Tag was beginning to think she had on way too many clothes. She didn't seem to mind, because she continued to taunt him with her soft, smooth fingers and her sharp little nails while she worked to remove the rest of his clothes.

"I think you're enjoying this as much as I am," Tag teased her as she returned to her feet, pushing his shirt off of his shoulders until the material slid over his biceps and then down his forearms, where he caught it with his hands before slinging it in the direction of the chair.

"Well, how can I not, with such a beautiful playground before me? Now, get on the bed. On your back," McKenna urged.

Tag did as she told him, lying on his bed, tempted to put his hands behind his head and let her do her worst, but as he watched, he realized she had other plans for him. The sneaky woman went straight to his closet, peeking through his clothes before she returned with two of his ties and a bewitching smile on her face.

With ease, McKenna tied his hands to the wrought iron headboard, and Tag didn't struggle. Had she been naked, he would've used the opportunity to tease her, but she was still fully dressed, but hopefully she wouldn't be for long.

The next thing he knew, she was standing above him on the bed, one foot on each side of his chest, which forced her tight denim skirt up her thighs to her hips, offering him a glimpse of what appeared to be red silk panties.

He watched, hypnotized, as she began to undress slowly, sliding her formfitting T-shirt over her head, revealing a barely there red demi bra that gave him a tempting view of her distended nipples and her perfect, pale skin.

When she unbuttoned her skirt, McKenna put one foot on his chest, which allowed her to lower the denim down her long, smooth legs. Once she was free of the skirt, she placed her foot back at his side, her ankles pressing into the sides of his chest.

The woman was wicked and so fucking sexy she made his tongue itch at the remembered taste of her. If he had his say in it, she'd lower her sweet, warm pussy down to his mouth and let him familiarize himself with her taste all over again.

He knew he didn't have a say in what she did, so he simply watched, waiting. He was just grateful that he had been blessed with the patience of a damn saint, because this woman was more than a handful, and she was proving it with every passing second.

McKenna kept her bra and panties on as she lowered herself down to the bed, sitting on his chest with her legs straddling him. With only his eyes, he roamed her face, her neck, each soft, round globe with the pretty, puckered pink nipples, and then trailed over her stomach until he was staring directly between her thighs. He could smell her arousal, and it made his body harden, but he didn't pull against his restraints, because as far as he was concerned, at least for now, he would allow her to believe she was in control.

She needed this, he knew, but not nearly as much as she needed him to show her exactly how easy it was for her to relinquish that strong, embedded urge to dominate. McKenna liked to call the shots; he had learned that quickly. Although, she enjoyed giving herself over to him more than she was willing to admit.

When her mouth lowered to his, her tongue darting out to flick his lips, Tag growled, knowing she wasn't going to give him what he wanted, so he just pretended that it didn't matter. It fucking mattered.

He wanted to crush her mouth to his, to feast from her lips until she was unable to breathe unless she was inhaling him into her lungs. His main goal was to infuse every cell in her body with his presence until they were still two bodies but only one soul.

That's what he wanted from McKenna. He wanted her heart, her body, and her soul. He wanted every single piece of her since she already owned every piece of him.

Although he had expressed exactly how he felt, Tag realized she was holding herself back. Even if momentarily, it wasn't enough for him only to have her body. Granted, he knew he had hurt her, and she was probably only trying to protect herself, but he had never been the man to have only part of anything.

"Your pulse is racing," she whispered before her wet tongue slid down his neck.

"That's what you do to me," he told her, relishing the feel of her warm breath and her soft tongue against his skin. "You make my body ache for you, to be inside of you…"

She lifted her head and gifted him with a small glimpse into her soul. "Every time I look at you, my pulse beats faster than before. It's like I can't get enough of you," she said, and he knew what it cost her to admit it.

Tag could barely breathe as he waited for her to continue. When she didn't, he said the only thing he could. "You're mine, McKenna. You can do to me whatever you want just as long as you understand you will always be mine."

For a second, he saw a sheen of tears in her eyes, but they were quickly gone when her mouth returned to his skin, her tongue tracing the artwork on his chest as she ventured lower. When she reached his nipple, Tag hissed as she circled it with her tongue, then used her sharp little teeth to nip the sensitive brown disc. He forced his eyes closed, letting the sensations consume him, allowing his mind to memorize every slight touch, every gentle lick, every stinging bite as McKenna continued to drive him wild.

When her warm breath teased his dick, Tag pressed his ass into the mattress to keep his hips from bucking off of the bed. There was no need for him to try and memorize what it felt like to have her mouth on his cock, because that was one feeling his body would never forget.

His eyes flew open when the head of his dick slid into the hot recesses of her mouth, her hands not touching him in any way like they had before. She wasn't stroking his shaft or massaging his balls this time, leaving the only sensation that of her sweet fucking mouth as she assaulted him with the tenderest of touches. McKenna didn't suck him into her mouth, she tormented him slowly, and he fought to keep his body rigid, not to press up into her, wanting to feel her lips wrapped around him, the head of his cock thrusting against the back of her throat as she sucked his release from him.

Being tied to the bed was the hardest damn thing for him to accept because Tag wanted to touch her, he wanted to control her movements, to flip her over and bury his tongue in her pussy while she writhed beneath him. Only McKenna had thought that one through, because his arms were held firmly, his legs spread around her as she knelt between his thighs, his iron-hard erection subjected to her wicked onslaught.

"McKenna." He was warning her, because quite frankly, Tag didn't know how much more he could take, and she hadn't even done anything more than torture him with her mouth. "Untie me, baby," he said, the words sounding like the plea that they were.

Her eyes met his as he peered at her down the length of his body.

"Let me touch you," he growled. "I need to touch you. Aw, fuck!"

His cock disappeared inside of her mouth fully, and the sweet suction she applied had his eyes damn near rolling back in his head. He didn't want to think about where she might've learned to give the most explosive blow job ever, but he couldn't help but be thankful for the skill she had acquired.

"Fuck, baby," Tag groaned, "that's it. Oh, God, McKenna. Suck me harder." He could no longer control his body as he tried to thrust upward, wanting to go deeper into that soft, velvety warmth as her tongue curled around his shaft, her teeth purposely grazing the hypersensitive underside while the vibrations from her moans shot fire into his balls.

Tag glared down at her, knowing he wasn't going to last much longer. "Please, McKenna," he begged, "please don't make me come yet, baby."

He was hanging by his fingernails, unsure whether the next delicate rasp of her mouth was going to send him over the jagged edge that he was fighting to hang on to. When she quickened her pace, still only using her mouth, Tag's muscles locked as he fought the demands of his body. "It's so fucking good, baby! Too fucking good. Don't make me come yet. Fuck." Tag knew he wouldn't last but a second more. "I need to be inside of you when I come. I need to feel you wrapped around me. Don't make me come, please, baby, not yet."

His words echoed in the otherwise silent room, but they must have worked, because McKenna slowed, gently releasing his cock from the heaven of her mouth. She was breathing just as hard as he was, and Tag knew she needed his touch the same way he needed hers.

"Let me go, McKenna. Untie me." Tag didn't move, didn't try to break free of his restraints, because, despite his need to take her in ways he hadn't ever taken her, he was going to give her this for as long as she needed it.

As he locked his gaze with hers, that's when Tag saw just how much she needed him. McKenna only thought she wanted to be the one in control, but he could see it in her eyes. He was breaking through that hard outer shell, one delicate layer at a time, and he only hoped that, before too long, she would give in to what she needed most.

McKenna Thorne didn't want to dominate, she wanted to submit.

MCKENNA KNEELED BETWEEN Tag's thighs, watching his eyes as he watched her. How was it that this man knew her better than she knew herself? Being in control had always been her way of protecting herself, making sure she never allowed anyone to get too close or to know too much. Somehow, when she hadn't been looking, Tag had gotten beyond that wall she had erected in an attempt to keep people out.

She had no doubt that she loved him. She'd figured that out a while back, but loving him and letting him in were two different things as far as she was concerned. Except, with Tag, they were the same thing.

She had inadvertently let him in, and the only thing she found she wanted was to be in his arms, to be lost to him, to let go. Trying to be the stronger, more assertive one was draining, especially when she was convinced, thanks to the way Tag had taken her body in ways she'd never imagined, she only wanted to be loved.

"Are you going to tie me up?" McKenna questioned him as she began inching back up his body. She couldn't resist letting her tongue graze his delectable skin.

"Do you want to be tied up?" he asked as he relaxed farther into the mattress.

McKenna had wanted to make him come, wanted to make him lose control, because Tag was a man who was always in control, and it was frustrating. It was also so damn hot to know that he would protect her. He was strong enough for both of them. He made her feel feminine when he was around, as though she didn't need to be the one holding the reins because he wouldn't take them from her, but rather he would show her what it was like to hand them over.

"No," she answered. She didn't want to be tied up. Not this time.

This time, she wanted to be wrapped around him in every way possible.

"Then I won't tie you up," he promised, and McKenna believed him.

Leaning over him, she easily unknotted the ties that were binding him to the bed. Once his hands were freed, she gently massaged his wrists before starting to move back down his body.

"Don't move," he demanded, pulling his wrists back and sliding his fingertips down her throat, over her collarbone, then to her breasts, where he gently cupped and lifted them while she watched.

"Beautiful," he mumbled, seemingly mesmerized as he continued to fondle her breasts, her body temperature rising to dangerous levels.

When he lowered the cups, pushing her breasts up more, he gently tweaked her nipples, pulling the aching tips closer to his mouth. McKenna couldn't stop watching as his tongue darted out to lave one and then the other, while he continued to pinch them between his fingers. The heat of his mouth brushing against the inflamed tips had her belly rippling with warmth. It was exquisite. That tiny bite of pain, chased away by the delicate glide of his tongue, had her slowly grinding herself against his chest, where she straddled him.

"That's it, baby," Tag urged. "Rub your sweet pussy on me."

McKenna groaned as the friction against her clit warred with the pleasure-pain he was inflicting on her nipples. Tag continued his sensual assault on her breasts for long minutes as she continued to grind against him, bringing her closer and closer to the edge that she wasn't quite ready to jump from.

"Sit up," he directed, his hands cupping her breasts once more, squeezing with just the right amount of pressure to have her arching into his hands.

As soon as the rough warmth of his palms left her breasts, McKenna wanted to beg him not to stop, but apparently he had other ideas. He maneuvered his arms beneath her legs until his biceps were trapped beneath her calves, but he remedied that when he scooted her forward on his chest, bringing his mouth dangerously close to her pussy. The only thing between his skilled tongue and her sensitive folds was her panties, and McKenna suddenly wished they would just disappear.

Tag found a solution for that quickly as he used his fingers to slide the damp fabric out of the way, exposing her to his mouth.

"Put your hands on the headboard and don't move them," Tag insisted, and McKenna immediately recognized his dominant side as he easily maneuvered back to being in control.

Oh, who was she kidding? Tag Murphy had always been the one in control, no matter what she thought.

Wrapping her fingers around the wrought iron detail in the headboard, McKenna held on, still looking down at him as his mouth disappeared between her legs, his tongue spearing through her wet folds.

"Oh…" McKenna threw her head back as his tongue pressed through the narrow entrance, mimicking what she desperately wanted him to do with his cock. Over and over, he continued to fuck her with his tongue, never paying mind to her greedy clit, and she was somewhat grateful, because there was no way she would've been able to hold out if he had.

Unable to control herself, McKenna began a slow, rhythmic grind against his mouth, aching to feel him deeper inside of her, but settling, for the moment, on having his tongue do delicious things to her.

McKenna was both relieved and disappointed when Tag pulled away, gripping her hips and turning her so she had no choice but to let go of the iron bars. When she tumbled to her back, he was kneeling between her legs, slowly and methodically running his hands over every inch of her skin, his mouth trailing his hands as he unclasped her bra before somehow discarding it without ever making her move.

Her panties were being peeled down her legs, and McKenna was suddenly breathing harder as she anticipated having Tag flush against her body. And then he was there, his mouth hovering above hers, his chest pressing against her breasts, his stomach against hers, and the hard ridge of his erection pressing intimately between her thighs.

"Don't wrap your legs around me," Tag instructed when she started to move. "Keep them on the mattress against mine."

The position had them touching from ankle to chest, his body blanketing hers in much-needed heat. Tag took her hands in his, twining their fingers and raising her arms above her head, where he held them. She felt the hard knots of his biceps against her inner arms, his forearms against hers as he held most of his weight off of her.

Every part of her was touching every part of him, and McKenna suddenly felt complete for the first time. When he angled his hips, the head of his thick, hard cock nudged just inside of her, she whimpered, not wanting him to stop until he was filling her.

"Look at me," Tag told her, and McKenna opened her eyes, not realizing she had even closed them. "Feel me," he said, his voice low and controlled. "Feel every part of me, McKenna."

Tag's hips thrust forward hard, his cock lodging inside of her, deeper, but he didn't pull back.

"Do you feel me?" he asked.

McKenna knew he wasn't just talking about the sensations that rocked her body from having him buried to the hilt inside of her. He wanted to know that she felt him penetrating every single molecule, every cell, every fiber of her being.

"Everywhere," she whispered. "I feel you everywhere."

"I want you to remember this moment." Tag's words were gruff, his breaths choppy against her neck, and McKenna hung on every word. "This is the first" — Tag punctuated his statement with a deeper thrust of his hips — "and the very last time I'll give myself to anyone."

McKenna's breath hitched in her throat, her fingers squeezing his as she let him know without words that she heard him.

"Do you understand what I'm telling you?" Tag's hips moved, his cock retreating, never fully removing himself from inside of her and never allowing any part of his body to separate from hers. "I love you, McKenna."

His words shredded her soul, inflated her heart once again to the point McKenna wondered whether she would be able to contain all of what she felt for him inside of her.

"With every breath I take, I love you more," he whispered, his lips barely brushing hers.

Squeezing his fingers once more, McKenna willed him to feel what she was feeling, praying that the next words that she spoke would never come back to haunt her, because no matter how she wanted to protect herself, she knew that there was no way to do that with this man. "I love you," she whispered in return.

When Tag's mouth came down on hers, McKenna was consumed by him. Every part of her became every part of him as he continued to move, deep, penetrating thrusts filling her until she was overcome with the strongest orgasm she had ever known. He never took his mouth from hers as they moaned their release together, her body clasping his, holding him to her as his cock pulsed deep inside of her.

It was in that moment that McKenna realized she had never known anything like the emotion she felt for this man. She could label it as love, but she knew in her heart that it was *so much more*.

Chapter *Thirty-Seven*

THE SUN WAS barely peeking through the slats in the wood blinds when Tag was woken by the sound of his cell phone ringing. He remembered bringing it into the bedroom the night before after he had ordered Chinese food. That was the first time Tag had ever eaten dinner in his bed, naked. He would never forget it, either. McKenna had been propped up against him, her bottom between his thighs, her head resting on his chest while they'd eaten and talked.

He could feel her against him now, her arm over his chest, her soft breasts against his side, and her leg across his. He wasn't sure he wanted to move, but when his cell phone rang again a few minutes later, he knew he couldn't stay there forever.

He eased out from under her, reaching over to grab his phone, and after hitting the talk button, he pressed it to his ear. "Don't you dare fucking ask me where I'm at," he greeted the caller.

Logan actually laughed, but Tag could hear the tension in the sound. "Fine. I'll just ask how long it will take you to get here."

"Where?"

"The club. Meet us in Luke's office in half an hour."

Tag was used to being summoned, and though it pissed him off, he knew he couldn't tell Logan no. "I'll be there."

"Hey," Logan said as Tag was about to disconnect.

"What?"

"I've been trying to get in touch with McKenna. Do you know where she is? I'd really like her to be here, too."

Tag turned to see the sleeping woman beside him and smiled. "I'll make sure she's there."

Almost an hour later, thanks to McKenna's insistence that they take a shower — together — they were walking into Luke's office.

Tag proceeded with caution as he took stock of the unfamiliar man standing near a corner in the back. Luke, Logan, and Alex were seated in the only three available chairs, while Cole stood in another corner, his arms crossed over his massive chest in a defensive stance. As soon as they approached, all three men immediately stood, offering McKenna their chair.

She smiled at them and then glanced over at Tag before taking the one closest to her and leaving Luke to stand.

"Thanks for coming," Logan said, sounding much more enthusiastic than he had on the phone. Surprisingly, he didn't even give Tag a hard time about being late.

"What's going on?" Tag asked, stepping around to stand behind McKenna's chair, placing his hands on her shoulders because he couldn't resist touching her.

"Tag Murphy, I'd like you to meet Chance Reed. Chance, Tag is Club Destiny's legal counsel."

Tag didn't move forward to shake the man's hand, but neither did Chance. Instead, they stared back at each other for a moment, both of them sizing each other up. Tag had seen the man somewhere, he just wasn't sure where.

Logan broke the tension once more as he introduced McKenna, as well. He briefly explained his reason for asking her to join them, which Tag understood to be due to the topic of Stephen Crawford.

"What's going on?" Tag wanted to get right to the point. Whoever this man was, there was a reason he was here, and Tag wasn't interested in trying to figure it out for himself.

"Chance is our newest member," Luke clarified, standing beside Cole, mirroring his defensive stance with his arms folded over his chest and a scowl on his face.

"So why don't you look happy about that?" Tag asked the obvious question.

"They aren't thrilled with the fact that I'm an undercover cop," Chance relayed, his eyes intensely focused on Tag.

"Is that right?" Tag felt his curiosity intensifying, but the tension in the room was thick enough to cut with a knife. "And how does that affect us?"

Chance leaned against the wall behind him, crossing one booted foot over the other ankle, his hands in his pockets. He didn't look concerned to have all eyes on him, nor did he seem to mind the permanent scowl etched on Luke McCoy's face.

Tag wasn't one to get intimidated easily, but then again, at six foot three, a solid two twenty, he'd gotten pretty comfortable in his own body. As for Chance, well, Luke definitely had a few inches on him, even though the cop didn't look much shorter than Tag was. And the only other person in the room who might've had the same breadth was Cole. Both men looked like they lived at the gym.

When Chance started talking, all eyes stayed on him. "I've been keeping tabs on Stewart Crawford for going on a year now."

"Stewart Crawford? The big oil tycoon out of West Texas?" McKenna asked.

"That'd be the one. You might not be familiar with him, but you're definitely acquainted with his son, Stephen."

Tag knew the relation because the McCoys didn't play around when they did background checks. He just wasn't sure why it was relevant.

"We know for a fact that Stewart's managed to get away with thousands of oil drilling violations in recent years. Mainly, as they relate to corroded pipelines that are leaking and in desperate need of repair."

"I don't understand," McKenna voiced. "Wouldn't that be something for the Texas Railroad Commission to investigate? Why are you undercover investigating it?"

"I'm not. Well, not anymore anyway," Chance clarified, and Tag noticed Luke's eyebrows get even closer as he regarded Chance.

"Then what are you doing?" Logan asked.

"I'm investigating Stephen Crawford." Chance didn't elaborate, and Tag felt the pressure in the room shift dramatically.

"Do we have to drag it out of you?" Cole bit out, standing more firmly in place.

"Stephen Crawford has managed to blackmail a handful of very influential people in this state, several of them members of your club."

"Sonuvabitch!" Luke bellowed and began pacing. "That's why that little motherfucker wanted in so bad. He's using us to get the dirt he needs."

Tag watched each person, noticing how Logan allowed his twin a moment to vent before he spoke up. "If Crawford's blackmailing government officials, I assume they are the ones who are managing to bypass the red tape as far as the environmental violations are concerned."

"That's correct," Chance responded. "Keep in mind, I'm undercover, and I've managed to get close to Stephen Crawford in the last few months. So, I was a little surprised to learn he wasn't just using his underhanded skills to protect his daddy's fortune but that he was now venturing down a new path of crazy."

Luke stopped moving and jerked his attention to Chance at the same moment Logan stood up. Tag didn't move from behind McKenna, keeping his hands firmly on her shoulders as he watched the two identical brothers. He recognized their immediate protective instincts.

"Chill out, boys," Chance said casually, never moving from his disinterested stance against the wall. "I'm here to help you."

"How the hell do you propose to do that?" Luke asked.

"Well, if you'd let me finish, I was just getting to the interesting part."

Chapter *Thirty-Eight*

MCKENNA SAT AT the table, drinking in the sight of Tag sitting across from her. She was supposed to be working, but for the last few minutes, she'd been too interested in staring at the sexiest man she had ever laid eyes on.

For two days, they hadn't spent a single minute apart, and during that time, she had even gotten used to the way he continued to touch her in the most innocent of ways. Like right now. They were sitting directly across from one another at his breakfast table, their laptops set up between them while Tag's bare foot methodically rubbed against hers beneath the table. Even that innocent, sweet caress was enough to send her hormones into a frenzy.

"You're supposed to be working," Tag stated, never looking up from his computer screen.

McKenna smiled. "I am."

"Yeah?" Tag's eyes came up to meet hers, and that sexy dimple in his right cheek winked as he grinned.

"I'm thinking about writing an article on the world's sexiest men. And I think you'll be the first one I write about."

"Well, darlin', I can assure you that your readers would be sadly disappointed." He grinned even bigger.

"Why's that?" McKenna didn't doubt how sexy her readers would find Tag, especially if they had as intimate a glimpse into who he truly was as she did. Not that she would ever allow that to happen, though.

"Because I'd never let you do the research on anyone else."

McKenna laughed. She loved how possessive Tag had become of her in recent days. Not that he hadn't been before, but now, he didn't seem to mind who knew.

From what she could tell, the only difference was that he was now giving in to his desire to be with her, versus trying to push her away as he had before. And since that road now traveled both ways, she'd been able to loosen up quite a bit, allowing herself to ease into the less dominant role. McKenna would never be a submissive, but considering Tag didn't seem to need that, she wasn't too worried about it.

"Keep looking at me like that and I'm going to make your clothes fall off." Tag smirked.

"How am I looking at you?" she asked, wanting to know so she could continue doing it.

"Like I'm dessert."

"I've never heard of having dessert after breakfast," McKenna said sweetly.

"Well, darlin', I think it's high time we try." With that confident, relaxed ease that was so much a part of him, Tag stood from his chair before crowding her on the opposite side of the table. "I think it's time we try a few things, actually."

That teasing spark disappeared from his eyes, replaced by a hungry gleam. Without conscious thought, McKenna's body responded immediately as she stood to her feet in front of him. When he lifted her, she instinctively wrapped her legs around his narrow waist and her arms around his neck.

"What did you have in mind?"

"I'll show you," he growled as he moved through the house, toward his bedroom.

McKenna fully expected him to toss her on the bed, but he changed course abruptly and led her into his bathroom. For the last two days, McKenna had fantasized about getting into that gargantuan bathtub of his, but once again, he turned, and they were suddenly standing in his oversized glass shower.

"We're a little overdressed for this, don't you think?" she asked when he turned on the water, still holding her. He didn't answer as he waited a moment while the water heated before submerging them both beneath the warm spray of water.

She was wearing one of his white button-down shirts and nothing else, while he had pulled on a pair of old, faded jeans that she found to be even sexier on him than those expensive suits. Especially when that was the only thing he wore.

As the water cascaded over them, the shirt she was wearing did little to hide anything, including the way her nipples puckered as they rubbed against his chest. As Tag's mouth ate at hers, the hungry desperation that only he made her feel quickly consumed them.

McKenna tried to hang on to him when he went to put her back on her feet, and Tag broke the kiss as he grinned. "I promise this will be worth it."

She knew it would, but she had no idea what he was going to do next. Lucky for her, he chose to rid them of the hindering garments before he moved around behind her, pushing her wet hair out of the way as he began suckling her neck, his hands fondling her breasts as she groaned.

Even though he was touching her, McKenna needed more. For the past two nights, they had come together as one, but each time, she'd felt as though Tag had been restraining that dark side of him that she had glimpsed before. He was sweet and gentle, yet he made her body come apart in the most exquisite ways possible. But standing here, feeling his teeth nipping at her shoulder, she knew he was unable to hold himself back much longer.

She tried to turn, but he pulled back, his hands holding her still. "Uh uh. Stay right where you are," he insisted firmly, his hands holding her hips in place.

McKenna fought the urge to take over, to turn despite his insistence and drop to her knees, where she could make him lose control the way he was attempting to make her. This was the part she had a hard time with. When she wanted something, she didn't want to wait, especially when it came to this man.

As his lips trailed lower, McKenna tried to distract herself by focusing on the water as it sprayed down on her, but his mouth was making it hard to think of anything except the firm press of his lips to her skin.

When he reached her bottom, McKenna pushed back against his mouth, trying to urge him to hurry because the smoldering kindling in her belly was quickly raging into a full-blown inferno. "Tag, touch me," she pleaded.

"I am touching you," he said as he nipped at her bottom.

She groaned. "Quit teasing me."

There was a time and place for everything, but this blazing lust was getting out of control, and for the last two days, he had drawn out their lovemaking until she was nearly blind with it.

Right now, she just wanted to be fucked.

Oh, Lord. Have mercy!

Tag's tongue stroked between her ass cheeks, and the rasp against the sensitive nerve endings nearly had her knees buckling. McKenna no longer had any way of distracting herself because the only thing she could focus on was the intensity of what he was doing.

"Don't stop," she moaned as she pushed back against him, shamelessly trying to get him closer.

The growl that tore from his chest pierced the humid air as he gripped her hips, forcefully pulling her back against him as he thrust his tongue inside of her in such a brutally intimate way. He was going to make her come with just his tongue…

When she thought the pleasure was too much, he proved her wrong by slowly penetrating her ass with one finger, gently fucking her before inserting a second. He continued, increasing the pace as she began pushing against him, needing more, needing him…

TAG COULDN'T TAKE much more, his dick was like iron, and he had been putting this off for far too long. Standing, he grabbed a bottle of lube he had placed in the shower that morning for just this purpose.

"Put your hands on the wall," he told McKenna, unable to disguise the pure, unadulterated lust that had swallowed him whole.

Having managed to get McKenna to relinquish some of that damned need to control everything, Tag had been fighting this urge for longer than he cared to admit. As far as they had come, he still had the urge to show her, to make her realize just how much he needed her complete submission.

With fumbling hands, he managed to lather his cock with lubrication before gripping her hip and aligning the engorged head against the tight entrance to her ass. He didn't press into her, though.

Leaning down so that his chest was against her back, his mouth close to her ear, he wrapped one arm around her stomach while guiding his cock slowly against her. "Tell me no, and I'll stop."

"Don't stop," she pleaded. "Fuck me, Tag. Take me right now." McKenna's voice was strained, sounding as though she were battling her own needs while wanting to succumb to his.

Pressing the head of his cock just inside the snug entrance, Tag placed his lips on her shoulder. "Tell me that you're mine."

"Yes," McKenna groaned as she tried to push back against him.

"No, tell me. Say the words." Tag knew they had broken through so many barriers they had both erected inadvertently during their brief relationship, but he still had yet to hear from her mouth what he needed to hear.

She said she loved him, and he believed her. He needed more than that. He continued to battle with his demons, and knowing just how much this one woman owned him, he still needed reassurance. He needed to know she felt the same.

"You own me," McKenna whispered.

Tag thrust into her hard, burying his cock deep in her ass. He stilled, holding himself back, resisting the urge to fuck her fast and dirty like he wanted. Nipping her shoulder, he held her body close to his as he slowly pulled back, then rammed home again. Over and over, he did this as she continued to beg for more.

He refused to give in to her until she told him. And this time, he wanted to hear it because she wanted to say it, not because she wanted to make him happy.

"Do you feel me?" He asked the same question he had before. He wasn't asking in the physical sense, because when the two of them came together, it was so much more than physical.

"I feel you," McKenna answered. "I need you, Tag. I will always need you." Her face turned to the side where his head rested, and he turned so he could meet her lips with his own. "You own me. Mind, body, and soul. I'm yours, Tag. Always yours."

He lost it.

Tag moved his mouth back to her shoulder, his teeth gently biting the soft flesh as he began ramming into her, holding her still while she used the wall to push back against him. He growled like the animal he felt he was right then.

Taking her like this, his cock buried in her ass, controlling her and knowing deep in his soul that she felt exactly what he was feeling, that she was giving to him what he knew she would never give another man — that hard-won control — Tag let himself go.

"Fuck," he groaned, biting her hard but not hard enough to break the skin as his dick pulsed once, twice, before erupting inside of her.

When Tag finally returned to his body after that earth-shattering climax, he gently pulled out of her, then turned McKenna in his arms. Looking down at her, he could still see the swirling need. She hadn't come, but he hadn't expected her to.

Quickly, Tag took the soap from the shower ledge, washed himself fully and then her before turning off the water and leading her out. They were both dripping, and his cock was once again hard as he sensed her building desire. He didn't even take the time to dry them as he urged her over to the bed.

Tag sat on the edge of the mattress before pulling her against him, pressing his mouth to hers and helping her to straddle him. With one arm wrapped around her back, Tag ensured she wouldn't fall while he gripped her hair with his other hand, wrapping his fist in the thick, heavy strands.

"Fuck me, McKenna," he told her as she began grinding her pussy against his throbbing cock. The more he thought about being inside of her, the harder he got, even after just having her.

McKenna didn't hesitate when she gripped his cock in her hand, guiding him right where she wanted him. Her body consumed him as she slowly lowered until once again her ass was resting against his thighs.

"Fuck me, baby. I want to feel your tight pussy on my cock. I want to feel you, watch while you make yourself come."

McKenna groaned, pressing her mouth to his as she began to lift and lower on his cock, then alternating in a back and forth motion as she ground her clit against his pelvis. It was so fucking hot to hold her in his arms, to feel her as she rode him with only one thing in mind.

"Aw, fuck." Tag didn't expect to be driven so close to the edge so soon. Her muscles were tightening around his cock while she continued to move on him.

"Tag," McKenna groaned, her eyes opening. "I need more."

Tag stood instantly, gripping her ass and moving until he had her back against the wall. He crushed her body between his and the wall as he began slamming his cock deep inside of her cunt over and over, harder, faster until she was begging.

"Fuck," he groaned as her pussy spasmed, her muscles milking him until he couldn't hold on any longer.

"Tag!" McKenna screamed, her body stilling, her nails digging into his shoulders as she came, pulling him over right along with her.

Chapter *Thirty-Nine*

BY THE TIME Monday rolled around, McKenna was ready to get back into the swing of things. She and the rest of her staff had been instructed by a very insistent Tag to stay away from the Sensations offices until he told them otherwise. He'd graciously informed her Sunday night that they could all return to work on Monday.

When she first walked through the door, she nearly stumbled in her heels, wondering whether she had accidentally entered the wrong office. So much for just paint, she thought to herself.

Tag had obviously worked magic, and her entire office had been redone. From the walls to the floors and every piece of equipment and furniture. Nothing was the same. That also went for the security guard who now had his own desk in the front lobby area.

Nice touch, Murphy.

By noon, McKenna and Whisper had successfully answered every email they could answer as well as put a couple of fun articles together for later in the week. As much as she continued to worry about the McCoys and the issues they were facing, McKenna was trying her best to resume life as normal. At least until they asked for her help.

Based on the conversation with the UC, Chance Reed, she wasn't so sure they needed her help anymore. From the sound of it, Chance had a bit more dirt on Crawford than Crawford seemed to have on Luke and Logan, which ultimately, if presented correctly, would work in their favor. According to Tag, both Luke and Logan were also a bit more optimistic.

As for Susan Toulmin, well, she wasn't speaking much at the moment. That could've been because she was introduced to Chance Reed by Stephen Crawford, and according to Reed, she had found a new obsession. He assured all of them that he had absolutely no interest. McKenna believed him. She also believed that there was something more to this cop than what they were letting on.

She hadn't mentioned her suspicions to Tag yet because she was truly trying to see how this would all play out. If it were true and Reed would be able to turn the tables on Crawford, the pictures might just die a sudden, much deserved death, and they could all resume their lives as normal. The only concern was whether Crawford had already released them since he had been so generous and sent them to McKenna. Remembering what she'd seen still made her sick to her stomach. Not because of what they were doing but because McKenna had no desire ever to see Tag with another woman.

"Hey, boss lady," Whisper greeted as she cheerfully walked into McKenna's office without knocking.

"Why are you so happy?" McKenna smiled back at her friend.

"No reason," Whisper lied.

"I find that very hard to believe. Sit down. Talk to me," McKenna told her assistant as she pushed her keyboard away and focused solely on the vibrant, glowing woman in her office.

She couldn't help but remember the last few times she'd seen Whisper. McKenna was pretty sure there were issues in her life, and she kept hoping her friend would reach out to her, but, unfortunately, McKenna had been wrapped up in her own drama.

"How's Anna?" McKenna asked, deciding to jump in with both feet.

"She's amazing," Whisper said dreamily.

McKenna smiled and cocked an eyebrow, waiting for Whisper to elaborate. She didn't. "Well, I could've told you that, so you're going to have to give me more than that."

Whisper laughed, and her husky, seductive chuckle echoed through the room and probably the rest of the building, if she had to guess. Her friend was definitely not anything like her name would suggest.

"I think we both realized exactly what we were doing."

"And that was?" McKenna felt clueless, and she wondered why Whisper seemed to be talking in circles.

Whisper grinned slyly. "Let's just say, we have decided not to take for granted what we have anymore. It took us a long time to find each other, and in less time than that, we'd somehow managed to start drifting apart. I love her. She is my world, and maybe, just maybe, I took a little *what not to do* from your book."

McKenna's eyes widened and then she laughed. Loudly. "What *not* to do? I know you did not just say that."

"Yes, boss lady. If nothing else, over the last few weeks, I've learned that you're supposed to go after what you want because *you* taught me that," Whisper said, pointing her finger directly at McKenna. "And I also learned that you aren't supposed to run away from it once you find it. I learned *that* from your sexy lawyer man.

"Then, most importantly, I learned that if you want something badly enough, it's worth everything it takes to get it. And it's worth every second invested after, because there are some people who are not as blessed to have found it. And you never know how long it might last."

McKenna sat back in her chair, tapping her pen on her thumb as she regarded her friend's words of wisdom.

She knew that what Stephen Crawford was doing was ultimately affecting lives. In many ways. Ways he probably wasn't even aware of. But she was damn sure he didn't realize that he had brought a couple back together because of his ignorance and his desire to tear everything apart.

To top it off, Susan Toulmin was bound and determined to ensure she hurt others the way she felt she had been hurt, and though McKenna absolutely didn't agree with her methods, she could almost understand her logic.

"Well, regardless of how this turn of events happened, I'm super thrilled that the two of you are working it out. You're both amazing women who deserve each other. You complement one another nicely."

"That we do," Whisper agreed. "Now, I think I better get outta here. I really do have a date this time."

"Be careful and have fun." McKenna watched as Whisper practically skipped out of the room.

Wow. It was crazy how things happened, but when they resulted in a woman who was as happy as Whisper, McKenna didn't feel the need to question it.

Glancing at her watch, she realized it was just after five, and she had one last thing she needed to get done. Sending off a quick note to Tag, inviting him to her house for dinner, she jumped right into the article she hoped to have out the following day.

By the time she was finished, McKenna was about half an hour late for meeting Tag. She glanced at her cell phone but noticed he hadn't called, so she figured he'd gotten tied up and would probably get there about the same time she did. After shutting down her laptop and dropping it into her bag, McKenna hefted the bag on her shoulder and grabbed her purse.

Walking down the hall, she dug through her purse for her keys and looked up in time to come almost face-to-face with Stephen Crawford.

"Mr. Crawford," McKenna said coolly, trying to ignore the painful pounding of her heart against her ribs.

"Ready to do that interview yet?" he asked, sounding eerily calm.

"Interview?" She knew there was no way to get out of this confrontation, so she could only hope if she pretended not to know what he was talking about, it'd give her at least a minute to come up with a plan.

Since she already had her keys in her hand, she couldn't very well reach back in her purse and grab her handgun, because he'd wonder what she was doing, and the last thing McKenna wanted was for this to go bad.

"Yeah, you know the interview you're going to run tomorrow because if you don't, I'm going to make sure pictures of your boyfriend and that whore, Samantha McCoy, are plastered all over cyberspace."

Infatuation

The memory of those photos made her stomach churn, but McKenna ignored it. Those were in the past; they didn't matter anymore.

Tag and Sam mattered, though. To McKenna. She cared about what happened to them, and she wasn't about to let this crazy bastard get away with ruining lives because he was a selfish, greedy asshole.

Shifting her bag on her shoulder, McKenna stared back at Stephen, seeing the crazed look in his eye. She still had a hard time understanding how he could've gotten so greedy that he resorted to blackmailing. She wondered whether his father even knew, but then again, if the Crawfords were working to cover up environmental problems that would ultimately cost them a fortune, she could see how he might.

"What did you have in mind, Mr. Crawford?"

"Please, call me Stephen. It's not like I haven't seen you intimately."

McKenna choked on the bile that threatened to come surging from her throat. She knew exactly what he was referring to, but it made her sick to think of what perverse things he might've done while looking at her pictures.

"Those were tastefully done, by the way," he added. "I would've much preferred to see more of your pretty pink pussy, but now that you're frequenting the club, I figure I might just get my chance."

"Not in this lifetime," McKenna bit out, her fury overshadowing any self-preservation she might've had.

"See, that's where you're wrong," Stephen said as he lunged toward her.

Before McKenna even knew what had happened, Stephen was flying the opposite direction, his arms flailing as he lost his step and went crashing into the wall.

In the next instant, she was in Tag's arms, and she wasn't sure whether she was the one shaking or if his rage was vibrating right through his limbs.

TAG DIDN'T KNOW how McKenna had ended up alone in her office, but the first thing he did after the police escorted Stephen Crawford off of the premises was call Alex. He demanded that the security guard now permanently assigned to Sensations, Inc. be there until everyone went home. And if he had a problem with that, he could find a new job.

The second thing he did was take her home. To her house. She was a little shaken up, but he was pretty sure he was more upset about what had happened than she was. Tag had to admit, he was rather impressed with the way she'd been handling Crawford when he'd showed up. Had it not been for the phone call he'd received minutes before from Chance Reed, things could've turned out very different.

He suspected Chance would've intervened if necessary, but he was still trying not to blow his cover. Since he was now a member of the club, with the same level of membership as Stephen Crawford, he at least could keep tabs on the guy.

Luke and Logan weren't thrilled with their newest member, because according to Logan, they were just layering a problem over a problem. If the other members got word that they had a UC in attendance, Club Destiny might just go to shit faster than if the member list was leaked.

But it wasn't like they had much of a choice these days. They could either continue to try and Band-Aid the problem or give up and allow the walls to come crumbling down around them. Fortunately, no one knew that Stephen Crawford had already sent the pictures to McKenna, and if Luke or Logan were to find out, Tag wasn't sure he'd be able to protect them from themselves.

He might've been slow in understanding the reason they would go to any extreme for the ones they loved, but since finding McKenna, Tag finally got it. And tonight, his only intention was to hold her close and ensure she knew just how much she meant to him.

Chapter *Forty*

THE FOLLOWING MORNING, Tag was sitting at the breakfast bar in McKenna's kitchen watching as she moved back and forth, effortlessly putting a breakfast together that was better suited for an army than just the two of them. She seemed a little nervous, but he wasn't sure why. The only possibility he could come up with was she was still shaken up from Crawford, although she'd seemed better than all right the night before.

Tag smiled as he remembered.

"What are you smiling for?" McKenna laughed as she turned on him, and Tag laughed right along with her.

"If you only knew."

"Oh, I think I've got an idea," she teased, turning back to the stove.

When Tag's cell phone rang, interrupting their perfect morning, he was tempted not to answer it. Since that had never worked for him before, he snatched it up from the bar and growled when he saw who it was.

"Murphy."

"Where the hell are you?" Logan quipped, and Tag almost thought there was a smile in his voice.

"Why the fuck do you always ask me that?"

"Because I can. Now answer the damn door." The line disconnected, and a second later, the doorbell rang. McKenna stopped in her tracks, staring back at him, but she no longer looked happy.

"I'll get it," Tag told her.

After walking to the front door, Tag pulled it open, expecting to see Logan, but he was not expecting to see everyone else.

There was a wolf whistle, followed by Ashleigh's voice as she said, "Holy shit! Did you know he had all that ink?"

Tag ignored her, then stepped back, allowing them all to file into McKenna's house. He only hoped she had time to put on more clothes than she had, because if not, they were about to get a show.

After shutting the door, Tag snuck into McKenna's bedroom and pulled a shirt from the closet, one he had placed in there the night before. Once he was at least semi-dressed, he returned to the kitchen to see everyone had managed to trap McKenna there.

"What's going on?" he asked as he slipped between Ashleigh and Sierra on his way to get to McKenna's side.

"Did you know about this?" Logan asked, his mouth a grim, hard line.

"What?" he asked, grabbing the small sheet of paper from Logan's hand. It looked like an article that had been printed out.

It only took a second for it to sink in, and Tag turned to look at McKenna. She looked terrified.

"I'm sor—"

She was quickly cut off when Sierra threw her arms around McKenna's neck, practically pushing Tag into the counter behind him. Following Sierra was Sam and then Ashleigh.

"I can't believe you did this. I don't know how to thank you," Sam whispered, but the whole room heard it.

"It wasn't that hard," McKenna said when the women finally gave her room to breathe. "It was just one woman with a broken heart talking to another. As easy as it is to lose control because you can't have something you think should be yours, it doesn't give you the right to trash everyone in the process."

Tag pulled the paper back in front of his face to read the article beside a picture of Susan Toulmin:

Strength Times Ten

I met a woman recently who told me that she wasn't strong enough to let go. That holding on was the key to happiness, the key to making the pain go away.

This woman is no different from you and me. She's beautiful, successful, and she bleeds red when she's wounded. She's a strong woman, an independent woman who has accomplished success all on her own. However, this woman doesn't define success by her career or her intelligence or even by those who love her. She defines success by the one who got away. In her eyes, she is a failure.

That's where she is wrong.

It was during my discussion with her that I realized I am that very same woman, except my life is defined by my strength and my success, and there is no need for anyone else to be strong for me. I don't need someone else to lift me up; I can do that all on my own. I've used brute force to get where I am, tenacity to show I can do it on my own, and my independence to prove that I am not dependent.

Until I spoke to this independent, tenacious woman who uses brute force to go after what she wants, I didn't realize that I had been going about this the wrong way.

Same as she had.

It was then that I acknowledged that I am still strong, I am still tenacious, and I am still independent. And now, because I have given my heart to someone who will not lift me up but rather will hold me up when I am not strong enough to do so, I've simply made myself stronger. In turn, I have made him stronger, too, because I am now strong enough to return the favor when he needs to be held.

During this conversation, she and I both realized that we are strong enough … to let go.

By doing this, I assure you, we will not lose touch with who we really are. However, we will forget everything we thought we knew, ignore all of the things we imagined perfection to be, and let go of all of the things we held fast to for so long thinking we weren't quite strong enough.

So, I'll tell you the same thing I told this woman:

Whether you are fortunate enough to have met him already or you are blessed enough to know you will have him one day … there is someone who is strong enough to be your equal, and you will know him when you meet him because you will finally be strong enough to love yourself and him…

At the same time.

-McKenna Thorne

Tag couldn't move. He couldn't think, he couldn't breathe, he couldn't… He was stunned into complete and total silence. As he let his arms drop to his sides, McKenna's beautiful face came into view, and the look of worry and concern that he saw there completely broke his heart.

"I love you," he whispered, not caring who was in the room or who was there to witness every emotion he had ever known.

"Susan said she was—" McKenna began, but he quickly cut her off as he reached for her.

"I don't give a damn about Susan. I. Love. You." Taking her hand in his, Tag found himself going down on one knee, realizing that this moment might never present itself again. "Marry me, McKenna. Make *me* stronger."

When her eyes filled with tears, Tag held his breath, unsure what that meant. The house was eerily silent, which was strange, considering the number of people standing around them, but Tag didn't exhale as he waited for McKenna to respond.

"Yes," she whispered, dropping to her knees in front of him. "Yes. I'll marry you."

Tag crushed his mouth to hers, holding her as close as he could get her and ignoring the whistles and applause that erupted around them.

Chapter *Forty - One*

MCKENNA SAT QUIETLY in the back of the room, grateful that she didn't have to speak to this group of people today. As each person passed her, she felt their inquisitive eyes on her, probably wondering why she was there. She wanted to save them the question, because she didn't know why she was there, either.

Luke and Logan had called an impromptu meeting, insisting that all members be present, and Tag had insisted that she come. At first McKenna had attempted to persuade him otherwise, but in the end, she had lost. Well, in actuality, she had won — big-time — but she wasn't going to think about that now. This wasn't the time or place for her to daydream about that man's sexy, wicked mouth and all the things he did to her with it.

She sipped from the bottle of water Tag had gotten for her as she waited for everyone else to show up. She recalled all of the faces as each person came in, realizing these were the full-fledged members. She was a little surprised when Samantha, Sierra, and Ashleigh filed in, their eyes scanning the room until they landed on her. She smiled.

McKenna didn't know what to think of this group of women. She'd had the pleasure of their company for the last few days, unable to say no when they'd invited her to lunch or the one night they'd insisted she meet them at the bar for drinks. They were an interesting bunch and as different as three women could be.

Despite the uproar that the images of Sam had caused, she still seemed to be trying to be the woman she wanted to be. McKenna didn't know her all that well, but she sensed Sam was battling some internal demons of her own these days. At one point, McKenna had heard that Samantha's usual method of coping with stress to this degree was to run. She hadn't, though, and she wondered whether that was due to her deep, profound love for the man she'd married.

They were an interesting pair, Logan and Sam. Not that McKenna liked to think about it, but she did hear about the couple's recent decision to avoid threesomes. At least for the near future. Apparently, Sam didn't think she was cut out for it. According to her, she enjoyed the thrill, but she didn't like knowing that one day, for whatever reason, it would come to an end. Since she had Logan for the duration, she felt her time and energy were better spent on loving him. McKenna admired her for that. For a woman many people called selfish, she seemed anything but when it came to her husband.

Then, of course, there was Ashleigh and Alex, and those two needed to get a room. McKenna couldn't stop the smile as she thought about them. It made sense that they hadn't been together all that long, but according to what she'd heard, they'd been fighting an attraction for many years. Well, in case they didn't know it, their attraction was still burning bright and hot. Sometimes, their reaction to one another was hot enough for even McKenna to feel it when they were close.

As for Luke, Sierra, and Cole, well, there wasn't much McKenna knew about those three, aside from the fact that they were totally in love with one another. Sierra's pregnancy was driving both men absolutely crazy, making them even more protective of her than they already had been. As Sierra would tell it, she wouldn't want to be anywhere else. McKenna couldn't blame her.

The one thing that still shocked the hell out of McKenna was the way Luke and Cole were toward each other. Being on the outside looking in, she'd originally thought that both men were in this for Sierra, but that clearly wasn't the case. There was a passion between the two men that was as rugged and unrestrained as the two of them were. They might not show it often, but McKenna had seen it a time or two, and, well, she had to admit, it was hotter than hell to witness.

As for her and Tag ... they were making headway. He was trying to dominate her, and she was learning to be dominated. There were a few things they still disagreed on, but that was something she knew would take some time to get used to. For two people who'd been determined to move through life solo, they were learning what it meant to have someone to lean on. McKenna loved him with everything she was, and she felt every bit of it in return.

As for the wedding, well, they were still arguing about that one. McKenna's parents were hoping for the whole nine yards, and for some reason, Tag wanted to appease them. She, on the other hand, would prefer to go to Vegas. Originally, Tag had liked the idea, but after her father had spoken with him, he'd changed his tune. She was working diligently to change it back. She smiled at the thought. She liked changing his mind.

"What's going on?" McKenna asked as Sam took a seat on her left, Sierra lowering herself slowly to the chair on her right while Ashleigh sat on the other side of Sierra.

"I guess we're about to find out," Sam stated in a noncommittal tone that set McKenna's sensors off.

On the drive over, she had questioned Tag relentlessly, but to no avail. The man wasn't saying a word. And now she wondered whether she was the only one who didn't know. Considering the crowd that was still filing in, McKenna figured it had to be big. There were more people than last time, that was for sure.

All eyes were drawn to the front of the room when Logan and Luke walked to the center before turning to address them all. McKenna was riveted to the two men because no matter how many times she saw them, she still couldn't get over how exactly alike they looked but how completely different they really were. She thought back to her interviews with both men and nearly laughed out loud. They were definitely interesting.

"Thanks for coming on such short notice. Luke and I wanted to address everyone at once. As you can see, we've only invited our full-fledged members, and after the last time, I hope we were able to answer your questions as to the status of our memberships," Logan said in the calm, firm tone everyone was used to.

"In recent months, we've found ourselves going through some rough spots, as many of you are aware. As of today, I'm happy to say that we've overcome some major obstacles thanks to the help of some really incredible people. Without them, I'm not sure we would've been as lucky."

McKenna noticed Travis Walker when he walked into the room, moving along the back wall and stopping just short of where she and the other three women were sitting.

"I personally want to thank McKenna Thorne," Luke spoke up, slowly pacing back and forth with that animalistic grace he had. "The day Tag told me what McKenna was hoping to do, I'll admit I wasn't thrilled with the idea. However, considering I trust Tag with my life and those of my family, I didn't have any doubts that, in the end, we would come out ahead. And we did. I'm not sure if any of you know what McKenna put on the line to protect my club, but I can tell you with the utmost assurance, not a single one of you would've done the same."

The hard edge to Luke's tone had a few people sitting up straight. McKenna even flinched at the statement. She knew the man was rough around the edges, and he was showing every single jagged ridge at the moment.

When Logan took a step forward, placing his hand on Luke's arm, he was shrugged away.

"Most of you know me fairly well," Luke continued, "and for those of you who do, you understand what loyalty means to me—"

"Luke." Cole moved to the front of the room, coming to stand beside him. "Don't do this."

Luke didn't say anything to Cole, nor did he shrug him off when Cole placed his hand on his arm in a similar manner as Logan had. He went completely still for a moment, his eyes roaming the crowd until they landed just to McKenna's right.

Sierra wasn't moving a muscle as she watched what was playing out in front of her, Ashleigh's hand being squeezed in the process. McKenna instinctively put her hand on Sierra's arm, and the other woman grabbed it and held on.

"We're behind you, baby," she said loud enough for the entire room to hear. "No matter what you decide, Cole and I love you no matter what."

McKenna swallowed a lump in her throat, fighting the urge to cry at the sentiment. The pure love in Sierra's voice could be felt by everyone in the room.

As the group began to turn around and face Luke again, silence once again descended. McKenna saw Cole squeeze Luke's arm slightly, but he didn't back away.

"It has come to my attention that there are some shady things going on with various people within this room. While I've been protecting and defending my family and the life I have built, I've also put my ass on the line for each and every one of you in this room. While we" —Luke motioned to Cole and Logan behind him — "stood up here, doing our best to protect your identity, every one of you turned your back on us. And all the while, I'm fighting a battle I knew I couldn't win because of the unethical, immoral behavior of the members of my club."

Luke paused for a moment, but no one moved a muscle as they waited for what came next. McKenna had no idea where Luke was going with this, but she knew, without a doubt, she would never look at Luke McCoy the same again.

TAG KEPT HIS hands in his pockets and his face expressionless as he listened to Luke. In all the time he had known the man, he had never seen him nearly as emotional as he was right then. He felt the fury in his words as they rumbled through the room. He knew exactly what Luke was feeling.

These people, the ones who depended on Luke and Logan to safeguard them so they could indulge in behavior frowned upon by many, although not in any way illegal, had turned their back on him at a time when he'd needed support. Neither Luke nor Logan had expected it, but nonetheless, Luke seemed to be having a difficult time dealing with the knowledge.

"I've asked Travis Walker to attend today because I want him to understand up front exactly what it is he is risking. Alluring Indulgence is going to change the industry as we know it, and everyone in this room had the opportunity to get in on the ground floor."

Tag stood up straight as he moved around to the back of the room, needing to be closer to McKenna. He wasn't sure what it was, but when she was around, she managed to settle him in ways he hadn't thought possible. Although, he wasn't sure he was the one who needed settling at the moment.

"What are you saying, Luke?" someone in the crowd asked.

Luke glanced over at Cole, then back at Logan before once again returning his gaze to the crowd in front of him. "I'm saying that as of today, I'm closing the doors of Club Destiny."

Tag stood motionless. He had no idea what to think. He definitely hadn't seen that one coming.

Chapter *Forty-Two*

"MCKENNA?" TAG CALLED her name from somewhere in the house, and McKenna finished what she was doing before going in search of him. Didn't the man realize they had a party to get ready for?

"Do you need help picking out a… Well, *hello.*" She smiled when she walked into Tag's bedroom, because what she found there was sinfully delicious.

Standing before her in a pair of tight black boxer briefs with an upper body hardened and covered with glorious ink was the most intensely sexy man she had ever met. As it would seem, it didn't matter how many times she saw him, McKenna still wanted him with an aching, relentless hunger.

"Keep looking at me like that and this is going to be a different kind of party," Tag growled, his vivid green eyes instantly turning inky dark with his restrained need.

"Yeah? I might be able to get into that," she said as she moved closer.

McKenna made the mistake of touching him, because the instant her fingers grazed his smooth, hot skin, they tingled with awareness, and immediately the rest of her body caught up, begging for the same satisfaction.

"McKenna."

She heard his warning but chose to ignore it because she just couldn't help herself. Touching him was beyond intoxicating, and she wanted nothing more than to get drunk on him.

The little voices in her head warned her that they would have company soon, but she just couldn't find it in herself to care. She had to have him, and she had to have him right now.

Easing around so that she was standing in front of him, McKenna trailed the outline of one of his tattoos with her finger before following the connecting lines that led to others down the center of his stomach. She didn't linger, just simply lowered herself to her knees as she let her finger slip into the waistband of his sexy underwear before pulling them down slowly, releasing his thick, steel-hard erection.

She took a moment to look at him, to absorb every minute detail of his cock, wanting nothing more than to take him into her mouth and pleasure him. Little did Tag know, but McKenna enjoyed giving him head as much as he enjoyed getting it. Maybe more. Not that she would tell him that, because there were days he liked to restrain her from getting what she wanted, but so far, he hadn't stopped her from going down on him.

Glancing up the long, muscular length of his body, McKenna stopped when their eyes met. He wasn't smiling. No, he was too turned on to smile, she knew. There was a hard edge to him that she'd seen before, the same one that made her panties wet and her clit throb for his attention. When he looked at her like that, McKenna longed to be taken by him in ways only Tag could take her.

"We will have guests arriving any second," Tag told her, but his eyes deceived his warning as they moved to her mouth.

"Then they can watch," she answered before using the tip of her tongue to trace the crest of his swollen cock.

The growl she received in reply made her pussy clench, but she ignored her own body's needs, because right now, this wasn't about her. This was about the man she loved and her attempt to push him over the edge.

Using one hand to stroke the satiny-soft length of him, McKenna wrapped her lips around the head of his cock and sucked while flicking her tongue down the slit, instantly receiving Tag's answering groan of ecstasy she'd been searching for.

When he slid his fingers through her hair, gently guiding her head until he was sliding his cock deep in her mouth, slowly at first, McKenna gave some of her control up. She loved when he did that — took control because he knew her in ways no one else did.

"Fuck, baby," Tag groaned as he began thrusting more adamantly, placing his other hand on her head to hold her completely still. "Put your hands down."

McKenna released his shaft after one final stroke, dropping her hands to her sides. Looking up at him, she let him see every ounce of her need for him in her eyes. She had learned that she didn't need to tell him what she wanted; he just knew.

"I'm going deep," he warned her as the head of his cock brushed the back of her throat before he pulled out again. He repeated the action numerous times, continuing to go slow but going deeper and deeper each time.

McKenna knew there was no way she could take him fully into her mouth because he was too big, but she didn't mind trying. To see the sensual satisfaction on his rugged face as he concentrated on going deeper while holding on to his control at the same time made her pussy spasm.

She knew they had to hurry, but she wasn't going to rush him because these moments were what she lived for.

TAG HAD CALLED McKenna into the bedroom because he wanted her to pick out a tie, but instead he found himself fucking her mouth with slow, torturous strokes, luxuriating in the feel of her soft lips and her smooth tongue wrapped around his cock.

He'd learned quickly that McKenna enjoyed doing this to him, tormenting him with her wicked ways, but he found he couldn't tell her no most of the time. With such exquisite precision, she somehow managed to coax his release from him, and he found himself daydreaming about this exact thing. Only in his fantasies, she was on her knees with her hands bound behind her, naked and just as damn horny as he was.

She was horny, all right, but there was no way they had time for more than this. That didn't mean he wasn't going to trap her somewhere later and show her just what it felt like when he lifted up that short tease of a skirt and buried his tongue deep in her pussy.

Holding her head still and trying to keep from coming too quickly, Tag continued to drive his throbbing dick deep in her mouth, listening to her soft moans.

"I love seeing my cock sliding in and out of your pretty mouth," he groaned, not sure how much longer he could hold out.

A subtle sound drew Tag's attention to the bedroom door. He wasn't all that surprised to see Travis Walker standing there, which told Tag more than he wanted to know. He didn't let his eyes linger, because for some reason, knowing the man was watching McKenna blow him with such brutal enthusiasm only made him that much hotter. It didn't get by him that Travis had an agenda all his own, and from what Tag could tell, the man was trying to tempt him. Him *and* McKenna.

For now, Tag wasn't interested in sharing this woman. He wasn't sure he ever would be interested, but he couldn't guarantee that the day would never come, and he was pretty sure Travis knew that.

"Aw, fuck, baby," Tag groaned when McKenna's mouth applied the sweetest suction. "Your mouth is so fucking sweet, so fucking hot. Shit yes! Suck me, McKenna. I need to come in your mouth."

Tag drove into her mouth with shallow strokes, trying his damnedest to hang on because their audience was still present, still standing in the doorway, shamelessly witnessing as McKenna proceeded to blow his mind.

Gripping her hair painfully hard, Tag stilled, his cock pulsing in her mouth, his seed emptying down her throat as she continued to stare up at him with just as much satisfaction in her eyes as the man standing in the doorway.

Two hours later, Tag was standing in a small group, McKenna by his side while Cole and Luke carried on about something wildly inappropriate, but a story everyone seemed to be listening to.

"Have you decided what you're doing with the club?" Travis asked when the laughter had died down.

All eyes turned to Luke as they waited to see what he would say. Tag honestly didn't expect Luke to say anything, because for the last week, he'd been hell-bent on being furious, which only made him stick to his decision to close down the club.

"We don't know yet," Logan interrupted as he walked up to the group. "We haven't talked about it much."

"Do you really think closing it down is the right thing to do?" McKenna asked innocently.

At the same time, Luke said yes, Logan said no, and Tag knew they were in disagreement, but surprisingly, Logan wasn't pushing either way. Tag figured he was just as pissed off at the members of the club for Samantha nearly having to take the fall. Considering it turned out certain members were being blackmailed at Sam's expense, it didn't make it any easier to swallow.

It was a risk they all took choosing to belong to such a risqué club, but now that Susan Toulmin had ceased her personal attack, things were calming down somewhat. Not to mention, Stephen Crawford was once again lying low. If Tag had to guess, that was probably due more to Chance Reed's interference than anything else.

"Have you thought about opening the club somewhere else?" McKenna questioned. Considering she was a journalist, they had all come to expect her to keep the conversation rolling.

"We've thought about it," Luke grumbled. "Not an idea I'm fond of."

Tag didn't think the idea was necessarily a good one, either. Club Destiny had shut its doors to the private members club only, not the general public club. Considering they were still on the front page of nearly every newspaper in the city, their popularity had only increased. Everyone wanted to visit the place that was in the news, and although no one truly knew what went on behind those double doors on the second floor, they didn't seem to mind.

"I think we should do the story we talked about," McKenna told Luke.

Tag watched the other man as he stared back at McKenna. Ever since Luke had made the decision to close the doors, he had refused to sign off on McKenna's exclusive. As much as it hurt her that Luke wasn't interested right now, she hadn't pushed it any further. She seemed to understand where he was coming from, and Tag did, too. If nothing else, through all of this, he'd learned one thing — you held on to what was important to you, protected it with your life, and anyone who didn't like it could go to hell.

Luke didn't answer, simply nodded his head as though he might consider it and then turned and walked away. Cole followed, as did Logan, leaving only Travis and McKenna standing beside him.

Tag hadn't yet said anything to Travis, nor did he reveal what had happened to McKenna. He had a feeling she knew, but she hadn't mentioned anything, either. He didn't know if that was more for his benefit or hers. When she squeezed his hip, her arm hidden around his waist beneath his suit jacket, Tag realized exactly how aware she was.

Apparently, the gentle squeeze was her warning for what was about to come out of her mouth, because what she said next blew Tag's mind.

"So, I take it you like to watch?" Her voice was calm and smooth, and her facial expression belied the way her hand tightened even more on Tag's hip.

She was turned on by the idea. *Holy shit.*

Travis at least had the decency to look somewhat ashamed, but more than that, he looked amused. "When it's as hot as that, I don't mind at all."

McKenna pulled her arm from around Tag's waist and smiled up at him before she turned back to Travis. "Well, if you boys could get over your macho bullshit, you never know what might happen." With that, she sauntered off, leaving both Tag and Travis staring after her.

"Don't even think about it, Walker." Tag laughed before downing the rest of his beer.

After managing to suppress the hard-on threatening to have him taking McKenna to the first available place with enough privacy, Tag decided he'd better wait a little while. Without another word, he and Travis returned to the house, and the instant Tag stepped inside, he heard the greetings that rang out. Apparently someone else had decided to join the party.

Tag still didn't know what the party was for, but according to McKenna — and the other women — they'd just needed something to look forward to. Nothing fancy, nothing formal. However, when Tag had agreed, he hadn't realized they'd use his house. He didn't really mind that, either. It seemed to make McKenna happy, and as it turned out, that's what he lived for.

"Travis, come over here. I'd like you to meet someone," Logan called from a group of people standing close to the newcomer.

Tag couldn't see past the big men blocking the view, but he continued over to the group right alongside Travis. As much as he hated it, he was still trying to be a good host. For McKenna's sake, of course. Granted, he'd much rather sneak her off into another room and do something much more satisfying, but that would have to wait.

At least a little while longer.

"Travis," Logan said as the group parted, "I'd like to introduce you to the newest member of the temporarily disbanded club." The group around them laughed, and then Logan continued, "Chance Reed, meet Travis Walker. If you like our club, you're going to want to get to know this man personally."

Tag noticed the sudden change on Chance's face as Travis moved closer. There was recognition, and although Tag couldn't see Travis's face, he noticed the man's sudden stillness. Travis knew *of* the man, although they apparently hadn't met. Travis had been present during one of their conversations recently, and despite Tag's reluctance to have him in on all of the Club Destiny secrets, Logan and Luke didn't have any issues considering he was their new business partner.

"Chance Reed, huh?" Travis's deep, southern drawl broke through the murmurs and had all eyes turning toward him. "Interesting, considering all this time I thought your name was Gage Matthews."

Epilogue

"DOES IT LOOK as good as you thought it would?" Tag asked, sitting in a chair beside her as she glanced over the published article she had put together for Luke.

McKenna was happy with it.

She should be, considering she had spent the last two weeks working on it. As it would turn out, Luke and Logan McCoy weren't as easy to write about as she'd originally thought.

"I wish they could've told me more," McKenna answered, looking up at him briefly before returning her gaze to her tablet computer.

Ever since her brief articles on Club Destiny had come out, Sensations, Inc. had been overwhelmed with interest on the bad-boy club owners and the decision to close the doors. So much so, McKenna had been hard-pressed not to put something together.

Due to Luke's abrupt closing of Club Destiny, McKenna had found it necessary to sit back down with him. She'd been fortunate that he'd agreed, as had Logan.

"Are we done?" Tag asked, causing McKenna to look up.

"Done," the man said.

"Looks like it's your turn, darlin'," Tag stated, standing up and moving toward her. "What do you think?"

McKenna couldn't hide the smile. Staring at the vivid ink, shiny from the layer of ointment the man had put on Tag's side, she still couldn't believe her eyes. He'd mentioned wanting to get another tattoo, but she hadn't expected this, and quite frankly, she'd tried to talk him out of it at first. There, in a very intricate black font: *The red-haired vixen belongs to me.*

Apparently that was a nickname he'd given her over the course of the last few months, and he'd insisted on having it added.

Now it was her turn, and as she stared down at the picture the tattoo artist had drawn up, McKenna was excited about her very first tattoo. It was the same symbol Tag had tattooed near his collarbone. After some research, she'd found it referred to as Serch Bythol, which was formed by using two *triskeles* that joined to create a circle representing an everlasting circle of eternity.

As far as she was concerned, it represented them perfectly, and although Tag hadn't known his reason for getting it at the time, he'd told her that it was obviously a sign of what was to come.

Two people joined in mind, body, and spirit, in everlasting love.

Club Destiny...
Where Do They Go From Here?
by McKenna Thorne

Deemed as Dallas's very own bad boys of the sex industry, Luke and Logan McCoy have successfully established what so many could only dream about. Not only are they the owners of Club Destiny, the hottest nightspot in the city, they've also managed to create one of the most sought-after fetish clubs, not to mention, keep it entirely on the down low.

At thirty-nine years old, the identical twins have successfully managed to establish themselves as two of the most prominent members of society — even if they put the "sex" in sexy. Although they look exactly the same, don't let that fool you. These two men couldn't be more different if they tried.

Luke seems to have settled down quite nicely with Sierra Sellers — his wife, as he refers to her, although they are not officially married — and Cole Ackerley, the man Luke refers to as his husband. That's right, ladies, this man is well spoken for. And don't go having dirty thoughts about Logan, because I've had the pleasure of meeting his wife. She's a protective little thing.

Although we've all enjoyed hearing about these two men in recent months, I can assure you, they haven't had it easy. In fact, recent events led Luke to shut the doors on Club Destiny's fetish club. At this point, according to both Luke and Logan, they aren't sure where they are going to go from here. They've admitted to having invested an undisclosed amount of money in the new resort, Alluring Indulgence, being built by Walker, Inc. Aside from that, they aren't sharing what their next steps will be.

Despite my interest, Luke hasn't given me any additional information at this time, but I can assure you, as soon as he does, I'll make sure you're the first to know.

TRENT RAMSEY SKIMMED the article on the screen, a smile tipping his lips. He was interested to see that Luke and Logan hadn't announced publicly whether or not they would keep the doors closed on Club Destiny.

He'd been a little disappointed that neither of them had thought to call him up when they were having issues, but he wasn't surprised, either. They were still trying to keep him out of the limelight as much as they could.

As much as he was already in the news, Trent respected them for that, but he knew it wasn't necessary. As far as he was concerned, it was high time he paid his partners a little visit. After all, closing the doors on Club Destiny temporarily wasn't a big issue for him, but in no way was he interested in shutting the doors forever.

Infatuation

He was all for investing in this new resort, Alluring Indulgence, but Trent had spoken with both Luke and Logan in the last couple of days, and he knew they were thinking the same thing he was… There was no way they'd let that resort outshine Club Destiny.

It was just time to make a few changes.

♥□□□□♥□□□□♥

I hope you enjoyed Tag and McKenna's story. Infatuation is the fourth book in Nicole's bestselling Club Destiny series. You can read more about Club Destiny as well as her other series on her website. Did you know that the Club Destiny and Alluring Indulgence series overlap? You can find the full reading order at www.NicoleEdwardsAuthor.com.

Want to see some fun stuff related to the Club Destiny series, you can find extras and details regarding what's coming next on my website as well. I keep my website updated with the books I'm working on, including the writing progression of what's coming up for the Club Destiny series.

If you're interested in keeping up to date on Club Destiny as well as receiving updates on all that I'm working on, you can sign up for my monthly newsletter.

Want a simple, *fast* way to get updates on new releases? You can also sign up for text messaging. I promise not to spam your phone. This is just my way of letting you know what's happening because I know you're busy, but if you're anything like me, you always have your phone on you.

And last but certainly not least, if you want to see what's going on with me each week, sign up for my weekly Hot Sheet! It's a short, entertaining weekly update of things going on in my life and that of the team that supports me. We're a little crazy at times and this is a firsthand account of our antics.

And, as always, thank you so much for reading. I hope you'll be able to leave an honest review, as this is the best way to share your thoughts about the book with others.

About Nicole

New York Times and *USA Today* bestselling author Nicole Edwards lives in Austin, Texas with her husband, their three kids, and four rambunctious dogs. When she's not writing about sexy alpha males, Nicole can often be found with her Kindle in hand or making an attempt to keep the dogs happy. You can find her hanging out on Facebook and interacting with her readers - even when she's supposed to be writing.

Website: NicoleEdwardsAuthor.com

Facebook: Author.Nicole.Edwards

Twitter: NicoleEAuthor

Nicole also writes contemporary/new adult romance as Timberlyn Scott.

Acknowledgements

I can remember the day I pushed that publish button for the first time back on July 29, 2012. That wasn't long ago. Conviction was the book I published and just like every other Indie author out there, I was hoping someone would get some enjoyment out of the book I had poured so much of myself into. In the months to follow, I learned about book tours and features and reviews and deleted scenes... The list goes on and on.

When I published Kaleb, I wasn't even sure what the first step was, so, I sent out some emails to a handful of the amazing book review sites that I had seen and let me say, the response was overwhelming. I didn't have the first clue about what I was supposed to do to "pimp" my book.

They did.

The amazing women that I met helped me through the steps and they were so very patient with me. I will forever be in their debt. I just want to say thank you for all that you have done to help me. I don't know what I would've done without you!

I want to say thank you to the *Rock Stars of Romance* for adding me to your page — I still have bruises from falling out of my chair when I saw that one. Literally — I was floored.

Reality Bites! Let's Get Lost! I think you were the first to respond to my emails and I felt so totally clueless, but you've been there for me with every question — no matter how silly. And *Shh Mom's Reading...* I'm truly speechless. Your inspiration is priceless.

There are so many others: *Sinfully Sexy Book Reviews, Sugar and Spice Book Reviews, Erotica Book Club, Three Chicks and Their Books, Stick Girl Book Reviews, Megan's Book Blog* and many more who have helped me along the way.

For the amazing fans, many of you I am honored to now call friends and I look forward to your emails because they are a true bright point in my day: *Carla, Jeni and Nicole (supa ninja)* — you ladies make me laugh and I hope you never stop.

Infatuation

I love you all! Thank you from the bottom of my heart.

By Nicole Edwards

The Alluring Indulgence Series
Kaleb
Zane
Travis
Holidays with the Walker Brothers
Ethan
Braydon
Sawyer
Brendon

The Austin Arrows Series
The SEASON: Rush
The SEASON: Kaufman

The Bad Boys of Sports Series
Bad Reputation
Bad Business

The Caine Cousins Series
Hard to Hold
Hard to Handle

The Club Destiny Series
Conviction
Temptation
Addicted
Seduction
Infatuation
Captivated
Devotion
Perception
Entrusted
Adored
Distraction

Writing as Timberlyn Scott
Unhinged
Unraveling
Chaos

Naughty Holiday Editions
2015
2016